RECKONING

INFINITY

By John E. Stith

RECKONING

I N F I N I T Y

J O H N   E.   S T I T H

A TOM DOHERTY ASSOCIATES BOOK • NEW YORK
TOR®

This is a work of fiction. All the characters and events portrayed in this novel are either fictitious or are used fictitiously.

RECKONING INFINITY

A Tor Book
Published by Tom Doherty Associates, Inc.
175 Fifth Avenue
New York, NY 10010

Tor Books on the World Wide Web:
http://www.tor.com

Tor® is a registered trademark of
Tom Doherty Associates, Inc.

Design by Lynn Newmark

Library of Congress Cataloging-in-Publication Data

Stith, John E.
    Reckoning infinity / John E. Stith.—1st ed.
        p.   cm.
    "A Tom Doherty Associates book."
    ISBN 0-312-86298-9 (acid-free paper)
    I. Title.
PS3569.T548R38   1997
813'.54—dc20   96-31888
                                              CIP

First Edition: April 1997

Printed in the United States of America

0 9 8 7 6 5 4 3 2 1

For Melissa Henning, Kelley Jones, and Stuart Rose,
Marian Berzon and Brian Simpson,
Barb and Dennis Ellis,
Marianne and Howard Jones,
Donna and Mike Wortham,
and Ann and Mike Thompson

I ▪ A D R E N A L I N E

Indications of pending disaster can be as clear and personal as the approaching squeal of tires, or as generic as a distant alarm buzzer and the muted thuds of running feet. The Tokyan Station alarm buzzer certainly wasn't nearly so direct as opening a fortune cookie saying: "Lieutenant Commander Alis Mary Nussem, you are going to have a terrible accident today. Yes, you, Alis," or even a horoscope telling her: "It's a good day to stay in your bunk."

Flashing cabin lights and a pulsating buzzer muffled by a bulkhead pulled Alis out of a deep sleep and put her on edge. Groggy, she realized she'd been asleep only a couple of hours. Was this a drill or the real thing? No way to tell. This was the month for a surprise drill, what the bureaucrats called a "planned non-scheduled drill," so the odds were high that this was the drill. And naturally it would be during her sleep period. Murphy's Law had been written before humans began living in space, but Murphy's ideas dated no faster than Leonardo da Vinci's.

Her feet hit the Persian rug beside her bed. Four steps brought her to the closet, and she popped an orange emergency suit loose from the overhead compartment. The plastic suit felt cool as she thrust her bare legs into it, and she wished she'd clipped her toenails more recently. Her hands reached the thin gloves at the end of the sleeves, and seconds later she pulled the zipper along the curve from hip to neck.

Despite her trim figure, the suit fit so tightly it showed her panty lines, and she could still feel the texture of the rug on her soles as she moved toward her compartment door. She checked an indicator beside the door and left the balloon helmet disconnected, hanging loose at the back of her neck. She might need it later, and she wouldn't want to waste her oxygen in a corridor that was still pressurized with safe air.

She released the door lock and slid the door aside just a centimeter, on the off chance that the indicator had been wrong about the pressure. Someone ran past the slit, and footsteps thudded down the corridor. Alis must have been the last one up. She slid the door all the way open and moved into a territory filled with controlled anxiety.

ISA Lieutenant Karl Stanton was in a shuttle on his way back to Tokyan Station when he heard a soft *ping* from somewhere. This first sign of trouble was tangible, but it still seemed innocuous. A moment later a warning indicator at the edge of his peripheral vision began to flash red.

A heat exchanger on the sunward side of the shuttle had failed. Vaguely puzzled that the equipment had failed without spending any time in a degraded condition, Karl took no action when the shuttle's auto-support system indicated that it was shutting down the unit, reassigning functions to a backup unit, and finally inserting entries in the failure log and the required-maintenance journal. Maybe he'd suffered a hit from a micrometeor large enough to punch through the shuttle's defenses.

For a moment, he wished he were a shuttle mechanic or a pilot rather than a biologist. This was supposed to be just a routine flight, one that would bore a pilot silly, and one well within the capabilities of anyone with the requisite short training course. For missions more complicated than a quick run of a few kilometers, trained pilots were always used. He wished one were here now.

Seconds later the indicator showed the backup unit functioning normally. On the main screen, Tokyan Station loomed, the enormous disk slowly spinning about a docking-station axis that pointed at the sun. Behind the station, the Earth's disk was dark, with just a thin luminous nimbus to mark the boundary between dirt and vacuum.

All looked calm.

In Tokyan Station corridor C-8, the buzzer was much louder. A recorded voice repeated, "Please evacuate this corridor." Alis closed her cabin door and turned on the *unoccupied* indicator so no rescue effort would be wasted there. A man and a woman ran past her, and she followed, jogging. The man hadn't donned his emergency suit. If this was a drill, he might gain points by reaching a safety area early, but he'd lose points for no suit. If this was a real emergency, the penalty for making the wrong decision could be higher than he'd want to pay.

Alis supposed the lack of emergency suit meant the man had been in the woman's cabin and had chosen not to wear a one-size-fits-all suit. She pushed aside a twinge of jealousy. Being a good ISA Tri-Service officer took too much of her time to allow diversions, but she had convinced herself that would change when she reached the next rank. In fact, she was so good at convincing herself to wait, she had done it twice. Two different boyfriends had patiently explained that she worked too much and they weren't getting enough of her time to stay involved.

She flashed past a series of cabin doors already set to *unoccupied*. She hadn't been as fast as she thought. Ahead of them the corridor curved gently upward. The pitch of the buzzers increased, and a huge emergency seal began to slide closed automatically. Beyond the seal stood a large group, milling in the hallway. The pair in front of her wasted at least a second or two in trying to decide who would go through first, finally settling on the woman, and the man squeezed through a gap in the seal that was hardly bigger than he was. Alis reached the door just as the seal closed in her face, and the two of them looked back apologetically through the hardened window. Behind them in the crowd were a few familiar faces.

Feeling sorry for herself wouldn't help anything, so Alis just turned away from the seal and started for the nearest set of double seals leading to corridors on both sides of hers. She could use the exercise anyway. In the absence of obvious air leaks and secondary warning indicators, she was more and more convinced this was the promised drill.

She retraced her steps through the deserted corridor. The beige passageway curved up and out of sight ahead, and color-coded tubes of red, blue, green, and black hugged the ceiling between two larger pipes, both beige. Alis sped past a *you are here* sign that said more about where she wanted to be.

Her path now carried her opposite the station's spin direction, so she felt fractionally lighter. Her shoulder-length hair bounced with each stride. She felt lucky that her body hadn't complained much about going straight from sleep to heavy exercise.

She settled into a rhythm, wondering why drills came during sleep shift and why she only met attractive men when she had temporarily sworn off relationships.

.   .   .

Karl reset the shuttle alarm indicator associated with the malfunctioning heat exchanger. Five seconds later it tripped again. Tokyan Station filled half the view screen already, and he couldn't afford to keep his attention focused on that single failure. He reset the alarm and deactivated the control bank that included the malfunctioning equipment and four other pieces of low-priority gear.

His current course had his shuttle headed five degrees away from the tip of the docking axis. The navigation system warned him of an upcoming course correction. Without taking his eyes off the view ahead, he said, "Do it," and allowed the nav system to proceed.

The burn pushed him back and sideways for almost five seconds.

Subconsciously he knew something was wrong even before the display verified it. The course correction thrust computed by the nav system was completely wrong. It had somehow been calculated 180 degrees off. Instead of heading more precisely for the docking axis, he was now heading directly toward the living quarters.

Karl's pulse accelerated. Sweat formed on his forehead, and he wished even more firmly that he were a pilot. What was happening here?

From somewhere behind him came a *pop* that he felt more than heard, and suddenly a third of his instrument panel went dark. Just as quickly, it flashed back to life and then died a second time.

In a semi-dark exercise control room near the central axis of Tokyan Station, Albert McIntyre and six other people watched displays showing the results of the drill in progress. The primary hologram showed the layer-cake image of the entire station, with each layer made up of concentric rings, each one a different circular corridor.

Portions of six adjacent corridors were highlighted, indicating the portion of the station being drilled. The six corridor segments formed the outermost layer of the station, stretching about a third of the way around the station's perimeter.

Up to that point, the exercise had gone strictly according to plan, but now a new warning indicator started to flash.

"Crap," Albert said. "This is early, isn't it? I'm showing an object entering zone three. Who the hell checked the mission plan?"

"I did," said Lori Wend, a redheaded woman wearing a lab coat. "That shouldn't be in there for another five—five and a half minutes."

"Well, just go ahead and let it run. But be more careful in the future."

"I *was*—right, I'll do it." Lori touched a few panels on the console, and a flashing red light turned to a solid pink.

A comm panel buzzed, and the face of a man in his forties showed on the screen next to it. Red Adams was calling from the main Tokyan Station control center.

"Yes," Albert said irritably.

"We're showing a shuttlecraft in zone three," Red Adams said. "We need to cancel the drill."

"That's *us*. That's part of the test data. I don't know how it happened, but the test plan calls for that to happen in just a few minutes. Somehow the test event got shifted forward. We'll take a hard look at it when we're done."

Red glanced away for a moment and then back. "How sure are you that—"

"I'm sure; I'm sure. What do you think—that the first stray in ten years would happen within minutes of the time the test plan calls for it? We've just got a glitch in the timing."

"Well, I don't like it. Next time, make damn sure all your

test activities are flagged that way. This one's showing up as a live event, and I've got a couple of people here about to wet their pants."

An anonymous voice called from the background. "Too late."

"You got it." Albert sent an angry glance toward Lori. "Sometimes it seems like if anything can go wrong, it will."

Karl's pulse quickened and his face grew warmer. He touched the comm panel and said, "Tokyan Station, this is shuttle 142. I've got an emergency. I'm presently on a course intersecting the station itself. I've had a control system failure, and I'm now trying to change course."

Karl tried the thrusters again. Still dead.

The comm speaker remained silent. Karl tried again. "Tokyan Station, do you read me? Tokyan Station, do you read?"

Silence. Karl couldn't tell if he had just a receiver failure or if the whole communications system had fallen victim to whatever equipment failure had blown out a third of the console. He locked the comm switch open and started a steady commentary of where he was, what had happened, and what actions he was now taking.

The station kept growing larger in slow motion. He couldn't even read the relative velocity, but it had to be big enough that the shuttle was going to do some serious damage. For an instant he considered abandoning ship, but he couldn't—not as long as there was a chance of stopping the shuttle. Besides that, he might not have time to avoid hitting the station anyway, and he'd be better off inside the shuttle. He tried not to think about what the crash would do to him. At least he had a cushioned flight web and the protection of being inside a large mass.

"I'm still on the way in," he said. "For God's sake I hope

you can hear me. It looks like I'll probably hit two or three corridors up from the southern rim. I would have tried to go outside and manually fire one of the thrusters, but I'm so close already, there's no time."

The station was near enough to entirely fill the view screen. As the station's spin became more and more obvious, Karl realized that the rotation rate would contribute to the damage.

Another huge section of the instrument panel went dark. "Tokyan Station, do you read? Answer me, damnit!"

Alis hadn't seen another person for over a minute. Probably the people who had originally started for other exits were already out. She sped past compartment after compartment displaying *unoccupied* indicators. The pulsating buzzer seemed to fade into the background, as if it had become just another station noise, just one more ingredient in the collection of normal sounds that might in another time and place have included chirping crickets, rustling leaves, and a squeaking screen door.

Far ahead, so far that it was concealed by the upward curve of the corridor, lay one of four connection points where Alis could move either to an adjacent corridor or upward to the next interior corridor. For the moment, she felt good, her body moving in an easy rhythm. She felt fit and alert now that the minor adrenaline surge had swept away the effects of sleep. She no longer resented the drill, and a second later she realized that it shouldn't have taken a drill to get her mind temporarily off work.

She smiled suddenly at the notion that a brisk run would trigger a reaction that told herself she needed to slow down. She was aboard the Tokyan Station, for crying out loud. She was in space, living her dream. She should be savoring this a little more, and being a little less single-minded about her job. She certainly didn't want to slack off in her duties, but work didn't have to consume *all* her off-hours. She wondered how long it had been since she'd gone up to the low-gee observation lounge and just watched the stars for an hour. She would do that at the end of today's shift, no matter what.

Alis suddenly felt more alive than she had in months. She had worked tirelessly in graduate school in Houston, spending hours upon hours in simulators and sometimes going with so little sleep that she felt perpetually light-headed. She'd been on scholarship, one of just five in her graduating high school class in El Paso who not only wanted off the ground but also tested high enough to have a chance. All that work, just so she could be here.

She made herself promise she wouldn't back out of her commitment to go to the lounge tonight, no matter how much more she could get done if she stayed late at work. She thought about some of her old classmates, destined to see the stars only through the dirty lens of the Earth's atmosphere, trapped forever at one gee, never even to see the far side of the moon. Yes, this drill had come at exactly the right time. This was a signal to shift her priorities.

As Tokyan Station grew large in Karl's forward view port, what used to look like small vague shapes resolved into huge expanses of bulkheads, antennas, safety tie-down loops, maintenance lamps, emergency access panels, and networks of welding scars.

At another time, Karl might have marveled that the transformation in view was like looking at something familiar under a high-power microscope. Right now, he was as near panic as he'd ever been. The instrument panel was completely dark, so he couldn't try to minimize the damage by adjusting the shuttle's attitude to make sure he hit with the largest possible profile.

He was fully suited, breathing his personal air supply.

The emergency beacon should be on, but he had no way to verify its operation. All he could do was wait.

Suddenly overpowered by frustration, Karl pounded on the dark control panel. It stayed dark.

He recalled a winter day on Earth, on a steep, icy hill, on a cold and overcast Minnesota morning. Even the anti-lock brakes were virtually ineffective as his Intruder slid down the hill. That morning he was able to maintain a weak sense of control by turning the steering wheel. Today he didn't even have that.

The comm panel near Albert McIntyre's fingertips buzzed again. Red Adams's face appeared.

"Can't it wait?" asked Albert.

"No," said Red. "We've really got a problem."

Albert moved his gaze from the drill displays to Red's face on the screen as Red continued speaking. "There really is a shuttle out there, and it's really on a collision course for the station. You've got to terminate the exercise."

"Oh, come on. We went over this. What you're seeing is exercise data that's incorrectly flagged."

"Wrong. We backtracked, and a science shuttle was on the way in before you guys started up."

"And you expect me to believe—"

"I expect you to react!"

Alis felt good. Normally one didn't run through the corridors. The exercise areas were available twenty-four hours a day for running and other conditioning. Unfortunately, Alis had conditioned herself to feel she was working when she went there. Here in the corridor, running was somehow fun, a little like breaking the rules.

The series of closed cabin doors gave over to a longer expanse of solid corridor wall as she reached one of the high-gee sick bays. The one low-gee infirmary was much closer to the station's spin axis, and reserved for only those patients whose condition required low gravity for recuperation. As she passed the first door, she relaxed further as she saw one more indication that this was, in fact, just an exercise, not a real emergency. The indicator next to the door said: *occupied*.

The sign made sense, Alis decided. There wasn't much to gain by moving injured people during a routine evacuation exercise. She kept moving.

At last she came within sight of her goal: the cross-corridor hatch. On her left was a recycling bay. On her right was still the sick bay. And not thirty meters away was the hatch. All she had to do was get through it.

Alis's exhilaration lasted less than a second. The floor shuddered under her feet, and suddenly, only ten meters in front of her, the steel floor buckled upward like a newly forming mountain range. Fissures formed. Bulkheads crumpled.

Alis stumbled as the shock wave hit her, and the blast of noise sounded like an explosion. This big a shock would have people on the far side of the station saying, "What was that?"

The air filled with a metallic crunching noise, as if some huge piece of machinery had been placed between two powerful vise jaws. There came an aftershock, or a second impact, and the sounds of destruction vanished, to be replaced by the hiss of leaking air. Within another second, the hiss became a roar.

Coming out of shock, Alis tried to back up. Already the blast of air threatened to sweep her bodily toward the damaged area and its jagged edges of curled metal. Her grasping fingers finally made contact with a recessed safety rung high on the wall.

Just in time. Her body blew at a forty-five-degree angle as the air from the corridor blasted through the hole and into space.

The pattern of the buzzer changed. The regular series of buzzes was replaced by a new code of long-short-long-short. A calm recorded voice began to repeat, "Hull breach. Please move to a higher level." Alis didn't need the extra encouragement. The sound volume already seemed to be tapering off as the air pressure fell.

She wouldn't have air much longer. Dangling by one hand as her body was buffeted by the escaping air, she tried with her free hand to pull her balloon helmet over her head. Her ears popped and her vision took on a faint red tinge.

The scene took on a nightmare quality as Alis dangled from the rung, her body whipped by the wind. The station designers expected occasional micrometeor impacts, but this was horribly wrong. Nothing the size of a pebble would do damage like this. This looked like some idiot had driven a shuttle directly into the station.

Karl almost blacked out on impact, but the webbing had helped absorb the worst of the shock. Immediately after the abrupt stop, he felt a sideways lurch. For just that second or two, the shuttle was stuck to the skin of Tokyan Station, like a piece of mud on a tire. But as soon as the station's spin had a second or two to act, the shuttle was cast loose, and Karl was in free fall again.

The only good news was that if he'd been flung off the station like mud slinging off a rotating tire, the one thing he couldn't do was cause any more damage to the station.

He wondered where he was heading. The impact had given the shuttle a several-rpm spin, and the only thing he was sure of was that Tokyan Station looked a little smaller each time it passed his field of vision.

In the silent, power-dead cabin, the slowly spinning star field generated a false sense of serenity.

Karl hoped they'd find him before his air ran out.

·   ·   ·

Now do you believe me?" asked Red Adams. His expression in the comm panel showed more satisfaction in being right than worry about damage to Tokyan Station.

"Okay, okay," said Albert. "We felt it, too. We're shutting down the exercise. But why weren't you able to talk to the shuttle? Nothing in the test setup disturbs communications."

"I don't know yet. But we did have a small bit of luck. The impact is in the area that was already evacuated for your test. Crews are on their way now."

Alis was a doll in a tornado by the time she finally managed to get her balloon helmet secured. She grabbed a different recessed rung and let go of the first one. The hiss of internal suit air was a welcome sound. Seconds later the clear bubble around her head snapped outward from the pressure. A faint vibration came from the air exchanger on her back.

The flow of wind buffeting her was slowing. Almost all the air in the corridor was gone now.

She grabbed another rung and held on with both hands as she turned to survey the damage. Several jagged slits like knife wounds showed black. She could see through to the blackness of space, but the corridor lights made the adjacent ripped surfaces too bright for her to actually see the stars spinning past.

Whatever had hit the station was big. The walls on both sides of the corridor showed damage. Even the heavy frame that surrounded the emergency door between her and the next section of the corridor was crumpled at the bottom.

The air was finally almost gone, and she hung limply from the rungs. Alis let go and stood up. Her legs felt shaky at first, but her strength was returning. She moved forward to the door, avoiding the sharp edges of metal that had been pushed up through the floor.

The door was jammed shut. Through the portal she could see workers on the other side starting repairs, but the work was obviously going to take a while.

She looked back down the hall toward her cabin. She'd have to go all the way back to the other end to get out. Surely they'd unlock it; they had to realize by now that something really had gone wrong.

As she moved back through the damaged area, she noticed for the first time the tiny jets spraying condensing atmosphere from the pressurized sick bay into the vacuum of the corridor. Damn! The patients left in sick bay almost certainly wouldn't have been put in life-suits or pressure-protection bags just for what had started as an exercise. Alis ran to the nearest emergency panel, popped it open, and searched in the locker for something to deal with the leaks.

She fetched a set of generic patches, ones that could be used for a leaking life-suit or anything else. As she pressed a few into place and stopped the biggest leaks, she realized that the leaks indicated good news and bad news. The good news was that the sick bay still held enough pressure to leak this vigorously. The bad news was that if the room was leaking into the corridor here, it could also have slow leaks to the outside. She had to get into the sick bay to patch the leaks there.

Think, she told herself. She couldn't just slide open the door and walk in. She'd lose too much air too fast.

She turned and ran back to the emergency locker. She could hear her labored breathing inside her helmet, but nothing else. The emergency buzzers had long since been squelched by the vacuum. The emergency panel held a blocker that she could use to seal the corridor, but she needed two of them to isolate this section of corridor. She pulled out the blocker and dumped it on the floor. She ran the twenty meters to the next emergency panel and grabbed a second blocker. She lugged it to where she'd need to activate it, and then returned to get three air tanks. She'd need all the air she could manage. When an air tank hit the floor, she felt the impact through her feet.

A meter from the sick bay door she stopped and knelt beside the blocker. She double-checked her plan, and then pulled the cord and stepped back.

The blocker inflated quickly. In an atmosphere, it would have gone more slowly and would have made sound. Here, the folds of material just snapped silently in place as the huge shape inflated. Within seconds it was a large ball almost as wide as the corridor. As it expanded, Alis moved to activate the second blocker.

This one was trickier. She needed it to be on the other side of the damaged part of the sick bay wall, but she needed to avoid the sharpest slices of damaged metal. She picked the spot carefully and pulled the cord on the unit.

A few seconds later, her horizons had compressed to a corridor only ten meters long, blocked at both ends by the two huge, inflated balls that had by now firmly wedged themselves into place. She twisted the nozzle on one of the air tanks, and then another, letting air spill into the sealed section of the corridor. While the corridor section slowly filled with air, she grabbed two more air tanks from the emergency panel that she still had access to, and piled her supplies just outside the sick bay door.

Alis tried to gauge the ambient pressure by the snugness of her life-suit. When finally her balloon helmet began to sag slightly, she figured it was close to normal. She slid the sick bay door ajar and stuck her hand in the gap. The airflow seemed to be pulling her hand gently inside.

Good. At least she hadn't made the situation inside even worse. She slid the door wide open, and her balloon helmet stretched a little tighter.

She grabbed some of the supplies stacked on the corridor floor and carried them into the sick bay waiting area. Three quick trips later, everything was inside the sick bay, and she closed the door again. She turned off the flow from one of the air tanks and left the other running. Nervously she cracked the seal between her helmet and collar. Enough air escaped to pop her ears again, but the pressure was adequate. She pulled her helmet back off her head and shut down her air supply. Air was also flowing into the room from overhead nozzles, but their flow was meant for circulating fresh air in a pressurized environment, not for replacing air escaping from an unexpected leak.

Alis took some of the patch sealer and moved into a corridor that paralleled the main corridor. She passed an empty office and a deserted surgery room. The first patient room was unoccupied, but the second held a comatose, bedridden man with a couple of monitors nestled against shaved spots on the side of his head. The trace lines on the monitoring panel made it seem to her untrained eyes that he was in roughly the same condition as he had been in before the exercise started.

She continued down the hall. She found another empty room, and then another patient. This one was a young girl, maybe ten or twelve, awake and wide-eyed, in bed and trying to sit up.

"What's wrong? What's happened?" the girl asked.

"I don't know for sure," Alis said. "But I'm sure things will be getting under control soon. Anyone else besides you and the guy back there in here?"

"I don't think so." The girl was obviously afraid, and obviously reluctant to admit it. Apparently she had a broken leg. Her right leg was constrained, and the casing sprouted several monitoring transducers, each no doubt transmitting data to the control panel. The girl looked tiny in the huge bed.

"Good. Look, I've got to patch a couple of slow leaks. The station suffered some damage, but more help is on the way. You going to be all right?"

The girl nodded quickly, then pushed a lock of hair away from one eye.

Alis moved back to the hallway and headed toward the damaged area. She passed a series of empty rooms and reached the end of the corridor. The corner where the corridor met the far wall was the focal point of the damage, and crumpled metal showed a series of cracks in the floor and both walls, as if the corner of the room had been crushed inward.

From this close, Alis could hear the hiss of escaping air. She retrieved a patching kit, including flexible squares of tough material, and slapped three pieces on the most obvious holes, two on the floor and one on the far wall. The worst of the risk was probably over. With internal air pressure working with the adhesive to push the patches firmly against the edges of the gaps, the leaks should be easily controllable.

Alis grabbed a spray can of mist and filled the corner with fog. A couple of smaller leaks showed up instantly as the fog funneled into the tears in the metal. She covered those leaks, too, and then sealed another smaller leak. Now the fog gradually dissipated in the room instead of leaking out. Considering the damage, she had been extremely lucky these leaks were so small.

She finally let herself start to relax as she took the last step. She took out another spray can and gave all three damaged surfaces a coat of gap-sap. The aerosol glue should form a rubbery layer over the whole surface and take care of even microscopic leaks until a repair crew arrived.

The girl looked very happy to see Alis return.

Alis set down her repair kit. "I think everything's under control. You're sure you're all right?"

The girl nodded.

"Okay. I'm going up front to find a comm panel and find out how long it'll be before we get some help."

As she walked to the waiting room, Alis remembered one

more precaution she should take, just in case the damaged area were to suddenly rupture. She found a supply closet and grabbed an air ball.

Back in the girl's room, Alis unsnapped the loop that held the fabric tight and began to spread it out. "Have you seen an air ball before?"

"Yes. Every few months they show us."

"Good. I want to get this one ready for you, just in case we have any more air problems." Alis spread the material under the girl's body and pulled a section up and over her leg. When inflated, the air ball would form a meter-wide ball with a contained atmosphere. Moments later, the girl lay almost enclosed by the material, and her hand held the interior zipper, ready to zip the bag closed if need be.

"I don't think you're going to need this, but I'd rather be safe," Alis said. "I'll take care of the guy in the other room if you can zip this up for yourself."

"Yes. I can do it."

"Good. I've got to make some calls. You're sure you're going to be all right?"

"Yes, thanks."

Alis smiled. After she did what she could for the man, she moved to the small office next to the waiting room. The comm panel was built into a desk that was in turn built into the wall. She tapped the icon for the operations center and waited for an answer.

The panel lit up and showed the face of a man she vaguely recognized.

Alis spoke carefully. "This is Lieutenant Commander Nussem. I'm in corridor C-8, in sick bay. We had a loss of pressure in the corridor, but the two patients here are safe as long as the air leaks don't get worse."

"Excellent. How are you doing?"

"Just a little shaken up. The corridor floor damage is just this side of the main doors. I inflated two blockers, one near the damaged area and one on the opposite side of the sick bay door. Between them is atmosphere. The rest of the corridor is still vacuum, I assume."

"Right. That's what we show here." The man looked away from the screen and up at someone standing next to him. Seconds later he was back. "Look, we've got another problem. A shuttle rammed into the side of the station. We're getting bad readings from the recycling station across the hall from you. There must be a rupture, because we're sensing a steady loss of gas. Apparently we're venting a huge amount into space. We're trying to get a crew on it from the outside, but meanwhile we've got to try to do it from the inside. Obviously we've got a problem on our hands. I'm not ordering you to go in there, but if you were to volunteer—"

"I can't just walk away," Alis said. "Anything special I should know before I go?"

"Don't think so. Just use your own judgment and give us an assessment when you get in. If there's anything obvious you can patch, great. We've got a team on the way, but it might be ten or fifteen minutes."

"Will do."

Alis stopped briefly at the door of the girl's room. "We've got some other damage I need to take a look at. You going to be all right?"

"I think so. Yes."

Alis flashed another quick smile at the girl and left. In front of the door to the corridor, she put her balloon helmet back in place. The sound of her breathing intensified, and she took a deep breath that almost sounded as if she had just emerged from one of the underwater training sessions back in Houston.

She slid the door slightly ajar. Air rushed neither in nor out. She slid the door open, stepped through, and shut it behind her, grateful that the sick bay would probably hold up just fine until the others arrived.

The two inflatable corridor blockers were still in place and doing their jobs adequately, or there wouldn't have still been air in the corridor. She moved down the hall and stopped in front of the door to the recycling bay. She realized with surprise that she didn't want to go in, and without the slightest effort she instantly traced the reaction back to Texas.

Growing up in El Paso, she and a group of the neighborhood kids had played hide-and-go-seek. It was a game Alis played not because it was fun, but because she wanted the companionship and didn't want to be an outsider. Almost invariably one of the boys would hide in the boiler room of the apartment complex. From that time on, Alis disliked spending time around large machinery. She just hated creeping through that maze of huge refrigeration units, water tanks, dripping pipes, and creaking metal, worrying that one of the huge water tanks would choose that moment to explode, and knowing that at any instant one of the hiding children might leap from a dark corner and scare her so badly her heart sounded like a drum.

A game like that made her think she could understand how some people could look at Russian roulette as a game, but it still couldn't make her understand how they might think it was fun. And yet here she was living in space, surrounded by machinery.

Alis shoved aside the memories. Wary of a vacuum beyond the door, she leaned away from the side of the door she intended to open and pulled the recessed handle. The door would not budge.

She moved her head closer to the panel next to the door. The indicator said the door was locked as a safety measure because vacuum was reported on the other side. She entered the emergency code 9911 on the keypad, and a warning light bright enough for a foggy runway began to strobe. A horn began to scream. She pressed her fingertips against the door, and soon she felt the *click* as the computer released the lock.

She pulled the door open a few centimeters, and air began

to screech through the gap. Damn, now there would be that much more gas lost in space. Her bubble helmet stretched tighter, and the noise from the air loss started to wind down as the pressure fell. She pulled the door farther open and tossed a couple of air tanks and a repair kit inside. She left one air tank to refill the segment of corridor, then closed the door behind her. The regular overhead lighting had failed inside the recycling bay, and the masses of equipment were garishly lit by wall-mounted emergency lamps. Vacuum intensified the contrast along the edges of shadows.

Back in the maze of machinery, numerous emergency indicators independently flashed on and off, creating a constantly changing patchwork of illuminated surfaces, an ant's view of the interior of an old-fashioned pinball machine.

Alis left the air tanks near the door and grabbed the patch kit. She realized her heart rate was up as she moved into the maze, walking carefully along a narrow corridor. She wished her emergency suit had a radio. A calm voice in her ears would be welcome.

The corridor turned ninety degrees, traveled a couple of meters, and then split into two branches. She took the one on the right, the one that led toward where she guessed the damage lay.

Another ten meters brought her within sight of the impact area. The damage here was worse than in the corridor. A hole almost a half-meter across showed in the floor, as if a huge blunt knife had ripped into the outside shell of the station. The patch material wouldn't do any good here.

Gas steadily jetted from a ruptured pipe, part of it turning to mist in the cold and funneling out the hole in the hull. For all Alis knew, that could be oxygen that was being wasted. Whatever is was, it was completely unrecoverable.

Alis moved to a nearby equipment cabinet door. She opened it, snapped two catches loose, and lifted the door from its hinges. She levered the door into place over the hole in the hull, making it into a giant patch. The raised lip of metal around the hole in the hull kept the door from lying flat against the floor. With one foot on one side of the door, she kicked down on the opposite side, wishing she were heavier. After several blows, the door bent slightly over the damaged metal of the hull, and the gaps between the edges of the door and the hull grew smaller.

She dug out the biggest patches she could find and started applying them to the perimeter of the door. After about a minute, she could see sections of the material starting to bulge outward. Good! The hole to the outside was growing smaller. She kept applying material, and seconds later completed her circuit of the door. So far the material was holding.

She sprayed mist and followed its path. At first it was hard to see in the shadow, but soon she saw that a hairline crack between two bulkhead plates was still letting gas out. She sprayed the length of the seam with gap-sap, and then sprayed all around the material surrounding the door. Suddenly the center of the door buckled outward with a *twang* that she could hear. The atmosphere was building up. Finally!

The pressure increased to the point that her bubble helmet no longer stretched tightly, and the door held. Next she had to repair the burst pipe or find a way to shut off the flow. She spun a valve handle a couple of meters from the broken section, but the flow continued. She traced the pipe on the far side of the break.

The pipe vanished behind a bay of cabinets. She raced back to the damaged section and tried to wrap patch material around it. She couldn't get a good seal. The surface next to the pipe was oily, and so was the pipe. Besides that, this time the pressure was working against the seal instead of with it.

She hurried back to see if she could trace where the pipe came out after going behind the bay of cabinets. At the end of the bay was a bulkhead wall, and she had to backtrack along the corridor to the branch and follow the other corridor.

Finally she came around to the far side of the cabinets and the stubby support bulkhead. There was a pipe—three pipes. She picked the one with the same diameter as the other section, and she traced it along a section of corridor, past another small maze of huge containers, and finally she found another valve. She closed the valve and finally started to relax.

She stayed in that semi-relaxed state only another ten seconds or so, because as her gaze followed the pipe to where it split into two paths, she saw a label on the pipe: *Hydrogen.*

Oh, God. That meant this entire bay must be full of hydrogen by now. And she had plugged the leak to the outside. A rescue crew could be coming along the corridor at any second—along a corridor now filled with oxygen.

She had to keep them from opening the door. If those two gases were to mix, and there were to be a spark, say caused by a metal boot scraping against the corridor floor or, worse yet, someone with a welding torch—

She ran. She sped along the narrow corridor. She careened off an instrument panel at a sharp bend in the corridor, and her feet pounded against the hull beneath her. Her breath was ragged inside the helmet.

She was within sight of the door. It was still closed. Thank God. She raced the rest of the way and slapped the lock into the *on* position. That had been way too close.

But the danger wasn't over. The emergency crew could override the lock. She had to get word to them.

She flipped on the comm panel next to the door, suddenly even more angry that emergency evacuation suits didn't have radios.

The light on the comm panel lit, indicating someone was on the other end. Alis took a deep breath and quickly removed her helmet.

"Don't let anyone in the recycling bay down here. It's filled with hydrogen!"

"Is this Alis Nussem? In the damaged section?"

"Yes. I've got the door locked, but the emergency crew will override it." Alis had to take a breath. "You've got to tell them—" Alis stopped. Her voice had turned into a cartoon squeaky voice. It was the hydrogen. She put her helmet back on and took a couple of deep breaths to fill her lungs with oxygen. Once again she tore the helmet off, and said, "You've got to tell them not to open the door."

"Nelson is calling them right now. Good work."

Even as the words came over the comm speaker, Alis heard a thump on the door. The emergency crew was already here. She grabbed the recessed handle and held the door closed.

Whoever was on the other side had already overridden the lock and was sliding the door open. A tiny gap opened at the side of the door.

Alis pushed as hard as she could to keep the door from opening farther. She was starting to grow light-headed from lack of oxygen, but she couldn't put her helmet back on without reducing her pressure on the door. She was acutely aware of the grim irony that on the other side of the door she was trying to hold closed was plenty of oxygen. If only the person on the other side of the door would get the word before she lost consciousness.

Through the gap came a narrow metal pry bar. The lever forced the door open almost as if Alis weren't making any effort at all.

"Keep the door closed!" she yelled. The pry bar kept moving, as if the suited worker couldn't hear her.

She gave up trying to hold it closed. As soon as the door had opened far enough for her to see someone in a full EVA suit, she gestured to indicate the door must close again. She yelled, "Hydrogen! Shut the door!" but her last breath of hydrogen again turned her voice into the high-pitched squeak that was neither very intelligible nor commanding.

The suited figure stood there motionless for a second as though dumbstruck by the spectacle of Alis struggling with her helmet. The person turned suddenly, as if to look back at someone else in the corridor, and the tip of the pry bar struck the edge of the door frame.

Alis didn't even have time to blink. The explosion was a belly flop from the high dive. She pinwheeled backward into blackness, unconscious even before she hit the recycling center bulkhead.

2 ▪ B I O F E E D B A C K

Dr. Tommy Weng was far enough away from the explosion, and muffled enough inside his life-support suit, that at first he underestimated the damage. Fortunately, he was close enough that he had time to be of help.

At the urging of rescue workers ahead of him in corridor C-8, he hurried forward and passed several other suited crew members. The injured people weren't in sick bay as he had suspected, though; the first ones were right out in the corridor.

The first man Tommy examined had apparently been slammed against the corridor wall. The man looked as if he'd fallen from a ten-story building. Crouched next to the body was one of the rescue team in a life-suit, a guy who'd just done one of the things no one wanted to do in a life-suit; he'd thrown up.

Sometimes death is absolutely unmistakable. Without

even removing the victim's blood-splattered helmet, Tommy could see the man had died instantly of massive brain hemorrhage. During Tommy's internship in San Francisco, an old man with skin so rough that shaving with a razor would have been really ill-advised had come in complaining of what he called a brain hemorrhoid. Tommy had told the old man he thought the odds were against it.

Tommy moved on and stopped at the side of a man who'd been several meters away from the open door opposite the first body. This man was already recovering. Tommy gave him a quick check, hampered by his suit and the other man's suit.

"Stay quiet," Tommy told the man. "I don't want you moving until I've had a chance for a more thorough check. Don't be a hero. Yell out if you feel light-headed or faint. Got that? Don't move."

The man nodded.

"I told you not to move."

The man gave Tommy a lopsided smile. "Got you, Doc."

Tommy signaled one of the obviously healthy emergency crew. "Get this guy out of here on a stretcher. And stay with him so you can call for help if his condition worsens. I want to know ASAP if he loses consciousness."

"You got it."

He found another dead victim, this one a woman with blonde hair. Moments later her body was transported away.

Tommy caught a signal from an individual inside the recycling bay that they'd been told was the problem area. A number of people were effecting repairs, shutting off valves, and sifting through damaged equipment. As Tommy moved closer he could see another victim.

The third victim was just in a thin emergency suit. That would be the woman who'd been working to avert the disaster. His first impression, given the blood loss and the woman's crazy posture, was that she was probably dead, too.

"Doesn't look good, Doc," said the woman who'd found the victim.

This was the part of the job Tommy hated the most—reaching people when it was maybe just a few minutes too late. He stooped next to the body. This was the kind of victim who, given a choice, probably wouldn't want to live anyway. Her face had been smashed in by the force of whatever hit her, and her eyebrows had been burned right off. It didn't take a physician to know that at least one of her eyes, probably both, would never be repairable. The fabric of her emergency suit was miraculously intact, but it still couldn't conceal the damage. One leg was twisted, and both legs had been crushed by a falling equipment cabinet. Her shoulder-length hair was so bloody she looked like a redhead. He touched the woman's chest and had a sensation like pressing on a water bed. Even with all his conditioning, Tommy felt sick.

The woman was almost certainly dead, but Tommy made the obligatory move to feel for a pulse as he considered whether a CPR effort would, in fact, just guarantee she'd die if she wasn't dead already. He felt his face go hot. Beneath his fingers beat a pulse. God almighty.

He looked up at the life-suited woman standing next to him. "She's alive. My God, she's alive."

Whether the woman would prefer to be dead or alive was no longer fuel for idle speculation. In her place, Tommy probably would want to be dead, but he would never presume to make that decision for another person.

He switched his life-suit radio from local to emergency and began to speak. "This is Dr. Weng on C-8. I want a full operating crew down here ASAP. Faster than ASAP. We've got a critically injured woman, probably the woman who made the emergency call. Find out who she is and get her records ready. While the first crew is on the way, I want a second crew on stand-by. We'll work in the recycling bay across from sick bay, then move her if and when we can. Bring a lot of blood. And

I want two of every life-support system we've got ready for instant use. Get Janny Rankine to head up the crew. No one else will do."

"Got it, Tommy," said a voice.

Tommy turned back to the woman's body. For a little while, the tight suit was working in his favor, acting as a mild tourniquet and reducing the blood loss. He switched back to local radio and said to the woman standing beside him, "We're going to need lots of light in here. And get someone to rig a water supply. Get started, will you?"

Other life-suited crew members started clearing the area.

Even as Tommy started doing what he could for the victim, he wondered, if she lived, would she come to appreciate this or to hate him?

Tokyan Station was barely more than a bright star by the time Karl Stanton saw motion against the rotating star field. At first he thought he was guilty of wishful thinking, but the next time the station slid past, he was sure he saw a slightly brighter object moving against the star field.

His head hurt, and the pounding in his temples kept him current on his pulse rate with no effort at all.

His air seemed to gradually grow stale, and soon the other craft blocked the whole view when his ship spun past that direction. Karl felt as if he were more than slightly drunk. He wondered how they'd board his shuttle while he was spinning like this.

He got the answer as something metallic *clicked* against the hull of his ship, a double-*click* as something magnetic hit the hull at an angle and then the magnet snapped the full surface against the hull. A second double-*click* sounded, from somewhere different if the altered texture of the sound was a good indication.

Finally Karl realized what was happening. The other ship

must have launched a couple of remote-control thrusters.

Sure enough. Seconds later he felt a series of twisting and tumbling lurches as the jets fired under computer control to zero out his spin. The star field slowed to a standstill.

Deeper sounds than before reached him, conducted through the hull. Apparently the rescue ship had made contact with his, and the two ships were magnetically locked together. Just as Karl was feeling proud that he had been able to figure all this out, he realized he must be suffering from oxygen deprivation. How could he have been unaware of this until now? Or had he already known it and forgotten it? He tried to raise his oxygen rate, but he couldn't tell if the control did anything.

The air lock finished cycling, and the wheel on the inner door spun, seemingly of its own accord. The door pivoted inward, and a space-suited figure entered the shuttle. Two people made the shuttle feel crowded.

The suited figure came closer to Karl and touched helmet to helmet. Karl hadn't even realized he'd put his own helmet on. He must have done that before impact and forgotten about it.

"Dr. Stanton, I presume?" said a metallic voice.

"I think so."

"Are you all right?"

"I think—where did you come from?"

"Just relax. Let's get you out of here."

"Out of where?" The next day, Karl would read those words on the transcript, but he wouldn't remember anything after the collision.

Alis Nussem had been hit by a car when she was twelve years old. The driver fled the scene, but a search of mobile phone records for vehicles in the area at that time had narrowed the search sufficiently that the Niponda van with blood on the bumper was located while waiting in line at a car wash, and the owner was arrested. As part of the driver's explanation for why he left the accident scene, he said he didn't know any first aid.

Both while lying in the road and later in the hospital, Alis had periods during which she floated in and out of consciousness. In the street, those brief spurts of awareness had been filled with dread, as she worried about whether she'd bleed to death right there or if a second driver would not notice her and run over her. In the hospital, her occasional surges of consciousness were more peaceful, as she assumed the situation was under control.

Lying in sick bay aboard Tokyan Station, where she should have felt subconsciously that her body was being tended to and she could just rest, she felt instead the same dread that she'd felt in that El Paso backstreet. There wouldn't be a car coming down the street toward her, but she was convinced that something terrible was yet to happen, that some unavoidable disaster was approaching.

As Alis slept, her fingers pulled tighter, as if she were trying to form her hands into fists.

Tommy Weng's legs hurt from standing so long, and he could feel the muscles in his lower back tensing. He and Janny Rankine, assisted by a large team, had been working on Alis Nussem for six hours already.

They left Alis's suit on at first, just cutting through sections of it and treating it like a second skin as they dealt with some of the internal hemorrhaging and tried to stabilize her life signs. After a half hour they had been able to move her across the hall to sick bay, onto a real operating platform. Equipment suspended over Alis's body trailed tubes into her arms and chest, and other tubes snaked up from the equipment housed in the operating platform itself.

Alis's shoulder-length hair had been cut short in most places, shaved to bare skin in others. Cutting the hair was purely superficial, but the change magnified the effects of the facial bruises and made her look like the loser of the world's longest fight.

Alis's soon-to-be-replaced heart was just idling roughly as an external pump kept the blood steadily recycling. A nutrient IV fed her a mixture designed to help her body recover strength. The muscles that normally tightened and relaxed to force air in and out of her lungs were assisted by a pump supplying a steady supply of forced oxygen and anesthetic. Four other independent systems kept vital body functions on track, ready to sound a warning if they detected trouble they couldn't handle. Working on a patient with this much damage was like trying to rebuild an aircraft in flight.

Janny's thoughts must have been tracking his own, because a moment later she said, "I need a quick in-flight refueling. How about you?" Her light eyebrows rose over calm hazel eyes. Her slightly too-wide ears parted her short blonde hair.

"Yeah. Just a sec." Tommy wished he had the confidence that medical school seemed to have instilled in all his classmates. Intellectually, he had a lot of trust in his abilities, but that didn't stop him from constantly worrying about mistakes. When that heightened fear of failure grew too large, and Tommy almost felt like running screaming from the operating floor, Janny's solid composure anchored him. He knew his droopy eyes made him look perpetually sleepy, but he was anything but.

Tommy laser-cauterized a damaged artery, then finished tying a couple of dissolving sutures, and an assistant sprayed temporary plastiskin over the area.

Moments later, the operating crew went on stand-by as Tommy and Janny sucked nutrient shakes and amphetamines from squeeze-bags. Tommy had lost track of how starved he was.

"So, what do you think so far?" Janny asked.

"It's going marvelously. I think she'll make a full recovery. A Tsuyoi heart should last a whole lot longer than the original."

Janny nodded. "We've got a Morganstern kidney ready to go in, too."

Tommy and Janny spoke in a form of code everyone on the operating crew knew. Because of the chance they were being overheard by the patient, they generally used the overly flattering rankings common on personnel evaluations, where "ten" meant "seven" and "outstanding" meant "fairly good." It was a language in which "I'm having a little difficulty here" started pulses racing.

"I'm really glad you're here," Tommy said. "The patient couldn't ask for a better doctor." This time Tommy had no need to resort to code.

Janny blinked, her only response to the praise. "Triage discussion sometime soon?"

"Right." Part of what Janny meant was that there was more work than they could possibly finish during even a twenty-four-hour shift. The key life-threatening situations had mostly been dealt with, and soon would begin the slower process of working on things like facial reconstruction and replacing the woman's eyes.

"I really am glad you're here." Sometimes Tommy had to prod Janny twice before she'd let herself accept a compliment.

Janny's surgical mask bulged almost imperceptibly at her cheeks as she smiled this time. Small crinkles appeared at the corners of her eyes. She lowered her voice. "Thanks, Tommy. I appreciate that. And you can certainly use all the help you can get." Her smile was more visible through the mask this time.

Tommy nodded good-naturedly. In contrast with a few of his egomaniac classmates, he'd become a surgeon because he genuinely loved the idea of bringing people back from the brink of death. Unfortunately, he also empathized well, too well sometimes. He could sometimes get lost for an instant, imagining he was the patient or one of the patient's loved ones. Janny could sense when he hit a momentary impasse and jog him out of it effortlessly, and in addition she was a truly talented surgeon. If Tommy were in fact the patient at some point, he'd want Janny to be the surgeon in charge, no doubt about it. Janny was the only person he'd acknowledged his "undoctorly" emotions to.

Tommy gestured at the woman's legs. "Once we've finished repair work on her heart and kidneys, I suppose the next thing to do would be work on the legs." Both kneecaps were shattered beyond repair, but worse, both femurs had been crushed. The longest and strongest bones in the body weren't powerful enough to withstand being crushed between a bulkhead and a heavy cabinet. If they tried to repair Alis's legs, the procedure would be long and painful, and the very best Alis could ever hope for would be confinement in very-low-gee environments. If they attached replacements, most people would probably never even know that anything had changed.

Janny nodded. "And I suppose working on her eyes will wait until the legs are mending."

Tommy watched Alis as he responded to Janny's question. Alis was the person the answer was for anyway. "Right. And Quentin is due for rotation at just about the right time. If anyone can do miraculous work on the eyes, it's Quentin." Tommy had to stop and close his own eyes for just a moment as he thought about how terrifying it would be to him if someone were to have to replace one of his eyes. He got queasy just sitting in the chair for his annual laser correction, suddenly imagining what it might feel like if, instead of the laser focusing on the bottom of the cornea and the pulse lasting just microseconds, the laser was focused deeper and the cutoff timer failed. Tommy made an even worse patient than the average doctor did.

They spent another couple of minutes planning, never mentioning the lengthy rehabilitation and counseling Alis would need. A number of patients with lesser injuries never had pulled out of the self-pity that began in the post-operation period. After going several rounds with tissue-rejection complications, on top of the documented feelings of mechanization that came with having so much of the body replaced, some patients seemed to suffer more from the psychological damage than from the original accident.

Janny finally said, "All right. Are you ready to go back to work?"

Karl woke in a hospital bed. For a few seconds he wondered if some guys in the Clean Tricks Gang had drugged him and dumped him here, along with a chart that said he had requested penis enlargement surgery.

No, that gag was part of his past, and Franklin Amarty had taken it with good humor, as had the hospital staff, fortunately. This must be a new gag.

Karl's head cleared a bit and he realized he hadn't even seen anyone from the gang for years. He lifted his left wrist, and looked at the date and time display on the skin-colored patch affixed to the base of his thumb. The Clean Tricks Gang hadn't been part of his life for almost ten years.

Karl realized a bracelet circled his right wrist. Perhaps it was a monitoring tool or a hospital patient identification tag. He also felt a couple of warm spots on his chest, and others on his neck and legs. The warm spots had to be monitoring disks stuck onto his skin.

A nurse approached, and as if the white-coated man were a catalyst, everything came back to Karl in a rush. The gently curving overhead ceiling, the lack of windows, the faint metallic odor the atmospheric purifiers never managed to get rid of, the almost undetectable hum of machinery conducted through all the beams and metal plates and rivets of Tokyan Station. He was in sick bay.

And the reason he was here was that his shuttle had rammed the station. He checked his chronograph again. That would have been almost twenty-four hours ago.

The nurse didn't seem as solicitous as Karl had anticipated. He just said, "Dr. Himalt will see you shortly."

Karl nodded. "Can you tell me if anyone was injured? Anyone else, that is?"

The nurse's expression changed to that of a bank officer deciding whether a patron qualified for a loan. His dark eyes seemed to be focused on something behind Karl's head. Finally he said, "Two dead, plus one probably won't recover. Actually it's amazing that casualties were so light."

Karl barely heard the part about light casualties. He heard the "two dead, two injured—one probably won't recover" and the pit of his stomach turned cold. He desperately wished this were, in fact, a prank being played by the Clean Tricks Gang. No matter how angry he'd be at being made to think he was responsible for a death and a near death, that still wouldn't be as bad as *knowing* he had done that.

As the nurse walked silently away, Karl was lost in an internal struggle of "what-ifs." Of course he didn't ram the station deliberately, and of course it didn't happen through negligence. But he had been at the controls. Pilot or not, he should have been able to figure out some way to avert the catastrophe.

His mouth felt dry. As he turned to locate a water tube, he got a better look at the bracelet on his wrist. It wasn't hospital-issue monitoring gear. This one was strictly judicial-issue equipment—a locator bracelet. As he realized what it was and he thought about the anti-tamper explosive, his whole arm tingled. But why would he be wearing this? Locators were meant for convicted inmates and defendants awaiting trial.

Things were even worse than he had thought. He stared at the shiny bracelet. He'd never seen one up close. It was fascinating in a morbid way. The surface was covered with what looked like small stainless steel ball bearings. Although it looked far from ugly, it would never be mistaken for jewelry.

Karl hoped the doctor would arrive soon. He had to find out what was going on.

The doctor turned out to be a very large woman with hair the color of bronze. Karl had a vague recollection of seeing her in the cafeteria, but he'd not known what her job was. Either the nurse had told her that Karl was awake, or she'd been alerted by a change in some monitored function.

The doctor didn't look too pleased with him as a patient, either. Karl had a sudden impression of being a patient in a deadly and infectious ward. Her expression remained severe even when she reached the side of his bed. Without acknowledging his presence other than by stopping nearby, she poked at the touch screen at the foot of the bed, obviously looking at a number of images that were off-limits to Karl. The name on the tag across her breast was new to Karl; she must have been a fairly recent arrival.

"Good morning, Doctor," Karl said mildly.

The doctor checked another few screens before she looked up and seemed to see Karl for the first time. "You've had a pretty busy day, Mr. Stanton."

" 'Horrifying' is a lot closer than 'busy.' "

"Well, it was a lot tougher on the other folks than for you, don't you think?"

"It's the other folks I'm thinking about."

"Maybe you should have thought of them sooner."

"What exactly is that supposed to mean?"

"I mean I thought pilots were supposed to stay awake on the job."

"I *was* awake." The sudden appearance of a very long needle wouldn't have made Karl more uncomfortable. "What gives you the idea this was pilot error?"

"That's out of my field. All I can say is, 'You'll live.' "

"That's all you're going to tell me? What the hell is going on around here?"

The doctor walked away without replying. Her retreating footsteps somehow grew louder and louder in Karl's ears.

The smiling man arrived not ten minutes after the doctor left. He had an air of nonchalance that made Karl feel more relaxed than he should have.

"Hello there," the man said. "You would be Karl Stanton if my guess is right."

Karl glanced around. He was the only patient in this section of sick bay, so he'd be a little hard to miss. "That's me."

"Great. That's great. If you're feeling up to it, I need to ask you a few questions about yesterday."

"Sure."

"I'm Leroy Barstow, by the way," the man said as he pulled up a chair, turned it to face him, and sat down, straddling the chair. "Anytime there's an accident, we have to ask a lot of questions. I'll get out of your hair in no time, though."

"No problem. It's not like I'm going anywhere today."

"That's a good one, Doc," Leroy said, still smiling. "You are a doc, right?" He pulled out a pack of gum and offered a stick to Karl.

Karl declined the gum with a wave of his hand. "Ph.D., not an M.D. In biology."

Leroy popped a stick of gum in his mouth and put the pack away. "Ah. So tell me about yesterday."

"What level of detail?"

"Whatever you think makes sense. I'll ask if I need anything more."

"Okay." Karl began a recap of the twelve hours before the accident, starting with dinner aboard Tokyan Station. He had been working midnight shifts during the last week as a team of biologists performed some experiments with microbe life housed in basketball-sized spheres that the team periodically left adrift in space far enough from the station that the man-made residual electrical and magnetic fields were effectively zero. It had been Karl's turn to leave another sample outside, which was why he had checked out the shuttle.

Leroy interrupted good-naturedly several times to clarify one point or another. He was quiet as Karl started describing the return trip. As Karl reached the time of the shuttle failure, Leroy quit chewing his gum.

Karl finished his tale with the impact and fuzzy recollections of what came later.

Leroy was silent for a long moment before he started chewing his gum again. "Mighty strange story, Doc."

"I agree. I've never seen a shuttle malfunction before, not with all the redundant systems they have."

"How much do you know about shuttles?"

"How do you mean? I know how to fly them. I don't know how to repair them."

"You don't know anything about electronics or the guts of the control system?"

"I know a little circuit theory and stuff like that from school, but I don't know the first thing about shuttle electronics. And even if I did, I couldn't fix a problem like that in a few minutes unless it involved pounding on the equipment panels. By the way, I can tell you that doesn't work; I tried it."

"How do you handle these rotating shifts, Doc? Don't they play havoc with your metabolism?"

Karl was surprised at the sudden left turn, but he answered the question. "I'm not crazy about it, but if you've ever worked shift, you'd know we've got some fairly good drugs that help resynch the circadian clocks. The first shift after you change is slightly worse than a normal shift but not much. By the second shift, you're fine."

"Those drugs ever make you drowsy?"

"Nope."

"What about your personal life, Doc? Any problems that make you lose sleep?"

"Nothing that I lose sleep over. Why do you—" Karl turned his head and looked directly at Leroy. "What are you saying, that you think this is pilot error? That's ridiculous."

"Is it?" Leroy was no longer smiling, and his face had somehow shed the good-old-boy expression.

Karl was abruptly aware that Leroy must be very good at his job. "This was not pilot error. I didn't fall asleep at the controls or make some stupid mistake. Something failed. Several somethings failed. I told you what happened. Why are you wasting your time and my time when you should be checking what happened by looking at the flight recorder?"

"Ah, there's one of those convenient snags, Doc." Leroy's serious expression made him look like a completely different person. "The black box doesn't have anything in it. It's completely blank."

"What do you mean by 'convenient snags'?" Karl asked, even as he realized where Leroy had been headed all along.

"I mean if I fell asleep and caused an accident that killed a couple of people and might as well have killed a third, and if I knew anything about shuttle systems, I might be tempted to destroy the black box and then claim equipment failure. With all the damage done to the shuttle, it might be a little difficult to prove I did it."

"You're beating up the wrong suspect. The shuttle failure was an accident."

"We'll see about that." As Leroy rose to leave, his expression was as icy as it had been jovial only a few minutes earlier.

Karl decided Leroy would make a good actor.

. . .

Tommy Weng put in more hours during the next couple of days than he normally spent in a week.

Alis's body seemed to be adjusting satisfactorily to the Tsuyoi heart, and the Morganstern kidney didn't seem to be causing any rejection problems. Tommy had replaced enough segments of arteries and veins with Everlast conduit that he felt like an electrician replacing wires in an antique radio. Tommy had never been involved with a patient with this much replacement work. Normally injuries as severe as Alis Nussem's were accompanied by massive spinal cord injuries or brain death.

The other factors in Alis's favor were that she had been in excellent shape and was under thirty years old. The same injuries would almost certainly have killed someone without those advantages. Alis's endurance was already being taxed to the limit. Even with her body motionless all day long, she consumed a high-calorie diet as her body's regenerative powers were called on to perform at peak rates.

In a sense, she was lucky to have so many transplants; if her body were also having to perform internal repairs on that many more organs, either her recovery would be significantly slowed, or the body might just quit. In much the same way hypothermia told the body to perform a set of autonomic protective actions, trauma could sometimes be so devastating that the body decided for itself that enough was enough, and just gave up.

All the way down to her white blood cells, Alis Nussem was a fighter.

Trips to the exercise room took Karl past the private room where Alis Nussem's body lay when it wasn't in surgery. Or what was left of her body.

The first time Karl had seen the hologram posted on the wall next to her door, he had been stunned. Now that he had seen it a few times, he was merely dumbfounded. In hospitals on Earth, medical status was closely guarded and private; in the confines of space habitats, privacy was more of a lucky break than a right. He supposed the hologram had been posted simply because so many people were constantly inquiring about Alis's progress. Despite his knowledge that the accident wasn't his fault, the hologram still made him feel guilty.

The hologram showed the work to date and the plan for Alis's body. The parts of her body that Alis had possessed prior to the accident were shown in various shades of gray and red. The non-organic replacement organs such as her heart were color-coded with metallic tints. Damaged areas that were recovering under the body's own mechanisms, like the broken bones in her arm, were shown in purple. Structural replacements, like the large bones in her legs, were shown in charcoal. Work yet to be done, like replacing her eyes, was shown in yellow.

Next to the hologram was a picture of Alis before the accident. Shiny black hair reached her shoulders. Intelligent green eyes that made her look alert and ready for anything life might throw her way. Her uniform might have made her square shoulders seem a bit wider than in reality. Her lips held the hint of a smile, as if she'd just noticed the photographer and was starting to react. Somehow the photo of her caught in that instant seemed to be a reminder of how brief certain moments can be, and how fast things could change.

Karl looked back at the hologram. He had taken enough peripheral medical training on the way to his biology degrees to know that if Alis had lived a few centuries earlier, any one of at least a dozen of the medical problems on the chart could have killed her. So much of Alis had been replaced, Karl could imagine doctors making tasteless jokes about how the replacement parts were rejecting the fragments of original tissue.

If only someone else had gone out on that mission. If only he'd picked a different shuttle, perhaps even made a change as simple as leaving five minutes earlier or later. If only.

Lieutenant Stanton is innocent," said Rog Dameko, the defender assigned to Karl.

Karl watched expressions. Judge Thompson was impassive, but one of his two assistants actually frowned, and the other compressed her lips just enough for Karl to see. Karl didn't look over at the prosecutor; it was a given that she wasn't on his side.

Fortunately, Karl didn't need to scan all the faces of a jury. There was no jury at this point. The preliminary hearing would decide the next step. Rog Dameko had assured Karl there would be no next step.

Judge Thompson cleared his throat. "Let's hear your arguments."

Rog Dameko stood. He was a spindly kid who had just received his degree a year earlier, but Karl was happy with him. He was sharp, and he at least said he believed Karl.

"I've got everything I'm about to say available for your more detailed examination later, but I can sum it up fairly quickly. And I'll be quite candid. Although I sincerely believe my client is a victim of an accident, and *not* guilty of dereliction of duty, the evidence I have to present is largely material that supports the accident explanation but does not prove he's not guilty of dereliction. Obviously my client doesn't have to prove himself innocent. I believe he is innocent, and I wish I could present a case that proves his innocence, but without the black box data I honestly don't think I can. What I do intend is to demonstrate that it's impossible for anyone to prove him guilty."

Judge Thompson remained unreadable. "Proceed."

Rog took a deep breath. "All right. One. The flight

recorder was somehow damaged before, during, or after the crash. The box itself showed no sign of tampering, and a search of the shuttle found no evidence of the special tool required to open the box.

"Two. Both power supplies showed damage due to what seems to be micrometeor impact. I've got a technical document provided by a shuttle designer who says that a simultaneous disruption such as what *seems* to have happened could, in fact, cause symptoms including flight recorder failure and massive control mechanism and communication sub-system failures.

"Three. Not one person interviewed can suggest a motive for the defendant to justify a deliberate action such as ramming the station, and no one interviewed expressed the opinion that it would be in character for the defendant to fall asleep at the controls or act in an irresponsible manner.

"In summary, I believe it is impossible for the prosecution to prove method, opportunity, or motivation for this accident to be described as a result of deliberate action on the part of the defendant, or the result of negligence. I believe this was a genuine accident, and I also believe that it's impossible to *prove* otherwise."

Karl would have been happier if the case for his character and for the impossibility of it being his fault had been presented more forcefully, but logic was the game here, and raising one's voice didn't seem to make a person any more logical.

On the wall behind the judge was the International Space Agency Tri-Service emblem with the eagle, wolf, and bear. The emblem's background combined motifs from the USA, the Japan-China Alliance, and the Russian Federation. In the gaps between the three showed designations of army, navy, and air force.

Karl's commission was with the ISA. If this tribunal were to revoke it, he would be shut out of the vast majority of space activity handled under the military ISA umbrella and relegated to scratching for work with GSSC, the General Space Support Corporation, a civilian outfit that scrambled for all the jobs ISA felt were too boring or too temporary to handle themselves.

Judge Thompson conferred inaudibly with the woman on his right and then the man on his left. None of them looked happy.

In the end, in the absence of proof that the accident had been Karl's fault, the judge really had no choice. Karl thanked Rog Dameko profusely for the time he had spent, and Karl tried to get on with his life.

By noon the following day it was obvious to Karl that his friends went along with the "not guilty" decision comfortably, but that strangers were less inclined to be convinced. From people he didn't know he got puzzled frowns, blank stares, and the occasional scowl, but no one actually confronted him and claimed the decision had been wrong.

A friend of Karl's back in school had been accused of theft. He wasn't kicked out of school, so obviously there had been no proof, but the incident had colored Karl's feelings. He realized now that the situations weren't all that different.

Karl had occasionally thought about trying to get an assignment aboard one of the Tri-Service ships that performed a variety of scientific missions throughout the solar system. By the end of the day, the idea had grown far stronger.

He resolved not to take hasty action. With any luck, the incident would soon start to fade from people's memories. ·

Alis drifted. She seemed to be in a noisy vehicle, listening to a radio that couldn't keep one station locked. A snippet of conversation would be followed by white noise, and then another station would come in strong for just four or five words, disconnected from whatever had gone before and whatever followed.

"Careful with the—" noise "—function better—" noise "—do you think she'll—" noise "—remember what—" noise "—both legs—"

Very gradually, so gradually she couldn't really detect the progress other than by the occasional sudden realization that the sentences were longer than before, the reception began to improve.

"Can you hear me, Alis?" noise "—heart seems to be stable, and blood pressure is within—" noise "—knitting well, but let's have slightly more current on—"

Over time, the reception became clearer, seeming less like a bad radio and giving her the feeling that the people speaking were actually somewhere nearby.

At some point Alis realized she wasn't in a vehicle. She was lying on her back in bed. And one of the voices was speaking to *her*.

"Alis? Alis Nussem? Can you hear me?" The voice was male.

"Look at the monitor, Tommy. I think she should be able to hear you." The second voice was a woman's.

"Alis, you're in sick bay aboard Tokyan Station, and you're going to be fine." The male voice sounded confident, trust-inspiring.

Alis tried to speak, but a sudden pain in her throat turned her word to a croak. "Hello."

"Alis!" said the male voice. "You can hear me. Just relax. Your throat may be a little stiff. Just take it easy."

Alis swallowed a couple of times. "What happened?" This time her voice was clearer.

"You were in an accident. You were trying to stop a gas leak, and there was an explosion."

"I don't remember an accident."

"That's not all that unusual. You suffered a concussion. The memories around the time of the accident may come back, or they might not."

"I can't—can't see." Alis tried to lift her arm to her eyes, but she couldn't.

"We've still got some bandages on your head, mostly for your protection." As the man spoke, the woman in the room said something soft that Alis couldn't make out. "Your arms have been restrained. Both of your arms were broken, so we didn't want you to accidentally do some damage if you woke unexpectedly. But don't worry about them; they're healing nicely, and as long as you're careful, we can loosen the restraints."

"They're healing nicely? How long have I been here?"

The man hesitated. "Almost two weeks."

Alis felt her fingers involuntarily clutch at the bed, and a mild stab of pain shot up both arms. "Whatever happened to me is a lot worse than two broken arms, isn't it, Doctor?"

"Dr. Weng. And Dr. Rankine is here with us."

"Hello, Alis," said the woman's voice.

"Alis, you were hurt pretty badly, but you're going to be fine. You've got some recovery still ahead of you, but you'll make it." Dr. Weng's voice didn't sound quite as confident as it had earlier.

"You're making me more nervous by not telling me what it is." Alis heard the waver in her voice, unsure whether it was from panic spilling into her nerves or just the result of disuse.

"I'm sorry. I just thought it would be easier on you if you knew you were going to be as good as new before we started in on what were temporary problems. You broke several bones. You damaged several organs, but nothing we couldn't deal with."

"Does 'deal with' mean something like 'amputate' or does it mean 'fix so I'll be just the same'?"

The doctor hesitated again. Alis didn't like the hesitation.

"I mean 'deal with' in the sense that you'll be just the same. Or better."

Alis felt a shudder of relief move through her chest. As she thought about the sensation, she realized she couldn't feel her legs. She tried to curl her toes, but she couldn't feel her body respond.

"Please, Doctor. Tell me the truth. Am I a whole person?"

"Yes, Alis. You'll have some physical therapy ahead of you, but I'm sure you're going to pull through it just fine."

Suddenly Alis couldn't hold it all in anymore. She started to cry, unsure whether from fear or relief. She couldn't feel the tears on her cheeks, but she had to sniff to clear tears from her nasal passages.

The doctors let her cry without trying to get her to stop, and for that she was grateful.

Several minutes later, Alis felt more in control. "What happened? You said an explosion?"

The woman spoke. "A shuttle hit the side of the station. You were trying to repair some of the damage when an accumulation of gases exploded."

"Was anyone else hurt?"

"Three people. Two of them died in the same explosion; the other is recovering. The shuttle pilot was a little banged up, but he's fine now."

"Who died?"

It took a minute for the doctor to find out. Alis didn't recognize the names.

"Who was the shuttle pilot?"

"Karl Stanton."

Alis didn't recognize that name, either, but that wouldn't stop her from remembering it.

· · ·

Alis slept. When she awoke, still in darkness, the same two doctors were there again. This time, she could feel more of her body, and low-level pain seemed to come from everywhere except below her knees. She flexed one arm and was comforted by its response.

"I think we're ready to take the protection off your head," said Dr. Weng. "But first we need to talk. You're going to be startled when you see yourself in a mirror, but your appearance is only temporary. Your nose and cheekbones were broken, and we had to do some reconstructive surgery. You're going to think you'll have terrible scars, but you won't. Within a few weeks, you'll never know."

"All right. I guess I can handle that. At least I'm alive."

"There's more," said the woman, Dr. Rankine. "Your eyes suffered some damage, so your vision might not be clear for a while. You *are* going to be able to see just fine, but you may have some difficulty at first. We're going to have the lights dim."

The idea of her eyes being damaged made Alis a lot more nervous than the question of whether she'd be attractive to look at. She swallowed hard. "All right."

As gentle pressure on her head told her someone was removing the padding that had been covering most of her face, Alis held her breath, afraid the doctors had miscalculated and she'd be blind.

Even after the padding came off and she felt cool air on her face, Alis kept her eyes closed. Now she could detect faint light through her eyelids, and she felt enormously relieved.

"All right, Alis," said Dr. Weng. "Can you slowly open your eyes?"

For an instant Alis thought her eyelids were stuck closed, but suddenly they popped open. Hovering right in front of her eyes was a red-and-yellow glowing mask. Alis gasped and clamped her eyes shut again.

"What's wrong, Alis?" Dr. Weng's voice was full of concern.

Alis took a deep breath and willed herself to relax. "Where am I?"

"You're in sick bay. Please tell me what you saw."

"A glowing mask. What have you done to me?"

Dr. Rankine said something softly and quietly to Dr. Weng.

"Oh," said Dr. Weng. "We know what's wrong. Listen carefully, Alis. In just a minute I'm going to want you to squint. I'll want you to contract those same muscles you normally use when you squint, all right? Pretend you're looking toward the sun, and your helmet screen isn't dark enough. I want you to squint and then relax those muscles, and I want you to do that four times in a row. One. Two. Three. Four. All right?"

Totally baffled, Alis complied, then said, "All right."

"Okay, now open your eyes again."

Afraid of what she would see, Alis opened her eyes slowly. The scene was blurry, but much closer to normal. Two separate images quickly resolved themselves into one stereo image of the room and two doctors. A dark-haired, sleepy-looking man in a white lab coat stood near the bed, looking down at her. On the opposite side of the bed stood a blonde woman in a white lab coat. The scene felt like dusk, but colors were still vivid despite the dim light.

"Thank God," Alis said softly. "I thought I was going crazy or something."

"All right," said Dr. Weng. This time she could see his lips move. "Tell me what you see."

"I see you, and I see someone who must be Dr. Rankine."

Dr. Rankine nodded. "That's good."

"My vision is a little blurry, but my color vision seems very good. But what did I see before?"

Dr. Weng sat down in a chair beside the hospital bed. "Alis, your eyes have been enhanced. I think you must have somehow activated an infrared viewing mode."

"Viewing mode?" Alis closed her eyes momentarily. "Enhanced? What an understatement."

"You're right. We gave you brand-new eyes. It was the only solution."

Alis was still for a long moment. She wanted to yell, but she gave her best effort at staying clinically calm. "This goes beyond eye transplants, Doctor. None of my friends sees in infrared."

"You're right. Your new eyes aren't from a donor. They were fabricated replacements, designed to be a lot better than the original. And they look very much like your old eyes."

"What happened to my old eyes?"

Dr. Weng turned to the woman, Dr. Rankine, who took over. "I'm afraid they were damaged beyond repair. We had two choices—not do anything about them, or give you something even better. The eyes you've been given are the latest product of an ongoing research effort. A decade from now they might be commonly available, but the initial versions are fairly limited in quantity. Your tear ducts are still functional; tearing will keep these lenses clean in the same way tears used to keep your old eyes clear."

Dr. Rankine said something more to Dr. Weng, who turned back to Alis. "The muscle tightening we had you do served to reset your eyes for normal vision. If you're experiencing no pain, we'd like to turn the lights up."

"No pain. But what do you mean, 'reset'?"

"Your new eyes are far more capable than your old eyes. What you see now is going to be your normal vision, but you can also see other views, like the infrared view you just experienced. All that power needs to be manageable, so there are tiny microprocessors that handle that for you. They read muscle contractions to do their magic."

"So by squinting four times—"

"You tell your eyes to use the normal mode. Can I turn up the lights now?"

Almost overwhelmed by the changes, Alis nodded. Her neck felt sore.

Dr. Rankine moved to the wall and touched the light panel. The lights in the room rose slowly and evenly.

Alis felt no pain at all as the light level increased to normal. Colors shifted hue slightly, and the contrast between light and shadow increased a fraction, but she felt no need to squint in light that might have been painful for normal eyes that had been inactive for two weeks.

Dr. Weng flipped a switch, and an eye chart lit up on the far wall. The bottom three rows of letters were blurry, but Alis could read the top rows. "Just watch the chart for a moment. I'm going to trigger a set of patterns that will tell your new eyes to perform a self-diagnostic so they'll be providing you with the best vision they can."

Alis watched as a rapid sequence of bright letters flashed across the eye chart. A second later her vision dimmed for just an instant, and when it came back, the bottom line on the chart was perfectly clear.

"Wow." She took a deep breath. "I've probably never seen this well." She looked quickly from side to side and then back at the chart. "And I don't see any of those funny little wispy things, I don't know what they're called—"

"Floaters, probably," said Dr. Weng. "They're the result of small particles in the vitreous humor, the fluid that fills the eye between the retina and the lens. You won't ever see them again. On the other hand, you might see different problems if your eyes are damaged. You might see dead pixels like on a display screen. They'll show up as tiny black or white spots that always seem to be in the same position relative to your field of view."

Dr. Rankine moved closer and she looked into Alis's eyes.

"You won't have blind spots, either. Where the optic nerve joins the eye, there are no rods and cones to pick up light. With your new eyes, there's no reason to replicate that deficiency."

Alis shut her eyes for a moment. "Do my new eyes take a lot of energy? I'm exhausted just from this five minutes."

"No," said Dr. Weng. "That's just your body telling you you're going to have to take it easy. Get some rest, and we'll come back later."

Alis nodded weakly. "You're saying I've got some more surprises in store?"

Dr. Weng hesitated. "Yes, you do. But in the long run nothing about your body is going to be worse than it was before. You've got some challenging recovery ahead of you, but you're going to be just fine. Better than fine."

"He's right," said Dr. Rankine. "I watched him closely, and he did a good job."

"Don't let her avoid credit that easily. Dr. Rankine did the tough parts. And a couple of experts did the work the two of us couldn't handle. If President O'Langley had an accident, she couldn't have gotten any better care."

The two doctors managed to quell some of Alis's fears, and she drifted off to sleep.

Sometime later Alis awoke. She couldn't see the time, but it seemed like several hours later. She thought about food and realized she didn't feel hungry. Two tubes snaked down from panels near her head, and she supposed they explained why she didn't feel a need for food.

Her body ached from her head to her thighs, and without the comforting presence of the two doctors, she started worrying about what other damage her body had suffered. The absence of feeling below the thighs was starting to scare her.

Her fear grew stronger minute by minute until the doctors returned.

"I'm glad to see you're awake again, Alis," said Dr. Weng. "That's good. You should have more energy than yesterday."

Yesterday? She'd been out that long? "What's wrong with my legs?" Alis blurted out. She'd meant to show more patience, but she had to know.

Dr. Weng and Dr. Rankine exchanged glances, and that just served to make Alis more nervous. The apparent result of the silent communication was that Dr. Rankine had been designated to give her the information, and that made Alis even more nervous. The woman seemed to be the one who got to deliver the worst news.

Dr. Rankine sat down in a chair next to the bed. "Remember what we said yesterday? That every change has been for the better? Please keep that in mind. I know this is scary, but you're going to be just fine."

"What about my legs?"

"Both your legs from just above the knee were crushed, and they suffered severe damage. Your kneecaps and the bottom section of your femurs, the thighbones, were beyond repair. You've got two new synthetic femurs, surrounded by your original muscle, tissue, and skin almost to your knees. Your knees and everything below them are prosthetic replacements that are stronger than the originals."

Alis closed her eyes and began to cry.

Dr. Rankine put a hand on her shoulder. After a minute she said, "I know this is difficult. But it's not all bad—"

Alis took a couple of deep breaths that hurt. "Right. I should think of the bright side. For one thing, I'll never have to clip my toenails again," Alis said bitterly. She could feel the tears streaming down her cheeks, and somehow that was a reassuring sensation. At least they hadn't taken that away from her.

"What I meant was," Dr. Rankine said gently, "that your new legs will be virtually immune to injury, and they're indistinguishable from your own legs. If we'd left you with shattered kneecaps, you'd never have walked normally again. As it is, within a few months you should be back to normal. Better than normal."

"Tell me the rest." Alis tried to stop crying and succeeded in reaching a precarious state of calm.

"The rest?"

"I want to know everything. How much of me is left?"

"All of you is left. You're the same person you've always been."

"What parts of my body are no longer flesh and blood?"

"Alis, you need to be patient—"

"Tell me now, goddamnit!"

Dr. Rankine hesitated. "All right. Besides what we've talked about already, one of your kidneys is new. We could have just not replaced it, but you'll be safer in the long run. Your left arm from just above the elbow is new. You've got a new heart."

"That's it?"

"That plus assorted stitches and stuff like biodegradable glue to help things like broken ribs heal. And, er, you're not going to be able to conceive conventionally. When the time comes we can be of help in that department."

Alis lay in stunned silence for a long moment. "God, I'm dead. I'm just running on life support. The only difference between me and some patient permanently hooked up to blood pumps and dialysis machines is that the machines are small enough to fit inside my body."

"I know this is upsetting—"

"*Upsetting?* I'm not a real human being anymore."

"It's not like that."

"Oh, it's not? And how would you know? How much of you is artificial?"

"Alis—"

"Go away. Please go away. I want to be alone." Even with her eyes closed, Alis could feel the glances being exchanged between the two doctors. She heard Dr. Rankine rise from her chair.

"All right, Alis. We'll let you be alone for a while. But think about this. A machine wouldn't be upset about its condition. Only human beings experience those feelings."

Alis shut her eyes until the room was silent. When the two were gone, she reached for the mirror she'd been afraid to use. The face that stared back at her was a Frankenstein's monster sort of face. Her black hair was clipped and patchy, like a radiation victim's. Her green eyes were gone. In their place were eyes with black, perfectly round irises, surrounded by a pure white that looked like it could never appear bloodshot. The eyes looked like the eyes of a stuffed bear. She closed her eyes and cried.

Standing up was all but impossible at first, so Alis spent some of her idle time experimenting with her new eyes.

The right sequences of tension in the muscles around her eyes could give her an infrared view, a view into the metallic-feeling world of ultraviolet, or her normal vision. She could even use her eyes in a telephoto mode.

The most annoying characteristic of her new eyes was that almost every time she sneezed, her eyes flipped into infrared mode. The doctor had talked about downloading new software for her eyes, and that somehow made her feel worse rather than better.

Sometimes she'd move her wheelchair to where she could see out a port and then sit for hours in the dark, staring out at the stars. With her infrared view, she could see young stars that were invisible to everyone else, and with infrared and telephoto mode she could see Becklin's Object inside the Orion Nebula.

Sometimes as she sat there in the dark, she'd occasionally have to blink to clear the lenses on her eyes. They didn't seem totally unaffected by tears.

. . .

The door to Alis Nussem's sick bay room was open, but Karl knocked on the door frame before entering.

"Yes?" said Alis.

"You don't know me, but I just wanted to say hello." Karl took a step into the room.

"Hello." Alis looked at the wall in front of her.

Karl took another step into the room, feeling foolish. Alis certainly wasn't making this easy. Dr. Weng had warned him that she was feeling hostile, but Karl had hoped the feeling just extended to doctors.

"I just wanted to say how sorry I am that you've had to go through all this."

Alis raised her eyebrows. Her face was still fairly black-and-blue. "Who are you?"

"My name's Karl Stanton."

"Karl Stanton. I know that name."

"I was piloting the shuttle that hit the station."

Alis suddenly gave him her full attention.

"You've really got a lot of gall coming here."

"I just came to—"

"To say you wish you hadn't turned me into a robot? You should have thought of that earlier."

"Look, when I say I'm sorry, I'm expressing sympathy for what you've had to go through. The accident wasn't pilot error; it was a result of some kind of mechanical failure. But I didn't want to get into that. I just—"

"From what I've heard, you can't back up that claim."

Even though he had been afraid of this reaction, Karl felt himself getting angry. "No, I can't, but I really am telling you the truth."

"Maybe the court sees it that way."

"I guess this was a bad idea. All I wanted to do was express my sympathy and see if there was anything I could do for you to help your stay here be a little more pleasant." Karl felt even worse than before he'd come.

"Actually, now that I think about it, there is one thing."

"Yes?"

"Get out and don't come back. I don't ever want to see you again."

Karl considered and discarded several responses, then finally just turned silently and left. Someone more theatrically responsive might have banged his head against the wall or slammed the wall with a fist. Karl just pinched the bridge of his nose and shut his eyes for an instant.

On the way back to his quarters, he berated himself for even coming here. His friends were still supportive about the accident, but he was extremely tired of being judged guilty by everyone else. He had still been toying with the idea of requesting a remote assignment. Maybe now was a good time to ask.

3 ▪ C A D A V E R

Cold and loneliness filled Karl Stanton's senses. He tried to tell himself both feelings were induced by the view, but he knew that wasn't entirely true.

Karl floated in space as his suit heater struggled to keep him warm without localized hot or cold spots. He glanced at the sun, which was no more than a bright star in a frozen sky. He had put five light-hours and ten calendar months between himself and Earth, but despite that distance, the accident was still as close as yesterday.

Time seemed to move at the proverbial glacial pace out here. He hung in orbit, tens of kilometers over the surface of Pluto, a frozen ball that took 250 years just to circle a sun so distant that a supernova millions of light-years away could trick one into thinking that was the sun instead. Cold pinpoints of red, yellow, blue, and white pierced the vast darkness beyond the dim red of his visor readouts. He basked in the light of a billion stars, and their collective warmth wouldn't melt an ice cube.

"You ready?" The slightly tinny voice of William Tocker, first officer of the *Ranger,* sounded in Karl's ears. William was a bear of a man, but hearing just his voice, it was easy to imagine a much smaller guy on the other end of the microphone.

Karl's brief reverie was over, and he was again acutely aware of the survey satellite floating just under him and the bulk of the *Ranger* fifty meters behind him. William floated to one side of the satellite.

"Sure," Karl said. "Step one. Activate stand-by power."

"Right. Go for it."

Karl reached out to the maintenance panel and slid the cover open. In the light from his helmet lamps, he found the big red button and pushed it. The result wasn't as satisfying as it could have been; two tiny counters illuminated and counted down from ten to zero. Nothing else changed, but the small fission power plant inside had passed the first test. Out here, solar panels would have to be too large to be practical.

"Ready," Karl said.

"Okay. Next?"

Karl went through two more steps toward bringing the satellite to life as William checked his progress. Minutes later they were ready for the critical step, unfurling the antennas.

"I'm ready if you are," William said. Of the small crew on the *Ranger,* William came the closest to being a friend, even though he was Karl's boss. Some of the others on the crew, once they had associated Karl with the shuttle accident at Tokyan Station, either shunned him or got on him too hard about it. Innocent until proven guilty was a fine principle, but reality didn't always conform to the ideal. William wasn't a friend in the sense that they swapped jokes or played cards together, but whenever one of the crew started in on Karl too hard, William put a stop to it. Karl could defend himself, but William's support meant a lot to him.

"I'm switching on the unfurling motor right *now,*" Karl said as he turned a switch. The whole setup sequence could have of course been run automatically, controlled by the on-board computer, but this was a good excuse to get out of the *Ranger,* and sometimes a hands-on approach could eliminate failures. Pluto was about as out of the way as anywhere Karl had been, and he didn t care for the idea of spending a few weeks coming back here just to repair a survey probe. Only a few ships exploring the Oort cloud or performing measurements at points far out of the ecliptic spent more time without contact with other ships.

The motor made the satellite shell vibrate. Slowly and evenly, two long struts extended from the cylindrical body. As they reached the end of their jackknife travel, two dish antennas began to unfurl like Oriental fans. The larger antenna, which would eventually be pointing at Earth, jerked to a stop halfway open, but then resumed its motion even before Karl or William could move.

Moments later both antennas were in full bloom, and their gentle vibrations damped to invisibility.

"Ready to spin up," Karl said.

"Go for it." William floated on the far side of the survey satellite, his face hidden in the dark behind his shiny visor.

Karl glanced back at the boxy shape of the *Ranger,* visible more by the fact that it blotted out stars in a rectangular area than by any light it reflected.

Karl put out his gloved hand and flipped a large toggle switch. At one end of the central shaft running through the satellite, a spin stabilization cylinder began to work silently up to speed. Stars mirrored in the shiny surface began to waver, as if they were reflections from a rippled pond. Karl focused on a control on his helmet visor and blinked. In response, his forward-pointing jet gave a short blast of oxygen. He drifted slowly back from the satellite as his suit computer gave a couple of microblasts, one from each leg jet, to stabilize his body.

Karl was a couple of meters back from the spinning section when he saw the first sign of trouble. Two or three dark forms spun off into space before he could react. "Clear the area, William! We need to spin it back down. Something's loose."

Karl had barely finished speaking when William's chest jet gave a burst of air. But instead of his suited body slowly drifting away from the satellite, William's body suddenly began to spin helmet over boots. Even if his suit computer had malfunctioned and had not activated stabilizing jets, the chest jet was close enough to his center of gravity that it shouldn't have spun him like that. Karl felt cold sweat on his face.

"William?" He waited a second. "William, speak to me. Are you all right?"

Radio silence. Seconds later Karl's helmet crackled with a voice, but the voice wasn't William's. "What's wrong out there?" The voice was that of Enrico Fernandez, the captain of the *Ranger,* a man in his forties who had already attained the crustiness more typical of people in their eighties.

"Don't know yet. William may be hurt. Tell the bird to stop spinning. I'm going to check on William."

"Damn. Give me a running commentary. Lucy will join you as soon as she can. I've sent the spin-down signal."

"Good," Karl said as he faced William's spinning and receding body, then activated a blast from his rear jets. His body tumbled ten degrees before the autojets stabilized him again. From the corner of his eye he could see the spin section of the survey satellite slow noticeably. Another flywheel on the far side of the satellite should be slowing down, too. "I'm moving toward William. He's spinning about one rev a second. I think his suit must have been hit by something flung off the spin section."

"Would have to hit pretty hard," came Fernandez's voice.

"That's what I'm afraid of." Karl tried to force aside his fear. In the rear-view strips at the side of his visor, he could see the *Ranger* had drifted and was now silhouetted against the dim surface of Pluto. Most of Pluto's horizon was dark enough that the arc of occulted stars was the only indication of the planet's presence. "I'm about twenty meters from him and gaining."

In Karl's rear-view, a rectangular swath of light showed where Lucy Ito was leaving the ship. Lucy was the assistant science officer, reporting to Karl. She was a whiz kid who often irritated Karl by expressing surprise that he was aware of some uncommon information or that he was able to work out something in his head that she was also capable of handling. Her reactions wouldn't have been bothersome if they were accompanied by words like, "You're pretty sharp." Instead they often came with, "That's pretty good for a guy," or, "I must be slipping; I thought that was tougher." Despite her unconscious arrogance, she was probably one of those most civil to Karl. He wished he knew how much of that was deference to the boss and how much resulted from Lucy maintaining an open mind about the shuttle accident.

The air lock closed behind Lucy, and her paired helmet lamps looked like distant headlights.

Karl said, "I'm about ten meters from him. I still haven't seen his arms or legs change position, so I'm worried that it's more serious than an impact just knocking the radio out."

"Roger," said Captain Fernandez, keeping emotion to a minimum as always. His normal range of displayed emotion was limited to the part of the spectrum between impatience with people and irritation with regulations. He gave occasional praise, but without warmth the words seemed to be the result of some perceived duty to keep the employees motivated by telling them they were doing better than they really were.

Now that the nearby reference points like the survey satellite were gone, it seemed to Karl more like William's suited body was approaching him than he was approaching William. William still hadn't changed posture. He tumbled through space, as if a mannequin with outstretched arms had been spun into the vacuum. "I'm almost there," Karl said. The closer he came to William, the colder Karl felt.

Karl braked with a jet from his chest pack. One of William's legs spun past his visor. Karl braced himself, and the next time the leg spun past, he grabbed it and hung on.

"I've got him," Karl said as his mass slowed William's rotation and the two of them tumbled slowly through space. The lamps on the sides of Lucy's helmet were much closer than before.

Karl got a grip on William's waist and gave a voice command to tell his suit computer to auto-stabilize. A series of tugs and pushes against his legs made the rotating star field slowly come to a halt. The limpness of William's suit reinforced Karl's worst fears. The suit couldn't be fully pressurized and still feel that way.

Lucy braked to a stop just a meter away. "Let's start for the ship," she said.

"Right."

Karl took one of William's arms as Lucy took the other. When they were ready, they both activated their suit jets. Seconds later the trio was speeding toward the *Ranger*.

Once they were moving, Karl turned his helmet lamps toward William and started checking his suit for damage. The search took just seconds. Karl pointed toward William's neck.

Lucy's helmet tilted as she bent to look. Her gasp was confirmation enough that Karl wasn't imagining the slit in the fabric and the outline of blood-covered metal jutting out through the gap. Even more obvious in the bright light from his helmet lamps was the steady mist of moisture condensing in the escaping air. Karl couldn't see into William's helmet, and at the moment he thought that was just as well. He didn't think he'd care to see William's face. His dreams already had too many recurring elements—the hologram showing Alis Nussem's medical chart, the pain in her face when he had tried to explain that the shuttle collision had been a genuine accident, the funeral for the deceased. He didn't need William's face in his dreams, too.

Karl now felt sick as well as cold as he accepted the obvious: William couldn't possibly be alive. Lucy reached for an emergency patch and then stopped, obviously as undecided as Karl. Put the patch over the piece of metal stabbing into William's neck? Pull out the piece before a doctor was near enough to get to William's body? Don't do anything until inside? Every choice had its horrible side.

"Well?" Enrico Fernandez sounded impatient, but this time his voice also held a slight hoarseness, perhaps actually a tinge of fear or concern. Even that faint tinge was the most emotion Karl had ever heard from the captain.

Lucy hesitated, not because she didn't have an opinion, Karl thought, but because either she was waiting for him since he was the boss or she didn't want to be the one to pass on the terrible news. The *Ranger* was growing steadily larger.

Karl cleared his throat. "I'm afraid William's dead. You'd better keep Robert standing by just in case, but William's suit's been penetrated by a sharp piece of metal, probably something spun off the rotor when it started up. It's hard to tell how much blood he's lost, but the pressure in his suit must have been virtually nil for several minutes. We could pull out the metal and risk further damage, or patch over it and risk driving it farther into his neck. If I thought there was actually a chance he was still alive, I'd say patch it so at least he can breathe, but—"

"Right," said Enrico Fernandez. This time his voice sounded tired, as if he'd just lost a lot of energy. It was all right to show that you were tired; showing sorrow was another matter. "Robert's ready. He's been ready."

Robert Vasquez was the *Ranger*'s medical officer. His

public range of emotions was broader than the captain's. Robert was quick to show anger, contempt, superiority, humor, and confidence. He only rarely allowed uncertainty and amazement to show. Despite the friction between Karl and Robert, Karl knew the man was extremely competent, and if there still were a chance for William, Robert would find it.

Karl fell silent as the *Ranger* loomed ahead, its boxy shape littered with antennas, tie-down loops, grab rails, small attitude-control jets, air lock frames, portholes, retracted waldoes, standoff shock absorbers for docking, and seldom-used gear bolted to the outside walls.

Karl and Lucy applied braking jets as the lights around the air lock door grew closer.

Lucy opened the outer door as Karl drifted nearby with William's arm in his grasp. The door slid open, spilling yellow light into the void. Lucy grabbed an interior handhold and reached for Karl's gloved hand. Slowly she drew Karl into the lock, and William followed.

The air lock door closed. Seconds later came the muffled sounds of inrushing air, and Karl's suit sagged, no longer ballooning outward. William's suit had felt limp to begin with, and Karl saw no change.

The inner door opened to the emergency-room mix of speed and suppressed panic. Robert was there with Gwen Sonderson, the backup medical doctor on this mission. While Robert was actively hostile to Karl, Gwen merely ignored him, even if they had to pass each other in a corridor. Karl soon learned the procedure—he was to hug one wall as she floated through down the center of the corridor. As Karl and Lucy maneuvered William's body into the bay beyond the air lock, Robert flashed Karl an angry look, as if the accident were Karl's fault. Gwen kept her focus on William's suit.

A huge, disk-shaped section of the *Ranger* could be spun to generate gravity. The speed was adjustable, depending on whether the need was for microgravity experimenting, heavy-gravity exercise, or moderate gravity for healthy living. It was the logical place to operate on a patient, but there was no time to get William there.

Instead, Robert and Gwen were fitted with harnesses, and a maze of elastic straps held their torsos in position while Belinda Penson helped them slice off William's suit. Belinda, the *Ranger*'s generalist, and therefore one of the busiest of the crew, tossed the discarded strips of William's uniform along the corridor leading inward, obviously knowing they'd be out of the way long enough that if they floated back she could deal with them later. A portable sucker, making the disgusting sound of a dentist's drain, was strapped to the wall, pulling melting blood away from the working area.

Karl and Lucy helped get elastic straps around William's ankles as Robert and Gwen used still more straps to keep his body held into floating position between them. When that was done, Karl and Lucy grabbed rungs on the wall behind them and held on as they removed their helmets.

Robert gingerly removed William's helmet as Belinda took away the last suit remnants near his neck. Gwen pressed a couple of monitor disks onto William's chest and glanced at a display screen fixed to the ceiling. Every line on the screen was nearly flat, the only ripples being the ones caused by placing the disks against William's skin. William's body twisted and Karl could finally see the metal piece lodged in his neck as Robert and Gwen surveyed the damage.

Seconds later, Robert's and Gwen's bodies sagged, almost as if they were standing in a high-gravity field. The relaxation of the neck muscles was almost as obvious as the fact that they both closed their eyes for a moment.

"There's nothing we can do," Robert said finally. "He's already dead, and he's been without oxygen too long. Even if we had caught him earlier, there's too much damage."

Karl felt sick. He was trying to figure out what to say in return when Captain Fernandez's voice came from a nearby speaker panel. "I understand." Obviously Robert had been talking for the captain's benefit.

After a long pause, the captain added, "I'll want a full investigation."

"Right," said Robert. He said William's full name, the date, and the time and then said, "Cause of death was loss of blood and extensive injuries to the spinal cord, caused by a foreign object approximately ten centimeters long. The object is rounded on one end, sharp on the other. If it was spinning, it probably had only one chance in three of being fatal."

"Understood. Lucy, I want you and Belinda to take a look at the satellite in a few minutes. Find out what happened. Take Daren with you if you feel you need him."

"Roger," the women said together.

A long moment of silence ended with Robert saying, "I guess you can take off, Karl. You've done enough for now." The words on a court transcript could have been read as neutral, but the expression on Robert's face and the harshness of his voice said he was certain the blame for the accident could safely be laid on Karl.

Karl normally just let Robert's antagonism slide off; at least that was what he tried to show on the outside. At the moment, with William's death a reality less than minutes old, he couldn't keep his anger completely contained. "You had as much to do with William's death as I had."

Karl didn't wait for a reaction or a reply. He just turned and kicked himself along the corridor. When he reached his cabin, he locked the door and switched on the *do not disturb* indicator. He sat in the center of the cabin, staring out the porthole view screen at the chilly emptiness of space.

Space looked cold and endless and dead as Alis Nussem stared at the wide navigational view screen aboard the *Potemkin*. The view, looking back at the solar system from beyond Pluto's orbit, showed virtually the same thing she would see from the other side of the solar system, except for the pinpoint of Sol and the nearby speck of light that was Venus. Computer enhancements showed the locations of other exploratory craft, one near Pluto, one way out of the ecliptic, and the others much closer to Sol or on the other side of the solar system.

Most of her friends were near Earth now, but she didn't really miss them. For some reason, being around people who knew her before the accident was uncomfortable. They were either embarrassed that she'd had to go through so much or, in some cases, seemingly irritated with her that she hadn't come through the ordeal and turned instantly happy at being furnished with "super" replacement parts.

She wondered if any of those people had ever bristled when, after losing a family heirloom in a fire, they were told it was no problem, that they could just buy a modern replacement. Her new legs were stronger of course, but she would never feel as balanced, as unaware of them, as she had before. Standing and walking would always have that instability. And to her, her new eyes still looked more like stuffed animal eyes than real eyes, no matter how many people told her they were "just fine." Both eyes and legs still had software bugs that caused her to lurch awkwardly at random moments or have to blink several times to reset her eyes to normal. Damnit, a human body shouldn't have to have reset buttons.

A few locations on her face and several spots around her body were still numb and would always be numb. Nerves damaged beyond the point of repair meant that some signals would never travel. When they'd rebuilt her jaw and some of her face, they'd either made an error or had run into another place where the signals would never travel again, because her smile was crooked now. It wasn't like she smiled much anymore, but she always worried that her lopsided smile sent the wrong signals to people watching her.

Her formerly jet black hair now had gray streaks, at her

age. The doctors said it was because of the trauma and had suggested hair coloring. It wasn't their hair after all. She sometimes thought they would have been content if she'd shaved herself bald, bought a wig, and tattooed her makeup on her face so she'd always look just fine and always look exactly the same.

Sometimes she got even angrier with herself, telling herself she shouldn't feel this way, that she should feel how everyone else told her she should feel. But some people who told her, "I know how you must feel," certainly didn't.

One of the heavy doors on the bridge opened, and Captain Tsilkovsky floated through it looking tired. She glanced at Alis as she shut the door behind her.

"Long shift," Tsilkovsky said. She pushed herself into a sling and pulled the strap across her waist. She seemed more at ease when they were accelerating because then she could put her feet up on the console. She was one of the oldest ISA captains on active duty, and she didn't care much about appearances. The longest hair on her head was about the width of a finger, as if she'd touched a hand to a Van de Graaff generator and let someone clip the sphere of electrostatically charged hair.

"I'm fine." Alis shrugged.

"Ready for a course change?"

"No problem."

The captain unzipped a midriff pouch and took out a pack of gum. She offered some to Alis, who declined. Captain Tsilkovsky studied Alis for a long moment, long enough to make Alis uncomfortable. The captain finally said, "I've been talking to the *Ranger*. That's the ship near Pluto. They had an accident while they were deploying a planetary survey probe. Their first officer is dead."

Alis didn't experience much of a reaction. Sometimes she felt death would be preferable to being alive and feeling dead. "I'm sorry to hear that," she said mechanically.

Tsilkovsky studied her. "We're going to rendezvous and take the body home. They've got another couple of months on their schedule before they head back."

"Do they need a replacement?" Alis asked, even before she thought consciously about why she was asking.

"They could use one, but their captain says they can get by."

"Send me," Alis said suddenly, realizing she wasn't ready to go back to Tokyan Station or Earth. Out here in the dead regions of space, this was where she fit. Not back there where she'd see families and life going on as if everything were normal. Not on the station where she couldn't hide on the bridge or in her cabin most of the time.

"I somehow thought you might feel that way."

"So you already know if they'd be interested?"

"Right. They'd take you if you really want to go."

Alis sifted through the pros and cons. "I do."

"All right then."

As Alis prepared for acceleration and activated a warning announcement for the rest of the crew, she realized she felt good about the change. Maybe her luck was improving.

Karl Stanton floated near the farthest corner of the largest compartment aboard the *Ranger*. The rest of the assembled crew clung to various spots on the walls as Captain Enrico Fernandez talked about what a fine officer William Tocker had been.

A cold, silvery storage cylinder now serving as a casket showed a patina of icy condensation. Tomorrow the cylinder would be returned temporarily to the cold of space, when the *Ranger* traded its dead first officer for a live replacement.

Karl tried his best to ignore the icy glances he got from various members of the crew. He would have preferred to say good-bye to William from the isolation of his own cabin, but he suspected that if he had, the chill he felt from the rest of the crew would grow even more frigid. At times he wished he were inside that cylinder instead of William, finally in a place where no one could sneer at him. Maybe the price of staying in space was just too high. When they finished with this tour, he would have to come up with a compelling reason before he'd consider another.

He could face the idea that somehow he was a jinx. What he hated was the feeling that at least some of the crew felt he was inept and unqualified. Sometimes space had a way of settling scores without the agonizing process of searching for justice, but the idea that someone might deliberately puncture his suit while they were outside together bothered him less than the feeling that he didn't have one friend left. The person on the *Ranger* who had come the closest to that label was frozen solid.

Karl hoped the next first officer would be as understanding and as slow to condemn as William Tocker had been.

Alis watched the *Ranger* loom in the *Potemkin*'s view screen. A blinking green indicator said the *Ranger* had the *Potemkin* locked into its near-range detection system. Both ships' radars were shut down for the corridor between them and instead the ships were in a non-stop position-change-reporting cycle that kept them both aware of each other's location without the health risk from high-energy RF.

All of Alis's personal belongings were stowed in a cylinder half her height and as narrow as her hips. She had never felt particularly materialistic, but somehow she felt she should have more to show for the years than a package smaller than a coffin.

Captain Tsilkovsky entered the bridge wearing a neutral expression. "Last chance to change your mind."

Alis shook her head. "I'm ready."

"All right," Tsilkovsky said. "It's your decision."

"If you were me, you'd stay out longer, too, don't you think?"

"Perhaps."

Alis took a long look at the captain and decided she wouldn't want to go back either. *Something* had kept her on duty this long. Going back to Earth or Tokyan Station must have held its own menace for the captain. Back there, the effects of gravity would be impossible to ignore. Back there, she'd be a smaller fish in a bigger pond. Back there, she'd have to answer to someone else too much of the time.

Alis looked at the time. "Let's do it."

Captain Tsilkovsky nodded. She tied herself into a sling and flipped open the communication channel to the *Ranger.*

Alis let herself loose from the web and floated toward her cylinder. She released it as the view screen filled with the image of Enrico Fernandez, captain of the *Ranger.*

"All set?" Enrico asked.

"Ready when you are," said Tsilkovsky.

Alis pushed herself toward the door, ready to say goodbye without a hug or handshake after six months of sharing duties and cramped quarters with a community of fewer than two dozen.

"Alis?" Tsilkovsky said.

Alis looked back at her from the door. She could see Tsilkovsky's fingers on the mute button. "Yes?"

"Take care of yourself. One day you'll come out of this funk, and you'll be ready to live again."

"Thanks," Alis said, not believing her.

Alis pressed the *release* button. A quick second of acceleration made it seem the *Potemkin* was suddenly pulling her back, and then the sensation faded. She floated in free fall, kilometers above the dark surface of Pluto, on a straight-line course for a blinking red light on the side of the *Ranger*. Her breathing sounded unnaturally loud in the confines of her suit.

Moments earlier she had precisely aimed the launcher and compressed the spring that eventually pushed her on her way, a little like being gently shot out of a torpedo tube.

She spotted a moving glint of light that must have been the coffin containing the body of the *Ranger*'s former first officer transferring over to the *Potemkin*. The dead man departed as Alis arrived. From dust to dust. Even living in space doesn't change the rules. She realized that she no longer feared death the way she once had. If it came tomorrow, she felt she could deal with that.

The *Ranger* slowly grew larger against the field of stars. It looked like a BoLock 3.1 model exploratory craft, a slightly older vehicle than the *Potemkin*. Near the main thrusters was a gray bulge she recognized as the housing for outboard tanks installed after the ship had been built. The *Potemkin*, a 3.3 design, was a meter or two longer, and most of the features the crews had complained about on the 3.1 models had been corrected in the *Potemkin*. A few 4.0 craft existed, but Alis hadn't seen one yet. They were all restricted to near-Earth missions until the beta test crews sorted out the bugs from the features.

The doctor on Tokyan Station had jokingly told Alis she was a model 1.1 human. She hadn't vocalized her response: that she felt like a model 1.0 android.

The *Ranger* drifted closer. *It must be a 3.15 craft,* Alis decided, seeing the reinforcing struts along the bow.

For just an instant Alis suddenly felt alone. She was leaving an old crew behind, unlikely to know anyone in the new crew, adrift in vacuum between two cold and dark ships, so far from home that if she died, news of her death would take almost six hours to reach home. Adrift—that was her.

She tried unsuccessfully to shake off the emotions, preferring no feelings to negative feelings. Her mother would take her death hard, if her reactions to Alis's father's death were any indication.

Alis had gone with her father to the neighborhood convenience store. As she sat in the car waiting, she had watched as the two guys in no-sleeve sweatshirts pulled to a fast stop and got out of their idling car. When she saw one tuck a gun into his belt at the small of his back, she scrunched down farther in her seat, suddenly afraid.

She was still angry with herself that she hadn't gone into the store and somehow affected what had happened, but she had at least done the level-headed thing and used the car phone to call 911. The cops got there in time to catch the two guys as they sped away, but not before her father and the store clerk had been killed. The huge plate-glass windows had afforded Alis a direct view, and it was only the glass—on the store and in her car—that had kept the robbers from hearing her screams. Her mother had taken the news even worse.

The *Ranger* soon blocked most of the view ahead, and the landing site grew larger. The circular, padded area a few meters across was criss-crossed with several loose cords. Alis made an attitude adjustment swinging her feet toward the *Ranger*. Seconds later she fired another jet, stopping her rotation just after the *Potemkin* moved up and past her field of view.

She hit the padding, and her legs buckled. She snagged one of the cords in her right hand, and she was floating alongside the *Ranger*. She grabbed another cord and pulled herself toward the air lock.

The air lock display said: *"No code required. Welcome."*

With one hand Alis gripped the handrail. She let her body float around until she could take one last look at the dark outline of the *Potemkin*. She suppressed a quick flash of indecision, swiveled back, and pressed the *open* button.

Caught in the sudden bright light of the air lock, Alis winced, knowing her irises would lock up. Sure enough. A second later the air lock seemed too dim as the program that controlled iris dilation glitched and left both irises at their pinpoint settings. Alis blinked four times rapidly to reset the program, and her vision was back to "normal."

Welcome aboard, Ms. Nussem," Captain Fernandez told her fifteen minutes after she reached the *Ranger*.

Alis nodded. "Captain."

Captain Enrico Fernandez was younger than Alis had guessed he might be, probably somewhere in his forties. He only *sounded* old and crusty. He sat in a chair on the bridge and made no motion to rise when Alis entered. "Gravity okay for you?"

Alis was surprised by the question. The bridge, quarters, and some work areas on the ship were spun for artificial gravity, but this felt about like the standard one-half gee, which was what most ships used as a compromise between comfort and health.

"Fine."

The captain was silent for a moment as Alis realized he must have just about used up his supply of small talk. Finally he said, "I, er, appreciate your coming aboard. We're still all a little shaken up."

"Yes, sir. I'm sorry to hear about your first officer."

"Yes, well, none of us expects this kind of job to be without risk."

"Right."

"You've been to your quarters?"

"Yes, sir. Daren Schrader showed me the way, and I stowed my gear."

"Good. Daren is communications and computing. And backup pilot/navigator. One of the three who'll report to you.

Good man. We've got a good crew. The other two senior crew are on the way here now—our medical officer and science officer."

"Yes, sir."

"And go a little easy on Mr. Stanton for a few days, will you? He was out with Mr. Tocker when he died, and I think some of the crew are giving him a hard time."

Alis suddenly felt too warm and closed in. She looked away from Captain Fernandez and tried to keep her voice sounding calm. "Ah, Mr. Stanton?"

"Karl Stanton. He's my science officer. A biologist, but he seems fairly rounded."

When Alis had entered the spin area and moved from zero gravity back into one-half gee, her stomach had wanted to rebel. Suddenly the nausea was back, even stronger. She tried to ignore the discomfort and turn back to the captain so she could see if there were still time to catch the *Potemkin* before it was too late. "Sir, I—"

One of the doors on the bridge slid open and a man maybe ten years older than Alis entered.

"Ah, here's Mr. Vasquez now," said the captain. "Robert."

Alis paid little attention to Robert Vasquez other than the automatic subconscious cataloging of dark eyes, strong frame, and unhappy expression. Robert didn't close the door behind him, and a couple of seconds later another man followed him onto the bridge.

"And Mr. Stanton. Karl."

Alis was somehow aware the captain had spoken, but her awareness was locked onto Karl Stanton. It *was* the same man, of course. How many Karl Stantons could there be in space? That stocky frame, the short sandy hair, the gray-green eyes, the cleft chin, all were etched into her memory. The instant his gaze met hers she could see his cheeks whiten, and he was staring back at her in disbelief.

"I take it you've met Mr. Stanton already," said the captain after a second.

Alis felt seasick. She forced herself to respond. "Yes. We've met before."

From the corner of her eye she could see a puzzled expression wrinkle Robert's forehead.

She faced Enrico Fernandez and held her arms rigidly at her side. "Captain, I'd like to go back to the *Potemkin.*"

"But I need you here. I thought—"

Karl Stanton spoke. "If you need her here, sir, I can transfer to the *Potemkin.*"

Captain Fernandez rubbed his forehead. "Let's just slow down a minute. The *Potemkin*'s on its way, and I need a first officer, so no one is leaving this ship. Now what's the problem?"

Karl was the first to speak. "I think it would be best for us not to be serving on the same mission, sir. Ms. Nussem feels I'm responsible for causing injury to her in the past."

" *'Feels'?* " said Alis. "You were piloting the shuttle, yes or no?"

"Look, we've gone through this before."

"You're the one?" Robert Vasquez said abruptly. "You're the woman who received all the surgery after Karl's little jaunt near Tokyan Station?" He was smiling for the first time.

"That's enough!" said Captain Fernandez forcefully. He even stood up to reinforce his command.

Alis watched him as he spent five seconds apparently considering the situation.

"All right," he said finally. "Back to business. Alis Nussem, this is Robert Vasquez, the medical officer who will report to you. Robert, Alis. And, Alis, this is Karl Stanton, the science officer who will report to you. You are both professionals, and you will act in accordance with the standards of the International Space Agency. I expect you to do your jobs to the best of your ability. When this mission is complete,

you'll have the normal opportunities for assignment changes."
He looked at the console date/time display. "Alis, I want your
first report in twenty-four hours. Karl will fill you in on our
current mission priorities. That will be all."

No one moved.

"I said, 'Dismissed.' "

Alis, Karl, and Robert said, "Yes, sir," simultaneously.
They all turned toward the door. Alis moved through the door
first, doing her best to ignore the smile on Robert's face.

She kept moving until she heard the hatch door close behind them. She stopped and took in several deep breaths. Her
wristcomp confirmed that it was in sync with the *Ranger*'s
duty-cycle clock. She looked at the time, performed a quick
computation, and turned to face Robert Vasquez and Karl
Stanton.

Without looking at either man's face, she said, "Mr. Stanton, I'll expect a briefing at sixteen hundred hours."

Karl matched her businesslike tone. "Yes, ma'am. Where
do you want to meet?"

"I'll find you."

"When would you like to meet the rest of the crew?"
asked Robert. His smile had transformed to something more
like a smirk, and it probably would have annoyed Alis even
without the sudden and unexpectedly painful pressure of seeing Karl Stanton again.

"I'll let you know." Alis turned away and left the men
without another word.

Alis locked herself in her cabin. The low gravity and the limited personal space made it hard to pace back and forth, but
she gave it her best try. She felt the unexpected urge to punch
something, or someone. This couldn't be happening.

It took her almost an hour to calm down. She considered
and discarded one alternative after another until she was left

with only one acceptable course of action: to try her damnedest to pretend Karl was just another subordinate, one with whom contact would be limited to that required by the job.

Resigned and dejected, she had her wristcomp fetch the *Ranger*'s personnel database. When it indicated it was ready to support activities aboard ship, she said, "Call Mr. Stanton."

A few seconds later the man responded, "Stanton here."

"This is Lieutenant Commander Nussem." She glanced back at the display on the ship's computer screen. "About the sixteen-hundred mission briefing. Will you meet me in conference room B?"

"Yes, ma'am."

Alis terminated the conversation and began a mental inventory of the contents of her cabin, the room that would be her prison for at least four months.

Karl Stanton was waiting for her when Alis arrived at conference room B. The room was in the same location as the "Green Room" had been aboard the *Potemkin*. Apparently Captain Fernandez preferred to use the utilitarian designations found on the original plans for the ship, rather than giving the rooms some more esthetic labels.

Karl stood a little too fast when Alis entered the room. So he was nervous. Good.

"Look," he said, "I know what you think, but—"

"We've got a job to do here," Alis said. "How about if we get started?"

Karl froze, as if a robot in an old-time movie had received conflicting instructions. Finally he swallowed, nodded, and said, "Whatever you say."

"So, what's first?"

Karl sat down, obviously still having a hard time shifting gears, but a moment later his face was businesslike, neutral. In the months since the collision, Alis had pictured his face with two alternating expressions, one whining and one a combination of anger and satisfaction. As she sat down across the table from Karl, she realized that neither picture had been accurate. In another time and place, she might have felt attracted to him, but at the moment it was hard to imagine feeling attracted to anyone ever again. And who would be attracted to a half-human collection of parts?

Karl glanced at her briefly as he started talking, and she immediately broke eye contact. "Starting at the top. The *Ranger*'s main mission is to deploy a series of long-term probes. Most of them will accumulate measurements for something like a decade, partly because a lot of the measurements are expected to be way down in the noise . . ."

Alis was curious about why he had said "the *Ranger*'s main mission," instead of "our main mission." Was he somehow an outsider here? She discarded the question and concentrated on his words, trying her best to shut off her anger and just do her job.

Alis finished her dinner in her cabin and carefully resealed the recyclable container so it would be ready to take back to the galley. After two weeks aboard the *Ranger*, she was already bored with the food selections.

She was also getting bored with looking at the drab cabin walls, but boredom was still more comfortable than dealing with the crew. Whenever she talked with Karl Stanton, the forbidden topic of the collision was constantly on her mind. Dealing with Robert Vasquez held its own difficulties, and for some reason those bothered her even more than Karl did. Robert seemed to view her solely as a medical oddity, and the conversation almost invariably gravitated to her series of operations. What did this feel like, how did that affect her.

She found herself digging in and deliberately withholding information from him. Her irises still locked in pinpoints whenever she was suddenly exposed to bright light. At midnight Greenwich time, a time that rotated around the shift clock, her legs would feel sluggish for just an instant, the result, she was told, of the microcomputer controllers performing a routine system recalibration. The doctors on Tokyan Station had told her next time she had a checkup they might be able to install a new software version that would operate more smoothly. She hated the feeling of being a beta-version human.

She'd had less interaction with Daren Schrader, the early-twenties communications and computer expert, and even less with Captain Fernandez. She gave the captain daily briefings, none of which lasted longer than five minutes. She had become more closed about her feelings since the accident; she had the impression that the captain had always been that way.

She leaned back in her bunk, her body so calm that before the accident she would have been able to hear the rhythmic thumping of her heart as a soft metronome. The replacement heart would last far longer than her original, assuming she wanted it to, but it was virtually inaudible, its mechanism operating with such a smooth rotary motion that her systolic and diastolic pressures were virtually equal, and hard to measure. She wondered if the same basic design was also used in pumps in factories and distribution systems.

Alis closed her eyes. She had lain there for less than a minute before her wristcomp sounded with Captain Fernandez's voice.

"Ms. Nussem?"

"Yes?"

"I need you and Mr. Stanton on the bridge. A long-range scan has picked up something we don't understand yet."

As Alis headed for the bridge, she thought back to all the conversations she'd overheard while in sick bay, and she wondered if this were somehow the equivalent of the doctor-speak: "I'm having a little difficulty here."

4 ▪ D I A G N O S I S

Alis entered the bridge and found Karl Stanton and Daren Schrader already there with Captain Fernandez.

The main computer screen showed the sky in the region of Taurus, with the large red disk of Aldebaran centered in the screen. Just above and to the right of Aldebaran was a square display box with a dot much smaller than the red sun in it. One corner of the screen showed a blowup of what was in the box.

Alis moved closer to the screen and stopped. The magnification box showed a computer-enhanced small dark sphere. The adjacent indicators said it was approaching at about three percent of the speed of light. The estimated range, around five light-hours out, coupled with its angular diameter, said the object was roughly 100 kilometers in diameter, which would make it just a little larger than Jupiter's moon Elara. Something that size was a lot smaller than Luna, but still huge.

"What have we got?" Alis asked.

Captain Fernandez just shook his head.

Karl turned and said, "Take a look. You can see the size and speed." He pressed a couple of indicators on the control panel and another image came up, filling a different corner of the main display. This picture showed the object's trajectory into the solar system. The trajectory looked like a straight line passing near Earth.

Karl pointed. "There's its path. And it's obviously not a comet. Velocity's way too high. It looks like it's coming from Aldebaran."

"So it's on the way here from Aldebaran. But it couldn't be a ship, at least nothing we'd call a ship," Alis said. "Not that large."

"Sure wouldn't think so," said Daren Schrader. "Not only that, the radar cross section is really low. I'd expect a moon or a piece of rock to bounce back ten times more. And a ship would probably reflect much more than rock." Daren was fairly even-keeled, a quiet guy, someone who seemed to Alis to occasionally be quick to anger, quick to defuse.

"And this certainly doesn't seem to be a stealth ship," she said.

"True," Karl said. "It's not transmitting anything we can find yet, but it's easily visible."

"So, what are we going to do?"

Captain Fernandez turned from the display. "I want to match course with it and take a closer look. Once it reaches us, it'll only take a couple of weeks to pass through the solar system. If we don't start looking at it soon, we won't have much of a chance."

Alis turned to Daren. "You already have a course projected?"

He nodded. "As soon as the captain gives the word, we start toward it at about two gees. We do that for about a week, then flip and give it two gees to slow down for another week. Then we keep accelerating on the same heading back toward Sol at about two gees for a little less than a week until we match course about two light-hours out from here."

Alis looked at Captain Fernandez. "You think we're likely to get the authorization?"

For only the second or third time in her memory, the captain smiled. "I'm not waiting for authorization. I've already sent a mission-change notification message, and I'm not about to wait ten or twelve hours for a confirmation. Ms. Nussem, I want the ship readied for two-gee flight. We've been a little lax in a couple of the cargo bays. Have your people make sure everything is properly secured."

Alis nodded, and she felt herself smiling, for the first time aboard the *Ranger*. Perhaps for the first time in months. Something new was out there. Something no one knew anything about. This was what exploration should be about—not just charting and measuring and documenting the fringes of the frontier, but actually coming in contact with something no human had ever seen before. For the first time in too long a period, she really felt interested in what was going on around her.

Alis said, "Anything else, sir?"

"Just make sure to take care of everything on the ops section of the preflight list. And notify the crew. I want you back here as soon as we're under way. I make that to be thirty minutes."

"You got it."

Alis grabbed a display pad and stylus from a compartment near the door and exited the bridge.

In the adjacent corridor she thumbed her wristcomp and said, "Belinda, this is Alis. I need you in storage room C."

Seconds later Belinda Penson's voice sounded. "Will do. How soon?"

"Now. And bring one of your staff."

Alis switched her wristcomp to ship-broadcast mode and said, "Attention, all hands. This is Lieutenant Commander Nussem. The *Ranger* is leaving station. Prepare for two-gee acceleration to begin in twenty-five minutes. Contact me or your supervisor if you have any problems. I'll brief you in conference room A in twenty minutes." Briefing the crew, some of whom were still virtually strangers, was definitely the least pleasant item on her list, but she couldn't avoid it.

Alis pressed an indicator on her wristcomp and sent the message into constant repeat for anyone who was still waking up.

She moved through the rotating interface between the gravity-spun section of the ship and into the zero-gee area. She reached the cargo bay just before Belinda Penson, the operations officer. Belinda was in her early forties, with the muscles of a gymnast. Alis got bored with most of the ways of keeping fit aboard a spacecraft, but Belinda didn't seem to have that problem. Belinda's disheveled hair made Alis wonder for an instant what she had interrupted.

Before Alis could say anything, Belinda said, "I've got Tim on the way." Tim would be the youngest on board, still in his early twenties, the man most people called Timmy instead of Tim.

Even as Belinda stopped speaking, Tim showed up. He looked a little flushed and a bit nervous, not making eye contact with Belinda. Alis suddenly formed a theory that would explain what these two had been doing when she had called Belinda. She suppressed the thought and went straight to business. "Besides this area, what else do you think we need to secure for two-gee flight?"

Belinda thought for two seconds and said, "This is it."

"Do we need any additional help?"

Belinda hesitated. "You mean beyond the two of us or the three of us?"

"The three of us," Alis said.

"We can finish in time."

"Fine." Alis noticed Tim nod, and glanced back at Belinda. "What do you recommend we start with?"

"Anywhere you see a net. And there are a few yellow tags that indicate temporary storage. Tim could take the far end, I could start in the middle, and you could start here."

Alis looked down the axis of the long, square storage area. It was about four or five meters wide and high, perhaps fifty meters long. Equipment was held against the sides, leaving a few square meters along the axis, where people could get to equipment or move items in and out of storage. Near the door was fastened some heavier transport equipment that would be overkill for the current housekeeping task.

"Fine. Let's do it." Alis hadn't progressed through the ranks by ignoring the advice of people in a position to know.

Tim launched himself straight along the axis of the storage bay and Belinda followed, leaving Alis floating there. She pushed herself to the nearest net, a temporary but convenient housing for keeping a collection of tools from floating all around the storage bay and getting lost, but still easy to access.

She hooked a leg and an arm into the netting and fitted the tools into their receptacles, as if she were performing the old psychological test of fitting round pegs into round holes and square pegs into square holes. A few seconds later she tucked the net into a corner of the housing and swung the cover closed. Three heavy snap-latches secured the cover.

Alis moved on to the next area. Farther down the axis of the storage bay, Belinda maneuvered a heavy EVA toolbox into position and started snapping latches shut. Most of the equipment was already properly stored, but a few tools here and there had been just tucked in loosely, perhaps at the end of a long shift.

"What's up with the change in plans?" Belinda asked after a minute or two of silent effort.

Alis tucked an EVA instrument pack more tightly into its cushioned housing. "We're going to rendezvous with an incoming object. It has some of the characteristics of a small moon. Round, about one hundred klicks across." That made it a good deal smaller than Luna, more like the size of one of Jupiter's smaller moons.

"And?"

"And the rest of the data's inconsistent. Normal albedo is high, but radar albedo is awfully low. It's moving at about point zero three c, so it's way over solar system escape velocity."

"Which says it's never been here before."

"Right," Alis said. "Unless someone's hollowed out a small moon and is using it as a spacecraft."

"But no signals."

"Nope."

"Maybe it's just a big rock," said Tim from the far end of the storage bay.

"Maybe so, but what got it going that fast?"

Tim had no answer.

All right," Alis said. "Any more questions?" The briefing had been quick, mainly because so little was known at this point. She sat in conference room A with most of the crew of the *Ranger*. Daren Schrader and Karl Stanton were still on the bridge with the captain. Belinda and Tim sat almost as far from each other as possible, perhaps because Belinda was uncomfortable about the rest of the crew knowing she was spending off-hours with such a young guy. As if she could keep a secret among a crew of fewer than three dozen, and as if a distance of four meters would help conceal their relationship.

"Thirty-second mark," said Captain Fernandez over a speaker in the ceiling. "De-spin commencing."

For several days, the *Ranger* would no longer need the

quarters and operations area spun for artificial gravity because thrust would do the same job. Alis put her arms down on the armrests. She felt a sideways push as counter-thrust was applied to the ship, gradually decreasing the centrifugal force. Her stomach rose as she and the others approached weightlessness, and she gripped the armrests more tightly. Metallic creaks sounded from places she found hard to localize.

"One-half gee to commence in ten seconds," said the captain.

Soon Alis felt tugged toward what had been the wall.

"We're stable," said the captain. "Full acceleration to begin in two minutes."

Alis and the others released their seat belts and dropped to the new floor. She twisted the seat interlock and pulled her chair loose from the wall. When she found the corresponding floor socket, she anchored the chair in the place it would occupy for the next couple of weeks. The rest of the crew took care of the other chairs, and a few seconds later the room had been converted, and the crew was strapped into their chairs again.

Two gees, when the full acceleration finally began, was even more uncomfortable than it had seemed last time. Several of the conference room chairs squeaked and groaned as the load increased, making more noise than the people they supported, despite the fact that the chairs could withstand a lot more force than their cargo could.

Breathing seemed to require a conscious effort at first; then slowly the new environment began to feel almost natural.

Once the acceleration had steadied, Alis glanced at the faces of the crew and saw no questioning expressions. She unbuckled herself and rose a bit shakily in the two gees. "Dismissed."

The crew filed out, everyone moving with more care than normal, with Robert Vasquez taking up the rear. He stopped at the door. "I'm curious," he said. "Does the higher gravity feel the same as it used to—before? Do you feel the need to breathe more deeply? Any new pains?"

Alis suppressed her irritation. Virtually every interaction with the M.D. reminded her she was a freak. Why couldn't he at least introduce a little small talk with his questions, make even the tiniest effort to show her he acknowledged her as a person, not a freak? "No, I can't say that I notice any change."

Robert nodded, then left. She had the impression he was disappointed. She realized that despite her anger toward Karl and the discomfort she felt when around him, Robert made her feel worse.

Alis exited the conference room walking carefully and straining with a body that felt twice as heavy as normal. She headed for the bridge. Suddenly she could easily imagine how it would feel to be three times her age.

Four and a half days of double-gee brought Alis to the point of feeling tired almost all the time. Daren and Karl were on the bridge when she relieved Karl, who seemed to understand that engaging her in conversation wasn't a wise idea. Karl nodded to Daren and left.

Alis was settling in for the shift when she realized something was missing. She glanced at Daren. "I forgot that cushion I've been using for my neck. Can you handle the bridge alone for a couple of minutes?"

"Sure. It's not like a lot is going on." Daren had his legs propped up and cushioned so the blood didn't pool in his feet.

Alis left the bridge, deliberately moving at a moderate pace so she didn't catch up with Karl. He'd be in his quarters before she reached that corridor, so she wouldn't have to worry about a confrontation.

Despite moving slowly, she almost caught up too soon. As she peered around a corner, she saw Karl still in the circular corridor, about to enter his cabin. She'd wait just a moment until he was inside; then she'd enter the corridor.

As she waited, she heard a sudden *crack* as a cabin door opened. Following that was a sound that seemed so out of place that it compelled her to look around the corner.

Karl had been thrown against the wall opposite his cabin door, and *water* was flooding out of his cabin. She stared in amazement.

For several seconds Karl just lay there as water spilled through his doorway, along the corridor in both directions, and slowly emptied through recycling drains. Slowly he got to his feet. His posture gave Alis the feeling that he was uninjured but tired, maybe resigned.

She backed around the corner, unsure what to do. A second later, her mind made up, she moved forward, doing her best to re-create the surprise that was now several seconds old.

Karl stood in the corridor as water up to the middle of his calves drained from his cabin. He faced the cabin, bent slightly forward in defeat or in reaction to two gees. Alis was within a couple of meters before he turned and saw her.

"What happened?" she asked.

He hesitated. "I guess I must have left the water on."

The flood of water had slowed to a gentle stream.

"And you must have also bypassed the liter counter. That must be a few weeks' supply of water."

"It would seem that way, wouldn't it?"

"And you must have blocked the drain." She followed Karl's gaze into the water-damaged cabin, seeing his bed was soaked, as was his clothes locker. His desk and the contents had obviously been submerged.

"Yeah," he said. "Sometimes I'm pretty forgetful."

Alis shook her head. "What's happening here?"

"It's just an accident, all right?"

"No, it's not. I want to know what's going on."

Karl looked back into his cabin and sighed. "Let's just say I'm not too popular around here."

"Because of Tokyan Station?"

"It's just—personality conflicts."

"Right. And things like this have been happening all along? You don't seem all that surprised by this."

"Well, no. This isn't the first."

"And you don't fight back," Alis said, suddenly sure that was right.

"And turn the ship into a war zone? Whoever it is will get tired eventually."

"You look tired already."

Karl turned his head and looked at her. "Some people I know have gone through a lot worse. I can take this."

"This is about the most unprofessional thing I've ever seen. So you're accepting this as, what, your 'punishment' for causing the accident?"

Karl took on a sudden new intensity and he moved a step closer to Alis. His voice was soft, but she could feel the frustration held just in check. "Look, I'm going to mention this one more time, and I won't bring it up again. *I did not cause that accident.* That it seemed like I did caused me a lot of pain before I got here, and I don't really expect to be free of it. I'm sorry beyond words that you were hurt, and I see those two people more often in my dreams than I ever saw them while they were alive. I've taken responsibility for a lot of decisions and actions in my life, and I know I should have double-checked the last burn the shuttle made, but I did not *cause* that accident."

Alis stood there with her gaze locked on Karl's, not knowing what to say this time.

The anger faded from Karl's face. "Look, I'm tired. What's done is done. The situation is under control. There's nothing I wish to report. Can I be dismissed?"

Without waiting for a reply, Karl turned and walked into his quarters, where the standing water still covered his shoes. He turned off the water in the sink and pulled tape off the drain. He unhooked one corner of the bed-web, then another, and he started rolling the material to squeeze the water out.

A couple of seconds later, Alis touched her wristcomp and called Daren on the bridge. "I'll be back in a few minutes. Call me if you need me on the bridge." Daren acknowledged.

She entered Karl's cabin and moved to the far end of the bed-web. She felt a mild sensation of cooling on her feet, but the sensation of being wet wasn't conveyed. She unhooked both corners and looked up to see Karl standing motionless, watching her. "Well," she said. "What are you waiting for?"

Karl started moving again. Together they squeezed most of the water from the bed-web and hung it in front of the fresh-air vent. Karl retrieved gear from a nearby maintenance locker and swept the remaining water out into the corridor, where emergency drains sent it on its way to recycling.

Alis picked up some soggy certificates and records and spread them out to dry. It was a useless gesture; the hard copies were water-soluble, meant for easy recycling. Her attention snagged on a deteriorating picture of Karl and three other people. It was a commendation photo, and Karl was the one receiving some award.

"Tell me you aren't helping me just so you can snoop," Karl said from behind her.

She turned and looked at him. She didn't know him at all, despite how much her thoughts focused on him, but she didn't think he was actually angry. He looked calm, but hard to read.

"No, I'm not. But curiosity is a hard thing to stop sometimes." She turned back to the picture and read the caption underneath. Karl was being awarded the Silver Star. She read the text, then turned back to Karl with surprise. "You're the one who rescued the Yoterro hostages?"

"Even screwups have lucky days."

"I didn't mean it that way. I was just surprised that it's someone I know. The media never knew who you were, because—"

"Because it's bad form to show the faces of intelligence operatives in the press."

"You were in intelligence? Why'd you quit?"

"You ask a lot of questions. Is this an official interrogation?"

"I'm curious."

Karl sighed. "I got tired of seeing my friends die. Smart move, huh? I thought it was the line of work, but maybe it *is* me." Karl took the soggy papers and tossed them in the recycle receptacle.

Alis looked around for anything else to help with.

Karl said gently, "Look, I really appreciate your helping me clean up, but I think this place is about as good as it's going to get any time soon. I don't want to be rude, but I guess I'd really like to be alone for a while."

Alis nodded. That feeling she could understand. She tried to think of something appropriate to say, but by the time she was in the corridor she still hadn't. She walked slowly back to the bridge.

The closer the foreign object came, the more puzzling the readings were. Now that it was only a day away from the *Ranger,* its image was still fuzzy, but clear enough to let the crew start making some new guesses. Karl kept eager watch on the series of enhanced images on the bridge's wall display.

Alis Nussem and Captain Fernandez sat nearby. Alis tapped a control and one of the false-color images shifted further toward red. "On this scale, it's bouncing back about as much light as a giant peanut."

Karl rubbed his cheek. The primary image was off-white, almost perfectly round. Features were nearly impossible to make out yet, but there was the suggestion of a couple of grid lines, giant circles. The markings, if that was what they really were, hadn't changed since they came into view, implying the object was not rotating.

The more complete the collection of data grew, the more excited Karl became. The regular shape, the lack of rotation, the seemingly regular markings, all suggested the possibility that this thing was the product of intelligent life, but definitely not anything produced in human history. Possibly it even carried intelligent life, or it had in the past. Karl chided himself for making such huge assumptions, but if this was simply a large piece of rock thrown into space by some ancient collision, he would expect a lot more irregularity to its shape, and it wouldn't be at all surprising for it to be spinning, even if slowly, from whatever chaotic process had flung it on its way.

The very cold surface indicated by the measurements was consistent with the idea that it was just a moon that had somehow escaped from a planetary body and had somehow attained a much higher than expected velocity, significantly higher than what was needed to escape a solar system. On the other hand, a cold surface could surround a warmer interior, given adequate insulation.

Mass was tougher to measure; they'd have to get a lot closer before getting a first cut on it. Definitely no measurable atmosphere. With that small a diameter, the body would have to have an enormous density to trap any free gas molecules. It was enough smaller than Luna that, if its density was similar to Luna's, it would have less than one percent gee.

"Is it my imagination," Karl asked finally, "or do you see a dark spot near the edge?"

"Which edge?" asked Captain Fernandez.

Alis looked at Karl, and then looked up at the display. At least she wasn't still flashing him looks that made him wish he were dead.

"I don't want to say. I'd like to hear where you think it is, if you see it at all."

Alis stared at the image for a long moment. Karl supposed that if she were looking at the actual object instead of a display, she could set her eyes into different modes, allowing her to see far more than he could. The bridge display was an equalizer, allowing no one an edge.

Karl leaned back in his chair, feeling tired. This final leg of acceleration was at 1.9 gees instead of 2 gees. At first he thought he could feel a bit less force, but after several days of tiring under the high gravity, 1.9 gees felt more like 3 gees.

A moment later Captain Fernandez said, "Ten o'clock," just as Alis said, "Upper left, maybe 160 degrees?"

Karl nodded at Alis, then glanced at the captain and raised his eyebrows.

"Curious," said Fernandez.

Karl returned to the bridge after forcing himself to take a sleep shift. It had been almost impossible to fall asleep, but he knew the most interesting period was just ahead, and he wanted to be alert.

Everyone aboard was excited about what they had dubbed "Cantaloupe." Karl suspected there might actually be a more accurate match, like maybe "honeydew," but all the alternatives Karl could think of sounded even dumber.

The antagonism Karl had felt from Alis and Robert and several of the others had dropped into the noise, either because his attention was focused on the new arrival or because everyone else's attention was focused there, too. He felt more comfortable than he had in weeks.

Daren Schrader and Lucy Ito were on the bridge when Karl arrived. They both acknowledged Karl's arrival with more animation than usual before turning back to the wall display. Daren was busy taking readings and saving them in the ship's computer. Lucy seemed captivated by the central image on the screen. For the moment she seemed more like a young woman entranced by her first sight of the Earth from space than an ensign and a brilliant assistant science officer who managed to consistently give Karl the impression that she should be the science officer and he her assistant.

Karl sucked in his breath when he reached a position that let him see the full view. Cantaloupe's features were now sharper, vivid, looking more and more like an enormous pale white melon with a regular pattern of dimples covering its surface. A number of fine almost-straight dark lines cut the surface, each of them seemingly a segment of a great circle, some of them long enough to stretch all the way around the visible surface, some only a tenth that long. The lines formed no particular pattern that Karl could identify.

The dark spot on the upper left edge of the image had become better focused. A section of the wall screen had been devoted to a magnified image of that section, but even in the magnified picture Karl couldn't tell what he was looking at, other than a small discolored patch. It seemed important merely because it was so unlike the rest of Cantaloupe's surface.

Just before Karl had gone off duty, the latest image of Cantaloupe had been clear enough that the captain had notified the ISA mission control that they might want to either send an additional investigation team while they still had time or at least set up some high-resolution scanning equipment in its path so they could learn as much about Cantaloupe as they could before it was through the solar system and gone. So far the spectrometry results had told them little more than their visual inspection. A steady data stream was flowing to ISA headquarters.

Karl was more grateful than ever that he hadn't lost his ISA commission. If he'd been relegated to the civilian contractor ranks of GSSC, he wouldn't be out here; instead he would be doing one of the boring jobs ISA farmed out to GSSC. GSSC managed to secure a few interesting jobs, but not many.

Karl glanced at a display insert that counted down hours and minutes. In less than an hour they would match course with the object, and finally they'd be able to see the other side.

5 ▪ EPIDERMIS

Attention," Captain Fernandez said. "Reducing thrust in ten seconds. Prepare for zero gee." He thumbed off the microphone switch and nodded to Alis.

Karl's stomach rose in his chest several seconds later, and his seat belt kept him secure in his padded chair. Besides Alis and the captain, Daren Schrader and Lucy Ito were also on the bridge, so the small room felt crowded. Most of the rest of the crew were in conference room A, watching a relay of the video from the main wall screen. The additional screens, including a ceiling screen, were all active.

Cantaloupe filled the main screen, now in live video. Stars around the perimeter shone much more brightly than normal because the gain was cranked up to make Cantaloupe's dim surface more visible. It hung no more than a hundred kilometers away, in sharp focus, a sight even more puzzling than before.

Within limits, most objects grow more and more random as the magnification increases, the way things work when a microscope starts zooming in on a sheet of paper. From above, the paper looks like a smooth, white plane. Get close enough, and the surface looks like mountain country. Up close, Cantaloupe, instead of looking more and more irregular, like Luna for instance, looked more and more regular, more like the product of intelligence than the result of natural disaster or typical planetary formation.

The dimples that they had seen from a distance were still there, filled in by yet smaller dimples, but the depressions weren't crater-like, varying in size, some of them obscuring others. Instead, the surface resembled that of a golf ball, with a regular pattern of equally sized and spaced dimples and intervening raised areas.

"Eerie," Alis said softly.

"Amen," said Karl. The object was like nothing the human race had encountered before, and Karl wondered if they might actually be coming up on a first-contact situation. At the very least, this had the potential for being the first actual indication that the Earth wasn't the only place that intelligent life had come into existence.

The series of arcs they had seen from a distance hadn't changed much in appearance. They still looked as if they were just faint dark lines drawn on the surface. A section of the screen showed a blowup of a segment of one of the lines, and on each side of the line was the normal dimple pattern. Now they were close enough to get initial measurements of Cantaloupe's mass, those were surprising, too. It seemed to have less than a third of Luna's density, suggesting that either it was composed of very light material, dense material with a lot of vacuum pockets, or it contained a hollow core. Just one of the mysteries so far was the reading of about 0.05 gee despite the low apparent density and Cantaloupe's modest size.

"Ready for orbit?" Alis asked.

"Yes," said the captain. "And let's start toward the dark spot." He flipped on the microphone and spoke to the rest of the crew again. "We're about to enter a forced orbit around the visitor." He was the only one who didn't call it "Cantaloupe." "While we're in orbit, we'll be applying a steady thrust well under one gee. I'll plan on giving a minute's notice when we're going back to zero gee, but don't count on it."

The captain watched the clock tick three or four seconds, then nodded at Alis.

Alis fingered her controls, and the *Ranger* smoothly pushed ahead until Karl felt about a half gee. They kept that up until the *Ranger* reached a velocity that would take them around Cantaloupe every twenty minutes; then Alis cut the thrust way back and aimed the business end of the *Ranger*'s thrusters directly away from Cantaloupe.

Daren Schrader started a new surface recording as the discolored spot gradually moved inward from the edge of the field of view and started turning to face the *Ranger*.

Karl kept his attention on the wall screen. The dark spot was now fully visible, and it was definitely the most anomalous feature they'd seen on Cantaloupe. The dark shade and the irregular circular configuration gave the impression that someone had stubbed out a huge cigar against the surface, forming a shallow crater. Near the center of the discolored area was a small, raised ring of material. Beyond the dark spot was more of the same regular dimpled area.

Cantaloupe kept slowly rotating under them, giving Daren good 3-D images of the dark spot.

Karl's eyes widened, and he suddenly glanced at the others to see if they saw it, too. They did. Something small and shiny had just come into view on the horizon.

"What is that?" Daren Schrader said softly. He fingered his controls, and a section of the display opened up with a magnified view centered on the glint of light on Cantaloupe's surface.

No one answered.

Magnification grew steadily until the object filled the sub-display blowup. No question about it, the new object on Cantaloupe's surface must have been the product of intelligence. What showed in the image looked vaguely like the site of an airliner crash, with small shiny fragments scattered in a large fan-shaped area next to what could have been an alien space-craft.

Nothing about the shapes of the apparently damaged craft, if in fact that's what it was, reminded Karl even faintly of human spacecraft designs. The largest piece looked a little like a deformed donut with a huge bite taken out. About a quarter of the area of the torus had crumbled away. The torus was supported by three other large sections, each tall and thin, all three stuck through the center of the donut. All the surfaces glinted like metal on a gun barrel, but instead of gun-metal gray the shade was yellow-greenish. Karl glanced at the status legend underneath the display and verified that it was a true-color display, not some broad-spectrum enhancement.

"Will you look at that," Alis said, apparently to no one in particular.

After a long moment, Captain Fernandez cleared his throat and looked at Daren. "You haven't heard anything on any frequency yet, I assume."

Daren shook his head and double-checked his instrument panel.

"Keep sending the canned 'please respond' message to them, and keep your ears open. Try every available transmission range. I'm not optimistic about hearing back, but we'd be stupid not to try. And turn on the black box transmitter."

Daren touched a couple of spots on the instrument panel

display and a winking red light appeared. The recorder was always running, storing the most recent ten hours of activity no matter what. Having the flight recorder also periodically sending microburst transmissions back to mission control was something typically done only when a ship was entering a situation so dangerous that there was a risk of the black box being destroyed along with the ship.

The tour of the far side of Cantaloupe showed them nothing different from what they'd already seen. More even arrays of dimples, no more discolored spots or possible crash sites. When they neared the dark crater again, Captain Fernandez had Alis change orbit, and they moved off at right angles to their former orbit, just to make sure they hadn't missed anything at the poles.

They hadn't. The dark crater and the crash site seemed to be the only anomalies on the surface.

By the time the dark spot was almost centered under them again, Daren had still heard nothing back from Cantaloupe. A short radar imaging test failed to reveal anything but the surface they could see visually.

"Well, if we're going to explore, this certainly seems to be the place," said the captain. "Take us out of orbit and put us in a fixed position."

Alis complied. A few moments of one-half gee slowed Cantaloupe's apparent rotation under them. When the visitor seemed to hang motionless in space, Alis hit the station-keeping command, to apply a thrust so weak that it was barely noticeable, just enough to maintain a constant separation between the ship and Cantaloupe. Finally, they spun the living area up for half-gee comfort.

"Well, Karl," Captain Fernandez said when the ship had stabilized. "What do you want to do? It's going to be at least a day or two before anyone else gets here."

"Time for some hands-on sightseeing," Karl said. "We've got the surface mapped and we've already taken most of the measurements we can from orbit. The wreck isn't that far from the dark spot." He glanced at the display and turned on a units projection. "Twenty klicks, roughly. Since one of those lines passes between the two sites, a landing party put down between the two could investigate the four most interesting features."

"Four?" said Daren.

"The crater, the crash site, the lines, and the undamaged surface."

The captain looked at Alis. "You want a science team down there on their own, or do you want to be there?"

"I absolutely want to be there."

"Good answer. So who should be on your team?"

Alis hesitated. "Besides Karl? Daren, in case we get some opportunity to communicate. I know the odds are low, but we only have a week or two before this thing is through the solar system and gone forever, and I'd hate to miss any chance."

Daren nodded.

"And Belinda. She's good with logistics. I think she'd be a cool head if there's an emergency."

"No one else?" Karl said at last.

"Who would you suggest?" she asked.

"Lucy for one, and probably Robert."

"I can understand having the assistant science officer going, but our medical doctor, too? That would make six of us."

"I have a couple of reasons for recommending Robert. One, we're investigating something alien. I think that might make the potential for injuries higher than normal. Two, Cantaloupe's density and surface appearance suggest something organic. A medical doctor might come in handy. As you say, we don't have the luxury of time."

Karl watched Alis consider the suggestion. He suspected she didn't get along with Robert any better than he did. Even though he could do without Robert personally, he was glad to see her nod when she agreed he should be there.

Captain Fernandez had been thinking while watching Alis. He twisted his body toward Karl. "Organic? What are you suggesting?"

"That's just a guess at this point, and only one of a thousand guesses. I could be wrong."

"But if you're right?"

"I don't know. Some bizarre life-form that grows like crabgrass over the surface of moons. Maybe it's an organically grown outer shell over a starship. At the wildest end, we could be looking at a starship that's been completely organically grown. I'm not saying this is likely, just that it's one of the possibilities."

"Starship?" said Daren. "Where's the propulsion?"

"No idea. It could be some technology we wouldn't even recognize. Could be it's all internal to the body, or it extends outward when it's needed. This thing's velocity is consistent with the idea of something moving under its own power. At least it's moving a whole lot faster than any hunk of rock we've seen."

Daren shook his head. "Even assuming that was true, wouldn't now be the time it would be slowing down?"

"Maybe. Maybe it's waiting until it's closer to Sol. Maybe it's just passing through. It might not be slowing down if the crew is dead or disabled." Karl looked back at the screen. "Maybe the dark spot is an indication of damage deeper down."

Captain Fernandez suddenly looked unhappy. "We still know almost nothing about this thing except for the fact that it doesn't look like something formed spontaneously in nature. I don't like the idea that this thing could suddenly start accelerating. I want all of you back alive."

With Karl's history, he felt uncomfortable talking about

the danger, but he said, "Just being aboard the *Ranger* is a risk. Besides, if Cantaloupe does start accelerating at any significant rate, its gravity is so low that we'll just fall away from the surface and be left behind. You can pick us up easily without having to match course with something that's accelerating unevenly. If it makes you feel better, ask for volunteers."

The captain wrinkled his nose. "So, among us here, who would like to volunteer?"

Karl, Alis, and Daren immediately raised their hands.

Karl said, "I'd bet Belinda, Lucy, and Robert will volunteer, too."

Captain Fernandez came closer than normal to a smile. "Well, I guess we'd better figure out the best way to get you down there. This isn't quite the normal station docking this rig is built for, and EVA suits might take some practice in a gravity field. We could just stand off the surface and drop you if we're dealing with pretty light gravity. Is that enough to hold you, or are you going to just bounce off?"

Daren pulled up a computer screen and selected a couple of standard equations. A moment later he said, "Escape velocity is well over a hundred meters per second, so we might bounce awhile, but we won't be in any danger of leaving the surface permanently, unless it started accelerating."

"Is there any better way?" Alis asked.

The captain scratched his chin. "Well, I don't think the *Ranger* should actually make contact with the surface. Even in a one percent gee, this thing will weigh tons, so we could break through the surface."

Karl nodded. "Especially considering its low density. It might turn out to be really strong stuff, but it might not."

The captain went on. "And it's not a good idea to aim the business end of our propulsion at the surface from up close. No telling what it might do. We could lower you on a long line, get you at least within a few meters of the surface before we had to drop you. And you should be able to jump that high in the light gravity."

"As long as no one's injured."

"If we have to, we'll get closer. I just don't want the ship any closer than need be."

Alis nodded. "That sounds good to me. How soon can you put us down?"

The captain glanced at the wall chronometer. "How soon can you be ready?"

"Fifteen minutes, but if we shoot for an hour maybe we won't forget anything we'll wish we had remembered."

"That'll give you time to make sure everyone's a volunteer?"

Alis smiled. "We can go with a smaller team if we need to. But I bet there's hardly anyone on board who wouldn't volunteer."

Alis was right. Lucy Ito, Robert Vasquez, and Belinda Penson all volunteered instantly. Robert took the longest—three seconds—because Lucy's exclamation of pleasure was loud enough that at first he didn't understand the question.

Alis surreptitiously watched the others as they got into their suits and prepared to leave the *Ranger*. Lucy was so excited that she had shed her normal superior air.

Karl was difficult to read. Alis had found herself watching him more since the cabin-flooding incident. Before that she had imagined him to be a whiner, constantly trying to escape blame for what he had done. Since then she had realized that he put up with a lot that he never complained about, taking hostility in stride, doing his job well despite obstacles presented by the crew. He must have had extremely strong feelings about the disaster to have reacted the way he did.

Often when Alis talked with Robert he seemed haughty, as if he were some Neanderthal who resented reporting to a woman. Now he seemed almost as excited as Lucy.

Belinda Penson strapped an auxiliary tool kit into a bundle of supplies that would be the first arrival on Cantaloupe, partly so they didn't drop it on anyone, and partly so its presumably successful impact would let the team know they weren't going to be crashing through some membrane-thin shell. She'd make a good assistant; she followed through on everything she was told, and she consistently tried to think one step ahead without making the mistake of assuming everything she anticipated would be approved.

Daren Schrader poked and prodded at a boxy piece of equipment Alis was told was a communications repeater, furnished with enough power to relay their transmissions to the *Ranger* even if it needed to pull back a moderate distance. The unit mounted on the back of Daren's life-suit. Their suit radios would be able to receive transmissions from the *Ranger*'s powerful transmitter under virtually any conditions.

Alis suddenly realized that she had been paying so much attention to everyone else that she had neglected her own feelings. To her surprise, she felt more energetic than she had in months. She couldn't say whether her fake heart beat any faster than before, but she could feel a slight adrenaline buzz. Despite being nervous about the mission, she couldn't imagine anything she'd rather be doing at that moment.

Activity-filled minutes passed. Air supplies were checked. Suit computers completed their diagnostics. A long list of equipment and supplies made its way into suit pockets and into the inventory of the auxiliary equipment pack. Glad they had the advantage of a low-gee environment, Alis made sure they had far more survival supplies than a routine day-long mission would require. This mission was anything but routine.

Alis slid her faceplate closed and switched on the air supply. She scanned the others, seeing one helmet status indicator after another turn green.

She glanced at the heads-up display on the inside of her

helmet and picked suit-to-ship communications by looking in the right spots and blinking. "We're ready."

"We're in position," said Captain Fernandez. "Good luck."

Alis waited for a thumbs-up from each of the other five, then entered the air lock carrying the line they would use to reach the surface.

As an astronomical body, Cantaloupe was only a small-ish moon, but compared to an asteroid big enough to see from Earth, Cantaloupe was enormous. The dimpled surface was much dimmer than it had seemed in the light-amplified bridge screen. Alis hooked one end of the line on an eyelet next to the air lock door and watched it fall ever so slowly toward the surface of Cantaloupe, unwinding as it fell.

Alis moved away from the air lock and clung to handholds on the *Ranger*'s hull. Looking down at Cantaloupe was enough to give her mild vertigo. Despite the fact that she could probably survive a fall from here in the ultra-light gravity, she still felt nervous, as if a split-second blackout could trigger a fall to her death. The smallest dimples on the surface looked to be several meters across and no shallower than a half-meter. Cantaloupe's horizon seemed perfectly even, its surface stretching to fill almost half her field of view.

Not far away lay the alien crash site. The largest piece of the wreckage, the deformed torus, showed a long damaged section where a gash in the body's side looked more like a torn piece of paper than sheared metal. The pieces of the debris could have been there a day or a million years. Alis had no way of telling just from their appearance.

A suited figure emerged from the air lock. Karl Stanton, judging by the helmet markings. He moved away from the air lock door and hung on handholds near her. For some reason she felt reassured by his presence, but the instant she was aware of the feeling she squelched it. She didn't need anyone else to make her feel safe, especially Karl.

A couple of minutes later, the whole team of six clung to handholds near the air lock door. Belinda was easy to pick out of the group since she was the one with the largest auxiliary equipment bag. Alis looked back at the cord she had released. It swayed very slowly as if a breeze was forcing it to one side, and it almost reached the surface.

"You ready, Belinda?" Alis asked.

"Yes."

"Go for it. And drop the equipment bag when you're halfway down. I want to give the surface a good test impact before we reach it."

"You got it."

Belinda maneuvered into position and wrapped the cable around her body and through a clip on her belt. She let go of her grip on the *Ranger,* and Cantaloupe's ultra-mild gravity started slowly pulling her down.

A few seconds later, Belinda applied a little more pressure to the cable, and she was sliding down the cable at a near-constant rate, about a meter per second. Her body began to sway back and forth as if on a huge slow-motion pendulum that seemed to move more and more slowly. Below her the rest of the cable swayed with its own frequency.

A minute or two later, Belinda's descent slowed to a stop. "All right," she said over the suit radio. "Ready to drop."

"Go," said Alis.

The equipment bag began to fall in slow motion. It very gradually sped up until it was about to hit the surface. It looked like it might have been dropped from the roof of a house in normal gravity.

It hit. It bounced slightly sideways. It seemed to bounce about ten meters high, still in slow motion. It would probably have bounced a lot higher if it were one elastic body instead of a sack of loose equipment. The surface where it had hit seemed unblemished.

"All right," Alis said. "Proceed."

Belinda resumed her friction-controlled drop while the equipment pack kept bouncing, lower each time. Within a minute she dangled near the end of the cord, no more than a few meters off the surface. "Ready?" she asked.

"Go," said Alis.

Belinda let go. She dropped for a few seconds and hit. She bounced higher than a trampoline rebound. "Whoa!" she cried involuntarily, then added quickly, "I'm okay."

Alis smiled at the antithesis of the "one small step" speech.

Belinda was able to stop bouncing faster than the equipment bag had, by using her legs as shock absorbers. "I'm okay," she repeated. "The surface has a little give to it, like a stiff foam pad on a hard floor."

"Okay. Stand clear," Alis said, and she grabbed the cable. She wrapped the cord around her waist and fed it through a hook on her belt, and left the *Ranger* behind.

Sliding slowly away from the *Ranger* and toward the bizarre surface of Cantaloupe was one of the most surreal experiences of Alis's life. For an instant she worried what would happen if the *Ranger*'s propulsion suddenly died, with her suspended between the ship and the dimpled surface below. Would the *Ranger* bounce, and, if so, how high? If she were on the surface, she could at least hide in one of the depressions and hope the *Ranger*'s mass wouldn't be enough to squeeze the small raised spaces between dimples that far.

Alis blinked the sequence that shifted her eyes into infrared. Belinda's backpack heat exchanger became a beacon on the dim landscape. The dimples and raised spaces forming Cantaloupe's surface changed in shade and their texture seemed to roughen slightly, but the different view revealed nothing new. She switched back to normal vision before the combination of bizarre situation and distorted reality became too much.

She increased her tension on the cord as she neared the end of it. Seconds later she swayed over the surface of Cantaloupe. She waited a couple of seconds, until her instinct told her the fall would land her on a small raised space instead of in a dimple, and she let go.

Several seconds of zero gee ended when her feet touched down. She tried to fall to one side and roll, rather than just absorbing her entire momentum with her legs. Instead of making a controlled fall, she felt more like a victim of a blanket toss. She was in contact with a resilient surface for a second or two, but then she was thrown back up, still whirling, the *Ranger* flashing past her view twice before she bounced again, totally unharmed, but feeling stupid. Bionic legs were obviously no guarantee of control.

It took Alis two more bounces before she was in control again. She looked up at the underbelly of the *Ranger*. Its dim rectangular shape was close enough to stretch across two-thirds of the sky. From here she could easily see the twin helmet lamps on each of the four remaining team members' suits. The pairs of lights could have been distant headlights on a clear, dark Texas night, but a quick look around her renewed her sense of awe. "All right," she said, louder than she'd meant to. "Karl, you're next."

She took a couple of quick breaths as she watched Karl start his descent. Strange, but if it hadn't been for Karl and the accident, the odds were that she would not be here right now, here on the surface of the strangest thing the human race had yet come across.

Alis moved away from the drop point, edging around toward where Belinda had joined the equipment pack. The surface of Cantaloupe was crazy. From here she could see rings radiating outward from her position, rings formed by the tops of the raised spaces between dimples, and she had a sudden image of an ant on a golf ball. The view seemed more like a computer-generated construct than something out of real life.

She skidded down into one of the depressions and had a

hard time getting up the other side in the ultra-low gravity. Jumping from place to place seemed easier except for stopping. She knelt on the surface and ran her gloved fingers across it. The low gravity had given her the feeling that the surface was slick, but actually it wasn't. Alis found it difficult to be sure through the suit, but the ground seemed to have a texture similar to the skin of an orange, but tougher, firmer.

Karl was halfway down the line by the time Alis reached Belinda. Alis took another long look at the horizon. The curve was so smooth, it made Cantaloupe seem small, and she had to remind herself that its surface area wasn't much smaller than that of Switzerland.

She turned back and watched Karl jump. He hit the surface tilted slightly forward, and as his body bounced he very slowly pivoted, so that he took his second bounce on all fours, looking vaguely like a high-tech mutant frog. She thought about how ungraceful she had been and decided his form wasn't all that bad.

Robert was the next one down, followed by Daren and then Lucy. Lucy's delighted cry when she bounced reminded Alis that despite Lucy's more usual demeanor she was hardly older than Tim. She windmilled her arms in an effort to stay upright, and she almost managed it. Moments later she was on the ground and stable.

When the group had assembled, all of them unhurt, Alis said into her radio, "Captain, the team has landed. We're all safe. Ready for you to withdraw."

"Roger, and good luck."

Overhead, the dark shape of the *Ranger* seemed motionless for a long moment, but then it began to pull up first slowly, then faster. Seconds later it was just a dark patch obscuring a fist-sized patch of stars.

Alis glanced around at the ring of helmets, grateful for polarizing visors that cut the glare from helmet lamps. She looked at the direction finder strapped to her wrist. "Belinda, tell me if you get tired of handling the equipment pack. Let's move out."

She turned in the direction of the alien crash site and let herself tip forward. With an easy tiptoe stride, she started propelling herself across the surface of Cantaloupe. The others followed her across a terrain where no humans had ever tiptoed before.

6 ▪ FATALITY

Karl jogged behind Belinda and Alis, using his toes to keep pushing himself along in the micrograv-ity. The motion took less energy than treading water. The bizarre surface of Cantaloupe seemed like some unending 3-D model of a mathematical function. Overhead, the sky was filled with stars that seemed closer than ever. Karl didn't ac-tually bother to pinch himself, but the whole scene felt unreal, disconnected with anything he had done before, and he did have to periodically remind himself that this *was* all real, that he should stay cautious and not let himself get lost in the dream-like quality of the surroundings.

Alis looked totally at ease with the running, her motions smooth and precise, just the right deft touch each time she pushed her body ahead. Karl wondered briefly, for the thou-sandth time, if he would have been as angry if he'd been the one to have to need artificial legs, heart, eyes, and the other prostheses Alis had. It seemed to him that in some ways the replacements made her better than human, but her attitude seemed to be that the accident had made her less than human. Karl looked straight ahead and tried to force her out of his mind.

After a couple of spills, the group had reached a comfortable speed that let each of the team bound from the top of one cross-like raised space to the top of the next. The motion summoned an old image of running down a railroad track, hopping from one tie to another, landing on every other tie. It wasn't very likely that they would have to worry about an approaching train, but Karl wondered what other dangers lay ahead.

Karl glanced in his helmet rear-view screen and made sure Lucy, Daren, and Robert were keeping up. The *Ranger* could help locate stragglers, but if the group became separated, the regularity of the surface could make it a real nuisance to find people. He started cataloging possible solutions to the problem, just in case it came up. For one thing, by using suit radios to coordinate a jump time, two separated parties could simultaneously jump as high as they could. He didn't attempt any mental calculations, but given the lack of obstructions on the surface, and given the helmet lamps that could be seen for a long way, he guessed it might be possible to spot anyone within a several-kilometer range.

Karl felt better, having a potential solution to a possible problem. He traveled several more very long steps before he saw a problem with the solution. If one of the parties were injured, unable to make such a leap, that would cut way down on the useful distance.

Cantaloupe didn't rotate. That meant they could describe the location of particular stars near the horizon, and by comparing what was below or above the horizon at various compass points, two parties could conceivably locate each other.

The gentle leaping from one raised space to the next grew extremely boring after a while, almost hypnotic. At least Karl knew they weren't drifting off course. As long as they kept moving in the same pattern, they were always precisely on the same heading, as if following a diagonal on a chessboard.

"I see it!" Belinda said suddenly.

Her voice in Karl's helmet moved Karl's pulse faster as the excitement instantly infected him, too. A couple of seconds later, he could see the tip of the alien probe, or whatever it was, poking over the horizon ahead. On the amplified-light screen aboard the *Ranger* it had looked yellow-green; here in the dim light it was closer to dark green.

They kept moving closer as they neared their goal, and the trio of tilted greenish spires grew taller and larger. Karl was surprised by just how tall the structure was. The group skidded awkwardly to a stop thirty or forty meters away. The tops of the spires must have extended twenty meters above Cantaloupe's surface.

Karl realized that the team members had spread out to look at the artifact, each person standing atop one of the small raised spaces for the best view.

"Wow." Lucy's voice was subdued.

Karl could feel the awe she must have been experiencing. The spires each seemed not to be long rods, but rather very gently tapered cones. The bottom end of the nearest one looked to be a couple of meters across, and it had sunk a little into the surface of Cantaloupe. At its top end, it was no wider than a person's head, and the very top seemed to be smooth, rounded.

Surrounding the trio of spires, hanging perhaps a meter and a half off the surface of Cantaloupe, was the huge, deformed torus, also the same metallic shade of green. The green was dark enough to be barely distinguishable from black in the dim ambient light, but helmet lamps gave it an eerie yellowish cast, not quite a glow. From this angle, the structure appeared to be intact. Even if Cantaloupe itself turned out to have some explanation that didn't imply it was the product of intelligent life, this craft had to be of non-human design. There had to be other life out there somewhere, or at least there had been at one time.

After a long moment of silence, Alis said, "I'm ready for a scan of the perimeter. Belinda, can you break out the cameras? Anyone else with suggestions?"

Karl waited a moment, then spoke into the silence. "Lucy, mark off an area we haven't trampled on yet so you'll have a pristine work space for taking surface samples."

"Right." Lucy's voice was completely devoid of the smug air of superiority Karl had come to expect. *They should discover strange stuff like this more often,* he thought.

Belinda had the auxiliary equipment pack partly open. She opened a padded box and withdrew cameras. One by one she handed them out to the other team members. Karl accepted his, and he carefully locked it into position on his left shoulder bracket. When he turned the camera on and switched his helmet display to it, he saw a crisp display of Daren's suited form a few meters away. Karl swiveled his body, and the view from the camera panned with the motion.

Karl left the camera on and switched his helmet display back to general status. Power was still at ninety-nine percent. The latest periodic, automatic health check reported no problems. Oxygen-nitrogen balance fine. Temperature control fine. Power plant fine. Stores of nutrients and emergency medication ninety-nine percent.

Karl opened his mouth as he directed his gaze at the proper control spot, and a nutrient pill popped into his mouth. He leaned forward and took a sip of water and washed down the pill. He liked being out in a suit, with the accompanying feeling of being on his own that being inside a ship never gave him. The only aspects he hated about long periods in a suit related to recycling. Intellectually he knew suit recycling was not really any different from a ship recycling plant or a city recycling plant, but the confines of the suit made the process harder to ignore. Apparently the suit designers were uncomfortable with the process, too, because they labeled components with technical identifiers such as *recombination chamber, fluid reclamation pod,* and *adaptive recycling bay.*

When Karl looked back at Lucy, she had already positioned a few flags around a section of Cantaloupe's surface, and she had a sample case ready to start filling. She knelt on the surface and applied pressure to a cutting blade. He moved closer, careful not to enter her working area. "Need some help with the samples?" he asked.

Lucy's helmet swung around, aiming her lamps at Karl. "All under control." Karl wouldn't have been surprised to have her leave it at that, but the expedition was still having its effect on her, because she added, "This is strange stuff. Nothing like the consistency of rock. More like very tough orange peel." She carefully deposited a sliver of material in a vial.

"Isn't it time we started looking around that—that vehicle—if that's what it is?" asked Robert. Impatience modulated his voice.

"We can afford to spend a little time here getting samples," Alis said calmly. "We'll investigate soon."

"Well, there's no need for my presence here. I could go on ahead, or do a perimeter scan. Daren and Belinda probably aren't needed here at the moment, either."

"Stay here for now. We're one team, and I don't see any strong advantage to splitting up just to save five minutes."

"But there's so much to—"

Karl cut in on the conversation. "You wouldn't like it if one of your patients started arguing about your diagnosis. Alis has a job to do; why don't we try to make it a little easier for her?"

A chime sounded in Karl's helmet, indicating a private transmission. Alis said, "Thanks, but I can handle him." The words were so quick that Karl wasn't sure if she was angry or just confident in her leadership.

A second chime sounded before he could decide, and Robert's private message said, "Why don't you take a long walk with a short air bottle?"

Replying would only make things worse, so Karl didn't. He went back to watching Lucy. She had a hand-crank drill fitted with a core sampler. As she turned the crank, a half-meter tube with the diameter of Karl's thumb dug slowly into the surface. Karl wondered whether they were digging through the surface of a balloon or something more like the name Cantaloupe implied.

Lucy's body shifted on the surface as the increased torque forced her to turn. "Can someone sit on my feet?" she asked.

Karl moved forward. Seconds later he sat on the surface, holding Lucy's booted feet.

Lucy started turning again, and Karl could feel her feet trying their best to turn away from him. After a long moment, he suddenly felt himself slipping along the surface, too. Alis and Belinda both sat down on the surface in front of him, and when his boots reached their suits, he came to a stop again.

Their combined friction was enough to let Lucy keep drilling. A few minutes later, she cried out, "I got it!"

Karl got back to his feet along with the others as Lucy slipped the core sample into a cylindrical enclosure and sealed it shut.

"I think I've got enough of the top surface," Lucy said. "I'd rather hold off on getting deeper samples. If we're lucky, when that probe-thing landed, it cut into the surface."

"Why do you assume it is a probe?" asked Robert.

"Why, do you think it grew here?"

"I have no idea. I'm trying to keep an open mind."

"Me, too. It's just a guess, all right? It looks damaged, maybe from an impact here. It doesn't seem to share any property we know of with Cantaloupe. It looks to me like Cantaloupe passed by some other life at some time in the past, and they were curious enough and technologically adept enough to send something out to investigate."

"I wonder if we'll find some dead aliens," Belinda said suddenly.

"That's preposterous," said Robert with conviction. "Even if that thing is a probe, and even if it were populated by aliens, the impact probably happened millions of years ago. They'd be dust by now."

"Sounds like an assumption to me, Doc," Lucy said. Karl could normally tell when someone was smiling just from the sound of the person's voice, and he was certain that Lucy was smiling.

"Don't call me 'Doc.' "

"Okay, people," Alis said. "We've got a job to do. If you're finished with your samples, Lucy, let's move out. I want to walk the perimeter before we go closer."

"Oh, good idea," said Robert.

"Dr. Vasquez, if you'd like to be relieved of your duty and sent back to the *Ranger*, I think we can manage just fine."

After an uncomfortable silence, Robert said, "I'm sorry. I'm just impatient."

"So am I. Let's go."

This time Alis took the lead. The group began to walk a large circle around the alien object, staying at least thirty meters away from it.

The object seemed symmetrical from a top view, in the same way a kaleidoscope view was. From a number of points, the object looked the same in both directions. Taken as a whole, the huge torus seemed to have as much in common with a pretzel as with a donut. Topologically it was a donut, but the surface curved and rippled as if the body contained huge coils that weren't lined up evenly, but braided.

They had made their way about sixty degrees around the probe, or whatever it was, when they came to the damaged area.

Even up close, the damage looked more like torn paper than metal ripped apart. Along one edge were stringy fiber ends. They looked small enough to be pieces of thread, but in the vacuum on Cantaloupe's surface, the fibers hung absolutely motionless, adding to the feeling that they were a lot stronger than thread.

Karl felt the urge to go closer, to be able to see inside the structure and to feel the damage with his own glove. He stayed where he was.

"Look," said Belinda. "There's some of the residue— some pieces from that thing."

Karl looked where she pointed and saw that they were almost on the discolored area of Cantaloupe's surface that had apparently resulted from being sprayed with fragments or gas from the probe.

"Let me collect a few samples before we walk on them," Lucy said. She moved ahead of the group, carrying her sample case.

A few meters away she stopped and started filling more sample vials. Karl looked back at the probe.

Inside the torus shell seemed to be an exposed cavity. Karl moved a couple of meters to his left to get a slightly different angle, but he still had a difficult time determining what he was seeing inside.

Minutes later, when Lucy had finished collecting samples of the debris, Alis gave the order to resume their sweep around the probe. The team went full circle without seeing anything new. They stopped again, facing the damaged section of the probe.

By now Karl really felt it was a probe, and he couldn't help mentally comparing it to exhibits in the museum on Luna. The thing was squat, almost certainly alien to its current location, and, with its low center of gravity, not designed for aerodynamic flight.

"I think it's time for a closer look," Alis said.

No one disagreed. Probably they were all as impatient as Karl.

"Let me just make sure the *Ranger*'s getting good views from all our cameras," said Karl.

"Fine."

Karl turned on the suit-to-ship channel and reached Captain Fernandez, who sounded more energized than Karl had ever heard him.

"Yes, all the cameras are working perfectly. I've got all six views on the wall screen. Fascinating stuff. Oh, Alis, let's just leave the ship connected to your voice and video for now."

"You got it," she said. To the team, she said, "Let's go."

The team began moving in, toward the probe. Without any conscious coordination, they formed a shoulder-to-shoulder line, rather than the single-file formation they had used earlier.

Helmet lights played slowly over the metallic-green surface and began to illuminate the exposed cavity in the side of the torus. The bottom of the torus was a meter and a half off the surface, and one of the tripod legs bit into the surface of Cantaloupe just beyond the bottom of the torus.

Karl continued moving forward, slowing as he neared the torus. The side of the torus now seemed much larger than it had. He reached up and ran his glove over the underside of the green surface. His glove slid over the surface with no discernable friction.

He moved to the damaged area and lightly touched some of the exposed fibers. They were no thicker than sections of yarn, but they felt rigid. He pulled as hard as he felt comfortable doing, and he couldn't feel any give at all.

Lucy was the first to break the silence. "I want to go under the torus and look at where the feet landed. Any objections?"

Karl said, "I'd like to look, too."

After a moment, Alis said, "Go ahead."

Lucy and Karl ducked their heads and moved underneath the torus. Even with the microgravity Karl felt nervous. This thing had probably been here for eons, but he still worried that it might finally fall.

The landing leg was huge. If he and Lucy had stood on opposite sides, he doubted that they'd be able to reach each other's hands. He knelt next to her and the base of the leg. Obviously it had torn into the surface when it landed, but the damage was analogous to that of a sharp cookie cutter forced into dough. The surface of the leg met evenly with Cantaloupe's surface, leaving hardly any gap between the two.

Lucy used a small tool to pry the Cantaloupe surface material away from the leg, but the material was fairly unyielding, and the effort looked to be as difficult as prying an inflated tire away from the rim.

"Couldn't be," Lucy said. Her voice was soft enough that she could have been talking to herself, but the voice-activation circuitry turned on her transmitter anyway.

"What couldn't be?" Karl asked.

"Well, look at the area of the surface around this landing leg, if that's what it is."

"Yeah?" Karl was aware of others coming closer.

"This lip of surface material matches up almost exactly."

"Yeah," said Karl, suddenly understanding.

"Yeah, what?" said Robert.

Lucy's helmet turned toward Karl's. Karl said, "Go ahead. You spotted it."

"Okay. This smooth surface suggests to me one of two things, one likely, one less likely. If this really is a probe meant to land on Cantaloupe's surface, would whoever sent it have made the legs with sharp cutting surfaces or blunt?"

"Blunt, I suppose," said Robert.

"I agree. Say you jammed the end of a large, blunt cylinder into an orange. Would you expect as even a mark as if you stuck a knife-edge into it?"

"Of course not, but what—"

"I expect the bottom of the landing leg isn't particularly sharp. I bet the reason this surface is so even is that it's been repaired since the impact."

"Whoa," Daren said. "That's a hell of an assumption."

"Sure," she said. "And that's all it is—a guess. But if this thing is organic in nature, like it feels, like the density suggests, maybe it's still capable of repairing damage to itself."

"Now I know you're wrong," said Robert. The satisfaction in his voice was unmistakable. "We've seen the dark spot, the section that looks damaged. Surely that didn't happen just a few days ago. I think it's been there a long time, without being fixed."

"Lots of possibilities," Karl said in Lucy's defense. "Could be the damage was originally much larger, and that's as far as repair has gotten. Could be the damage is such that it *can't* be repaired, or whatever part of Cantaloupe that handles repairs was also damaged."

"Even if that's so," Daren said, "that gets us back to the question of what Cantaloupe is."

"My vote is that it's an organic starship," said Lucy with no hesitation.

Robert laughed. "That's preposterous. If that's true, why haven't we been greeted?"

"Again, lots of possibilities," Karl said. "Could be the crew's dead. Could be that damaged area is like a spot on a fruit, indicating lots of concealed damage. We just don't know enough yet to make intelligent guesses. This is just a theory we can start testing. If we find evidence that makes it impossible, or if we find evidence that suggests something more likely, we'll start tearing *that* theory apart."

"Right," said Alis. "Let's keep exploring and taking samples. We'll have time later for speculating, and if we're lucky we'll spot some things that answer a few of our questions."

Lucy was obviously not ready to quit voicing ideas, but she followed orders. Karl watched as she tried to take a scraping off the metallic surface and the scalpel just slid over the surface. "I want to see inside," Lucy said finally.

"Me, too," Karl said.

Alis hesitated. "I don't want to take too many chances. Karl, you and Lucy can go in, but I want everyone else out here for now."

Karl and Lucy walked side by side toward the opening in the side of the torus. When they reached it, they hesitated.

Alis said, "Just a sec. I want to see your video while you're in there."

Karl waited another moment while Alis switched her helmet display over to his video or Lucy's.

"All set," Alis said.

"You want to go first, or me?" Lucy said.

Karl supposed it was nervousness that made her deferential for a change, but he was willing to take deferential over abrasive any day. "I'll go." He gave a vertical test jump and let his helmet lamps play on the inside of the craft. His jump was slightly low, and he still couldn't see much. The blown-away section was about twice his height and almost as wide.

Karl jumped. This time he pushed off harder and jumped forward.

The jump was just about right. He cleared the lip of the surface without hitting the damaged section at the top. His motion was slow, but he was still nervous because a few of the edges looked pretty sharp. The floor was uneven, and he landed crookedly.

In a few seconds he stopped moving. He bent forward, directing his helmet lamps toward the floor, then farther into the interior. "All right, Lucy. Be prepared to fall when you get inside—the floor's uneven. But it looks safe enough so far. I'm moving out of the way."

A few seconds later, Lucy landed about where Karl had. She fell, too, but came to a stop soon enough.

"Oooh," she said as she swept her helmet lamps around the inside.

"Let's hear some chatter," Alis said. "Everything seems fairly dark."

"Nothing like Kansas," Lucy said. "The chamber is filled with equipment, I guess it is, but nothing looks even remotely familiar."

Karl said, "The hub of the torus is a wall-to-wall array of stuff that does look vaguely like equipment. Or maybe an equipment bank that someone sprayed with black paint. You can see panels and shapes and a few protrusions here and there, but the whole surface is an even flat black."

Lucy went on. "Even where the stuff is damaged by whatever happened, it's still black. It's like the stuff was carved out of a big black block of something."

Karl ducked. "Crawlway running around the ship, it looks like. In some places the equipment comes close to the outer shell, but I can see quite a way along the lower outside wall."

"Same this way, too," said Lucy.

"Looks like we might be able to go a lot of the way around the ship with the crawlway," Karl said. "I can go this way, making a video record. You want to take the opposite side?"

"Sure."

Karl had just enough space to duckwalk deeper into the ship. He could have crawled, but his boots were a lot tougher than his suit's knees. Fortunately, the ultra-light gravity put hardly any stress on his knees.

Belinda's voice came over Karl's helmet speakers. "I'm still on the outside, following the direction you're going, Lucy. Here's something different. There's a large circular ring on the bottom of the torus. I think I can see into the ship from here. Do you see my light on the inside?"

A few seconds went by before Lucy responded. "Yes! I can see it. And there's something blocking part of the crawlway here."

"Can you be more specific?" asked Alis.

"It doesn't seem like the result of damage," Lucy said. "It seems like part of the equipment just extends into the crawlway. Bizarre."

Lucy was silent for a few seconds, then said, "I think I can get past it, Belinda. How wide is the ring you can see?"

"Oh, maybe a meter."

Karl was seeing more of the same stuff they had seen just inside the opening, banks of equipment-like stuff, nothing like what Lucy must be near. He kept moving forward, grateful for the light gravity.

Alis spoke again. "I'm going to move around it. Can you see my light on the other side of the ring?"

"No," said Belinda. "No, wait. Yes."

That was Belinda's last transmission. A second later, Lucy screamed, "Oh, God!" and a rumbling noise carried with her voice.

Karl, Alis, Robert, and Daren must have all simultaneously said, "What's wrong?" Karl was already feeling a sense of dread and expecting the worst when Alis said softly, "Oh, my God."

Karl tried to turn around and almost got stuck, but seconds later he was moving quickly back the way he had come.

"Get out from under the torus, now!" Alis said. She would have had to be talking to Belinda, Robert, and Daren.

"What's wrong?" Karl asked as he scrambled toward the opening. "Lucy, are you all right?"

"I guess," Lucy said slowly, sounding dazed. "Oh, my God."

"What the hell's going on?" Karl said.

"An accident," said Alis. "Belinda's dead."

Instantly Karl felt extremely cold. He wasn't sure how Alis could be so sure, so fast, but seconds later he reached the opening in the side of the torus and leaped out. He drifted to the surface and bounced, wanting to turn around to see what was going on, frustrated at the delay. Just as he began turning, Alis started talking again, apparently mainly for Captain Fernandez's benefit.

"Belinda is dead," Alis repeated. "Crushed."

Karl could see part of the accident scene finally.

"Something from the probe extended fast. Belinda was beneath it. There's no chance she survived."

Karl's initial reaction was that this still was a pretty big assumption to make so quickly, but as he got closer he found no way to disagree. A column almost a meter in diameter had apparently been driven through the bottom of the torus toward the surface of Cantaloupe. Belinda's body was virtually bisected, her head and shoulders underneath the column. Her suited legs extended outward from the blood-spattered column, and the pressure suit hadn't been able to do much at all to minimize the damage. The gap between the exposed portion of Belinda's body and the column made it obvious that it had acted a little like a giant hole punch. Karl had to turn away. His stomach churned and his vision blurred.

Voices blended in his head for a few seconds until he heard Daren's shaking voice say, "—hard to tell. Some of our early probes had seismic measurement equipment. Things that either set off explosions or dropped large mass. This could be something similar or maybe not."

Seconds later, Lucy's suit showed in the opening on the side of the probe and she jumped out. She lost her balance when she hit and went rolling and bouncing.

Daren and Robert stood a few meters from Belinda's body, their helmet lamps unsteadily illuminating the accident scene.

Karl said silently to himself, *Don't throw up. Don't throw up. Don't throw up.*

"My God, I didn't mean to—" Lucy said after a moment. "How horrible." A moment later, she began crying, her sobs loud enough to trigger the voice-activation circuit in her transmitter.

"It's not your fault," Alis said. Her voice sounded as if someone's hands were around her throat. "We're fooling around with something we don't understand."

Seconds later, Lucy started to regain control. "It must have failed to move when the probe landed, and I must have triggered it somehow or freed it to move. One second everything was normal and the next this thing was sliding down past me, fast."

"Hey, if we wanted safe jobs, we wouldn't be here," Robert said gently, his voice a bit ragged, too. That was the kindest thing Robert had ever said in Karl's hearing.

Karl sat down on the surface. Gradually his stomach began to recover.

"Are you all right, Karl?" Alis asked.

"I guess I will be. I'm—just a little unsettled."

"Well, at least—never mind."

Karl wondered what she had intended to say. At least it wasn't his fault this time? Shakily he rose to his feet.

"Robert," Alis said, "is there anything you can do—I don't mean can you—God, what am I trying to say?" Alis took a couple of breaths that were loud enough to carry to Karl's helmet. "Captain? I don't want to try to retract that leg. For all we know, there *is* no mechanism to retract it. My recommendation is that we cease our examination of the probe. If you can drop us a supply of cords and hooks, and some tape, we can rig it so you can hoist the probe off the surface. That way we can have as long as we want to examine it. And we'll secure Belinda's suit to the probe, so you'll be able to retrieve her body, too. What do you think? This way gives us more time to explore the damaged area, too."

After a moment, Captain Fernandez said, "Give us ten minutes, and you'll have your supplies. In the meantime, stay put. I don't want this falling on top of you."

"You got it."

Karl had recovered to the point where he felt more comfortable approaching Lucy. He moved in front of her and stood close. He activated a private message, and quietly he said, "I'm really sorry we've lost a friend. But no one blames you. It just happened. It would have played out the same way no matter who was in the probe."

Lucy slowly nodded her helmet. "Thanks, Karl."

Karl realized he had lost all interest in exploring Cantaloupe. For a moment, he wished he were back in a desk job, able to close the door for an hour or go home for the day. He stared at the horizon and took a few deep breaths. He thought about Tim, impatiently waiting aboard the *Ranger,* listening and maybe watching as his lover and the rest of the team explored the surface. No one would have been more surprised and more hurt. To lose someone you loved in no more time than it took to blink. Karl closed his eyes for a moment.

Less than ten minutes later, the *Ranger* grew from nothing into a rectangular shape large enough to block out almost half the sky. "Bombs away," said Captain Fernandez.

For several seconds, Karl saw nothing happening, but then a blinking red dot showed against the dark hull, and the *Ranger* began to shrink again. The equipment pack tied to the warning light fell slowly, finally hitting the surface of Cantaloupe at least a hundred meters away. Karl and Robert reached it almost as soon as it stopped bouncing.

Alis took the job of taping the remains of Belinda's body to the tripod leg. She'd searched for an alternative, but hadn't found one as reliable. Karl and the others looped cables over the torus near each tripod leg and secured them. When they finished, they had the ends of three long cables joined with the end of a much longer cable. On the far end of the single cable was a strong magnet. Karl felt sick, operating from moment to moment and trying to get the image of Belinda's broken suit out of his mind.

Alis called the *Ranger* back, and by the time it once again hung low over the surface of Cantaloupe, the cable was carefully coiled next to a small launcher. Karl and the others stood well back as, on command from the *Ranger*, Alis pressed the remote-control button and activated the small rocket carrying the magnet tied to the end of the cable.

In the small gravity, the rocket was the fastest moving thing Karl had seen in hours. It shot toward the *Ranger* as the cable rose from its coil, the world's fastest and longest charmed snake.

They were lucky; they got it in one try. Before the rocket began to fall back under the light weight of the extended cable, the *Ranger* had the magnet snared on another much stronger magnet. Karl and the others moved even farther back as the *Ranger*'s crew secured the cable adequately and the ship began to rise so slowly that the only way to tell it was moving was to watch the three cables on the probe slowly tighten.

Finally the cables all looked tight. The scene didn't change for several long seconds, and Karl wondered idly how much the *Ranger* could change Cantaloupe's path by pulling on it this way. Then one leg of the probe suddenly lurched upward a half-meter. And the other legs were free. Belinda's body stayed with the smaller extension that had launched downward from the probe. Karl felt a lump in his throat as her suit ripped loose from the frozen blood that stained the surface.

Suddenly the probe seemed to be sliding sideways, directly toward Karl. Obviously the *Ranger* wasn't pulling from precisely over the top of the probe. Fortunately, before the probe had traveled more than a third of the distance toward them, it began accelerating rapidly upward. A half-minute later, it was just a speck against the receding hull of the *Ranger*.

Only when the ship was nearly invisible again did Karl finally let go of the fear that the cable might break and the probe would come tumbling back down. Low gravity or not, inertia was an unthinking killer.

Karl moved toward the probe's former resting place. As he approached the spot where the nearest tripod leg had stood, he caught motion to his side and realized Lucy apparently had the same idea. The two of them stopped at the circular depression and aimed their helmet lamps inside.

An elephant footprint in mud was the image that suggested itself to Karl, despite his never having seen one. The depression was perfectly round, no deeper than one handspan.

Karl's suit helmet sounded the private message *bing*, and Lucy said, "I've got to stay working. Otherwise I'm afraid I won't be any use to you."

Karl's gaze flicked to activate the "private reply" indicator and said, "That's fine. I didn't know Belinda as long as you did, but I think I know how you feel."

Lucy walked around the hole, keeping her helmet aimed at the depression, no doubt so she'd have the complete video record to work with later. After a pause, she said, "I'm sorry you've had such a tough time aboard ship. You've always treated me fairly, even when your temper must have been stretched pretty thin."

Karl wondered if Belinda's death had Lucy suddenly aware of her own mortality, and he reflected that he wouldn't want to die now, with so many things unsaid, so many things untried.

"Thanks, Lucy. It has been a little tough, and I appreciate what you've said."

"Tell me. Were you really—no, scratch that. I don't have the right to ask that."

"Was the station accident really my fault? No, I really don't think it was. But somehow that doesn't keep me from feeling guilty. You know yourself that your heart and brain don't always agree. If only I'd doubled-checked the nav computer, if only I'd left a little later, or if only I'd had a different job to do that day, if only, if only."

"I think I understand," she said, and she sounded as if she actually did. She continued her slow path around the depression.

After several seconds of silence, the communications indicator in Karl's helmet flipped from *private* to *public* and the warning chime sounded to warn him that anything he said now would reach everyone. He moved out of Lucy's way once, then knelt next to the lip of the depression.

The surface didn't look as if it had been cut by the tripod leg. Rather, it looked as if a couch leg had been standing on a carpet for a few years. The material at the bottom was flatter than the surrounding surface, and the seam around the rim didn't show any cracks or tears.

Lucy began to take more samples, some from the bottom of the depression, a bit from the seam, more from the sides, and some from the untouched top surface. When she spoke next, it was almost as if talking to herself. "It does seem like this material has been repaired. If this were rock or soil, I would have expected fractures, or crumbling or tearing, some sign of actual damage beyond compression."

Karl agreed with her, but a subtle faraway quality to her voice kept him silent. Finally he turned to see what the others were doing. Daren and Robert were investigating one of the other tripod depressions. Alis was sitting near the spot where Belinda had died.

As if the flash from Karl's helmet brought her out of the space she was in, Alis suddenly said, "Okay, people. It's time we move on." Her voice was still a little ragged. Her initial reactions to Belinda's death hadn't seemed as strong as those of the others; perhaps it was all catching up with her now.

No one objected. In the next couple of minutes they determined the direction of the damaged spot visible from the *Ranger*. Between it and their current location was one of the fine dark lines that cut along the surface. Before long, they were once again propelling themselves along the surface, all leaning forward almost forty-five degrees.

Running soon grew monotonous. Karl imagined he was running in place as Cantaloupe spun ever so slowly beneath his feet. The repetitive motion coupled with the unchanging landscape put him in a mild trance, and he almost missed what they had been looking for. He managed to notice the dark line on Cantaloupe's surface, but only after he had already overshot it.

Karl managed to come to a stop without falling over this time. A minute later he and the others were playing their lamps over the marking. The dark strip was a little narrower than a highway centerline. Karl straddled the line and jumped straight up as high as he could. The line stretched over the horizon. It was perfectly straight, running through a series of tiny adjacent valleys.

When he had settled on the surface once again, he knelt next to the dark line. It seemed just as straight on a microlevel as it did from his high view. The edges could have been painted on with a ruler.

He looked at the line from a different perspective, and he saw a tiny shadow running parallel to the edge.

"Lucy," he said, "could I have a knife?"

Lucy found one in the tool kit and handed it to Karl. He first knelt next to the dark line, then changed position until he lay flat on his stomach, his faceplate close to the dark line. He pushed the blade retractor back and locked it.

He gingerly inserted the knife blade under the side of the

line that seemed to have a gap running along it. There was a slit. The knife blade penetrated several centimeters without any force necessary.

"So there's a gap there," said Alis.

Karl realized he lay in the center of activity. Four suits all shone their helmet lamps on his work area. "Right," he said.

"What do you think it means?" Robert asked.

This really was a day of firsts. Karl didn't think Robert had ever solicited his opinion before. Karl hated to say he hadn't the slightest idea, but he admitted the fact.

"How about if we try something larger?" Lucy said. She knelt beside the line and tried to fit the end of a small pry bar into the gap. By pushing on the end of the pry bar, she was able to wedge the tool about ten centimeters into the gap.

Daren broke a long silence, saying, "If we want to see what's under the surface, maybe we should just wait until we get to the crater."

Alis said, "Makes sense to me. Karl, you or Lucy have a problem with that?"

Karl said, "Fine," at the same time Lucy said, "I guess that's okay."

Seconds later the team was in motion again.

Alis breathed comfortably as she kept up the even motion of a medium-speed run over the surface of Cantaloupe. The gentle pushes required to keep herself moving were about as exerting as tapping a balloon away from her. She led the team as they moved from the site where Karl and Lucy had investigated one of the surface markings and headed toward the dark crater.

For the moment, despite the fact that they had learned a little bit about Cantaloupe, she had the feeling that she knew even less than when she had started. For long moments she had to force herself to think of the crater ahead. This should have been the kind of thing that had her excited about the next step of learning more, but instead she repeatedly found herself seeing Belinda's bloody suit flattened against the surface.

Belinda's life had been her responsibility; her death was Alis's fault. Sure, no one had said that out loud, but Alis was the one who should have shown more caution.

In particular, Karl had avoided blaming Lucy or Alis. Alis's first inclination had been to think that of course Karl would take that position, because it made him seem less guilty for the accident he had caused. After the first several minutes of shock, though, she started thinking about the possibility that Karl really was innocent of having caused the station accident. That maybe Belinda's death and Alis's trauma had just been random acts of a mean-spirited fate, events that no one person caused or could have prevented.

Alis found she had a petty reason for denying the theory. If her accident hadn't been Karl's fault, then she owed him a huge apology. He'd been unfairly persecuted for no fault of his own, which was of course what he'd maintained all along. Of course if he were really guilty, he would have said the same thing.

Alis blinked. The surface ahead was more of the monotonous tiny peaks and valleys. But wait. At the top of her next stride she thought she saw a dark stretch on the horizon. Her next stride confirmed her initial observation. "It looks like we're almost there, people."

As they came closer and closer, they slowed to a walk. A couple of minutes later, the five of them stood on the rim of a small crater maybe a hundred meters across and less than twenty meters deep. Its shape suggested a volcanic origin rather than a meteor impact, but the crater rim was level with Cantaloupe's surface, and the idea of Cantaloupe having volcanoes felt all wrong.

Lucy set about taking a number of samples from the crater rim. Alis announced her intention of walking the perimeter of the crater, and Karl followed her.

The surface of the crater was a mottled charcoal color that looked somehow unhealthy when compared to the color of most of Cantaloupe's surface. The spoiled fruit analogy wouldn't leave her, even though the crater definitely seemed to indicate an impact rather than some unusual crater-shaped sinkage.

As Alis walked along the crater rim, she realized that the mound of surface material right at the center of the crater wasn't symmetrical. Instead of the hemisphere she had thought it to be at first, it looked more like an old band shell, or like someone had cut a very large ball in half, cut one of the halves into two more pieces, and left just the one-quarter of the ball.

As she moved farther around the crater, a dark spot under the lip of the overhang grew more prominent.

"I'm going into the crater to take a look around," Alis suddenly announced.

She heard no objections, so she sat on the side of the crater and let the extremely gentle gravity slide her gently down the curving crater wall. Her body came to a rest on the crater floor, and she got to her feet. She took a ration pill and a gulp of water. From reflex she checked her suit's status, and nothing was under ninety-nine percent full. Her suit's fusion pack and recycling pod were still doing everything they should.

"Mind if I come down, too?" asked Karl.

"No objection. The surface here feels just as solid as up there. I want at least two people out of the crater at all times, though. We might need a rope assist to get back out."

Alis waited for Karl to catch up, and together they cautiously approached the center of the crater.

The shell material seemed to be slightly lighter in texture than the crater floor. It reached about twice as high as Alis's helmet. As they came closer, the dark patch remained a mystery, reflecting almost none of the helmet light.

Alis and Karl slowed their approach even more as they came within a couple of meters of the black patch, and from this distance they could see that it was a hole in the surface, apparently charred or blackened by something. The hole was about two meters wide. The depth was hard to gauge.

Alis edged closer.

"Careful," Karl said.

Closer. Alis stood just a pace away from the lip of the hole. She couldn't angle her helmet lamps down far enough, so she backed up a couple of steps, then lay down on the surface. She edged her way forward until her head extended over the hole and she could look straight down. The effort required to breathe was suddenly much greater than normal.

"Amazing," Alis said. "It's like a mine shaft. This hole must be enormously deep."

Karl edged himself to the lip of the shaft, and the combined lumens from their helmet lamps weren't enough to illuminate the bottom of the shaft.

She thought for a moment, then stated the obvious. "You know, we really can't *not* go down here."

7 · GRADIENT

Karl stood with the other members of the team in a semi-circle facing the shaft leading into the interior of Cantaloupe. The *Ranger* would be dropping another supply pack any time now.

They still didn't have a good estimate for how deep the shaft was, or what had caused it. The surrounding crater-like damaged area suggested an impact, but what had hit, and how long ago?

If the shaft had been a horizontal tunnel, Karl could have walked upright through it, with the curved ceiling just over his head. With the shaft being vertical, and given the tiny gravity, he could probably climb down the shaft by keeping his feet against one side and hands against the other like someone climbing between two closely spaced walls. What he didn't know was how long he could last and how far he would fall when his strength gave out.

The team had discussed dropping a shoulder camera from one of the suits, but ultimately their innate curiosity had again proved to be one of the world's strongest motivations, more powerful than even fear, and no one wanted to wait on the surface. If they ran into trouble, the *Ranger* could drop some more of the crew. Karl's somber thoughts went back to Belinda's crushed body. The drop could be dangerous, but at the same time, he knew how much he'd hate himself if all he took back from this part of the expedition was the experience of hearing some of the others say how fascinating the interior was and that he should have been there.

The *Ranger* began blocking out stars overhead, and its rectangular outline grew again to the point that it seemed about ready to flatten them under its bulk. Finally Captain Fernandez's voice came on their suit radios and warned them the ship was about to drop the latest bundle of extra equipment.

After a slow-motion fall, the equipment bounced a few times near the lip of the crater. The mass of the package made it a little awkward to handle, but Karl and Robert were able to bring it near the shaft opening, where they unhooked the straps that kept everything in a bundle.

Alis, Lucy, and Daren helped Karl and Robert unpack and ready the equipment. In ten minutes they had a stable tripod positioned over the shaft, and a remote-controlled winch stood ready for operation, wound with 2,000 meters of strong cord.

If the five of them had been the only people in the area, one or two would have stayed on the surface as a safety precaution. Since the *Ranger* was ready to drop more people if an emergency arose, they fastened five handholds on the cable, at five-meter intervals.

Karl was nervous about the idea of going inside something they knew so little about, but he didn't voice his fears. By silent consensus, neither did anyone else, but in the terse speech that flowed back and forth as they got ready, he thought he could hear similar nervousness from everyone.

At the same time, the very thing that made him nervous—the idea of going somewhere no human had been before—also excited him. Besides that, if the trip turned out to be really interesting, maybe at some point he'd be thought of as one of the people to explore Cantaloupe, instead of the idiot who ran a shuttle into the side of Tokyan Station.

Karl fastened a small equipment pack to the end of the cord. After a short discussion, Alis took the lowest handle on the cord and spoke the computer commands required to give her suit priority control over the winch. She stepped into the void and vanished. Karl went second, and his suit was set to issue controls to the winch if Alis's communication link were interrupted.

Karl took a step off the lip of the shaft and he was falling.

His grip on the slowly moving handle brought him to an easy stop, and he hung suspended by one arm. He tilted his helmet downward and could see Alis hanging from a strap below him. "I'm fine," he said for her benefit.

"Roger." Alis gave another command to the winch.

Karl felt weightless for a second as he fell deeper. He wondered what lay below them. Was Cantaloupe, in fact, the product of intelligent life? Amazement at being here washed over him.

Seconds later, the winch stopped again so Lucy could get on. Two stops later, the entire team was ready to go. Alis signaled the start of the journey downward, and she gave the winch another command.

The others in the team were silent for a long moment, or they were exchanging private messages Karl couldn't hear. He wondered what they would find below, and despite trying to assure himself everything was totally under control, he kept imagining that the walls speeding up past his helmet were slowly growing closer, as if they were letting themselves down a very gradual funnel. If they were, Alis had a higher risk of getting wedged in the bottom.

Karl tilted his head upward so he could see the three teammates above him. Since the only thing visible through the hole far above was a dim star field, he received the impression that they were already hundreds of meters deep, though they couldn't possibly have gone that far yet. He took some comfort in knowing the winch would detect when the end of the cord was near and would automatically slow their descent. He tightened his grip as his imagination summoned an image of the sensor failing and having the team suddenly stripped off the cable as it made a sudden dead stop. That was one of the few times he wished his imagination weren't so vivid.

None of their quick and dirty efforts had yielded an estimate for the depth of the shaft. There was nothing to say they could even reach the bottom with two kilometers of cable.

"Oh," Alis said suddenly, without elaboration.

A second later Karl saw what she'd reacted to. A side tunnel slipped upward and past his view fast enough that he didn't have an opportunity to aim his helmet lamps directly into it, or to turn and see if there was a matching opening directly opposite. The gap in the side of the shaft had been about half the diameter of the shaft they rode down—large enough to crawl through but not walk through.

"We'll take a longer look if we have time on the way up," Alis said.

The texture of the side of the shaft hadn't changed much at all, as far as Karl could tell. He reached out and brushed his glove against the moving shaft wall, and was surprised by the impression of sponginess. As they continued downward, suddenly the color of the wall changed, darkening. During the next minute, the wall went though several oscillations between dark and light. Karl convinced himself they had just gone past some color bands, and that the change was totally independent of his having touched the wall earlier.

He touched the wall again, finding a rougher feel this time, and feeling happy that he saw no new apparent changes in wall texture. He backtracked his thinking and realized that the soft texture above had convinced him they were inside something mostly organic, rather than inside an asteroid or moon covered with some strange organic outer layer.

"Another side tunnel," Alis said abruptly.

The warning gave Karl time to get ready, and this time he was able to direct his helmet lamps directly into the side tunnel as it flashed upward. He had the strong impression of winding, or screw threads around the perimeter.

The trip down seemed to take forever. Karl glanced at his helmet chronometer and realized they'd been dropping no more than two minutes. They traveled downward about a meter a second, so that put them at 120 meters. About as deep as a forty-story building. If they didn't hit bottom, they could drop for about a half hour before running out of cable.

Compared to the diameter of Cantaloupe, they were still only skin-deep, but it still seemed like a long way down. The steadily moving surface of the tunnel was almost hypnotic, and occasionally Karl had the feeling that he was stationary and an incredibly long pipe was rising past him.

"Still no end in sight," Alis said.

"This thing still looks organic," Robert said.

Daren spoke for the first time in quite a while. "What do you suppose those side tunnels are?"

Lucy spoke first. "For all we know, this is a huge organic starship, and it's honeycombed with tunnels and living spaces."

Robert laughed. "That tunnel wasn't very wide. That would make the inhabitants fairly small. So you're saying this is a giant rabbit warren? Space rabbits?"

They dropped several more meters down the shaft before Robert added, "Besides, just because we've seen some tunnels doesn't mean the Cantaloupe is riddled with them. Maybe we just are in the right place."

Karl said, "Maybe, but the odds suggest a lot of tunnels, assuming this shaft is randomly placed."

"Right," Lucy said, and Karl found that it felt good for someone to agree with him. "This shaft *seems* to be caused by something external to Cantaloupe, so we don't have any reason to say this isn't a random location. Maybe a second probe hit here."

Robert's voice still sounded argumentative. "This shaft seems awfully uniform to be the result of an impact."

Alis said, "You maybe wouldn't say that if you saw the results when a tornado pounded a straw into an oak tree or when someone shot an arrow through a watermelon."

"True," said Lucy. "And if this shaft was caused by a probe, maybe it deliberately burrowed straight down to get interior readings. Or maybe this thing has vertical shear lines, so a probe that was meant to penetrate a few meters into rock instead drilled a really deep hole."

"Here's another tunnel," Alis said. "A big one."

The shaft had cut through the side of a larger tunnel, leaving an oval gap at the intersection. This tunnel definitely looked larger than the first two, at least three times wider than the others. It had the same screw-thread texture around the perimeter. A suited human could have comfortably walked through that tunnel.

The drop continued.

After another minute of watching the shaft walls pass upward, and noticing occasional dark spots on the wall, Karl said suddenly, "Those dark spots. They're very small tunnels. Or holes. What's the word for very small tunnels?"

"Very small tunnels," Robert said helpfully.

"Can we stop?" Daren said.

A second later Karl felt slightly heavier as Alis commanded the winch to slow to a halt.

"What is it?" Alis asked.

"I want to plant another transmitter. For the *Ranger*'s imaging."

"Go for it."

"Can you lower us about a half-meter? I see one of those small tunnels. The transmitter's likely to stay put more safely if I stick it in there."

Karl felt himself drop slowly until Daren called, "Stop! Perfect."

Karl touched the wall in front of his face. It was spongy, with the resiliency of a slightly under-inflated basketball.

"All right," Daren said after a few more seconds. "It's all set."

Alis spoke a little louder than normal, saying, "Captain, do you copy?"

Captain Fernandez rubbed his tired eyes and replied, "Got it on my screen. Thanks."

The ceiling screen contained the view from the camera Alis carried, so he could watch it while he leaned back in his chair. On one of the ancillary screens, a status box showed him the frequency and average power output from the new transmitter. Another screen indicated normal status also on the transmitter Daren had left on the surface near the shaft opening, along with the status of five other transmitters that had been dropped at equally spaced intervals on the surface of Cantaloupe, marking four points on an arbitrary equator and the two poles.

Ten minutes ago, the *Ranger* had finished deploying a series of receiver/transmitters in a number of mapping orbits. The ship had already begun gathering data relayed from the orbital receiver/transmitters, with the goal of generating a 3-D map

of the interior. It was too early to tell if the various interior elements of Cantaloupe would differentiate themselves well or
poorly when it came to signal absorption.

Mapping such a large volume could put a sizable demand
on the ship's main computational array. As a kid, Fernandez
had played with his personal computer, trying to find the limits of its computational ability. He had come close to bogging
it down by having it generate larger and larger 3-D fractal
images in motion. The problem at hand made that early experiment seem like something he could have done on a wrist
computer.

At the moment, Captain Fernandez felt they'd be lucky
just to get a sense of how Cantaloupe's density varied by depth,
if it did. A holographic projection hung in a darkened corner
of the bridge, but so far it just gave the impression of a solid
sphere.

Fernandez looked back at a screen carrying the image
from Alis Nussem's shoulder camera. The steady movement
down the shaft reminded him of interior views of arteries as a
fiber-optic camera snaked deeper and deeper.

In their first few hours of investigation, they had realized
that whatever Cantaloupe was, it was certainly not a moon.
Looking at these pictures, Fernandez decided that knowing
what it wasn't sure didn't seem very helpful yet in finding out
what it was.

The team dropped a long time without spotting any more tunnels, of any size. Karl figured they were at least a kilometer
deep already.

The shaft walls abruptly changed color, from a mottled
gray to a more uniform dark blue.

"I don't believe it," Karl said suddenly.

"What?" Lucy was the first to ask.

"Arne Saknussemm. Did you see the lettering? We just

passed some scrawled handwriting that said: 'Arne Saknus-semm was here.' "

Alis laughed, but no one else got it.

"Okay," Lucy said. "What's going on?"

"Just a feeble joke," Karl said. "Arne Saknussemm was the man who went down before the rest of them in *A Journey to the Center of the Earth.*"

"In what?" Robert asked.

"Never mind," Karl said. "So you've read Verne, Alis?"

"He's one of my favorites."

Mine, too, Karl thought. "The originals, or the updated versions Saint Paramount put out?"

"The originals."

"Isn't anyone else surprised that we're not dragging against one side?" Robert said, jarring Karl back to the mission.

"Meaning what?" Lucy asked. "That this shaft is perfectly vertical?"

"Exactly."

Karl shook his head. "Even if the shaft isn't perfectly vertical, the gravity's so light that an occasional boot scraping against the shaft wall is enough to counteract any horizontal force."

Alis said, "As a matter of fact, I have bumped against the wall from time to time. Probably the fact that I stay centered in the gap is enough to keep you folks from touching as often."

Robert let the subject die.

The dark blue shade of the shaft wall seemed to be darkening ever so slowly, so slowly that Karl couldn't be sure if it was his imagination or not. After a couple more minutes, he felt sure the surface was darker.

They went deeper still. The surface of the walls kept darkening until it was black.

By the time Karl estimated they were at least a kilometer

and a half deep, Alis said quickly, "We may be near the bottom. I think I see something."

Karl looked down, but Alis's body blocked too much of the view.

"So, what do you see?" Robert asked impatiently.

"I can't tell yet. I'm just seeing some light reflecting from down there."

Karl felt the deceleration as Alis commanded the winch to slow their rate of descent. He guessed they were moving downward about a half-meter per second. The shaft wall felt firmer here than it had above.

Karl kept his view focused on Alis and whatever he could see past her body. Finally he, too, could make out something of a glow, a faint greenish tint. Whether it came from ten meters down, or a hundred, he couldn't say.

As they moved deeper the glow resolved into a larger area with a dark spot at its center. They kept dropping.

"Whoa," Alis said at last.

"What does that mean?" Robert asked, his exasperation plain.

"You'll see for yourself in a minute."

Below Karl, Alis's body dropped into a pool of dim green light, and seconds later he followed.

Karl took a deep breath and felt the adrenaline rush make the skin on the back of his neck tingle. They had dropped through a hole in the top of a huge tunnel more than twenty meters high. The tunnel was slightly wider than that, and extended far enough in opposite directions that they couldn't see where it went. A number of large splotches on the exposed wall surface emitted a faint green glow after being illuminated by helmet lamps. The combined effect of a small amount of light from so much area was enough that Karl imagined he could tell the color of someone's eyes without the benefit of any additional light.

Below them, in the floor of the tunnel, was a dark hole, the continuation of the shaft they had ridden down in.

Alis kept dropping as the teammates above Karl came one by one into view. When she finally slowed the descent and came to a full stop, all five of them were in the tunnel.

Alis said, "Let's make a short stop here." She turned the winch until her feet were close to the bottom surface of the tunnel, and she swung her body to one side. After a moment of imbalance, she stood on the tunnel floor.

One at a time, Alis lowered the cord until each of the others could get off conveniently, and finally all five teammates stood on the floor of the bizarre tunnel.

"Amazing," Lucy said so softly that she could have been talking to herself.

Karl switched off his helmet lamps and dropped gently to his knees. The tunnel surface seemed spongier than the outside surface of Cantaloupe. He was pushing his glove against the surface when a sudden drop in the light level to his left made him swivel. Lucy had turned off her lamps, too.

"I'm not picking up any significant radiation levels," Lucy said. "This material appears to be bioluminescent. But if it is, that sure doesn't go along with the possibility that Cantaloupe, whatever it is, has been dead for millions of years."

Robert moved closer to Alis and Karl. "What if this is some huge starship?"

Lucy snorted, then caught herself and turned slightly more deferential. "Very interesting theory, Robert."

Robert's voice grew hard. "Hey, I'm just throwing out ideas. If you know exactly what we're dealing with, feel free to enlighten us anytime. In the meantime, I think it makes sense to generate a few hypotheses and see if they stand up. If you wanted to move a huge population to a new solar system, it would probably be a lot more efficient to design an enormous craft rather than build hundreds of thousands of small craft, each with their own separate propulsion, life support, communication systems, and all the rest. A sphere maximizes the interior volume for a given outside surface. An extremely thick protective layer on the outside would provide some protection from radiation and moderately small collisions."

"So this could be a huge generation ship?" Lucy said. "Or cryogenic storage for a whole population?"

"I don't know how likely it is, but I think either is possible."

"If it's a ship," Alis said, "why no response to our hails? Why no response to our presence?"

"Could be everyone's dead," Robert said. "Could be only parts of the ship are still functional. Could be this shaft, whatever caused it, did some critical damage that can't be undone. Could be our transmission methods have nothing in common. Could be lots of things."

Karl noticed that while the discussion went on, Daren put another transmitter in service. He positioned it on the tunnel wall near the floor, and pressed an anchor into the surface.

Karl turned his helmet lamps back on, then pushed against the tunnel wall. "If you want something to last a long time, designing it to be self-maintaining makes sense. You could build a ship that had lots of redundant systems, but I can see the appeal of an overall organic design for perpetual life. You design it with the ability to steadily repair any failure, and eliminate the unnecessary aspects, like the equivalent of growing fingernails that have to be cut off. Done correctly, and furnished with a constant supply of energy, a bioengineered system could last a long time."

Lucy said, "So there might be a fusion source or some other kind of power plant down here someplace?"

Karl shrugged despite the fact that no one would notice the gesture. "Could be, or I suppose it's possible that Cantaloupe just has an enormous battery and absorbs energy from occasional passes nearby a star. Or, given the volume of Cantaloupe, it could even turn out that a fair amount of the space

is devoted to huge internal chemical fuel cells that could provide power for a long time."

Karl walked farther down the tunnel and spotted the
mouth of a smaller offshoot tunnel. It was less than half the
diameter of the main tunnel, angled downward at about forty-
five degrees. Given the fact that low gravity made surfaces
more slippery than they would seem in Earth gravity, he
guessed that without a rope an exploration of that tunnel
would be a laundry chute experience. Visualizing the results
of a dead end, he moved on.

After a minute Karl was aware that others were following him. He stopped near another smaller adjoining tunnel, this
one branching off from halfway up the side of the main tunnel, and not much taller than a suited human. He aimed his
helmet lamps into the smaller tunnel. It went straight at a
slight upward slope for twenty or thirty meters before it bent.

Karl glanced at the two suited figures near him. He
couldn't see into their helmets, but their biceps patches identified them as Alis and Robert. "I'd like to go in there and take
a quick look. Any objections?"

After a hesitation, Alis said, "Fine, but stay in sight."

"You got it." Karl made a vertical test jump to gauge how
hard he'd have to jump to get to the smaller tunnel opening.
After he landed and turned back to face his destination, he
jumped again, this time slightly higher and at an angle.

Karl felt a touch of pride in landing just on the lip of the
smaller tunnel opening, even though the leap really wasn't
that much of an accomplishment.

The sense of pride almost died a second later when he
slipped as he started into the smaller tunnel. He almost fell
back into the main tunnel, but was able to catch his balance
just in time. He pushed his hands against the roof of the tunnel, and that gave him better balance and more friction.
Cautiously he moved up the gentle slope, as if he were a bug
crawling up a slightly tilted straw.

The texture of the walls of this smaller tunnel seemed very much like that of the larger tunnel, still showing large blotches that gave the impression he was crawling through an artery of someone in very ill health.

Karl reached the bend in the tunnel and aimed his light toward the end. The tunnel dwindled to a distant point, but he couldn't tell if that was because it grew progressively smaller or he was just seeing a typical perspective illusion in a tunnel that went on forever.

Less than a couple of meters from the bend, a yet smaller tunnel met the side of the tunnel he was in.

"Can you see this?" Karl asked. He supposed that by now Alis had switched over to monitor his shoulder video, but he didn't know for sure.

"Got it," she said.

"I assume I'm not the only one who's thinking this entire tunnel structure vaguely resembles the network of progressively smaller arteries servicing a human body."

"I'm way ahead of you," Robert said. "That's part of why I'm here. My medical skills may well be the key."

Karl gritted his teeth. "I can't tell you how glad I am to hear that, Robert. I was afraid you were sent along in case anyone might need an enema."

"Why don't you just suck—"

"Boys, boys," Alis said. "Is this the kind of thing you want on the expedition records?"

Karl shut his eyes for a moment and felt himself growing calmer. He turned back toward the main tunnel and began gingerly making his way out. He didn't say anything more, and neither did Robert. As Karl cooled off, he realized that instead of feeling insulted by Alis's comment, he appreciated how easily she had defused the situation.

He reached the lip of the smaller tunnel and realized that the others had the same fear of his losing his footing, and they stood well back from where he would land. He sat on the lip of the tunnel and slid down the rest of the way.

"You might want to look at this," Daren said.

Karl looked around and spotted Daren's suit about fifty meters down the main tunnel. Karl started moving, and a minute later the rest of the team stood looking at what Daren had found.

The tunnel curved to the side at about forty-five degrees, and from here they could see that about thirty meters from them the tunnel was blocked.

The whole team moved closer. The blockage was nothing like a rockfall. Instead it again reminded Karl of anatomy far more than geology. All around the perimeter of the blockage, the tunnel wall had expanded, as if swollen by disease. The swelling cut the diameter of the tunnel almost in half, leaving a smaller circle at the center. Filling the circle was a mass of what vaguely resembled large leaves, packed so tightly that they seemed to be a solid mass. The perimeter of the mass was more or less even with the swelling around the rim of the tunnel, but the center of the mass formed a cone extending toward them.

Karl looked back at the open tunnel behind them. At intervals of about ten meters, a faint discoloration marked a ring on the tunnel wall, as if each of those locations could be capable of swelling to constrict flow through the tunnel.

"No more guesses, Robert?" Alis said finally.

"I'm not sure I need any more abuse." Robert hesitated. "But I wouldn't be surprised if this was a reaction to the hole we just came through. It makes me think of an artery that's been clotted with platelets."

The same idea had occurred to Karl. He tried to make his response as non-inflammatory as possible. "That makes a lot of sense to me, Robert. But do you have any theory on why the seal occurred here, rather than closer to the damage?" Karl moved and pointed. "These rings make me think the tunnel could have been sealed at any of several places."

"I wondered about that, too. Here's another guess, but it's only a wild guess, all right? If this tunnel has been blocked by some kind of self-repair or damage-control mechanism, in a way vaguely like the way the human body repairs itself, maybe the damage extends to self-repair mechanism itself, and this portion of the whole is like a scar that won't ever heal, or maybe it can't be healed until the repair mechanism is fixed."

Lucy moved in to take some more samples from both the swollen area of the tunnel and the clogged section in the middle. She had to stand on Daren's shoulders to reach the middle.

"If that's true," Alis said, "are you saying that normally something flows through this tunnel—a liquid or a gas?"

"I think that's possible." Robert said. "It could even be that in this ultra-low gravity there's no need for a carrier fluid. I suppose it's possible that repair mechanisms like those platelets, or whatever they are, get released only when something detects a problem and they're charged with one polarity while the 'wound' is given an opposite charge, and they just bounce through the tunnel until they wind up where they're needed. I'm sure there are other methods that haven't even occurred to me."

Silence lengthened until Alis said, "I think we've spent enough time here. Unless there are any objections, I want to keep exploring down the main shaft."

No one objected. As the team walked back toward the cord, Alis spoke to Captain Fernandez aboard the *Ranger.* "How's our signal strength, Captain? I want to go deeper."

"We're reading you at ninety-five percent," said the captain.

"We've still got you at a hundred percent," said Daren. The black lump stuck to the back of his suit was the high-power transponder responsible for boosting their suit communications so the *Ranger* could see and hear despite the distance and a moderate amount of potential interference or shielding inside Cantaloupe. The *Ranger*'s transmitter was powerful enough that they'd be able to hear the ship no matter what.

As they moved closer to the vertical shaft, Karl felt relieved to see the cord still in place. Maybe a little paranoia was a healthy thing, but he never liked seeing it in himself.

Minutes later Karl and the rest of the team were once again moving steadily downward through Cantaloupe's shell, Alis still on the bottom. Long minutes passed during the silent descent. The walls of the shaft seemed to keep growing darker, as if the black material was becoming more and more light-absorbent, but the process was so gradual that Karl couldn't tell if maybe his eyes were just slowly adjusting.

Just as Karl started trying to decide how much more cable was still wound on the winch far above, Alis said, "I see more light below. It looks like a reflection."

Captain Fernandez broke his long silence. "The interior scans still aren't showing much detail, but there is a dark spot forming about a hundred meters below you. Its RF reflectivity is high enough compared to the rest of this thing that it's conceivable that it's foreign."

"Meaning we could be near whatever made this hole?"

"Exactly."

Karl felt his pulse pick up a little speed as they dropped closer to whatever was causing the reflections. He wondered if Alis's replacement heart was doing the same.

The winch far overhead kept playing out line. Finally Karl felt the faint tug that meant Alis was slowing the winch. They must be close.

"Something's down there all right," Alis said.

8 ■ HEMORRHAGE

Alis switched her eyes back into normal mode. The reflection below vanished.

She blinked the sequence to put her eyes back in telephoto mode, and the reflection was there again, along with a reddish tinge and a faint outline of something directly below her. For the first time since starting the most recent portion of their descent, Alis couldn't see a black spot directly below them.

She waited a few seconds before switching back to normal mode. The reflection was just now becoming visible.

"I see it, too," Karl said finally, and Alis reminded herself that his view was partly obscured by her own presence farther down the cable, so even without the telescopic advantage he wouldn't have seen the reflection as soon as she did.

She looked up, and all she could see was the diminishing

string of helmet lamps. It had been a long time since she'd had a hope of seeing a star field beyond the opening of the shaft, even with her telephoto mode.

For a second, she considered whether it might be dangerous to explore whatever lay below. Exploring on the surface had already cost one life. She realized the danger didn't bother her, and suddenly she saw how appropriate her presence on the mission was. Who better to send on a potentially dangerous mission than someone who didn't care whether she came back?

But her feelings weren't as dead as she had thought; otherwise she wouldn't be feeling so bad about Belinda's death. It would have been better for everyone involved if she had died instead of Belinda. Belinda would have a life, and Karl wouldn't have an angry, accusing presence in his life, constantly reminding him of the consequences of the crash. Of course if she died in an accident down here, if Karl could in any way share the blame, he'd be sure to get all of it.

Closer. The reddish reflection seemed no more than thirty meters away. She had to check to make sure her eyes were in normal mode. Once, back on Tokyan Station, she had left her eyes in telephoto mode and didn't reset them for a couple of minutes as she walked along the corridor, experiencing the unsettling sensation of seeing people plaster their well-wishing smiles over their concerned frowns as they came closer. As she approached the stairs in the exercise room, she'd almost fallen on her face when she started "climbing" before she actually reached the stairs.

She supposed this was a sign of insecurity, but she feared looking stupid even more than she worried about breaking a bone. At least she didn't have to worry much anymore about breaking a leg. Any accident severe enough to damage her replacement legs would probably do terminal damage. Now if she could only get something to protect herself from ever making a social gaffe or otherwise putting her foot in her mouth.

Karl seemed to deal pretty well with all the pressure he got from the crew, and the discomfort she gave him. Was he as unruffled on the inside, or did he share the same neurotic feelings?

Fifteen meters. Below her was a large cavity, and maybe five meters under the point where the shaft met the cavity was what looked like a metallic reflection from a weathered red surface, a surface vaguely like the hood of an old car that had started with a shiny red paint job and then been left in a junkyard under the desert sun for fifty years.

Ten meters. The red surface was dimpled, as if made of leather rather than some metal alloy. She slowed their descent even further.

Just below her feet was the biggest deformity she'd seen in the entire length of the shaft. The opening into the cavity below was not perfectly round, as was the rest of the shaft. It was vaguely circular, but distorted, as if someone had used a cookie cutter to remove some dough from the center of a cookie but had then baked the rest, causing the dough to melt and flow toward the center of the hole. The opening was large enough to admit a suited body, but there wouldn't be much room to spare.

"The shaft narrows here," Alis said for the benefit of her teammates farther up the cord. "I think I can lower myself through it. If anything happens to me, you know the chain of command."

Alis took a deep breath and resumed the downward journey, moving very slowly. Her suit was sturdy, but the lip of the hole could be sharper than it looked.

Her feet dropped through the opening. Careful seconds later, her helmet was through, and she halted.

She hung at the top of an irregular cavity. Four or five meters below her, the red reflective surface resolved into a circle with the same diameter as the shaft. This could well be the bullet that had been shot into the surface.

Above her, Karl's feet dangled just above the irregular opening in the ceiling. From this perspective, the opening still looked fairly safe—no sharp edges visible.

She continued the descent. By the time her feet were almost touching the red surface, Karl's body was in the chamber, too.

The chamber walls looked little like the tunnel walls above. Instead of the relatively smooth and deliberate appearance of the tunnels, the chamber looked a little like the crater on top of a hugely magnified candle, as if it had been partly burned, partly melted, perhaps by the presence of the object under her feet. The chamber was maybe thirty meters across at its widest, and unlike the faintly luminescent tunnels above them, it was dark except for where her helmet lamps splashed light.

Alis's feet brushed against the red surface. She let herself drop another few centimeters and put pressure on the object. It didn't give at all. The light gravity didn't give much of a test, so she lifted one foot and kicked a heel against the surface. The sensation was nothing like kicking the hood of a car, but more like kicking the top of a boulder.

"There's a large object down here," she said. "It looks to be the same diameter as the shaft, possibly what made the shaft in the first place. It's solid, and we could probably stand on it without doing any damage, but I'd rather get to the floor of the cavity."

She let herself down farther until finally she was able to reach the edge of the round surface and start dropping down beside it.

Her feet swayed underneath the lip of the surface, and for a moment she wondered if the object were nothing but a disk supported in space, but as soon as she could see beneath the top surface, she realized that she had just started downward next to an opening in the side. Moments later she stood next to the object towering over her head.

The rest of the team slowly entered the cavity one by one as Alis walked the perimeter of the red object. Every visible surface had the same rough texture and red tint. From about head level to the top of the probe, assuming that was what it was, was a ring of eight smaller cavities, all but one of them empty. Apparently, for each of the cavities, a door slid downward into the base of the probe, exposing the cavity. The eighth cavity was still occupied; the door had evidently jammed halfway open. By jumping, Alis got a glimpse of something still inside, something also red-tinted, something mechanical with numerous panels and openings and small protrusions.

Below the ring of compartments was a smooth cone extending downward, farther into Cantaloupe's interior. If the buried surface really was a cone, it must have driven another twenty or thirty meters into the surface.

In another minute Lucy, Robert, and Daren had joined Alis and Karl in the area around the perimeter of what more and more she was convinced was a probe.

Robert asked, "Did you see this?"

Alis found him near one of the dark irregularities she had seen near the base of the cavity wall. "What do you have?"

"This isn't just a small pocket. I think it's a tunnel."

"And?"

"And the surface doesn't look like the other tunnels we saw." Robert moved back so Alis could take a better look. "This looks a lot smoother, much more regular."

Alis looked. Robert was right. The tunnel into the partly melted surface of the wall looked even more regular than the shaft they had come down. The tunnel curved off to the left in the distance, in a very gradual curve. The tunnel was a claustrophobic size, not much wider than Karl's shoulders.

Alis stepped back and Karl took a look. She glanced around the uneven perimeter of the chamber and spotted four more apparent tunnel mouths.

Robert said, "You realize that the size of this tunnel is

pretty close to the width of that, whatever it is, that thing still stored in the compartment up there."

He was talking about what Alis had mentally labeled a sub-probe. His thinking was tracking with hers. If this large red object was a probe designed to make maximum penetration through the surface and to distribute a smaller set of remote-controlled or autonomous secondary probes, she hadn't yet seen anything at odds with the theory. "So you're thinking that the empty slots on this thing—" she gestured toward the huge object in the center of the cavity "—released these smaller probes, and they've been tunneling through, maybe exploring and reporting back?"

"Seems like a reasonable hypothesis to me."

Alis turned back to Karl. "You agree, Karl?"

"Oh, sure." Karl's response was so quick and offhand, she had the feeling that he, too, had already toyed with the same theory and found no reason yet to doubt it. She wondered why, if that was the case, he hadn't volunteered any guesses already.

"But if that's the case," Karl continued, "I'm still not sure what happened to the material they scooped out as they cut their way through Cantaloupe."

"Easy," said Lucy. "This whole area's exposed to vacuum. All the probes would have to do is vaporize material in their path. The gas they spewed out as they traveled would just get continually sucked out into space." She turned back toward the huge red probe. "It could be the main probe here vaporized stuff in its path, too."

Apparently no one had a better theory yet, so they let the subject drop.

Alis toured the perimeter of the chamber more thoroughly than before as Daren sat down and the others made their own way around the circumference. She found six tunnels altogether and puzzled over where the seventh was until she finally realized that one of the tunnels branched just inside the tunnel mouth, as if two probes had started in the same spot and then their paths diverged. She pointed out the spot to the others.

None of the tunnels went up. Two of them seemed to go out roughly horizontally, and the other five went deeper into the interior at angles ranging from about thirty degrees below horizontal to one going nearly straight down.

Karl said, "I'd like to get a better look at the probe left behind. Any objections? Maybe we can even take it back with us if we can get it free."

"Go for it," Alis said.

The panel concealing the trapped probe was over Karl's head. He jumped and grabbed the top of the half-open panel. He hung there a moment without any sign the panel had moved at all. Alis wasn't too surprised. His weight hardly amounted to much on Cantaloupe.

She watched as he kept his grip on the panel and pivoted his body almost upside down, at which point he put his feet against the top of the opening and started applying pressure on the panel. For several long seconds, nothing moved; then suddenly the panel slid downward, opening the compartment.

Karl tumbled to the floor of the chamber. As he was bouncing on the floor, trying to turn himself over and regain his footing, the probe inside the compartment slowly toppled out. It dropped toward Karl in slow motion and might have landed on top of him except that Alis grabbed Karl's outstretched hand, kept her other hand locked on a section of the larger probe, and pulled Karl out of the way.

Karl said, "Thanks!"

"It's okay," she said as the probe hit the floor and bounced. "In this gravity it probably wouldn't have done you any harm, but I'd rather not take the risk."

"Well, I still appreciate it. You could have just let me struggle."

"Is that what you think of me?" Alis said, suddenly hot. "That just because you caused my accident I'd be so vindictive that I—"

"I didn't cause that—look, all I meant was you're right, I probably would have been okay, but I appreciate your help just in case."

"Right." Alis felt her anger dissipating rapidly. "I was out of line. Sorry about that."

"It's okay. I didn't say what I was trying to say."

By now the probe had stopped bouncing. It looked completely lifeless, and Alis was glad to see that it hadn't sprung to life and started eating through whatever was close as it began some programmed search course.

"You're lucky that thing's turned off," Lucy said. "If it does vaporize its path ahead of it, that could be kinda painful."

"Oh, please," Robert said. "That thing must have come from some other solar system, and it must have been here for centuries, if not hundreds of centuries. Whatever powered it must be long dead."

"Thank you, Doctor Science," Lucy said. "I was kidding, all right?"

"Yes, of course you were."

Alis gritted her teeth, wondering if she'd have to haul in Robert's leash, but fortunately, he and Lucy let the argument drop. Why did high intelligence too often go hand in hand with idiocy about the way people work? Why couldn't more intelligent people take a time-out and make some discoveries about how to function around other people, and understand that you don't get people's best when they're harassed? Constantly condescending to people did nothing but throw obstacles in their own paths. Karl seemed every bit as bright as Robert, but Alis didn't see Karl throwing his IQ around.

One moment she was thinking about how Karl might not be such a bad guy after all, and the next instant brought back an image of a shuttle careening into the side of Tokyan Station. She shook her head and got back to business.

Aboard the *Ranger,* Captain Fernandez intently watched the images coming back from the exploration team, trying to make sense out of the situation and feeling no smarter than Alis Nussem and her team.

A comm chime sounded the one-second ripple of tones that was shorthand for "Incoming Message from Home," and the ship's comm computer said, "Message from ISA headquarters is now being received. I'll file it for later unless you want to hear it as it comes in."

"Play the message," Fernandez said.

A formerly blank section of screen lit up with the ISA Tri-Service emblem with the eagle, wolf, and bear looking as if they naturally got along well together. On the wall in Fernandez's cabin hung a slightly altered version, showing a roadrunner with Fernandez's bushy eyebrows peering over the wolf's shoulder, the inscription at the bottom of the image saying: "*To Enrico Fernandez, from the crew of the* Shark. *May you never lose your skill at taming bureaucrats and declawing politicians.*"

Yet another new face filled the image area and the young woman began speaking. Text along the bottom of the image said the authorization code had been checked and verified.

"Captain Fernandez," the woman said, "just a few minutes ago, the high-fidelity course calculations were completed for the object the *Ranger* is accompanying. At the moment, it looks like we have a problem. The path in the latest calculations still misses the Earth by a comfortable margin, but it now appears that it will intersect the orbit of the high-loft Hamilton Station."

As the woman continued talking, Fernandez pulled up an image of the station, alongside a computer image of the station's highly elliptical orbit.

"Given the circumstances, the timing couldn't be much better, because Hamilton Station reaches perigee in just a few hours, and engineers are making calculations now so Hamilton can use its orbit maintenance thrust at the point where they'll give the station the most leverage. They'll try to change the orbital inclination as much as they can, and may be able to make sure the station isn't near your object as it passes through. The downside is that the station's thrusters are meant for fairly small corrections. Evacuation of Hamilton Station has already begun, but we won't have time to get everyone out.

"Given the distance and time span involved in the calculations, as a backup we're sending out a trio of high-gee scout ships with three of the largest asteroid-deflection explosive devices we have in the ISA arsenal. The ships will be placed under your command, and, should the next iteration of calculations deem it necessary, you will have to direct crews to plant those devices at locations we'll calculate and, if need be, activate them when the time comes.

"We will start a series of updates to be sent out at a minimum of four-hour intervals. Have your crew ready for action. Please confirm receipt."

The screen went dark and an instant later the trio of animals and the ISA crest were back on the screen. Fernandez spoke a quick command, then leaned back, pursed his lips, and thought for a long moment before activating the comm link to talk to Alis Nussem.

After he updated Alis, he would need to assemble a packet of video data for ISA Headquarters. Obviously they were going to be concerned with saving human lives on Hamilton Station, but the more they knew about the first-contact potential here, the more cautious they'd be about taking action that threatened the new arrival and his crew. Whatever this object turned out to be, the video certainly suggested that it was something the human race could learn a lot from.

Understood, sir," Alis said. "We'll be ready to get out of here whenever you say the word."

"Right. I'll keep you posted. There's obviously no rush since it'll take them at least a day or two to match course." Captain Fernandez fell silent, and a second later the voice-activation circuitry shut off the background noise on the bridge.

"What a jinx," Robert said. He swiveled his helmet lamps toward Karl.

"You talking to me?" Karl asked.

"Good guess. You sure have a knack for hitting stations, don't you?"

"Maybe I do. But I'm as much to blame for Cantaloupe's path as I was to blame for the shuttle accident."

Robert hesitated, obviously realizing he'd made a tactical error.

"Look," Karl said. "I'm really tired of this whole discussion. I don't accuse you of becoming a doctor so you could see people naked, so stop accusing me of something I didn't do."

"I went into medicine because my mother died when I was a kid. I thought maybe—that I wouldn't have to watch anyone die needlessly again."

"See? We were both wrong."

Alis was just about to step in and squash the argument, but it was already over. Both men turned back to exploring the chamber. Lucy's helmet swiveled from side to side a couple of times, as if she were shaking her head. Daren busied himself looking at the small probe.

Alis turned back to the large probe, training her helmet camera slowly over each section so the recorded data would have maximum usefulness later. The seams where planes met each other were perfectly formed, making it appear that either the probe had been cut from a single block of material or, once assembled, it had been heated to a temperature high enough to melt all the seams until they flowed together.

She made a complete slow circuit of the large probe as the others played their lights over every nook and cranny in the chamber. She moved from the probe to investigate the nearest small tunnel mouth.

The small round tunnel angled down at about thirty degrees below horizontal as if someone had put an organic air duct right there. She felt the smooth surface with her glove. The texture seemed closer to leather than glass. She wondered if there would be enough friction to let her ease herself into the tunnel and keep from sliding all the way down to who knew where. Stories about people getting caught in chimneys suddenly seemed more vivid than anything else in that high school class. Some of the stories involved people whose bodies weren't found for years. She shivered.

She switched her eyes into telephoto and examined the farthest section of tunnel before it dipped closer to vertical and out of sight. The tunnel surface seemed fairly uniform the whole way. She switched to infrared, but the view wasn't very helpful. The uniform blotchy black simply said the tunnel wall was consistently cold.

A suited body knelt next to her. Lucy. "Might be interesting to see what's down there, huh?"

"Yes, it would." Alis hesitated. "How would you feel about going down there?"

"I'm ready."

Alis was a little surprised to hear the quick, unreserved statement.

Karl spoke up. "I think it might be interesting, too, but it's awfully cramped. Maybe for a first look we could just drop a suit camera on the cable."

"Good idea. Just so we can call these tunnels something

short, I'm going to number them, starting at the one closest to this failed sub-probe, clockwise around the rim of the chamber."

By the time Alis had finished talking, Daren was already detaching his shoulder camera. Seconds later he handed it to her.

Alis struggled for a moment as she tried to feed the cable through a gap in the mounting bracket. Soon she had the camera secured.

"Tunnel number one is nearly vertical," Robert said. "That's probably a good place to start."

Alis let the end of the cable carrying the camera dip into the tunnel. She held it suspended there while she switched part of her helmet screen to watch the view from the camera. She pulled the cable up and readjusted the camera until it pointed as close as possible to straight down and fed it back into the opening.

Much better. Now the view showed a central dark spot surrounded by climbing tunnel walls as she fed the cable downward.

"I wish we had a lamp to send down with it. I'm not sure how deep we're going to be able to go before running out of usable light."

Alis ran out of free cable and gave the command to the winch far above to let out more. Slowly the cable snaked down through the opening at the top of the chamber and fed into the tunnel leading farther into the interior. The view transmitted from the camera to her helmet screen looked vaguely like something one would get from remotely inspecting a pipe, or perhaps something a doctor would see while sending a tiny camera through an artery.

The camera flopped from side to side in the light gravity, but the stiffness of the cable kept it pointing downward.

"Do we have enough cable left to go all the way?" Robert asked.

Alis shook her head. "No idea how deep 'all the way' is. We'll probably run out of light before we run out of cable."

Alis kept one of her helmet lamps pointing down into the hole, letting the light bounce along the length of the tunnel to provide as much illumination as possible. Ever so gradually the view from the camera lost contrast and moved slowly toward a uniform gray as the camera's automatic gain control tried to make use of the dimmer and dimmer light.

The contrast was on the verge of vanishing when they finally noticed a subtle change in the view ahead. The central dark spot no longer seemed as dark.

"Got something maybe," Alis said. On the display from the camera far below she could just make out a series of concentric rings. She stopped the winch.

Alis sensed motion behind her and turned to see what was happening. Karl was turning the sub-probe on one end. He had it positioned so that her intuition said the business end was down. On the top side was a flat plate with six concentric rings etched into the surface.

"Dead end, huh?" Lucy said. "That thing just burrowed as far as it could go and then died."

"Looks that way," Alis said. She let the camera descend a bit more, and the rings went out of focus.

Alis started the winch back up and waited for the camera to surface.

The next tunnel was maybe ten degrees away from vertical, and the cable snaked into it fairly easily, too. This tunnel turned out to be shorter, and at the end of it they found another back end of a sub-probe. This one was easier to make out, because they already knew what they might find and the light was stronger since the sub-probe had stopped nearer to them.

The third tunnel was deep enough that they ran out of light before spotting anything. Alis let the cable continue to run down the shaft.

Minutes later the cable stopped.

"Have we hit something?" Robert asked.

"I don't think so," Alis said. She checked the winch status. "We've completely run out of cable. That's as deep as we can go."

Running the winch back up was the most boring period Alis had spent since leaving the *Ranger*. She realized her arms felt a little tired, and she wondered how the others were doing but didn't ask. Her replacement eyes felt fine. They always felt fine. Before the accident, her eyes were usually the first part of her to get tired after a long day, and she had idly speculated that tired eyes were somehow nature's way of providing an early warning to the rest of the body to take it easy for a while. She eventually decided that having tired eyes was one aspect of her former life that she didn't regret leaving behind.

The next tunnel was close enough to horizontal that the camera and cable wouldn't cooperate and kept getting snagged. The experience was only slightly different than trying to push a rope, and it was ultimately an uninformative failure. By that time the camera had lost most of its charge, so Daren plugged it back into his shoulder mount long enough to bring it back to full power.

Only one other tunnel was steep enough to have a chance of getting a camera down it. They fed the cable steadily downward as the view again kept losing contrast.

"Something different this time." Lucy said suddenly.

Alis saw it, too, and began slowing the cable's descent. When she halted it completely, the view was nothing like the previous pictures.

"It looks like the tunnel's completely blocked," Robert said. "Where's the probe?"

Alis looked intently at the display coming back from the camera. The end of the tunnel seemed melted shut. In the center of the view was a smooth surface blocking the camera's path, and around the perimeter of the circular area, the material from the walls seemed to be blended as if everything in the picture were made of wax that had been exposed to a hot flame for just a second—long enough to let the surfaces run together and short enough to keep the tunnel in its familiar round shape.

"The probe must have gone that way, don't you think?" Lucy said.

"Makes sense to me," Alis said. "The alternative is that it backed up along its path, and then it would have had to follow the path of one of the other existing tunnels, or we would see it here."

"So," Karl said slowly, "either the probe caused that to happen, or maybe Cantaloupe caused that reaction because of the damage the probe did."

Robert drew in a loud breath. "Okay, but if it was Cantaloupe itself doing, say, a job of self-repair and damage control, that leaves another question. The implication is that the probe hit while Cantaloupe was still able to repair itself—it seems organic after all—but if it did, why did it stop there? Why not repair the entire tunnel, all the tunnels, this chamber, and the shaft to the surface?"

"Puzzling, isn't it?" Karl said. "But it could make sense if Cantaloupe shared some characteristics of the human body. We get cut, and the skin heals. A virus attacks and the body's immune system fights the infection. But if the damage is greater than the body's designed to repair, say the loss of a leg—ah, bad example—"

"Go on," Alis said evenly.

"Sorry. Anyway, if the damage is bad enough, the body can't do the repairs on its own."

"There's another explanation," said Robert. "If the damage is done directly to mechanisms that do the repair, for either the entire body or just for localized parts of the body, then the body can't heal itself either."

"So," Lucy said, "if Cantaloupe is self-repairing, it's still possible that this probe damaged some mechanism to the point that it can't repair this section, or maybe can't do any repairs?"

"Possible," Robert said. "But almost impossible to verify, given how little we know so far." He looked up. "But it's within the realm of possibility that one of those larger tunnels the shaft cut through above was a critical one."

Karl added, "Or that one of these secondary probes managed to do significant damage as it cut deeper into the surface."

Robert nodded energetically enough that his helmet moved. "True, or it could be some combination of all the damage."

Lucy said, "So you think that if we knew what to fix, we could help Cantaloupe repair itself?"

"Really hard to say," Robert responded. "We're already two or three levels deep in what-ifs. It could also be that Cantaloupe as a whole is dead now, either from the damage done by the probe or because it was designed to last a certain span of time, and traveling between solar systems, maybe a lot of solar systems, is far longer than its design life."

Robert went back and looked up the shaft to the surface. "We've talked about the theory that Cantaloupe is a huge organic spaceship. If that's so, the fact that this damage hasn't been repaired also suggests the crew is long dead. Presumably, if Cantaloupe suffered unusual damage, the people who built it might be able to figure out how to repair it."

"If they had the necessary resources," Karl said.

"Cantaloupe is enormous. It seems to me that this must be something built for the long haul. If some of those initial assumptions are true, it seems to me the crew, and passengers, should have brought along everything they needed. Even allowing one percent of Cantaloupe's volume for repair mechanisms would give a huge volume."

"It's always possible, though," Karl said, "that having a probe blast into the surface and start spreading additional probes that cut even deeper, doing even more damage, isn't one of the things the designers felt was really likely. It could even be that the probe somehow did enough damage that it killed the inhabitants."

"Certainly possible," Alis said, "but I think we should get back to gathering data. There'll be plenty of time later to go over the data and try to make sense of it all." There would be plenty of time later, too, to grieve for Belinda. She sensed that people were grateful that their puzzling surroundings were helping them from sinking into a morass of depression.

"I've pretty much covered this area," Lucy said. "I've got lots more samples collected, and we must have enough video upstairs to recreate a mock-up of this chamber in detail."

"So, what does that leave? We could start back up the main shaft and explore the side tunnels more thoroughly. Or we could talk about finding a different way to explore these smaller tunnels that we haven't seen all the way into yet."

Lucy spoke up. "I'm still ready to go in."

Alis's body shook with reflex. The idea of crawling into one of those tunnels and getting stuck bothered her even more than the first time the image had sprung into her head. "That wouldn't bother you?"

"I think I can handle it. There's one way to find out. But if we're going to do it, let's do it. Don't give me a lot of time to think about it."

Alis would have been uncomfortable ordering anyone into one of the tunnels, but Lucy seemed so ready to go, she said, "All right. Let's try the tunnel where we ran out of light before getting to the end. We can tie the cable to one of your legs and lower you down."

"Just make sure it's secure."

Alis shuddered again and said, "Absolutely."

Lucy tilted her shoulder camera so it pointed straight up. Robert tied the end of the cable to Lucy's left ankle, as if she were about to be used as bait for some giant aquatic creature.

After Alis double- and triple-checked the arrangement to make sure the cable was tight enough not to slip off the boot and loose enough to avoid constrictions, Lucy crawled head-first into the tunnel. The tunnel walls cleared Lucy's shoulders by about the length of a finger on each side.

"Here we go," Alis said as she let the winch start letting cable out slowly. "Tell me instantly if the tunnel seems to get any narrower."

"Count on it."

"And count or chatter or anything to make sure I know the comm link is still working. If you get out of range, I'm pulling you back up right then."

"Fine by me. I'm willing to do this, but it's not like I'm crazy about it."

Lucy's body disappeared inside the tunnel and Alis switched part of her helmet display to watch the view from Lucy's camera.

"Thanks for doing this," Alis said. "I'm a little surprised by the absence of male volunteers. You'd think this kind of thing would put them in testosterone heaven."

"Actually," said Robert, "I'm afraid my shoulders are so broad I might not fit."

"Me, too," said Daren just as Karl said, "Right, my thought exactly."

Daren sounded just as serious as Robert, but in Karl's voice Alis could hear his undisguised smile, and Alis smiled to herself.

"Men," Lucy said. "Okay, so far so good." After a few seconds of silence, she added, "This is actually a little spookier than I thought it might be. I wonder if this is how chimney sweeps felt?"

Alis had no idea. "You want us to pull you back up?"

"No." Pause. "Yes. Er, not all the way back up, but could you pull me up just a meter or so? Just so my head knows how easy it's going to be."

"You got it." Alis stopped the winch, waited a second, and started it up for a couple of seconds. "How's that?"

"Better. I'm ready now."

Alis let the winch start playing out more cable again.

"At least in this ultra-low gee, the blood isn't rushing to my head the way it would normally," Lucy said, and proceeded to ramble about the texture of the tunnel walls and how the view was not changing. "You know this isn't really what I had in mind when I left home and told my parents I wanted to explore space."

"On the other hand," Karl said, "being able to explore something alien that must have come from a lot of light-years away isn't something that most people get to do."

Daren moved closer to the tunnel and peered down it as the cable snaked farther and farther down. "I'll just be happy if we don't stumble onto a nest of vicious acid-spitting, flesh-eating aliens."

"Oh, good timing, Daren," Lucy said. "As if I don't have enough to worry about already. And hanging from one ankle isn't really a strong position of power."

"Oh, don't worry about him," Robert said. "The odds of that happening have to be well below fifty percent."

"When we're back on the ship, I'm going to get even with you guys, even if it takes the rest of the mission."

Robert chuckled. "Not good to make threats while you're in a position like this. If the cable were to get accidentally cut, we still have enough for the rest of us to get back to the surface."

"Okay, okay," Alis said finally. "We're a team, and teams should be supportive, not spreading infectious paranoia among ourselves. We've already lost one teammate; let's make the rest of this mission a little smoother." As soon as she finished speaking and heard the sudden silence, she suddenly had second thoughts about reminding people of Belinda's death. The group needed to be concentrating on the job at hand, not dwelling on the gruesome scene above.

Karl said, "You're right. Lucy, we really do appreciate what you're doing. I, for one, would find the job really uncomfortable."

"Thanks, Karl," Lucy said. "It's a dirty job . . ."

Alis silently thanked Karl for helping get things back on track. She had no doubt that he was a perfectly capable leader in his own right, but she was appreciative that his chosen role was so supportive, reinforcing her own leadership rather than constantly trying to whittle away at it, the way Robert often did.

"Am I past the point where we ran out of light yet?" Lucy asked.

Alis did a quick mental calculation and said, "Yes. You're probably a hundred meters past that point already."

"Good. The tunnel doesn't seem perfectly straight like the shaft above did. This is more like the path of an insect trying to burrow in a straight path and not quite making it."

Several more minutes passed as Lucy dropped deeper and deeper.

"Hey, I think I see something," Lucy called suddenly.

Alis could just made out a change in the center of the display. The image jittered as Lucy dangled on the end of the cable, so she couldn't tell what was ahead.

"Slow me down," Lucy said. "It looks like the butt end of another probe."

Alis had a better view now that Lucy was closer. She let Lucy drop lower until she was just above the probe and Lucy called out to stop. The now-familiar concentric rings on the back of the probe were plainly visible in the center of the display, but they looked dirty.

"The back of the probe seems dusty," Lucy said. "I want to collect a sample before you pull me back up."

"Roger. Just say when."

"Take a look at this," Karl said.

Alis turned and found Karl crouching next to the probe that had failed to deploy. He was looking at one end of the probe and pointing at the chamber wall on the other side of the probe. At first she didn't know what he meant her to see, but then she saw the circle of light wavering on the wall. She moved. The light was coming from Karl's helmet lamps and shining through a hole that apparently ran through the center of the probe.

Karl went on. "If the probe vaporizes material ahead of it as it moves, this hole could be for venting the exhaust gas behind it. And if the probe does operate that way, it would be fairly easy for material on the edge of the beam, or whatever it cuts with, to crumble into dust or small particles that wouldn't get sucked into vacuum. That could be the 'dust' Lucy just spotted."

"Makes good sense to me," Alis said. She assumed it made sense to Robert and Daren also, because they didn't say anything.

Lucy seemed to have an awkward moment or two as she maneuvered upside down in a cramped space, but she managed to get her samples. "Okay, haul me up. But take it slow at first. If my free foot catches on the tunnel wall, I could wind up jammed down here."

"You got it." Alis started the winch back up at about one-fifth the speed Lucy had traveled down at.

After a few minutes Lucy said, "Okay. Speed me up. At this rate I'll die of boredom or old age."

Alis ramped the speed gradually up to a more comfortable rate.

Captain Fernandez's voice sounded in her helmet. "We've got slightly more detail starting to show up on the internal scan. I've just transmitted a new version to you. The first frame is a blowup of the region near you. The others are slices of the whole, identified by latitude ring number. I'll transmit an entire new holographic image every hour, or more often if there are significant changes."

"Thanks very much. I'll take a look." Alis brought up a display of stored images and picked the first one. She was sure the others on the team were doing the same thing.

At the center of the image was an elongated dark spot that she assumed was the main probe. A small lighter balloon was formed around the probe, with the top half of the probe inside the bubble and the bottom half extending below the bubble. Slightly below Lucy's position was a very faint small dark spot, presumably the probe she had just visited.

The most interesting feature on the image was a ghostly faint suggestion of another open area below and to one side of the chamber housing the main probe. Alis flipped to another view to get a better sense of orientation.

After circling the part of the chamber and watching the inertial reference display in her helmet viewer, she stopped next to one of the other tunnels and found herself standing next to Karl, as if he'd been doing exactly the same thing.

He said, "If any of these tunnels reach that other open area, this one's the best bet, don't you think?"

"I agree."

The tunnel they stood before was the one that started out almost level and then dipped downward several meters inside. On her display, Alis could almost imagine she saw an ultra-faint line leading from the chamber down toward the other open space, but she supposed the vision was as trustworthy as early astronomers seeing canals on Mars.

Lucy spoke up. "You're saying that as soon as I get out of this thing you've got more work for me?"

"If you're willing," Alis said. "We only have the one cable. I'm still ready to share the assignment if I hear any other volunteers."

Her helmet was filled with nothing but the sound of her

gentle breathing, a soft whoosh of circulating air, and a slight circuitry hum. No clamor of volunteering male voices intruded on the steady sounds.

Finally Karl said, "Aren't you glad you're not saddled with one of those macho crews where everyone fights over who gets to do the dangerous stuff?"

As Alis tried to decide whether to respond, Lucy said, "Not really."

Robert said, "There is something we could do while we're waiting. We could try to dislodge the main probe. There's a chance we could take it with us when we're done exploring. That way it could be examined in more detail with better tools."

"Makes sense," Karl said after a moment. "In a week or so Cantaloupe will be through the solar system. We'll probably never see it again until there's a new generation of star drives. Anything we can keep gives us the potential for that much more information."

Alis looked at the main probe. In normal gravity she could safely predict freeing it to be a waste of time, but here, who knew? "Okay. If you do manage to get it free, we could hoist it up behind us when we leave."

Robert moved to the probe. "Give me a hand, guys. Spread around the perimeter. Let's see if we can lift it."

Karl moved to take his position and said, "Weight may not be the only issue. This thing may be lodged in place."

"Well, let's see what it feels like."

Alis stayed near the mouth of the small tunnel, monitoring the cable pulling Lucy back up.

Robert, Karl, and Daren positioned themselves around the probe and spent a moment looking for adequate grips. Robert said, "Okay, when I say 'now,' let's see what happens." He hesitated. "Now!"

Alis hadn't heard that much grunting and groaning since

her dog Puffer got stuck crawling under a fence while chasing her cat.

"Okay, okay," Robert said. "Let's rest a minute and try again."

More grunting and groaning. The probe seemed to move slightly, but Alis thought that could have been just her imagination.

"It moved a little," Robert said. "It feels like it's stuck. We pulled it up a few centimeters, but the tension increased."

Alis said, "Lucy's not far now. When she's back, the five of us could all pull. Maybe that would be enough to free it."

"Sounds good," said Karl.

"How are you doing, Lucy?" Alis asked.

"Fine. How much longer?"

Alis made a quick estimate. "A couple of minutes."

"Good. Can I stay on my feet for a few minutes before you send me back down?"

"I think that can be arranged."

Hardly more than a minute later Alis could see Lucy's boots come into view. She slowed down the winch and finally Lucy was back in the chamber.

"Maybe I should just leave the winch cable attached," Lucy said. "It got me back safely the way it is."

"Fine." Alis reversed the winch again and let out enough cable that Lucy was free to roam the chamber. "You ready to try to lift the main probe?"

"Almost." Lucy took a few deep breaths. "Okay."

All five of them surrounded the large probe. It took Alis a couple of tries before she found a grip that gave her some leverage.

"Everyone ready?" Robert asked.

Everyone was. On Robert's command they all strained against the uneven footing and tried to life the probe. Alis immediately understood what Robert had said about it feeling stuck. The sensation was more like pulling on a strong spring than like lifting a heavy weight. It was as if the tip of the probe was stuck in something gooey and elastic.

Despite the loudness of the grunting and groaning, the probe stayed stuck.

"Let's try rocking it," Robert said. "Pull up, on my command, and let go when I say so. Let's try at least three or four cycles. Okay, everyone. Lift."

They alternated between grunt-and-groan mode and relax mode several times. Alis had just about decided the effort wasn't going to pay off when on the next pull, the probe suddenly lurched upward.

"We got it!" Robert shouted.

"All right," Karl said.

The probe definitely seemed loose despite its weight even in the low gravity. Together they lifted the probe almost a half-meter before Alis said, "Hold on. If we pull it high enough, it'll block the way out. Let's just leave it for now, and when we're ready to go, we'll secure the end of the cable to it."

Robert said, "We could tie it now and the winch could hoist it up while we're still exploring. That way if we found anything else to take, we'd still be able to."

"Maybe, but I don't want to risk having that thing getting stuck in the shaft. If we're on top and can cut the cable below us, that's different. Besides, I want to use the cable to get Lucy down that other tunnel now."

The group let the large probe sink back into the depression. It stabilized slightly higher than it had originally rested.

Alis turned to Lucy. "Are you ready to go exploring again?"

"That's a nice way to put it. Yes, I guess so."

Both Alis and Lucy double-checked to make sure the cable was still safely secured to her boot. The tunnel mouth was a half-meter off the floor, and the tunnel started out at a very slight slope before, about twenty meters away, it started angling downward. Lucy crawled into the tunnel mouth with the cable trailing behind her.

Alis watched her as she pulled herself deeper into the tunnel. Alis didn't bother telling the winch to pull up the slack, but instead held onto the cable herself. With her feet planted on either side of the tunnel mouth, she would have the leverage to tug against Lucy's low weight until the slack was gone.

Lucy paused near the section where the tunnel dipped downward. "Are you sure that when you pull me up, the cord won't start cutting into the tunnel wall?"

"Trust us," Robert said with an all-too-audible smirk.

"Can it, Robert," Alis said. "Unless you want to trade places with Lucy."

Robert fell silent.

Alis cleared her throat. "How about if we lower you just a few meters and pull you back? You can take a look at the tunnel surface where the cable rubs and see what you think."

"Sounds okay to me." Lucy crawled ahead and within seconds she had vanished from sight. Alis was having to apply gentle tension so Lucy wouldn't just keep sliding downward.

Alis caught a hint of motion to one side, and she turned to see Karl with the cable in his hands, feeding it to her, obviously ready to back her up if the tension suddenly increased. She turned back toward the tunnel, relieved that she didn't have to fight with everyone.

"Okay, can you pull me back up?" Lucy asked.

"You got it." Alis started pulling on the cable, and without much effort was able to get Lucy back to the nearly level section of the tunnel.

"I think it'll be all right," Lucy said tentatively. "The surface here shows a little rubbing, but I think my weight is small enough here that the friction won't be a big problem."

"Good. You ready to go again?"

"Okay."

Lucy vanished from sight again, and Alis kept slowly letting out cable. From her helmet view of Lucy's camera output, it was hard to tell if the shaft was now nearly vertical or not, but the modest weight change had made it seem that way. A minute later, the cable went taut. Alis looked up and realized she had run out of loose cable. "I'm ready to start the winch again. Are you still okay?"

"I think so," Lucy said.

Alis started the winch unwinding cable, letting Lucy drop farther into the interior of Cantaloupe.

"The tunnel's curving again," Lucy said moments later. "It's been almost vertical, but now it's curving to maybe twenty degrees from vertical. It's a little hard to judge up and down right now."

"If the tunnel takes enough turns that you're worried about us being able to pull you back out, just say so."

"Guaran-damn-teed."

This tunnel went deeper than the first. Lucy kept Alis up-to-date on the twists and turns as the tunnel kept angling steadily downward.

"Hey, this could be interesting," Lucy said.

"What?" Alis could detect a change in the view ahead, but she couldn't tell what it represented.

"It looks like I'm coming toward another cavern or at least a large opening. I'm not—hey!"

Alis didn't realize what was wrong at first, and she couldn't move quickly enough to help.

The cable supporting Lucy had been cut. The loose end came racing into the chamber, flipping back and forth like a piece of spaghetti being sucked into a mouth. Alis scrambled to grab the loose end, as did Karl, but it flipped just out of reach and sucked itself into the tunnel mouth as Lucy began to scream.

"What the hell?" said Karl, as Daren and Robert both made noises expressing amazement and concern.

Lucy's long scream and following uncharacteristic string

of obscenities were cut short. Silence. The view from her camera was a chaotic series of flashes of tunnel walls.

"Lucy!" Alis shouted. "Lucy, are you all right?" She moved toward the center of the chamber so she could look up, in hopes of getting a clue to how the cable broke. Karl and Robert were there, too, craning to see.

Something seemed to be blocking the shaft to the surface, and the rest of the cable that had been attached to Lucy's foot was gone.

"What is going on?" Karl yelled in obvious frustration.

"And what the hell is *that?*" Robert asked immediately.

Alis looked where Robert pointed. In the depression around the perimeter of the large probe, a greenish fluid was bubbling up into the chamber.

9 ▪ INFECTION

Panic reigned for precious seconds.

Karl stared in amazement at the greenish fluid welling up around the perimeter of the large probe. Its viscosity was changing, and in a matter of seconds the texture changed from pea soup to something more like green axle-grease.

The view from Lucy's camera finally stabilized, but the view was mostly dark and it was hard to tell what the camera was looking at. Alis hadn't been able to get a response from Lucy.

Even before Karl finished mentally cataloging all that was going wrong, a new factor was added. The probe lurched up-ward, moving itself out of the depression it was in.

Robert shouted, "It's going to seal the opening!" He pointed at the circular hole in the ceiling over the probe.

Daren just quivered at the side of the chamber as Alis tried again to hail Lucy.

Captain Fernandez said nothing during the panic, no doubt because he had nothing to add and didn't want to contribute to the pandemonium.

Robert jumped high enough to get atop the probe, in an obvious effort to get out of the chamber before the exit was sealed. He wobbled on top of the probe, and then, as fast as he had gotten up, he scrambled back down and started bouncing around the chamber.

Karl saw the reason. The shaft above was already growing closed. Had Robert stayed where he was, he would have been crushed between the ceiling and the probe, which kept rising.

The goop started to spread away from the base of the probe just about the same time the probe reached the ceiling. The probe pushed maybe a quarter-meter into the ceiling before it finally stopped moving. Their exit was plugged.

Robert said, "We're sealed in! We're dead."

"Keep it to yourself," Alis snapped. "Lucy's down here, too, and she may be in worse shape." Alis called out to Lucy again, but still received no answer.

Suddenly Daren was yelling incoherently and in motion, propelling himself away from the chamber wall.

Karl found what had set off Daren. More green glop was slowly pumping out one of the small tunnel mouths.

"I'm okay, I think," Lucy said unexpectedly. "What the hell's happening up there?"

Captain Fernandez said, "Ditto."

Alis said, as much for Captain Fernandez as for Lucy, "It looks like we're about to be engulfed by some fluid that's pumping up from beneath the main probe, and the way out's been sealed. It's as if Cantaloupe is suddenly trying to repair the damage or something."

Alis hesitated. "Let's try to push the probe back down. Maybe that will cut off the flow."

Karl was already convinced that would do no good and they really had only one choice for getting out of the chamber, but he helped in a frantic effort to push down the probe. His weight was nothing compared to the probe's, so he flipped upside down and tried to push his legs against the ceiling while pushing the probe downward.

They might as well have been trying to push a two-ton boulder up a slope. The probe didn't budge.

More fluid swelled onto the chamber floor.

Karl said what he had to say as economically as possible. "I think the only way out is to follow Lucy."

"You're out of your mind," Robert said. "We should cut diagonally through the ceiling next to the probe and get closer to the surface."

"We don't have time. And Lucy's still down there."

"It's better that one person dies than five people, don't you—"

"That's enough," Alis said suddenly. "Karl's right. If we argue much longer, this goop will reach the tunnel mouth, and we won't even have that choice."

"This place seems safe," called Lucy. "It looks like a natural part of Cantaloupe. It won't collapse."

Robert said, "But if Cantaloupe is repairing itself, that tunnel could be filled with goop. Even if it isn't yet, it could close up while we're on the way down."

"The longer we argue, the worse the odds are," Alis said. "Karl, you first."

"I'm willing, but you should go first since you're smallest. If the tunnel does collapse or if one if us is too big to get through, we'll all die if the biggest person goes first."

"Right. I'll go. Everyone follow."

Karl could hear the nervousness in Alis's voice as she crawled into the tunnel. He felt even more nervous, but he was right. As bad as it looked, this was their best chance to survive.

As soon as Alis had disappeared, Karl said, "Next?"

Robert said, "No way."

Daren seemed petrified.

The goop was still rising just as fast. Karl grabbed Daren's arm and pulled him toward the tunnel. "You've got to do it."

As if he were an automaton, Darren got into the tunnel without saying a word. He hesitated inside the tunnel mouth, and Karl thought he'd have to push him, but as soon as Karl touched Daren's feet, the man jumped forward like a frog being prodded.

The green goop had almost reached where Karl stood. "Robert, we've got to go!"

"It's crazy."

"Yeah, but it's the only way!"

Robert stood there frozen. It was only when green goop suddenly started gushing from a tunnel mouth near his feet that he suddenly sped toward the escape tunnel.

Robert was about the same size Karl was, and Karl gulped as he saw how little gap there was between Robert's shoulders and the tunnel walls. Robert squirmed awkwardly into the tunnel mouth, cursing the entire time.

Even before Robert's feet disappeared down the bend in the tunnel, Karl started in, feeling he was entering a hose stretched wide by unseen hands that were tiring.

Alis was still falling, from the sounds of her gasps and cries as she shook through bends and twists. Karl prayed the tunnel wouldn't suddenly close, or start filling with green glop.

Moving himself through the tunnel with so little clearance was nerve-wracking. Daren wailed loudly as he fell, but in a sense the sound was comforting, because it meant Daren was still alive. Karl reached the point of no return where the tunnel bent deeper into the interior, and he wasn't even sure if he could have managed his way back at this point if he saw green

glop welling up from within this tunnel. From the screams of
the others, they were still hurtling unimpeded through an open
tunnel, so he bit his lip, took a breath, and pushed himself forward until he felt his body sliding helplessly forward.

No amusement park ride had prepared Karl for this. He
felt a groan spring unbidden to his throat. Amusement park
rides were at least theoretically safe, and they wouldn't suddenly run into a dead end. He accelerated slowly, but the tunnel was *deep,* and every second brought a slight increase in his
rate of fall. Plenty of time to fall more than made up for the
low gravity.

Karl felt himself speeding faster and faster until the tunnel walls were a blur. He tried to brake himself some by extending his gloved hands, but worried about tearing a glove
on some unanticipated sharp obstruction.

He tried to keep his thoughts off what would happen if
the tunnel walls began closing in on him as Cantaloupe started
healing that section of its interior. Or worse, if the walls closed
in on Robert or Daren, and Karl rammed into Robert and they
were both stuck for eternity inside a congealed mass of green
goo. With his arms outstretched he wouldn't be able to manually shut off his suit air, so he'd be conscious for a long time,
held upside down, glued motionless in the blackness.

He tried to keep his thoughts off what might happen if he
miraculously made it all the way through the tunnel and then
rammed into the suited bodies of his unconscious teammates
at a crushing speed.

He hit a bend in the tunnel that forced his hands and head
back in an almost spine-snapping curve. Only after he was
through the curve did he realize that if he'd hit this section
going more slowly, he might have been stuck right there.

The tunnel twisted to the right and turned back fast to the
left, still heading downward, vibrating Karl's brain and vision
to the point that for a short time he could no longer concentrate on his fears.

The cries of his teammates seemed softer now, but he couldn't tell if that was because his own voice was blotting them out, if they had all made it through the tunnel, or if they were all dead or injured, just waiting for him to pile into them. If he did get stuck forever in the tunnel, he hoped the impact would mercifully kill him. How could he have been stupid enough to suggest this way out?

He'd never ridden a toboggan except in VR, but this down-the-rabbit-hole fall seemed like a vertical toboggan.

Another spine-bending twist. Why couldn't the small probe have just kept going straight at maybe ten degrees below horizontal? Then the ride could almost have been fun. Of course if the least viscous green slime had reached the lip of the tunnel mouth, he'd wish he were traveling even more rapidly.

Faster. The tunnel walls were flashing past. If they were abrasive enough, his suit could tear at any time. Damnit. Why couldn't he think of anything positive?

Karl kept his hands extended over his head, fingers clamped together. He had quit trying to look ahead, partly out of concern that doing so gave him a larger profile and hitting his helmet on an obstruction could snap his neck.

He hurtled through the descending tunnel, scraping harder against the bottom surface as the tunnel made a gradual turn toward horizontal. As he absurdly worried that either the tunnel would start upward now and strand him or the journey might never end, he was suddenly free of the tunnel, in a large open space, flying toward whatever lay ahead.

He curled into a safer posture just before he hit. His last recollection was of flying toward the wall of a new chamber, passing over the suited bodies of his teammates.

He must have been dreaming. Karl struggled to lift heavy eyelids, and somewhere in front of him a circular tunnel mouth gaped. As he watched, the dark circle slowly lightened, turning the same shade as the surrounding material.

He blinked. The surface was smooth, as if no tunnel had ever broken the surface.

Awe-filled whispers in his helmet made him finally come to the realization that he was awake. Others had been watching the same thing he had just witnessed.

"Is that what I think it is?" he asked, his mouth dry.

"You're awake!" Alis said. Her voice gave the impression that she, too, had only recently recovered.

"Prove it."

"Do you feel any pain?"

"You don't?" Karl started to stretch, but increased pain cut the gesture short.

"Where do you hurt?"

Karl thought for a moment. "I think, I'm not sure, but I think one of my left toes doesn't hurt. No, wait. I'd guess I'd have to say everything hurts."

"Anything more than the rest?" Robert sounded tired or groggy. His bedside manner had never been what Karl would have called adequate, and now it was below par for even Robert.

"Who's the moron who suggested we try the tunnel?" Karl asked.

"You're that moron," Alis said. "At least you were the first moron to suggest it out loud. It's not all that bad, though. If we had stayed, we'd probably be dead—sooner or later anyway. You saw this tunnel just seal itself."

Karl suddenly imagined himself inside the tunnel as it sealed itself, and experienced a brief blast of the shakes. "So we all survived?" So far Daren had said nothing, but that wasn't unusual.

"If you call this surviving," Lucy said. "We're trapped thousands of meters below the surface, and we'll be passing out of the solar system in a week or two. I think the only improvement would be if we had just a couple of minutes of air left."

"We'll make it out of here," Alis said with a matter-of-fact tone that had to be carefully cultivated. "If nothing else, the *Ranger* can cut us out of here."

"How can you be sure?" Robert asked. "If this thing is repairing itself again, it could be that even if the *Ranger* cuts a new shaft, it won't stay open long enough."

Karl said, "It could be the *Ranger* won't even make the attempt. If Cantaloupe is still functioning, there may be a lot of pressure to write us off and let this thing go on its merry way without harm."

"Without harm?" Robert said. "They were talking about having to use asteroid-deflection charges. They might just blow the crap out of it. And us."

"Well, *there's* a cheery thought," Lucy said.

"Hey, I'm just being realistic."

"Well," Alis said. "Let's focus that imagination on getting back out."

In the following silence, Karl finally noticed a slowly blinking status indicator on his helmet display. He told his suit to give him the full diagnostic display. A series of green flashes sped up one side of his helmet display. Only one yellow. The circulation coils on his left arm were apparently damaged, but still operating in a degraded condition. Thank God for no reds. Down here, a red wouldn't simply mean an uncomfortable few minutes. It would probably mean death. The suit said his food, water, air, and energy were still at the ninety-eight percent level. Karl added a silent prayer of thanks to the suit designers who had found ways to build energy-assisted recycling into a two-week survival suit.

Karl got to his feet, shaky because of the low gravity and the recent spill. They weren't in a cavern after all, but rather they were in another large tunnel, this one wider than it was tall, but still at least twice as tall as he was. In one direction, the tunnel extended straighter than any tunnel he'd yet seen, shrinking to a dot in the distance. In the other direction, a nearby bend in the tunnel blocked the view.

He walked several paces and reached the spot on the wall that he was sure used to be a much smaller tunnel mouth. Suddenly he was sure of nothing. The wall appeared completely unscathed.

Motion beside him. Lucy reached forward and touched the area Karl thought used to be an open tunnel mouth. He reached out, too. The surface felt just like the surface a meter away, firm but not rock, somewhere between a thinly padded chair and a slightly under-inflated basketball.

"Incredible," Lucy said softly.

Karl imagined himself caught just at the last moment, with only his two gloved hands sticking out of the wall, like some practical-joke trophy. He looked behind him at the spot on the opposite wall where they must have all hit one by one. A couple of scuff marks told him their predicament was all too real.

The situation must have been getting to Daren. He sat on the tunnel floor with his arms surrounding his pulled-up knees, and his head tilted forward. Karl moved slowly over and sat in front of him.

"You all right, buddy?" Karl asked.

Silence.

"Alis is right. We really are going to make it out of here. The *Ranger* has some fairly hefty firepower if that's what's needed. We still have our brains. Well, Robert's always been that way, but the rest of us—"

"We're screwed," Daren said suddenly. "We're cut off."

"From the *Ranger?*" Karl finally realized that he'd heard nothing from up top since before the emergency.

"Yeah."

Karl noticed the small group forming around him and

Daren. "Are we out of range? We really didn't drop that far compared to how deep we already were."

"I know. The repeater unit on my back must be fried. I suppose I hit it on the tunnel wall. We're screwed. We can hear them, but our transmitters aren't strong enough."

"Let's not give up too fast. Let me take a look."

"We're screwed. Aren't you listening?"

"Let me look at it anyway. If we're screwed, we're going to have lots of time on our hands." Karl figured that actually, even with a power source and recycling unit that early space explorers would have killed for, they really had only about a week before true discomfort set in, and probably no more than a day after that they'd all be dead.

Daren bent forward so Karl could get at the unit on his back. "Don't you get it? The *Ranger* will think we're all dead. They won't have any reason to think we need help. We just vanished off the map."

"Oh, so what you're saying is we're screwed?"

"Now you got it."

"Lie down on your belly. I can't get a good look at this thing."

Daren obeyed, but not before he repeated his assessment of them all being screwed. He could really be focused when he wanted to be.

"He's right you know," Robert said. "If we can't talk to the *Ranger*, we really are—"

"I really don't want to hear it," Karl said. "Let's just wait a few minutes before assuming the worst."

The unit on Daren's back did, in fact, look damaged. The case was square, about the width of an outstretched hand, a self-contained unit housing a receiver/transmitter and antenna. The cover showed a large dent. This wasn't the kind of thing that would be easy to repair, since it probably contained just one integrated module, and it wasn't the kind of thing they'd thought to bring a backup for. Under normal circumstances, if it had failed, they'd just head back up to the surface.

Karl snapped off the interlocks on the cover and pulled it back. A black square showed a light spot about where the dent was. The small antenna, the one part they might be able to jerry-rig, looked fine.

As Karl handled the unit, another voice sounded in his helmet. "This is the *Ranger.* Reply, anyone." Captain Fernandez's voice was calm, but Karl knew he probably wasn't that way on the inside.

"You fixed it!" Lucy said. "Maybe we're not screwed."

"All right!" said Robert.

"Don't get your hopes too high," Karl said. "This box is just the relay to boost our suit transmissions. We're hearing the ship without the benefit."

"We're screwed," Daren said.

Karl made sure his suit communications were set to transmit to the ship. "Captain Fernandez, can you hear me?" He hesitated. "Do you read me?"

No response.

Karl lifted the repeater out of its shell, reflecting that this really was Daren's job—as if Daren could work on equipment in the middle of his back. He felt stupid as he stared at the flat pack with the thin lead going to the antenna. Obviously there was no way to repair it. The unit was sealed, probably all of the active components embedded in some flexible circuit gel. He bent the unit slightly. "Can you hear me now?"

Nothing.

Karl flexed the unit in a different direction. "*Ranger,* do you read?"

Nothing.

He flexed the unit on a corner-to-corner axis. "Anything now? *Ranger?*"

"I read you, Karl." Captain Fernandez's unemotional voice had never been so welcome.

Karl's ears were blasted by an immediate chorus of, "All right!" and, "We're on the air," and "We're still alive down here."

"I was worried that you folks were dead," the captain said, without worry or its aftereffects sounding in his voice.

Karl said, "Go ahead, Alis. Make the most of it, because I don't know how long this will last."

Alis talked rapidly. "We're all alive. Our ability to transmit to you is impaired and could fail at any time, so don't assume that no word from us means we're dead."

"Understood."

"Please keep transmitting updated maps of the interior as soon as there's any significant change. We need to find a way back to the shaft if there is a way."

"The shaft is closed."

"What? Already?" Alis's faceplate turned toward Karl.

"Apparently. I've got Lambert and Chow down on the surface investigating."

"All right. We'll have to find another way out. As the map gets more detailed, maybe we can find a tunnel that'll take us upward."

"Roger."

"What if we can't get all the way to the surface?" Alis asked. "You think ISA will let you cut us out?"

"I haven't asked them," Captain Fernandez said carefully. "I don't intend to ask them. I've got the responsibility here, and I'll do whatever I need to, to protect my crew."

Karl suddenly had a deeper appreciation for the captain's ability to deal with bureaucracy. Carefully deciding what questions you don't want someone else's answer to and not bringing up the issue gives you that much more control. Karl could think of at least two bosses who, whenever they didn't want to honor a request but also didn't want to be the bad guy, would make a point of asking questions designed to elicit a "no." He felt especially lucky to be under the command of someone at the opposite end of the spectrum just now.

"I do have some concerns about cutting into the surface, though," the captain added, "now that we know this thing is still alive or still functioning. On the other hand, if it can repair itself, that lessens the downside. Just get as close to the surface as you can."

"Right. For the time being—"

"I've lost your signal again."

Karl realized he'd relaxed his grip slightly. He flexed the panel a little more. He looked up at Alis and nodded.

"How about now?" Alis asked.

"Got you."

Karl cleared his throat. "I'd like to suggest that for now, we're going to be off the air most of the time. If you really need to talk to us, please say so, and if we really need to talk, we will. I'm concerned that this repeater may fail altogether if we bend it very often."

Alis agreed.

The captain said, "Roger. The latest map should be in your suit computers. We keep getting a little more detail, but it's still pretty murky. This would be a good time to tell your suit to transmit everything it's stored since the uplink was severed. Maybe we can spot something you've missed."

As Alis complied, Karl read between the lines. If they were all killed soon, or if they were all permanently stranded down here, at least the *Ranger* would have most of the information they came for.

"Okay, that should do it," Alis said. "We'll give you a new dump each time we talk."

"Good." Captain Fernandez hesitated. "You're all doing a fine job down there." He said it the same way a son would tell his father he loved him, so the son was sure of telling the father before he died.

Karl wished the captain hadn't said it. At least he hadn't added, "Be careful."

"Thanks, Captain," Alis said. She nodded toward Karl.

Karl put the repeater back into its housing and snapped the cover shut. "All right, Daren. You can get up."

Karl collected what was left of their cable, coiled it, and secured it to his suit. Moments later the team stood in a circle, facing each other. Karl still felt a little jittery, and he supposed the others did, too.

"Let's find out a little more about where we are before we start worrying about where to go," Alis said. "We've got more time than it'll take to get out of the solar system, because the *Ranger* could stay with us until we're out, as long as the supplies will last for the return trip. And they'll have the chance to transfer even more supplies from the other ships."

She was right, but the facts were self-evident, so Karl wasn't sure if she was saying them to boost morale or if they were really for the benefit of Captain Fernandez, so he wouldn't forget to make the requests.

"That assumes the new arrivals won't blow the crap out of Cantaloupe before we even get out of the system," Robert said.

"Let's try to think positive for a few more hours before we give up." Karl kept the thought to himself that Cantaloupe was so alien and so unknown that the lives of five explorers were fairly inconsequential in comparison. The probable priority sequence would be first the safety of Hamilton Station, second the preservation of Cantaloupe, and third getting the five of them out if possible.

"I'm not giving up," Robert said indignantly. "I just think we should be realistic."

"Whatever."

"Things could be worse," Karl said, and aimed his helmet lamps at where the small tunnel mouth had been.

"All right," Alis said. "Karl, you and Lucy check that direction. I'll go this way with Robert. Daren, why don't you just get a short rest."

"More of us could get a rest," Robert said.

"I want to play safe. For now let's stick with the buddy system for people who are moving around."

Robert shut up and the group split up.

The tunnel they were in was fairly level. Karl and Lucy walked slowly away from Daren, passing walls that seemed smoother, less blotchy than Karl remembered. He wondered if other changes were taking place besides the repair of the intruding tunnel.

Karl reached out with his gloved hand and pressed against the side of the tunnel. He couldn't press very hard without tipping himself in the low gravity, but when he pulled his hand away from the surface, his fingerprints seemed lighter than the surrounding area. He turned his head until he could just see the spot from the corner of his eye. With his hands, he blocked the light from his helmet lamps, putting the spot in shadow. The fingerprints were luminescent.

"Wow, that little guy was sure busy," Lucy said.

Karl looked where she pointed. At the side of the tunnel was a downward-leading smaller tunnel about the same size as the joyride that had brought them down to this level. For the benefit of the others, Karl said, "Lucy's found what seems to be the next leg of the path the small probe took."

Lucy took a long look, then moved aside so Karl could see. The tunnel they had slid down had been generally straight for much of its length, but it had certainly meandered. This tunnel looked perfectly straight, as uniform as a kilometer-long sewer tunnel plunging downward maybe ten degrees away from vertical.

By the time Karl stepped away from the opening, two

more suited bodies had showed up: Alis and Robert.

"We could drop you down there, Karl, if you want to investigate."

"I think I've had enough of small tunnels for today. For the whole week."

"I wonder why this tunnel hasn't been repaired yet," Alis said, "assuming it really was cut by the probe."

Lucy said, "Could be this one doesn't register as damage that needs to be fixed. Maybe it doesn't hurt anything."

Karl said, "Or it could be that it *is* being repaired, starting at the bottom. Or that this tunnel cut through some critical mechanism responsible for repair."

"If that was so," Robert said, "then how was the upper tunnel repaired?"

"Could be the interior is divided into repair zones, like the human body. You can cut your finger deep enough to scar and still not prevent the body from repairing a gash on your cheek."

Alis said, "I still don't understand why, after all this time, the repairs started."

Karl said, "I still think that by moving the large probe we must have unjammed some repair mechanism."

"Could be another reason," Lucy said. "We're coming closer to the sun. Maybe Cantaloupe is finally getting enough energy to start functioning again. Maybe it's been in some hibernation mode between the stars."

"Interesting," Karl said. "I hadn't thought of that."

Robert made a *tsk-tsk* sound that almost always presaged a derogatory comment. "Yeah, there's a lot you haven't—"

"Robert." Alis's voice was soft, but carried a big stick.

Robert shut up.

A "private conversation" chime sounded and Robert said to Karl, "Lucky you have a woman to stand up for you."

Karl used his glance to activate a private reply. "I really don't have any quarrel with you. If we work together, either we'll find a way to get out of here, or our last days will be a little more pleasant. This is looking more and more like a biological/medical problem, which makes us the experts. How about agreeing to a truce for a little while?"

Robert made no reply. Another chime sounded, indicating the end of the private conversation.

Alis and Robert moved off to explore the main tunnel in the opposite direction.

Karl entered his current position at the mouth of the small tunnel as another 3-D point on his internal navigation map and moved on with Lucy.

"If Cantaloupe *is* an enormous starship," Lucy said, "you have any ideas on how to contact the inhabitants?"

Karl considered the question. "Could be we just have to do some damage and that'll attract them. Could be they're on the way already. This is a big place, and it may be only recently that we did anything that had a high probability of being noticed."

"It could be the inhabitants are in hibernation, too," she said, as if she'd already had the idea when she'd asked Karl.

"Certainly possible."

Karl stopped, at first unsure why. He looked more closely at the tunnel wall and realized that subconsciously he'd noticed a new feature. A hairline seam ran from near the tunnel bottom to near the top, so fine that it was almost invisible. Karl moved along the tunnel and a few meters later stopped and scanned closely. Another seam.

"What?" Lucy asked.

Karl ran a finger along the seam without touching it. Lucy moved closer to the wall to angle her helmet lamps, and the seam became slightly more visible. Karl did the same for her so she'd get a better view when she looked at the seam straight on.

"Interesting," Lucy said.

"They could be everywhere or just in spots. There's another one back a few meters."

As they moved ahead to see if there was another seam, Robert asked what was going on. Karl told him.

A minute later Robert and Alis confirmed that there were seams in the section of tunnel they were investigating.

"Any theories?" Lucy asked.

Karl pushed against the wall along one of the vertical hairlines, but it felt no different than anyplace else. "None at all."

Lucy was silent rather than admit she didn't have a theory either.

For a second Karl considered taking out his utility cutter and slicing into the tunnel wall, but discarded the idea before ever getting serious about it.

"I see one of the lines near me," Daren said.

Karl looked back and saw they'd moved about thirty meters away from Daren as they inspected the tunnel. "They may be along the whole length of the tunnel for all we know."

About twenty meters farther along the tunnel, Karl and Lucy stopped before a circular outline on the wall. The circle was almost as tall as the tunnel they stood in.

"What do you make of this?" Karl asked.

"Don't know." Lucy reached out and touched the area inside the circle. "Whoa!"

"Whoa what?" Alis said sharply.

The tunnel wall inside the circle had suddenly changed shape, pulling away from Lucy's hand and forming the shape of a funnel. Around the perimeter the surface changed very little, but the very center pulled deep into the wall, revealing a small dark hole at the tip.

Lucy touched the surface again, and the section of the wall pulled even farther back. The hole at the center grew larger.

Karl explained to the others what was happening as Lucy

touched the surface again, harder. By now the surface had pulled back so far that a stubby tunnel was revealed. The off-shoot was no deeper than three meters, and the pushed-in surface of the main tunnel wall seemed to be nothing more than a discoloration around the mouth of the small tunnel.

In a matter of seconds, Alis, Robert, and Daren had joined Karl and Lucy, and the group stared at the dead-end tunnel. The interior surface was dark, with small textured wrinkles that made it look like leather.

The covering surface began to loosen itself from the wall around the perimeter of the opening, as if it were going to gradually return to its former position and cover the hole. Lucy touched it again, and it moved back out of the way.

Karl was suddenly reminded of the way some plants react to touch by curling up their leaves. For an instant he imagined a fly's reaction to a Venus's-flytrap.

He wished they were on a trek in the woods, where they could easily find something disposable to throw into the opening and watch what happened. Especially now they were cut off from the *Ranger*, nothing they carried with them could be treated as disposable. Except maybe Robert.

"What the hell is this thing?" Daren asked.

"No idea," said Karl. "A closet?"

"No, I mean what is Cantaloupe?"

"Oh. No idea."

The walls began creeping back into closed position. This time, Lucy let them alone, and no one else stuck a hand into the opening.

Karl still had no idea what function the mechanism served, but it made him uncomfortable, and grateful that it had been on the side of the tunnel and not on the floor.

"I don't know about the rest of you," Robert said, "but instead of feeling smarter and smarter about this place, I'm feeling dumber and dumber."

Karl held his tongue. Lucy's faceplate turned toward Karl, then away.

Alis said, "As long as we're together again, let's keep going this way."

The five of them began moving again. Karl checked his navigation display again. If the hologram map became complete enough to help them decide if Cantaloupe had any symmetry other than spherical, they could assign poles and latitude, longitude, and depth that made at least a little internal sense. As it was, he had to get by with the fact that they were, rather than heading "east" or "north," moving in a direction of increasing x and decreasing y from an arbitrary coordinate system defined by the location of the shaft, a shaft that apparently no longer existed. He marked the location of the shaft in case it vanished from newer scans.

The next section of the tunnel, for no apparent reason, began to change shape at regular intervals, at first flattening as if someone had pressed huge fingers above and below and squeezed. The following section was vertically squeezed, so it was taller than before, and narrower. The pattern continued to alternate between the two shapes for several cycles.

A few minutes later, Robert said, "Hey, what do you think?"

On the tunnel wall was another circular outline, but this one was far more pronounced, as if meant to be deliberately noticeable. It was about two meters tall, and the area inside the circle was almost white, contrasting sharply with the mottled gray of the rest of the tunnel surface.

Again it was Lucy who reached forward to touch the surface, her curiosity obviously outweighing caution by at least a small margin.

This surface moved, too, but the effect was much different than the first opening. This material simply dilated open, as it some elastic tension had been holding it closed, and sud-

denly the force had been turned off and the material pulled itself into a small roll surrounding the opening.

What was on the other side looked a lot different, too. The
first cavity had looked vaguely threatening to Karl, but this one
looked somehow functional. The cavity beyond the opening
was nearly spherical, as if someone had started with a sphere
and cut a two-meter opening on one side by slicing off a circle about half the diameter of the sphere. The insides glowed
with what seemed to be a weak bioluminescence.

Most of Cantaloupe had a distinctive organic feel to it, as
if it could be some enormous living ship, but this—this was like
a strange blend of flesh and technology. The surface still looked
as if it could be organic, perhaps the inside of an enormous and
highly regular orange peel, but the evenly spaced rows of what
could be handholds and the precise way the sphere seemed to
fit with its surroundings gave the feeling a surgeon might have
when performing an autopsy and coming upon an artificial
heart. Whatever this was, it fit here naturally, but at the same
time it felt foreign, constructed.

"Maybe we really do have a starship here," Robert said
softly.

Karl understood what he meant. This cavity looked *designed*, deliberate. And the odds of the entirety of Cantaloupe
being a designed entity, as opposed to being some very unusual
life-form, had just jumped an order of magnitude. And if it really was a starship, what better way to handle maintenance and
accidents than by making it a self-repairing, virtually living entity?

After a minute of inactivity, the surface that had been
curled up around the perimeter began to stretch back into
place, shrinking the hole at the center until the small black dot
in the center disappeared and once again the surface matched
the contour of the tunnel wall.

"Curiouser and curiouser," said Alis.

"Hey, what the hell!" Daren's voice held that undefinable

tinge of panic that probably told parents their little one was really in trouble and not just screaming as part of playtime.

Karl turned rapidly, trying to locate Daren.

Daren had apparently wandered twenty or thirty meters away. He held a knife in one hand, and he was busily hacking away at what vaguely resembled a large white snake.

Karl moved as fast as he could in the low gravity.

The "snake" had wrapped itself around Daren's leg. As he tried to cut it away with his knife, three more of the long white creatures started wrapping his body, one on his other leg and two around his chest.

Daren screamed, "Help me! These things are strong."

Karl readied his utility knife as he moved toward Daren. The creatures on his legs were squeezing him tight enough that Daren's suit legs looked like a balloon that someone had snapped a tight rubber band around.

A fourth creature emerged from one of the vertical slits on the walls, and it snaked toward Daren.

Daren let out a pitifully anguished cry just as Karl reached him. The creatures encircling his chest were obviously applying a horrific pressure. For an instant Karl's helmet lamps flashed at an angle that let him see Daren's face. Daren was gasping for air, unable to breathe.

Karl began hacking into the creatures circling Daren's chest, trying desperately to avoid slashing into Daren's suit, or getting slashed by Daren's spasmodic swings with his knife.

The creatures were tough. Karl's knife was strong, but trying to sever one of the creatures was like trying to cut a cable that had been dipped in water and then frozen.

Daren stopped moving. The creatures around his chest had tightened so far Karl thought maybe Daren was already dead.

The blade finally cut through one of the creatures. No blood or any fluid was released, but the creature was suddenly two limp pieces of rope instead of an active force. Neither end seemed to sport anything resembling a head or eyes. Both ends could have been the back end of a giant flatworm.

Karl managed to cut through the second creature before he was aware of anyone else helping. Lucy was cutting the creature on Daren's left leg.

A few seconds later, Karl started to feel they finally had the situation under control. But Daren might already be dead.

Daren's body, with the suit still pressurized, lay on the tunnel floor. Karl glanced back toward Robert and Alis. Robert held his knife out as if he wanted to help, but he just stood there motionless.

"Daren, can you hear me?" Karl asked.

"I think you're going to have to ask him later," Alis said suddenly. "Look back that way."

Karl looked where Alis pointed. The slits in the walls farther along the tunnel wall had opened, and dozens of the white snake-like creatures were swarming toward them.

"My God," said Lucy.

Karl picked up Daren's body and started moving away from the approaching creatures. He got no more than a few meters before spotting motion ahead. More creatures.

"We're pinned in!" Robert said.

"This way," Alis said.

She stopped in front of the white circle and poked it. The material dilated open again.

"Go in there?" Robert said.

"We don't have a lot of choices, do we?"

Karl moved, still carrying Daren. The cavity was large enough to hold them all, but he still felt nervous, not knowing the purpose of the chamber. Still it was hard to believe this would be worse than dealing with the snakes.

Alis joined Karl and Daren in the chamber, followed by Lucy. Finally Robert joined them. The snakes were no more than ten meters away.

"Move to the rear," Alis said. "The covering isn't closing."

"Maybe it won't close with anything inside here," Robert said.

Alis yanked him backward. "If it doesn't, we're dead."

Miraculously, the material even with the tunnel wall began to iris closed.

"Thank God," Lucy said.

In a few more seconds, the opening had closed entirely.

"Now what?" Robert said. "Wait here until those things go away?"

"Unless you've got a better—whoa!"

Karl almost cried out involuntarily, too. The chamber had suddenly tilted sharply. It kept turning.

Karl was upside down, then right-side up. Down, then up. And the chamber was still spinning.

The chamber spun faster and faster as bodies tumbled over bodies and Karl began to feel like a rag doll in a clothes dryer.

"What is this?" Lucy cried.

No one answered. The spin stabilized at a rate fast enough to keep everyone pinned to the walls. Karl thought about the indentations that looked a little like handholds.

"We're moving," Robert said.

"No, really?" Lucy said.

Karl understood what Robert meant. The surface where the door had been was gone, and in its place was a flat, featureless panel that had just enough texture for Karl to see that it was moving, sliding across the opening where once the door had been. They were no longer in the same starting position behind the wall.

Once the spin stabilized and Karl's pulse was no longer strong enough to call attention to itself, he forced himself to think, to analyze what was happening.

A glance at his inertial navigation display said it was currently useless. The display kept blinking the same word, "up-dating," because it couldn't keep up with whatever was happening to them.

The spinning motion seemed to be uniform, generating a constant moderate pressure forcing him against the wall. He took several seconds before he made sense of the observation. He convinced himself he could no longer perceive any periodic feeling of being heavier and then lighter, the way he would if they were still spinning around a horizontal axis in a gravity field.

So, either they were spinning around a vertical axis now, or they were somehow headed even deeper into Cantaloupe.

10 ▪ JAUNDICE

Alis felt as if she'd been tossed into some kind of carnival ride. The spinning motion was vaguely reminiscent of a training centrifuge, and she could feel her face grow hot from the tension and the extra blood forced to her head and face.

She "lay" facedown against the wall of the spinning sphere. A shift of her body flipped her onto her back and brought her in closer alignment to the "equator" of the sphere, and the pressure on her head now felt more direct. The rest of the crew were plastered against the sphere walls at awkward angles, their helmet lamps creating a jumble of random lights on the sphere walls.

Once Alis had aligned her body with the spin axis, it was easier to imagine that she was just held to the bottom of the sphere by gravity. She moved a hand to one side and felt the lateral push of Coriolis force. Definitely still rotating.

"I think we're going deeper," Karl said.

"Naturally," Lucy said, exasperation slowly moving out in front of fear. "Things weren't bad enough already."

"Why do you think—" Robert started.

"Daren?" Karl said. "Daren, how are you?"

Silence from Daren. Alis realized that it was Daren's body that was almost directly across from her. Robert and Karl were the closest to him, and they both shifted closer to him.

"Daren, speak to us." Karl's helmet was close to Daren's now, his helmet lamps focused on Daren's faceplate.

Alis was just about convinced Daren was dead when he finally spoke.

"I've felt a lot better than this." Daren's voice was faint, but the words tricked Alis into thinking he might be in better shape than he probably was.

"Where do you hurt?" Robert said. In their environment, with both patient and doctor in pressure suits, it was a fairly pointless question from the point of view of actual medical assistance, but Alis supposed it would make Daren feel better that a doctor was at least near.

Daren ignored Robert's question or didn't hear it. "Karl? Are you here?"

"Yeah. Right next to you."

"I'm not going to make it."

"Sure you are. But you've got to tell Robert—"

"I've got to tell you something. I don't want to die without—consider it a—" cough "—what you'd call a deathbed confession."

"You're going to be fine. And anyway, I'm not a priest or anything. I haven't even been inside a church for ten years."

"Just shut up—and listen. I know about the accident. And Tocker's death—they made me mess with the probe."

"What are you trying to say?" Karl asked. He was motionless.

"They made me. If I didn't—" Daren coughed several times, nasty-sounding wet coughs. "There's this group—people who want to get rid of ISA and stop government military involvement. They want the private area, GSSC, to do the work instead."

"That's been true for a long time," Karl said. "A vocal minority have always wanted the private sector to be doing more, and the government just watching."

"Everyone talks about it, but—these people *do* something about it."

Spinning in the enclosed space of the sphere, Alis thought this must have been the most surrealistic experience she'd had while awake.

Daren coughed again and went on, his voice weaker. "They make accidents happen. Accidents that—make ISA look bad, so people will figure GSSC—the private sector—should be doing more."

"But why are you telling—" Karl suddenly drew in a breath deep enough to be heard over the suit radio.

"Exactly. The shuttle accident."

Alis's attention suddenly grew a thousand percent more focused.

Karl said nothing for a moment. "You're really—if that's true, I'm not the person you should confess to. Alis is right here with us."

"I suppose. But she's alive—she survived. Other people died in that accident. And I saw what you—went through on the *Ranger.*" Daren's coughs were interrupted by a pitiful cry of pain before he went on. "You didn't deserve all that."

For an instant, Alis wished she'd been one of the dead ones, not the living half-woman/half-monstrosity.

Karl said, "Those people were killed deliberately?"

"No, no, no. Just supposed to just try to make—ISA and the government look bad, not—" Another coughing spasm shook Daren's body. "I really don't feel very—"

Those were Daren's last words. Another coughing spasm ended in silence and relaxation. In a morbid moment, Alis figured those last words might not actually be all that rare, but they didn't seem to have been reported very often.

Robert had moved his helmet closer to Daren's and now he took a close look through Daren's faceplate. Alis felt a little numb as she watched Robert connect a shoulder-to-shoulder plug.

Moments later, Robert said, "I'm afraid he really is dead. He must have suffered massive internal injuries from the pressure those snakes, or whatever they were, applied."

"This just can't be happening," Lucy said softly.

"And now we are four," Robert added.

Alis had a sudden vision of Belinda's smashed body clinging to the probe pedestal. At times Alis hadn't cared whether she personally lived or died, but that didn't stop her from feeling guilty that a third of her team was now dead. She tried to tell herself the deaths weren't her fault, but somewhere in her gut, part of her didn't buy it.

And had Daren been telling the truth? Or was he just a good friend of Karl's who had chosen this opportunity to help out his buddy by telling lies that could probably never be disproved?

"You know," Robert said in a slightly stronger tone of voice, "I think Daren might have been right."

"What?" Karl said. "About the accident?"

"No. About us being screwed."

The sphere kept spinning, and the silence lengthened. And Alis kept thinking about the accident.

Lucy cleared her throat. "You know, Doc, I've been meaning to talk to you about something."

"And that is?" Robert said.

"I seem to recall that while I was dangling in that tunnel and things started happening where you guys were, you said something about one death being more tolerable than five."

"At the time—"

"I just want to say that if that's my reward for taking risks, you can find yourself another dummy. And you can kiss my—"

"That's enough," Alis said sharply. "We didn't leave you to die, Lucy. Suppose Robert had been the one at risk and you had to decide whether to let him die or risk the rest of our lives?"

"Robert's life, huh? Well, that changes things."

Alis guessed maybe she had made her point, but she still wasn't happy with how the exchange had gone.

In the following silence, Karl rolled Daren's limp body until the back of his suit was exposed, and Alis thought about the repeater again.

Karl carefully undid the protective cover, and slid the repeater out of its pouch. She saw the damage almost as soon as he must have. The repeater was in two pieces, obviously damaged beyond any hope of repair. The snake-like thing that had encircled Daren's chest had done more than just kill Daren. It might have killed them all. They could continue to hear transmissions from the *Ranger,* but they no longer had the means to transmit a strong enough signal to reach the ship.

Alis carefully kept the worry out of her voice. "Looks like we should have brought a spare, huh?"

Karl nodded, and the reflections on his helmet visor bobbed. "We don't have the tools to do anything with this. All we can do is hope that Captain Fernandez sticks to the plan and doesn't abandon us because we can't call him and prove we're still alive."

"I trust him. Of course, there may be limits to what he can do if we can't get back to the surface, or at least near it."

"I trust him, too. He's one of those people you just know will always do the right thing."

Funny, Alis thought. *That was one of the things a mutual friend had said about Karl while she was recovering aboard Tokyan Station.*

"This is a touchy subject," Karl said, "but we should consider transferring Daren's resources."

"His body isn't even cold yet," Lucy said, with more surprise than indignation.

"I know, but we might get to where we're going soon, and this might be the calm before the storm."

"I don't know that we even need his resources," Robert said. "If we're not out of here before we use up what we've got, I don't think I'll want to be alive."

"If you want to shut off your air at some point, that's your decision. If something unexpected happens, I'd rather have the choice."

"Go ahead then," Robert said.

Karl took his time with the transfer. No one objected to Karl taking it all because they each knew they could transfer it from Karl if anything happened to him, too. He popped a small dual-tube connector out of one sleeve and snapped it to Daren's biceps socket. Status lights that even Alis could see winked on and off as the remaining life-support supplies were sucked from Daren's suit into Karl's, and the non-recyclable remains from Karl's suit were off-loaded into Daren's suit. Suit designers had obviously been familiar with the risks that suit wearers were exposed to.

When Karl finished with that, he keyed in the override sequence three times and disconnected Daren's power unit. He fit the power unit into a pouch on one leg. At least in the tiny gravity here he'd have to deal only with the extra inertia.

Daren's suit was left dark. No helmet lamps. No green bar across the top of the helmet, and no reflections from Daren's eyes or face of the interior helmet status panel that was now dark, too.

Alis supposed that Daren's cooling body would soon start to freeze. She forced away the morbid thought that he'd be easier to carry that way.

What a place to die. What a place for your body to rest

for eternity. They'd probably never be able to get Daren's body back to the surface, even if they were alive to try.

"What were those snake-things anyway?" Lucy asked suddenly, as if she couldn't deal with the silence and the presence of Daren's body. "Were those the residents? Have we just added murder to breaking and entering?"

"Get serious," Robert said. "Those things weren't intelligent."

"Thanks for sharing that knowledge, O wise one," she said. "I didn't know you could evaluate alien entities so rapidly. As long as you're so far ahead of me, why don't you tell us where we're going now and where the real residents are?"

"How would I know?"

When Lucy failed to prod him again, Robert added, "This is obviously a huge place. Even if the residents are still alive and aware of us, it could take them a long time to reach us. They could be in suspended animation, and not even aware that anything's changed."

"And the snakes?"

"Maybe defense mechanisms. If Cantaloupe was designed to be self-repairing, there could be all sorts of ways it limits damage."

"So we could be the equivalent of invading germs in a human body?" Karl said. "Or foreign matter, like a splinter."

"Exactly." Robert actually sounded relieved that Karl had spoken. Alis supposed that to him anything was better than being attacked, especially by a woman. "The human body has a lot of defense mechanisms. Platelets help block an exit wound to keep blood from being lost. White blood corpuscles attack invading organisms. The body temperature rises in a controlled way to fight infection. The stomach regurgitates to cleanse itself of potential poisons. Tears help eject foreign matter. Kidneys filter out damaging waste."

For a moment Alis had difficulty resolving Robert's matter-of-fact tone with the spinning reality of their situation.

Karl said, "Okay, I can accept the idea that those snakes are some sort of defense mechanism—and that maybe implies the presence of other defense mechanisms. What's to say we're not inside a defense mechanism right now? We could be on our way to the equivalent of kidneys."

"Or the anus," Lucy said.

"Maybe. My gut says no, that this is something that we entered deliberately, something designed for a purpose other than defense, but I could be wrong."

Suddenly the sphere seemed to be shrinking, closing in from all sides. Alis blinked hard. The walls receded, and everything felt "normal" again.

Lucy said, "Okay, I admit that theory makes some sense. But couldn't those things have been pets—or parasites?"

"Could be. Could be something this large has all kinds of symbiotic relationships with special-purpose, er, things."

"Well, whatever this is," Karl said, "we've sure been moving for a long time. I'm worried that we're going a lot deeper into the interior."

"Maybe that's our best choice anyway," Alis said. "Getting back to the surface by brute force is an almost non-existent possibility now. If we can find the control center, or at least learn more about this thing, maybe we can learn enough to find our way out."

"That's a lot to accomplish in a couple of days," Lucy said.

"It's still a lot more realistic than, say, using our cutters to slice our way to the surface. By now we could be several kilometers below the surface. If we were to cut through, what, a meter a minute, we'd still be way too deep before we ran out of fuel. Assuming we didn't run into some more snakes or other defense mechanisms."

"You're not suggesting we give up, are you?" Robert asked.

Alis shook her head needlessly. "No. I'm just being realistic."

"She's right," Karl said. "Knowledge is the only way we're getting out of here. Either that or massive quantities of good luck."

"Well, we're really on a roll so far," Lucy said.

"In a matter of speaking," Robert said.

Lucy groaned. "That's grounds for justifiable homicide, don't you think?"

A painful silence followed, as Alis stared at Daren's lifeless suit. At times she had felt that she wanted to be dead, and if a handy, painless means had been at her disposal she might have done more than think about the possibility. But now, faced with the reality of Daren's body, she felt the decision would be a lot tougher. Wouldn't that just be a hideous irony if she didn't really feel positive about staying alive until she wound up in a situation that looked more and more like a sentence of death.

She took another food pill and gulp of water and checked her suit status again. Resource percentages were still well in the nineties. The recycling system made her more uncomfortable as time went by, but at least her life wasn't being threatened by that aspect of existence in a suit.

The foursome held their thoughts private. Alis closed her eyes not because they were tired—they were never tired—but to shut out the rest of the world.

A long time later, Lucy said, "What's happening?" At the same instant, Alis realized something had changed.

A wobble. She felt heavier, then lighter, in a repeating pattern. The oscillations grew stronger, cycling her from what felt like two gees at the heaviest. At the lightest, she worried about separating from the wall.

"I bet we're slowing down," Karl said. "We're nearing our destination."

The light-heavy oscillations kept up for several long minutes as Alis kept anticipating that at any time they would stop.
Finally, when she had just convinced herself that the cycle
would continue for a much longer time, the oscillations did
stop. The sphere resumed its uniform spin, evidenced by the
fact that everyone was still pinned to the perimeter. Gradually
she felt lighter and lighter, as though the spin were slowing to
a stop.

"I think we're here," Karl said as they all began to come
loose from the walls and float slowly toward the side of the
sphere that Daren's body rested on. The surface next to the side
of the sphere was no longer in motion.

"Is everyone ready to move?" Alis said.

No one said no, so she reached out and touched what
might have been the door, if this place acted the same as their
origination point.

The material dilated open, revealing surroundings dis-
tinctly different from where they had left the snakes behind.
Alis stepped out of the sphere.

For the first time, the interior of Cantaloupe felt big. They
stood on what vaguely resembled a long ledge, deep in a mountain chasm. Twenty meters away, a drop-off loomed, and rising far above them was an open slit. Except for random dark
blotches, the entire surface glowed faintly blue-green.

"Wow," Lucy said softly.

Thankful for small advantages, Alis noticed that the ledge
ramped up very slightly as it approached the drop-off. In the
low gravity and low friction, if the ledge tilted the other way,
it would be all too easy to slide off the ledge and into the abyss.
She couldn't see how deep it was yet, but her gut said it was
going to be very deep.

"Let's get Daren's body out here," Alis said before everyone had exited the sphere. She re-sheathed her knife, periph-
erally aware of the others doing the same thing. In the absence

of an immediate threat, a sharp knifepoint near a pressure suit was dangerous, too.

As Karl pulled Daren's body out, Alis tried to ignore how stiff the frozen suit was. She glanced away and found her gaze fixed on the far surface of the fissure.

The far wall was easy to see, probably no more than thirty meters away, but the fissure extended to the left and the right for what could have been kilometers before the sides met or the fissure curved. And the surfaces were so very regular, as if a truly enormous scalpel had sliced through, leaving just the tiny gap.

Alis let her helmet tip back and experienced a moment of vertigo as she looked up and focused on the dark hairline at the top of the chasm. For an instant her brain gave the wrong answer, saying she was looking down into the world's deepest ice crevasse. Especially in the ultra-light gravity, it was hard to prove she wasn't falling unless she held onto something.

Karl broke in on her thoughts. "My inertial navigation unit is back on the air. It says we're almost twelve kilometers below the surface and more than three kilometers sideways from the spot we entered."

"I get the same results," Lucy said.

Alis looked back at the smooth, off-color disk on the wall that now covered the point they had exited. Its coloring was just enough different that it was easy to see if you knew to look for it. Daren's suited body lay right next to it, marking the spot.

Karl lay down facing the chasm and started creeping slowly toward the lip.

She was curious, too, about what lay below, and a moment later she was creeping forward beside Karl. Someone braver, or more foolish, than the two of them might have walked to the edge of the ledge, but with the footing so slippery, she sure wasn't going to try.

Alis moved more slowly as she approached the edge.

When she looked down, her breath came more raggedly than it had when the elevator or whatever it was had started spinning. The chasm seemed to extend even deeper than it rose above them. She had never seen anything this deep.

She might well have flown higher than the distance from here to the bottom, but there was something different about being part of the scenery, touching the same surface that seemed to extend forever. The bottom looked even farther away than a planet's horizon, because the chasm went straight down without gradually curving out of sight. Low gravity or not, a drop would still give a fast ride, probably even faster than on Earth since here no atmosphere would limit the speed to terminal velocity.

When she had been a girl, the other kids liked to deliberately scare her when they caught her already a little scared. They'd grab her arm right as the killer on the screen ripped a knife out of the darkness, or they'd pop out of the bushes when she walked home in the dark. Matthew what's-his-name, the kid who used to complain whenever the teacher extended a due date for homework he already had ready, had come to school with an amazingly real-looking fake severed hand, and Alis was his first victim. Right now, if anyone had nudged her foot and then claimed, "Just kidding," she probably would have shoved the offender off the edge and said, "That's three dead. Who wants to be next?"

Beside her, Karl made a sound somewhere between a groan and a grunt. The inarticulate sound still managed to convey his sense of wonder.

Karl pulled back from the edge and so did Alis. Robert stood a couple of meters from the edge, close enough to get a sense that the crevice was deep, but not close enough to see how deep. Lucy stood near the wall near Daren's body.

"We're really screwed, aren't we?" Lucy said as Alis and Karl made it back.

"Things are going to be difficult," Alis said.

"Difficult? I just looked at the repeater. Karl's right; we're never going to be able to fix it. The *Ranger* can't hear us, they can't find us, and we're ten kilometers down. We can't climb this without tools." She gestured at the vertical cliff wall. "If we go back up in this thing, who's to say the snakes won't still be there?"

"If we even can go back," Robert added helpfully.

Alis was about to speak when Karl said, "Hey, so we die here. Look at the bright side. Our names will go down in infamy—they might even name this thing after us. We'll see things no one has ever seen before. We'll go places—we're already going places—no human has ever been before. We'll be heroes, as long as we don't start gibbering near the end. And if things don't go according to plan, and the totally unexpected happens, and we can find a way to work together without panicking, we might actually even get back alive. So why don't we just assume we're going to die and be pleasantly surprised if it doesn't work out that way?"

Robert said, "You know, you really are a moron."

Karl didn't give Alis a chance to squeeze in a word. "Sure, I am. Who else would be down here with you? All I'm saying is that Alis is right. We keep our heads and we try to find out as much as we can about this place, and maybe we'll be lucky. If not, at least we'll be a little smarter. But if we concentrate on how to brute-force our way back to the surface when the brute-force way is just going to run out the clock, we're not using our heads. We've got one realistic chance to get out of here—follow Alis."

Alis gave Karl high marks in leadership, especially for someone who was on the surface claiming to be a follower.

"Look," Lucy said. "I'm okay now. I'll be fine."

Robert just sighed.

Alis waited for the second thoughts, but none came. "All right. We need to do some exploring along this ledge, see if we spot any other—elevators or whatever these things are—or anything else. If we don't see any other way out of here, we can try going back to where we were. At a minimum, we'll have a lot of pictures of this place stored in memory."

She glanced at the other three. "And we're leaving Daren's body here. I don't like doing it, but we can't just drag him wherever we go. Does anyone care to say a few last words for Daren, and for Belinda?"

A long silence was broken by Karl, who knelt next to Daren's body and placed a gloved hand on his suit. "Daren, you and Belinda died a long way from home. You probably won't be part of the dust-to-dust cycle, except in our hearts. But you'll be there in everyone's memory. And you'll be part of our history, remembered in tales of explorers, stories that have been accumulating since Homer. And every year there will be a few more little boys and little girls who hear your story and say to themselves, 'Those were brave people. I wish I could be like them someday.' And a few of them will be."

Karl slowly got back to his feet and leaned his back against the cliff wall.

Alis was surprised to feel in Karl's voice such a strong sense of pride in two people she'd hardly known, and such strong sorrow at their loss. She realized that she hadn't felt this strongly when Daren and Belinda had actually died. More than that, she hadn't felt anything other than anger this strongly for a long time.

She wondered if Daren had been telling the truth. Was Karl really a victim just like she was? She didn't trust herself to speak for a long moment, and when she did, she simply said, "Thanks, Karl."

No one else spoke, and finally Alis said, "Let's see what's down this way." She led the way and let the others follow at their own pace.

The wide ledge stayed level, and its width stayed uniform. Alis kept to the cliff wall. Spotting the discolorations that might indicate the presence of additional passages was more difficult while she was close, but slipping over the edge seemed like a terrible way to die. The cliff wall texture remained unchanged, more like leather than rock.

The ledge followed a gradual sine wave against the broad ripples of the cliff wall. The wall on the other side of the chasm seemed to match the wall Alis walked next to, so the distance between the walls was always the same.

"What purpose could this chasm serve?" Lucy asked after they had been walking for several minutes.

Alis didn't have the vaguest idea, and apparently neither did anyone else, because no one even hazarded a guess. The chasm felt like a deliberate aspect of Cantaloupe, rather than the result of some bizarre accident, but even that was a total guess. The "elevator" stop seemed to be much like the one far above, and if the chasm hadn't been here, there would be no reason to have a stop here.

"A map update just came in," Karl said just about the same time Alis noticed the small indicator in her helmet display.

A second later, the captain's voice sounded in her helmet. "We've just loaded a new map for you. This one is actually starting to seem marginally useful. Start checking in on the hour if you can, so we can keep current on the data you're recording."

"I wish," Alis said to herself as she stopped walking. She shifted her gaze to the control spots on the helmet and brought up the latest map.

Most of the volume of the map was a uniform gray, but sections with higher density were darker, and sections with lower density were lighter. The gray-scale wasn't easy to distinguish, so she shifted the map into false color, so the neutral area turned green, while densest areas turned red and the lightest areas turned blue. Her suit's navigation unit supplied a blinking white dot to show their current position.

"Wow," Lucy said, "I can see the chasm, kind of."

Alis saw what she meant. The blinking "you are here" dot overlapped a shadowy blue plane in the display. She shifted perspective a few times. The chasm seemed to reach almost to the surface, and it extended almost halfway to the core. About 150 degrees away, almost opposite them on the other side of Cantaloupe, a similar blue plane showed in the display. The blinking dot said they were almost halfway down the wedge-shaped plane, which was narrower near the core.

The core itself showed as a sphere-like volume containing a feathering of both red and blue. Farther out, at a point between the two matching planes, was the hint of something large and vaguely dumbbell-shaped. Above it was a trio of fainter planes forming a triangular volume. The entire shell of Cantaloupe seemed faintly darker than the rest of the sphere.

In seemingly random places were threads so faint that they could have been no more real than the canals of Mars had been. Many of them were roughly horizontal, but a large number ran at steep diagonals.

A faint vertical line, so faint it was on the verge of imagination, extending downward from the surface, showed the shaft they had come down. In a magnified view, a tiny red dot showed what was probably the large probe they had found. A diagonal line so faint that it showed only disconnected segments led from a spot below the probe to a spot very near the blinking dot. Another ultra-thin line led downward at about a forty-five-degree angle from their current position, pointing toward a hazy-looking section that held some variations in density.

Alis felt comforted by the display. They were just as far below the surface as they had been five minutes ago, but she no longer felt quite so stranded.

Robert said, "It looks like there are passages leading down from the elevator stop here and back up. Any theories as to how to tell it we want to go back up?"

"I didn't see anything remotely like controls," Karl said.

"It could be we don't have any choice. The passages might be more like a grand tour mechanism than elevators."

They resumed walking as Alis contemplated the possibility that the only way open to them now was down.

"That stuff Daren said before he died," Lucy said. "What do you think about that? Karl?" What had started to be an open question was focused on Karl just a second after she completed the question.

After a moment Karl said, "I can't deny the appeal of an explanation that says I wasn't the incompetent jerk everyone decided I was."

"But do you believe it?"

"Not enough evidence. But it would help explain what sure seemed unlikely—having a shuttle hit the station right during an exercise designed to test reactions for a shuttle impact. And there's certainly precedent for dirty tricks between GSSC and ISA."

"You don't buy that old conspiracy crap, do you?" Alis said. Despite the convincing nature of Daren's dying words, if he had told the truth, then she had been persecuting an innocent man. And her condition had been the result of a deliberate act of destruction.

"You mean the old NASA stuff?" Robert said. "That isn't what I'd call proven information."

"What old NASA stuff?" Lucy asked.

Karl said, "Back in the early twenty-first. There was a whole series of congressional hearings because some people claimed that a series of NASA disasters were the deliberate result of actions taken by a private group that wanted the space program taken away from NASA and put directly into private industry's hands. They claimed a whole list of disasters were not accidents but, in fact, sabotage."

"Stuff like what?"

"Lots of different stuff. *Apollo 13,* a shuttle explosion, the first and second Hubble telescopes, a launchpad fire, a space

station gas leak, a Mars probe that got almost all the way before blowing up. I don't remember the whole list."

"You think people would really do stuff like that?"

"People have done a lot worse," Karl said. "I've seen
Robert eat with his mouth open."

"But do you think your accident was really set up?"

"I don't know. All I can say is that it wasn't the result of
negligence."

"So you say," said Alis.

"So I say," Karl said tiredly.

The group walked another thirty or forty meters. Alis
veered slightly closer to the chasm, then pulled back.

"Oh, I had an interesting thought," Robert said.

"Get serious," said Karl.

"If we buy Daren's story, it follows that maybe he was also
supposed to sabotage the mission. So what's to say there
couldn't be *two* saboteurs?"

"Just the odds. If there really is a conspiracy to discredit
ISA, the more people in on it, the more likely someone would
have already blown the whistle."

"Sure, that's just what *they* would say."

"Wow," said Lucy, "are we getting a little paranoid here?"

"That's *also* what—"

"Robert, give it up," Karl said. "Alis was the biggest living victim of the 'accident.' I was the second biggest. You
know whether you're a saboteur or not, and that just leaves
Lucy."

"Right," Robert said. "They'd hardly trust the secret to
a woman."

"What's that supposed to mean?" asked Lucy irritably.

"No," Karl said. "I didn't mean that. I meant Lucy's
mother is a honcho at ISA. It's not very likely they'd approach
Lucy in the first place, even if she were receptive."

"A honcho? Oh, right, I knew that." Robert's transpar-
ent re-evaluation of how to treat Lucy was so unsubtle that Alis

almost laughed out loud. "But what kind of honcho? I seem to have forgotten."

"A sector director, no less."

Lucy said, "So, Karl. Is that why you've been so nice to me?"

"Oh, you caught me. That's why I was always so rude to Daren and Belinda. They didn't have any important relatives."

"Sorry, that *was* kind of stupid of me."

"You're entitled. You do have a powerful mother after all."

"Hey, I said I was sorry."

"I'm sorry, too." Karl hesitated. "I'm just tired of people interpreting my actions in the worst possible light. Could we have a cease-fire from being judgmental while we're down here?"

"Sounds fair to me," Lucy said.

To Alis's relief, Robert let the conversation drop. She felt a little warm despite the cool air flowing through her suit and helmet. Seconds later, to keep the conversation from drifting back, she said, "I still don't have even a guess as to what purpose this chasm serves."

No one else had any ideas they cared to put forth. Alis stopped on the next outward bend of the ledge and blinked her eyes into telephoto mode. Ahead, the ripples of the ledge against the cliff wall pulled closer to her, and she could see maybe a hundred back-and-forth ripples. For as far as she could see, the ledge looked the same as here.

No one complained when she gave the order to retrace their steps.

Daren's body provided a grim position marker that let them know when they had reached the transport mechanism.

Alis moved toward the large circle on the wall next to Daren's body. "I've seen enough of this place. I think it's time to see whether this takes us still deeper, or if the snakes are still where we left them."

11 ▪ KELOID

Karl was the last one into the transport mechanism. He really didn't like the idea of just leaving Daren's body on the ledge next to the chasm, but he knew Alis was right. They couldn't lug him along with them. He made Daren a silent promise that he'd come back if he could. He hoped he'd be alive to carry it through.

He pulled himself far enough into the transport pod that the circular covering over the entrance started spreading back over the opening. Seconds later the small gap in the center closed completely.

For a moment, nothing happened, but then, as before, the pod again began to rotate faster and faster, creating its own artificial gravitational field around the perimeter. Karl crawled to a more comfortable position and settled in for the ride.

Robert said, "I think we're going down again."

Karl felt the smooth pressure against the pod wall and came to the same conclusion. If they were headed upward, or even staying in the same horizontal plane, there should be a bumpiness to the pressure, or there should be a pressure at an angle to the fake gravity. He wasn't sure whether going farther down was good or bad. Alis's theory about the key to getting out being more knowledge of the interior sounded sane, but at the same time it had the feel of reaching farther down into the piranha tank to retrieve a dropped hamburger.

"Move your foot, would you, Robert?" Lucy shifted herself into a more comfortable position. When she finished, the four of them ringed the pod's equatorial perimeter. "It's still possible this mechanism isn't meant to be an elevator, but a grand tour—a programmed path from A to B to C. I don't see anything that looks like a control panel."

Karl said to Alis, "Have you scanned the area in infrared and UV in case there is some information here but not in the spectrum our eyes pick up?"

"Sure, but there's nothing." A second later she added, "How much do you know about my eyes?"

"Enough to know I'd like a pair."

Alis snorted.

"What?"

"You'd like your eyes ripped out and replaced by instrumentation? To become more like a machine than a human being?"

Karl hesitated. "You say that like it's a bad thing."

"Pretty flip for someone who hasn't been there."

"All right. Let's cut the flip. You've now got attractive eyes that, I assume, never get tired, allow you to see at great distance and ultra close up. You can see in infrared and ultraviolet when you choose to. On the surface, yes, that sounds like a good thing."

"Attractive? Maybe the way wigs look attractive to you."

"I don't honestly think anyone who didn't know your

background would suspect your eyes aren't original equipment."

"You make them sound like an option on a car."

"In a sense they are."

"You don't know what you're talking about."

"You have an artificial heart, right?"

"So?"

"So, what if I told you Robert has one, too?"

"Really? No, I didn't know that."

Robert said, "You didn't know it because it isn't true."

"Right," Karl said. "But don't you see? You can't tell. Parts are parts. It doesn't matter whether you have original equipment or replacement parts." Karl checked his inertial navigation display, but again it refused to tell him anything other than the fact that it was so busy computing updates that it couldn't tell him whether they were rising or falling.

"So I'm the only one with a new heart. You're just idly speculating."

"What was the favorite birthday present you had when you were a kid?"

"A bicycle. A green one with a little *whoosh* noisemaker so it sounded like a hovercraft. So?"

"So that's who you are."

"You've completely lost me."

"If you had said 'the laser gun' or 'the pink party dress' you'd be someone else. You might be Robert."

Robert said, "Ha ha. I would have said 'the telescope.' "

"Oh, that's insightful," Alis said. "That one question determines my entire personality?"

"No. But add a few thousand more questions like it, or a million questions like it, and you begin to home in on who you really are. You're not 'standard woman with new eyes, heart, and legs.' You're a woman who got into ISA by ranking number one in her class during almost every year of school. A woman who grew up in west Texas and saw her father die in an act of random senseless violence when she was young. You're a—"

"How do you know all that?"

"After the accident, you were in the news a lot, even if you weren't aware of it, and I had a reason to watch the news. All I'm saying is the fact that you've got new eyes and a new heart doesn't change who you are. I don't mean to belittle the damage, or to say it hasn't changed you at all. I'm just saying you're not *defined* by those things any more than I'm defined by having a replacement tooth."

"Oh, please," Alis said. "New eyes are a bit more intrusive than a new tooth."

"I agree. I'm just saying the fact that you've got new eyes and a new heart doesn't make you a robot."

"I didn't say that."

"I know. I sometimes exaggerate to make a point, like George Bernard Shaw and his offer to a woman."

"So you see things as black and white, no shades of gray?"

Karl thought a moment. "Maybe I see the same things you do, but I draw different conclusions. Reasonable people can do that."

"It sounded more like you were trying to convince me to change my point of view."

"Maybe I was, unconsciously. I didn't mean to. So, if someone knocked on the door and said, 'Excuse me, but you can have your original eyes back in fully working condition if you like,' you'd say, 'Yes'?"

"Well, of course—" Alis suddenly fell silent.

"Or maybe you'd have to think about it."

Since the artificial gravity was uniform, Karl couldn't tell how many times the pod spun before Alis answered, but he guessed it must have been five or six revolutions.

"You know, I thought I knew the answer to that."

"Well," Robert said. "I wish my eyes weren't tired right now. If this thing takes a lot longer, I'm going to take a nap."

"What I really wanted was a trip to Earth," Lucy said suddenly.

"You've never been down?" Alis asked.

"No. My mother kept talking about it, but we never did it."

Karl said, "I would have thought with a mother as far up the ladder as yours, you would have been down several times."

"You'd be surprised at how busy she always was," Lucy said with a subtle tone of sadness that let Alis mentally hear her complete the sentence with, "too busy for me anyway."

Alis said, "We should probably all take a little while to relax. This is probably the safest place we've found, and we're obviously not getting back out of here on schedule."

Karl let the silence lengthen. The interior of the pad, with the darkness cut by only the four pairs of helmet lamps, was a surreal nest of miners. His eyes were tired, too, and he let them close.

Alis's anger formed a pretty effective barrier, but Karl still found her an intriguing person, an appealing woman who had entered an altered state and still hadn't come out the other side. He wondered what she would be like when she emerged, and he wondered if he would have held up as well as she had.

He was independent enough that he liked to make his own decisions. On rare occasions he had decided to do something different than he might have just because someone else had told him what to do. Sometimes he could admit to himself that, in the absence of the other person's input, he would have done exactly what was requested anyway. Perhaps Alis was the same. Perhaps if someone had asked her ahead of time if she'd rather have a heart that would run forever or her old one, she would have chosen the new heart, but when presented with a fait accompli she resented not having been able to make the decision on her own.

He relaxed in the moderate gravity, and his thoughts drifted from Alis back to what Daren had said.

He would certainly never know the truth about the accident. There were only so many people who would die in his presence, and if a modern conspiracy had been held such a tight secret that he had never heard a whisper about it, there was no chance of him stumbling onto more information about it, but it did ease his pain a little. And he could sense a subtle shift in Alis, a hesitation that hadn't been there before, a tiny chink in the armor. She had talked with him more as one person to another just now than she ever had before.

He supposed it would be just his luck to finally break through that facade and make peace with her just before they all died. When he was a child, he'd nursed a cat injured by a car back to apparent good health, only to see it contract one of the new virus mutations that killed it in less than a week. That the vet had a new vaccination available six months later was little consolation. That wouldn't be any more useful than the *Ranger* locating them a week after they ran out of air.

He tried to force his thoughts into a more positive mode. He hated the part of him that constantly ran the worst-case scenarios for his current situation, whether the scenarios dealt with the distance out of the solar system a scout ship might track them before it had to turn around or run out of resources, or they dealt with how long it would take him to die from nitrogen narcosis if he came up too fast from a dive.

Despite the ease with which the worst-case scenario could happen, he told himself everything would work out just fine. Everything. But then he thought about Belinda and Daren again.

Karl shut his eyes tighter and tried to think of nothing at all. After a time his eyes relaxed, and he was more successful.

Someone was shaking Karl awake, or so it seemed at first.

He opened his eyes. Lucy was stretching her arms as if

she'd just awakened. They were all still inside the rotating pod, and no one was touching Karl.

The vibration that had brought him awake was the same bumpy feeling that had signaled the end of the first leg of the pod trip. They must be slowing down.

Sure enough. Several minutes later, the pod finally slowed to a halt that for a moment resulted in all four of them bumping into each other and bouncing around the center of the pod.

Robert was able to reach the pod opening first. The cover dilated all the way open.

Beyond the opening was another tunnel, this one with more color in its walls and a higher degree of luminescence. The walls glowed with a reddish hue, and the material seemed light-sensitive. The path of Karl's helmet lamps on the surface left a trail of brighter red that slowly faded back to normal, as if he were sweeping an electron beam across the business end of an ultra-slow cathode ray tube. One at a time they stepped into the tunnel.

The footing seemed even more tenuous than before. They each lost their footing trying to make their way down the gentle slope of the tunnel wall to the rounded bottom.

Karl took a look at his inertial navigation display. "We're much farther down, and that's why we're even lighter."

"We're lighter?" Lucy said. She jumped very gingerly, not much more energetically than just flexing her feet so her toes pressed on the ground, and she hit the ceiling, protecting her helmet with her outstretched hands. She fell back awkwardly. "Ulp, you're right."

"Lighter why?" Robert asked.

"Because the gravity here is a function of just the mass that's deeper than we are." Before Robert could ask the next question, Karl added, "The mass that's farther out than we are just cancels itself out from a gravitational point of view. The mass right over our heads is pulling us up the strongest, but all the other mass is pulling us down slightly, and the math works out that the sum is zero."

"So at the center there's no gravity?"

"Right. If you want to be picky about it, there is a gravitational field at the center, but it's the sum of being pulled equally in every direction, so you couldn't tell it from zero gee."

This tunnel seemed more regular than the others Karl had seen. It, too, was circular, but almost perfectly round, about three meters in diameter, and the walls seemed smoother and more uniform than the previous tunnels. The tunnel gently curved for the whole visible length, giving the impression that it formed a very large horizontal ring. The circular opening they had just come through was a dark brown. Unlike the doorway to the transport pod at the chasm, this one stood out visually, nearly impossible to miss.

Karl checked his internal navigation unit as the others stretched their legs and looked around. They were easily a third of the way to Cantaloupe's core. He tried not to think about how fast they were headed toward Earth and the sun, and therefore how fast they would soon be headed out the other side of the solar system.

By silent consensus they turned to the right and started walking single file along the tunnel floor, Alis in front. Just twenty or thirty meters away was another circular discoloration on the tunnel wall, this one on their left, on the inside of the ring, on the opposite side of the tunnel from the transport pod that had brought them here. The large circle sported a pattern of maybe a hundred concentric circles, making it hard to mistake for the plain circle covering the transport pod.

With his visor controls, Karl brought up the latest interior map overlaid with their current position. They had indeed arrived at the position that looked blotchy on the display, and when Karl blew up the display it showed them currently at the edge of the blotchy area, which looked vaguely doughnut-shaped. He blew up the display still more, but what looked a little vague at one resolution looked more like wispy, indistinct clouds at the next.

"The interesting area may be that way," Alis said, pointing to their left, and the inside of the ring, voicing the same conclusion Karl had just reached. "But let's keep going. I want to see if there are any other ways in, assuming this—" she gestured at the circle "—is a way in."

"I wonder," Lucy said, "if this really is a huge starship, maybe we're finally getting nearer the living quarters."

"I hope you're all safe," Captain Fernandez's voice said abruptly in Karl's helmet. "I haven't heard you check in recently, but I just want you to know I'm assuming that simply means the repeater has failed completely. If you can still communicate with the ship, or more precisely if you can still talk to the ship, let me know as soon as it's convenient. We're probably a few hours from the arrival of the GSSC ships carrying the deflection explosives, and the more recently I've heard from you—to prove you're still alive—the better ammunition I have to postpone any action."

When it was obvious that Captain Fernandez had said all he was going to say, Robert said, "That's just great. If those are GSSC ships and it's really true that some people within GSSC want to make ISA look bad, what better way than to be the saviors who knock Cantaloupe off course? And if we're still inside and wind up dead, then *we* look bad for screwing up the mission."

Karl thought Lucy was going to take the same side, but she surprised him.

"Robert, do you lie awake worrying about whether a patient will die on your next shift, or if an asteroid will hit a space station?"

"I fail to see the connection."

"You worry too much. About things we can't control."

"And you never think any farther ahead than whether to whine or moan?"

"That's enough," Alis said, and the conversation stopped just as Lucy had sucked in a load of air.

Karl actually felt a bit of sympathy with Robert on this one. The same potential ISA/GSSC conflict had occurred to him, too, and Karl himself had certainly been known to worry about things beyond his control. He envied people who could focus only on what was changeable, but he wasn't wired that way.

Ahead on the left was another of the large circles filled with a cut tree-trunk set of concentric rings. Karl thought they had come about ninety degrees around the ring, but he hadn't paid close enough attention to be certain.

Alis stopped in front of the circle. "I want to take a look through there. My map display makes it seem like this isn't a transportation pod, but a doorway."

No one voiced any nervousness about the plan.

Alis jumped for the circle and fell just a little short. She recovered her balance and tried again. This time she touched the circle before she fell back.

Sure enough, the circle opened. From Karl's vantage point, he couldn't see what was on the other side, except darkness. The circle stayed open for five or ten seconds and then slowly began to close.

Alis jumped again and caught the edge of the circle before it had completely closed. It started back open. She hung on, and a couple of seconds later it had opened wide enough to admit her. She stood just on the other side of the circle, holding it open, and said, "Next?"

Robert, then Lucy, then Karl jumped, one at a time pulling themselves through the circular opening.

Beyond the circle was darkness like the transport pod, but the volume wasn't a sphere. Instead it was another round tun-

nel that went perhaps ten meters before ending with another
large circular covering, the same size as the entrance.

Rather than let the circular opening close, Alis held it
open. "Karl, see if the other end opens."

Karl moved past Lucy and Robert to the far end of the
short, dark tunnel. He pressed on the circle at the far end.
Nothing happened.

"Maybe it's locked," Robert said.

"Or broken," Lucy added.

"Or this is an air lock," Karl said. The words "air lock"
sounded with an echo as Alis said the same words at almost
the same time.

Alis let the entrance close. "If something goes wrong, we
can always cut ourselves out of here."

As the entrance opening shrunk to a pinhole, Karl hoped
she was right.

At least they were right about it being an air lock, or a
similar double-door interlock. As soon as the entrance was
closed, a touch on the far surface opened the circle.

Karl didn't have any sense of air in motion. He put his
gloved hand near the opening while it was still fairly small and
felt no push that might indicate incoming atmosphere.

Karl gave it another long moment before he said, "My
suit's still reading well under a tenth of an atmosphere, so I'm
not sure why there needs to be an air lock."

Behind him Robert said, "There's more than one rationale
for interlocked doors. Decontamination stations, for instance."

"Well, I'm guessing this isn't the crew's quarters," Karl
said slowly, once the door had dilated far enough to let him
see what was on the other side.

"I'd say that's a safe bet," Alis said softly.

Karl walked through the doorway and stopped, standing
upright on a flat brown surface that extended at least a few
hundred meters before it met the far wall. The surface seemed
circular, as if it were, in fact, bounded by the circular tunnel

just outside. The floor wasn't solid, though. Like an enormous shower drain, the surface was broken by a regular series of holes each about a meter wide. In what was probably the center of the area was a thick vertical column.

The ceiling was like a different magnification of the same view. The surface of the ceiling was a few meters over their heads, but it, too, was regularly perforated by large holes, larger than the ones in the floor. The ceiling holes might have been two meters across.

Karl moved farther out on the floor and peered down one of the closest holes. The surface of the floor was about as thick as his hand. Through the round hole in the floor he could see a surface about two meters below, that one also perforated by round holes, offset from the ones in the surface he stood on. Gauging the distance and dimensions left room for error, but the holes in the lower level floor seemed to be closer together and only about three-quarters of a meter wide.

Robert whistled. "I was going to say it goes without saying that the whole interior of this place is bizarre, but I guess it does need to be said. This place is crazy."

Karl glanced back and saw that the other three had fanned out, each looking through a hole in the floor or ceiling. "I want to jump up a level and see what it looks like. Any objections?"

"Go for it," Alis said. A different leader might have said, "Be careful," and Karl wasn't sure exactly what to read into her speech.

"Right. I'll be careful." Karl tried to gauge how hard to jump.

"That's okay," Robert said.

Karl's jump actually fell a little short, and he wound up hanging from the lip of the hole in the ceiling. He'd been so careful not to jump too high in the low gravity, he guessed wrong. Fortunately, getting the rest of the way up to the next level was simply a matter of applying a forceful two-handed grip to the surface and twisting his body into an arc that landed him gently on the flat surface next to the hole.

He carefully got to his feet. This level was like the one below in that the surface formed a very large circle with a thick vertical column running upward through the center.

He looked up and his helmet lamps shone through more round cutouts in the ceiling, these even larger than the one he had come through. The beam illuminated a level above that one, and he spotted the edge of an even larger hole in that level.

Karl moved back to the hole he'd come through. He looked down and made sure none of his teammates stood under him, and levered himself back into a position where he hung from the lip of the hole. He let go and when he lightly hit the floor, he crumpled as well as he could, to keep from bouncing. If he explored the level below, he wanted it to be his deliberate choice, not the result of bouncing around until he fell through one of the holes in the floor.

"It seems the levels continue, with bigger and bigger holes," he said.

Robert said, "No, really?"

Karl ignored him. "I'd like to go down to the next level."

"Not yet," Alis said. "Let's check out the center first."

The foursome began walking toward the fat column in the center of the area, jogging from side to side to avoid the holes in the floor. Karl felt like a bug in some giant cheese grater. At least the holes in successive levels were staggered, so a misstep would result in a fall of only one level.

"Is anyone else getting a bad feeling about this?" Lucy asked.

Karl was, but he said nothing. This whole place gave him a bad feeling.

As they walked cautiously, Karl experienced a moment where suddenly nothing in the universe seemed real, this place especially, and as quickly as it had come, it was gone. He blinked, and moved forward, wishing the sensation had been valid, that his surroundings were merely the product of his expectations, and that by changing his mind about what he expected to see he could be instantly back aboard the *Ranger,* safe and sound and ready for a nap. Apparently that wasn't meant to be.

The view diagonally down through the next hole was something like witnessing a perfect planetary alignment. From where he stood, the hole in the floor below was totally visible through the hole in this floor. Centered in that lower hole was a view of a slightly smaller hole in the next level down, followed by the lined-up image of the level below, and the level below that. The successively smaller holes seemed to go on forever until the farthest hole was nothing but a dot.

Karl looked up and behind him, and the opposite view of the diagonal lineup looked equally strange. The hole two levels above, since it was both larger and farther away than the nearest hole, looked about the same size, forming just a slightly lit fringe around the hole. The pattern continued, forming a round tunnel with a perspective error, since it didn't shrink to a distant point but instead seemed to be a constant-diameter tunnel. Karl told himself he wasn't looking at a tunnel, but instead seeing a long cone, but it still felt like an arcade optical illusion. His light wasn't bright enough to reflect from the far end, and the darkness at the center gave him a feeling of looking all the way to the surface of Cantaloupe.

As they came nearer to the vertical cylinder at the center of the area, markings on the cylinder wall became visible. Fine spiral lines wound up or down, depending on your point of view. The pitch was narrow, as if they were looking at a surface of a bolt.

As a group, they walked around the perimeter of the cylinder. Karl estimated it was several meters in diameter.

Robert said, "I'd feel better if we got out of here. This definitely isn't the crew's quarters."

"I agree," Alis said. "And we've got plenty of video now. Let's head back to the same door we came in."

The instant she quit speaking, the surface of the cylinder was suddenly illuminated, as if a light had switched on inside it. A second later it went dark again, and then the cycle kept repeating. Bright—dark—bright—dark.

"Let's move," Alis said.

The group had covered less than a third of the distance when Karl stopped. He waited for his body to settle down in the low gee. "You feel that? Vibration." The floor under his feet swayed lightly, the sensation something like standing on a sandy beach in an earthquake. Behind him the cylinder was still flashing on and off.

"Yeah," Alis said a moment later. "Probably all the more reason to get out of here."

The group kept moving for the distant doorway, now with a stronger sense of urgency.

In the light gravity, most of the time Karl's feet didn't touch the surface, but in each brief footstep, the vibration seemed more pronounced. He moved faster, worried about making a misstep and falling through one of the holes, but more nervous about what the flashing column and the rumbling meant.

They were about halfway to the door when in the middle of one of Karl's strides he looked up. His helmet lamps flashed through one of the overhead holes and he was sure something was moving up there. And then the image was gone and he was past the point where he could see. "I thought I saw some—"

Suddenly green liquid began pouring from an overhead hole in front of them. "Pouring" made it sound faster than it really seemed. The liquid started oozing through the hole. The liquid appeared runny rather than highly viscous, but in the low gravity it still just oozed, falling at a leisurely pace.

"What's that?" Lucy cried.

"Oh, crap," said Robert.

Karl tried to move to avoid it, but traction was worse than sock feet on a slick floor. As he maneuvered, he spotted more liquid coming out of yet more holes in the ceiling. For a morbid second he wondered if, should anyone ever find their bodies, their last words would be studied like black box recordings for pilots. Abruptly self-conscious, he said nothing.

The liquid started oozing from almost every hole in the ceiling. Karl thought about the hole-sealing fluid they had encountered nearer the surface. He shuddered.

"Keep going," yelled Alis. "We've got to get out."

Karl was in total agreement, but the liquid came faster and faster, the volume increasing steadily.

Lucy said, "I hate this goddamn job."

The surface underfoot turned even more slippery, and Karl went down, bouncing and sliding on his back. For a moment he thought he'd stop before getting too close to the lip of one of the holes. He was wrong.

He started slipping over the edge as more green liquid pooled around him and slopped over the edge of the hole. He couldn't get any grip. He was falling.

A hand grabbed his arm.

Alis said, "Don't fall, damnit." Her hand held him place for an eternal moment, and then she, too, started to slip toward the edge. "Oh, no!"

A boulder bounced off Karl's back as he fell. At first he thought it was just Alis's body smashing into his, but in the twisting glare of his helmet lamps, a huge green half-meter-wide ball bounced past him and fell through a hole in the next level down.

Karl hit the floor and bounced. Alis's grip came loose, and they were both sloshed through a hole in the next level down.

Karl said, "Thanks anyway!"

He was suddenly immensely grateful that the size of the holes decreased as he fell deeper and deeper, and he was sloshed first one way, then another by a strengthening current of green goo mixed with round balls no bigger than his head, all the way up to balls a half-meter across. The only thing that kept him alive was that they seemed to have a density closer to that of croutons than that of ball bearings.

Karl could hear an almost steady stream of groans and grunts and "oofs" as the others were swept along by this bizarre torrent. His faceplate was abruptly smeared with green goo, and he couldn't see anything clearly. Fortunately, his helmet lamps were outside the faceplate, or else he would have been able to see nothing but the readouts inside his helmet and the reflection of his face. As it was, he could make out indistinct shapes, as if someone had smeared a lot of green petroleum jelly over his faceplate.

He hit another level and slid sideways. Another hole. He felt himself sliding over the edge. Slipping. He stretched out his legs and spread his arms.

This hole was significantly smaller than the ones above. His feet touched the other side. For a second he thought he'd be able to keep from falling deeper, but something slammed into his back and pushed him though. Simultaneously, an "oof" that sounded like Lucy's voice came through the suit radio.

He fell again, this time landing on the lip of another hole, and he went through it before he could try to grab the edge.

Karl tumbled as he fell, buffeted by the large balls in the soupy mess. He hit. Pain spiked through one leg, and he gasped. He had fallen on his back with one leg partly bent under him.

He grabbed for anything he could reach and felt nothing but more fluid splashing down. The fluid thickened, and suddenly he was whisked out of control like a leaf in a whirlpool. Down another hole. At least the pain in his leg was subsiding. Maybe it wasn't broken after all.

He landed on another surface and for the first time suddenly managed to get a grip on something, the edge of another hole. His body stretched prone, facedown on the surface, with his hands just reaching the lip of a hole.

He held tight and spread his feet. A toe slipped over the lip of another hole. Instantly he pulled his toes forward, to try to hook himself in place. He moved his other foot next to the one hooked over the lip, and it found purchase, too. As the green fluid continued pouring over him, he shifted position slightly, now with both feet hooked over the lip of a hole, and his outstretched hands gripping the lip of another hole.

For the first time in minutes he felt secure. Liquid and smaller irregular balls kept cascading over him, forcing him from side to side, but he was able to keep his position.

The flow increased, and for a while he felt virtually submerged in the messy fluid. For the first time, he was again able to form a semblance of rational thought. This liquid obviously couldn't be water-based, given the cold. Perhaps a methane base; it would be a liquid at this temperature.

And what had they stepped into? Was this a tiny part of a monstrously large kitchen or heating system or maybe a part of the system that supplied nutrients to the body of Cantaloupe? If Cantaloupe was, in fact, an organic spacecraft, he supposed that implied the need to provide tissue with the supplies it required to survive or repair itself.

The flow continued with no indication of lessening. Karl's arms and legs grew stiff with the constant tension of trying to hold himself in place, but the pain in his leg kept gradually decreasing, and soon he was convinced that he might have sprained some muscles but hadn't broken the leg. One of the great things about low gee was that he'd still be able to get around, even with a bad sprain.

On top of the other pain, though, he felt colder and colder. His suit was extremely well insulated, but the demands placed on his suit's fusion pack and the heating coils had to be a lot rougher than that in the design envelope. At one point he was sure he saw some of the fluid bubbling as the heat from his visor sent it to the boiling point.

Just as Karl concluded the fluid flow could last for hours or days, it started to diminish.

"What is this crap, anyway?" Robert's voice said suddenly.

"Rhetorical question, right?" Karl said.

"I'm all right, too," Alis said.

"I think I survived," Lucy said.

From their voices alone Karl had no way to tell if they were all within a few meters of each other, or if they'd been separated by a kilometer. As long as they were within nominal range, error-checking transceivers made sure voice transmissions were clear and complete.

The fluid flow kept diminishing. Karl looked around, trying to see as much as he could despite the smeared view through his faceplate. In his limited sample area, it seemed that one hole out of ten was plugged by a round boulder-like object slightly bigger than it. With a forearm he tried to wipe his faceplate clean. The result was mostly just further smearing of the green goop, but the effort did clear a strip in front of his eyes, and he peered through there, like an old-time car driver in a mud storm with defective windshield wipers.

Karl ran a thorough suit diagnostic, and it agreed with the routine background check. His suit was still safe.

"We need to regroup," Alis said. "And then get the hell out of here."

The flow had diminished to the point that it was more like dripping, with one persistent drip falling softly in the middle of Karl's back.

He was just about to release his grip and get up when he felt his body begin to move sideways.

"What's going on now?" Robert asked.

"Oh, no!" Lucy cried. Her voice started to trail off, but then it ended abruptly with another, "Oof!"

The surface Karl clung to was moving, beginning to push him sideways as it accelerated. Karl tightened his grip. Seconds later the speed had increased to the point that most of the force he felt was on his outstretched arms. He was in an enormous centrifuge, his hands nearest the column in the center, which had to form the rotation axis.

The whole situation was so outrageous that he lost several seconds of decision-making time. He could let go and get to the edge, where, if the walls were stationary, he might be safe. But if the walls moved along with the rotating floors, he'd be at the point of maximum force, and there was no guarantee that the force would be within his limits.

He could hang on, and hope that the force didn't increase beyond his ability to hold on, because at that point he'd be flung at the wall at a far faster rate than if he'd let go immediately.

In the end, he hung on. By the time he'd thought through the choices, he had only the hanging-on choice left.

From the sound of her grunts and groans, Lucy hadn't had a choice. She must have been tumbling toward the wall.

The tension on his arms increased slowly. His hands began to hurt. A boulder-like ball dislodged from a hole between him and the axis bounced past him, its low mass being the only reason it didn't kill him when it hit his helmet. As it was, it just made his ears ring.

Lucy fell silent, and the silence was far more threatening than her cries of pain.

Another boulder bounced past Karl. He craned his head up, worried that that would make him a bigger target but wanting to see what else might be on the way.

Gooey green fluid moved toward him and past him as if blown by a silent gale. He could feel no sensation at all of spinning, despite knowing that had to be what was happening. The murky view through his smeared faceplate slowly began to clear as the artificial gravity and surface tension proved strong enough to counteract adhesion. The view toward the cylinder at the center of the huge area now seemed a lot higher than he was, as his body's reaction to the outward force tried to trick his brain into thinking the whole plane had tilted and gravity had increased a hundredfold. Intellect told those false reactions to shut up, but it was still difficult to entirely disconnect them, especially when the result of letting go would be the same as it would be if his fooled perceptions were accurate: a long fall into darkness.

Streamers of green fluid kept swishing through the fringes of the area illuminated by Karl's helmet lamps, as if little green creatures were running for their lives.

His hands ached. A dark spot formed in front of his face, and for an instant Karl thought this was the end, that he was about to black out and lose his grip and go spinning into the distant wall. Seconds later he could still see, and he was still conscious.

The pressure on his hands actually seemed to lessen, and he worried this was some symptom like hypothermia tricking the victim into feeling warm. What a cruel trick.

But it didn't seem to be a trick. The pressure genuinely felt smaller, and he could feel his arms flex. When the pressure had been at its peak, that flexing would have been impossible.

"Spin cycle complete?" Alis's tired and disembodied voice said.

"Maybe so."

"Thank God," Robert said.

Karl heard nothing of Lucy's voice. "Lucy?" he called.

Silence.

"Uh-oh," Robert said after a pause long enough to give Lucy time to reply, if she were alive and conscious and within communication range.

Karl was sure Lucy must still have been within communication range. "Lucy!" he called, as if yelling would make his voice travel farther.

More silence. Karl suddenly remembered meeting Lucy for the first time. He'd told her that some people said he'd caused the Tokyan Station accident. She had replied, " 'They' say lots of things. Someone once told me 'they' say men are brighter than women." She'd shaken her head and gone back to work. Lucy hadn't seemed all that friendly to him—Lucy wasn't all that friendly with anyone—but she'd made it clear that she was the kind of person who generally needed some basis to form opinions on, and Karl liked that a lot.

A few seconds later Karl felt the mild sensation of falling that always told him gravity was lower than it had been. He finally relaxed his grip on the edge of the hole.

When he stood up, he almost hit his head on the level above. Besides the size of the holes shrinking as the levels went deeper, the levels obviously grew closer together, too.

"Lucy!" Alis called.

Again no answer.

Into the silence, a soft *beep* sounded, indicated a message coming in from the *Ranger.* Captain Fernandez cleared his voice, and something unusual about the sound made Karl tense.

"This is Captain Fernandez," he said unnecessarily. "I hope you can all still hear me and that you check in as soon as you can. You need to get out of there posthaste. The projections are still being refined, and there's still room for error, but at the moment indications are that if this object misses Hamilton Station, you're still not home free.

"The current projections say this object, after it leaves the Earth's gravity well, will be on a course that takes it too near the sun. If these figures are to be believed, the orbital arc will take it through the corona—far too close for it to survive the transit.

"I repeat. You need to get out, and you need to get out soon. There is still of course the issue of the asteroid-deflection explosives, which are now less than twenty-four hours away. I will endeavor to delay that action as long as possible, and to prevent it, should last-minute calculations deem it unnecessary.

I just want you to know that even if you all survive this complication, you must get out soon. We will not have the luxury of tracking you farther through the solar system, as we once thought."

Karl formed a newfound appreciation for the phrase "ignorance is bliss."

"Lucy!" he called.

No answer. Somehow the continued silence from Lucy and the brand-new silence from Captain Fernandez seemed additive, and even worse than the earlier silence.

12 ▪ L E S I O N

Lucy!" Karl called again.

"What does it matter?" Robert asked. "Cantaloupe is going to either be blown to bits or burn up in the sun. It doesn't much matter if we find her or not, does it?"

"If you're so sure we're all going to die, why don't you just turn off you air right now?"

"Why don't you just suck—"

"Lucy!" Alis called, even more loudly than Karl had called. "Lucy, respond if you can hear us."

Karl abandoned the flare-up with Robert. There were more important things to worry about. He switched off his helmet lamps and scanned the darkness. On this level he could see no other helmet lamps, neither those of Alis nor those of Robert but, more important, no sign of Lucy's.

He flipped his helmet lamps back on and jumped through

a nearby hole up to the next level. "We need to regroup so when we spot a light we'll know if it's Lucy or not."

He was about halfway between the central column and the dark wall. The pattern of holes stretched out uniformly in all directions, with a larger pattern of holes on the ceiling.

He made another scan with his helmet lamps off and spotted a refection of light from one or two levels up. "I'm on a level that's just taller than me, and the holes are about a meter wide. I'm moving up. Are you above or below me?"

"I'm above you," Alis said promptly. "I'd guess two or three levels. And I can see a lamp from someone a level above me."

"That would be me, I think." Robert said. "Did the light just go off?"

"Right."

"Yes, that's me. I'll come down to your level."

While Alis and Robert had talked, Karl moved up two more levels, and now he could see two pairs of helmet lamps. "So this is the three of us, right?"

Alis and Robert both said yes.

"I'm pretty sure Lucy was below this level," Karl said. "I think that was her body that crashed into me. I suggest we drop a level at a time and look for her light."

"You got it," Alis said.

The three of them dropped one level down. "I checked this level already," Karl said, "but on the off chance that her radio is dead and she's moving around, trying to find us, let's make a quick check with lights out."

A second later, with all the helmet lamps out, and with Karl's helmet display turned off, the area was so dark that all Karl could see was the quivering darkness of random retinal responses that could have been hundreds of fireflies on the distant verge of visibility.

They switched on their helmet lamps and moved downward again.

They completed another scan of the dark horizon before Robert said, "I hope what happened five minutes ago doesn't happen every fifteen minutes."

Karl and Alis ignored the comment.

The next level down was also dark, but something moved in the distance.

"See that?" Robert asked.

"Yes," Alis said softly. "Let's see what it is."

Karl understood why she chose those words. He couldn't make out what was moving in the distance, but he could see enough to tell that it wasn't Lucy, light or no light.

The closer they got, the more round it looked, whatever it was.

"What in the name of—" Robert fell silent. Karl wished he would shut up more often, not just when they came upon a bizarre creature that looked vaguely like a medicine ball. At least he assumed it was a creature.

The round thing, a half-meter-wide leathery brown ball, was rolling around the level they walked on, rolling around in a remarkably orderly pattern. The trio stopped at what seemed to be a consensually safe distance and watched the ball as it rolled around the perimeter of one of the holes in the floor. After it completed the circuit, it rolled in a pattern that seemed to cover every spot in the area surrounded by more holes.

Alis said, "Do you think we've finally met one of the residents?"

"My bet is that it's closer to one of the snakes than to the residents," Karl said. "This really doesn't look very smart to me. And it hasn't reacted to our presence."

"Maybe it doesn't see in the spectrum our lights are on. And with no atmosphere, it couldn't smell us or hear us even if it had the right organs."

"I think Karl's right," Robert said. "I'm getting the feeling that we're looking at something like a very remote cousin of the white corpuscle."

"Meaning it carries nutrients or attacks invaders?" Alis asked. "My medical knowledge is pretty rusty."

"I mean in general, not in specific. I think this is some bodily mechanism that's designed for a particular purpose and does it. I don't know what the function is, unless it's just cleaning up after the influx, doing the alien equivalent of cleaning the cell walls. If Cantaloupe is an enormous living ship, self-repairing and all that, I suppose it makes sense to think of it as an enormous body."

"So for all we know we could be in the lungs or the kidneys and this cleaner-upper is essentially an automaton designed for that one purpose?" Karl said.

"Could be. Could also be that in a body this size, especially if it's been designed, it could have the equivalent of a hundred kidneys so the failure of one or two would be inconsequential, or so that each one could serve a specific region of the body."

"Like the snakes could have been some kind of bodily defense mechanism?"

"Right."

The round blob kept rolling around the area in what seemed to be a programmed path that almost never recrossed the same point.

"And there's a chance that this thing could have its own form of defense?"

Alis said, "You're talking about a general defense mechanism? Whoever designed this could hardly have predicted we would show up, so the body would just be equipped to detect anything that isn't 'normal' and deal with it."

Robert said, "That's as good a theory as any."

The ball-shaped thing was gradually moving closer to the group. Karl said, "Let's stay clear of this thing and keep looking for Lucy, okay?"

"Right," Alis said, and she called out to Lucy again.

After a long silence, the trio moved well away from the

cleaner-upper and dropped down another level. Here, Karl
had to bend his knees to avoid hitting his head on the ceiling.

The next level down had just the right height to give Karl
a killing back pain if the gravity had been a lot higher. He had
to bend over quite a bit, and tilt his head up sharply to see. He
sat down.

They all switched off their helmet lamps again, and Karl
stared into the darkness, letting his eyes adjust. "If this thing
is like a giant body, it's too bad we don't know enough to make
it throw up."

"Or even worse than that," Robert said. "We might be
able to figure out how to make—"

"I don't think I want to hear this yet." Karl turned to look
in another direction.

"Me, neither," said Alis.

Karl's pulse picked up. Was that a flicker of dim light in
the distance? He couldn't see anything more by looking directly
at the spot, so he looked slightly away from the place he
thought he'd seen it. He couldn't tell if it had been his imagination or not. "Alis?"

"Yeah."

"I might be wrong, but I thought I got a glimpse of something very faint. Can you turn on your telephoto view and take
a look?"

"Okay, but I don't know where you're looking."

"I don't want to move, or I might lose track of where I
thought it was. Can you find me? I'll point in the direction so
you can feel my arm."

"Go ahead and point. I can see you now in infrared."

"Oh, right. I forgot."

Karl pointed.

Long seconds went by. Finally Alis said, "No, I can't—
wait. There may be something there. Yes. I see some light. It's
below us, can't tell whether one level or more."

"All right."

Alis flipped her helmet lamps on. "Let's move."

Karl and Robert flipped on their helmet lamps, too. Karl blinked a couple of times in the sudden light, and tried to pick a spot where he pointed on the far wall that he could use as a goal.

"It looked like the light was all the way against the wall," Alis said as the three of them began to move.

"Makes sense," Karl said. "If she lost her grip, or never had a grip, she could have been thrown against the wall during the spin."

"I hope she's all right," Alis said.

Karl had certainly made his share of mistakes in interpreting tone of voice, but Alis sounded genuinely concerned over Lucy's fate. In Karl's limited interactions with Alis to date, she had always seemed remote, some would say robotic and impersonal, constantly tense and judgmental, as if buffered from the world by a thin, hard veneer of anger. He didn't comment on the change, but just said, "Me, too."

Karl moved in the direction of the light. Given the cramped ceiling and the light gravity, he wound up in more of a swimming motion than walking. At each new circular hole in the floor, he reached forward and pulled hard enough to propel his body over the hole and land on the space between holes, ready to go again.

Two minutes brought them close to the wall. This time when they turned off their helmet lamps, Karl didn't need to ask Alis what she could see. The light below them was faint, but definite.

One at a time they dropped through the nearest round hole to the level below. The light was brighter.

Karl lay on his stomach next to a hole about a half-meter wide and looked into the next level down. "I can see her!" he said.

Seconds later, as if two more people had stuck their heads under the surface of a lake to look for fish, Alis's and Robert's lamps brightened the area around Lucy's body.

Lucy was motionless, lying against the outer wall. Her helmet lamps were on, which was why they had been able to locate her in the first place.

"Lucy," Karl said. "Can you hear me?" After he said the words, he was aware that he had yelled when they had been far away and now that they were close he had spoken in a normal voice, as if they were all outdoors someplace and proximity made communication easier.

No answer.

"She looks like she's higher than she would be if she were resting on the floor. What's holding her there?" Robert said.

"I don't know," said Karl. He pulled himself through the hole and onto the next level. This one was only about half his height, so he had to crawl toward Lucy's body. Bouncing lights in his peripheral vision said that Alis or Robert or both had joined him on this level.

As he got closer to Lucy's body, it became apparent that the wall was covered with an uneven green crust. Lucy's suited body formed a bizarre Statue of Liberty, with one arm flung high and stuck to the wall.

On the wall about ten meters away from Lucy's body what was left of one of the balls that had been carried along by the green fluid was stuck to the wall like a half-scoop of ice cream or a huge barnacle.

Karl reached her. "Lucy? Are you alive? Can you hear me?" He gripped one arm and squeezed. At least her suit still held pressure.

"Lucy?"

"Mmm?" Lucy's voice had never sounded so good.

"Lucy! We're here. Wake up, will you?"

At the same time, Alis said, "Thank God!" and Robert murmured something that sounded like relief.

Karl pulled on Lucy's arm, but it was stuck to the wall. He pulled on a leg, but it was stuck, too. "Lucy, wake up!"

"I'm—I'm—" she started. "Something's not right."

At least she was still alive and could speak. Karl moved closer and lifted one arm as far from the wall as he could. It didn't move far. He shifted position so he could see better.

The greenish crust on the walls seemed to have glued Lucy's suit to the wall. As if testing wet paint, Karl carefully touched the wall, first lightly, then pressing harder. The substance seemed dry and not at all adhesive.

He pulled out a utility knife and carefully wedged it between Lucy's arm and the wall. As cautious as a new surgeon, he tried to cut some of the green substance loose without risking a cut into Lucy's suit. After a moment he pulled the blade back. He had made a cut through a section no wider than his thumb. Apparently the process of freeing Lucy was going to be like cutting her loose from melted plastic, but at least it was a lot weaker than epoxy or evergrip.

"I'm going to need help cutting her loose," Karl said, and explained.

As Alis and Robert moved closer, Robert said, "I sure hope we can get done before this cycle starts again. If we all wind up glued to the wall, we're dead."

"Let's think positive," Alis said.

"What's going on?" Lucy asked.

"Just relax, Lucy," Karl said. "Everything's under control." Things were at least as much under control as they were when the police were spraying a run-amok soccer crowd with fire hoses. "Parts of your suit are stuck to the wall here, but we're getting you loose."

"That's nice," Lucy said, as if she were a patient with too much medication.

Moments later, Robert had picked an arm and Alis had picked a leg, and they were all busy carefully cutting Lucy free. Karl had to change position frequently in the cramped space, but he silently thanked whoever had included knives on the standard equipment list. He could have used his oxyacetylene cutter, but the area was a little too cramped for that to feel safe. Plus that, given their situation, he didn't like using up any non-recoverable substances.

Alis said sometime later, "This stuff is even worse than tree sap."

"What's that?" Robert asked.

"Doesn't matter."

Lucy finally spoke again. "We're still inside Cantaloupe, aren't we?"

"Yes," Karl said gently.

"Crap. So we're still screwed then."

Karl was sure that Lucy would have flung her head back against the wall if it hadn't already been stuck there.

"Easy, easy!" he said suddenly as Lucy struggled to get free. "Your suit is stuck against the wall and we're cutting you loose. Jostle us too much and the blade might go where it shouldn't."

"You're kidding, right?"

"You tell her, Alis. She knows you never joke."

"He's telling you the truth," Alis said. She hesitated. "I'm that humorless?"

"Less."

Lucy said, "Maybe they took out the humor gland when they took out—I can't believe I said that. I'm sorry. What is going on around here?"

"I think you're still a little loopy from the fall," Karl said. "Do you remember having this place start spinning? You must have been thrown here."

"That does seem familiar. I'm stuck here? What, did my suit melt or something?"

"Don't think so. Apparently the residue of that green fluid is kinda sticky." Karl had cut loose about half of her suit arm so far, and his hand was starting to cramp.

"I'd really like to go home now," Lucy said softly. "I'm tired."

"You and me both." Karl kept chipping away at the layer between her suit and the wall.

"This is taking forever," Robert said helpfully.

"Do you hurt anywhere, Lucy?" Karl asked, partly to prod Robert into medical mode.

"I have a headache."

Robert took the hint. "Localized sharp pain, or more like a typical headache?"

"Maybe a bit more pain than normal at the back of my head, but mostly like a normal headache."

"You have any sense of *no* feeling anywhere?"

"I don't think so."

"One at a time, so you don't risk getting cut, I'm going to ask you to tighten the muscles in your arms and legs. Okay?"

"Okay."

"Karl, stop cutting for just a sec. Okay, Lucy, try to make a fist with your right hand. If you don't feel any pain, keep increasing the pressure until you can't squeeze any harder."

After a long moment, Lucy said, "I guess everything seems okay to me. No significant pain."

"Good. Now let that arm totally relax again so Karl can keep cutting."

Robert continued the grand tour, asking Lucy to tense the muscles in her calves when the time came. She reported nothing in addition to the headache.

"How much longer?"

"Maybe ten minutes," said Karl.

"Can't you cut any faster? I have a patch kit if something goes wrong."

"I think we're going as fast as we can safely go. You wouldn't want us to cut your suit in a place where we couldn't get a patch to it in time."

"Well, I guess ten minutes is tolerable."

"I'm not so sure," Alis said. "Take a look that way."

Karl looked where Alis had directed her helmet lamps while Lucy said, "What, where? I can't turn my head."

"Uh-oh," Karl said.

" 'Uh-oh' what?" Lucy said, more loudly.

"What the hell is that?" Robert asked, even louder.

"What the hell is what?" Lucy demanded.

On the wall about thirty or forty meters away, just on the other side of the hemisphere of goop stuck to the wall, something seemed to be moving toward them. The thing vaguely resembled a very fat and very large worm. It was as tall as the gap between the level they crouched on and the level above, and was about as wide. Karl couldn't tell for sure from this angle, but it seemed to be two or three times as long as it was wide. The side facing the wall conformed to the wall, and the side away from the wall was rounded, with striations along its length. Karl gave Lucy a rough description.

Alis said, "Robert, check it out."

"Check it out?"

"Get closer; see what it's doing; see if it's a threat."

"How close?"

"Get moving!"

Robert started moving. Karl concluded that doctors must be so used to having other people follow their directions, they weren't well equipped to follow other people's orders.

"Hurry," Lucy said, but whether she meant to cut faster or for Robert to speed things up, Karl wasn't sure.

Karl tried to cut faster, but his occasional glances toward the worm-thing probably resulted in the same overall speed as before.

"It's definitely headed toward Lucy," Robert said moments later. "It seems to be cleaning the wall. Behind it, the green stuff is all gone from the wall. It's almost to this large ball of stuff that's stuck to the wall."

"Great," Alis said.

"At least you guys can get out of the way," Lucy said.

Robert sounded more nervous the next time he spoke. "It's eating into the goop. I can't tell what mechanism it's using, but the goop is just disappearing into what looks like pores in the wall."

Karl frowned and checked a helmet display. Sure enough, the reading indicated pressure. "This place has been pumped up somehow. I'm reading a bit over a tenth of an atmosphere, but no indication that it's breathable. If that thing grinds up the remaining stuff on the walls, the pressure could be pushing it out the pores."

"Well, that's all very educational," Lucy said, "but maybe Robert should be back here helping to cut me loose."

"Agreed," said Alis.

"It's making fast work of this green stuff," Robert said as he hurried back. "It might finish it in five minutes."

"Hurry!" said Lucy.

Karl kept his head down and cut as fast as he could. He finished with the arm he'd been working on and started on Lucy's upper back. "I'm making faster progress now," he said, to comfort her.

"You're just saying that."

"No, really," Karl said, trying to be more convincing this time.

"Damn, I'm gonna die."

"We're all going to die," Robert said.

"I know that. I just wanted to be a little older first."

"No, I mean we're all going to die in two or three days. If we survive the deflection explosion and we avoid a collision with Hamilton Station, we're headed for the sun."

"Let's go into this later," Alis said.

Robert reached Lucy's side and resumed his cutting duties.

"Is what he said true?" Lucy asked.

"Well," Alis said, "it's what we were told. But there's lots of room for error. If they detonate the deflection charge, that might put our path farther away from the sun."

"Or change it to a more direct path to the sun, right? I mean their first priority will be to make sure we miss Hamilton Station, not to worry about four lives."

"Five," Karl said. "They still think there are five of us alive."

"Oh, I'm relieved to know that," Lucy said. "Of course if there are *five* lives at stake that changes everything."

Karl felt a little stupid and decided to concentrate on cutting. Let Alis try to make Lucy feel better.

Alis tried. "Besides that, there's still a good chance that we can get out of here. The interior maps sent down from the *Ranger* are showing a little more detail each time, and we may well learn something critical anytime there's a new update."

Lucy arched her back and pulled her arms forward, straining against the wall. "I've got to get out of here."

"Easy," Karl said. "We don't want to cut you."

"That worm-thing is already halfway through the lump of green stuff," Robert said.

"Damnit," Lucy said. "Look, my arm's free now. Put a knife in my hand and guide it back to the back of my helmet. I can be cutting there at the same time, and that's safer than cutting near my suit material."

"Good idea," Alis said. She retrieved Lucy's knife from a leg pouch and guided Lucy's arm into position.

Karl glanced at the approaching worm-thing. It seemed to be chewing through the mound of green goop as fast as a snow plow churning through a big snow bank, except that the mound was simply disappearing.

"It just isn't fair," Lucy said. "I still haven't visited Olympus Lookout or walked on Titan or—oof, this stuff is hard to cut."

"No kidding," Robert said.

"And the thing that's approaching is just slicing through it?"

"Pretty much."

"We don't know for certain that it'll be dangerous for you, though," Karl said. "It could be spraying some chemical specifically meant to dissolve the green stuff, and your suit might be impervious to it."

"You don't plan on trying to find out, right?"

"Of course not," Karl said. "We'll test it with Robert's suit."

"Ha."

"It's almost through that pile of stuff," Alis said. "We probably have only a couple of minutes."

It was going to be close. Lucy was still held against the wall by part of one leg, her helmet, and some of her back. In no more than a minute, Alis would have to move out of the way of the worm-thing. Karl's hand was getting really sore, but he couldn't quit now.

"Oh, I can see it now," Lucy said finally, as she was able to turn her helmet. "It's really big."

"You can say that again," Karl said. "Robert probably doesn't hear that very often."

"Bend over, funny boy."

"Boys," Alis said, "I've got to get out of the way."

Alis shot away from the wall, just clearing the front edge of the worm-thing, which had finished disposing of the pile of green stuff and was now making even better speed as it dealt with the thinner layer of green rust. The front end of the worm-thing held a vertical lip of tissue next to the wall, as if it were applying a squeegee to push aside excess fluid. Next to the lip was a wide strip of glistening diamond-patterned skin that looked like a rattlesnake's skin had been stretched into that space and then sprayed with water. In front of the squeegee seemed to be a column of mist that was being sucked into the wall.

They were down to seconds, but Karl still thought there was time.

"We don't have enough time," Robert said.

"Alis," Karl said, "get a patch ready. We may have to pull her loose."

"Got it."

There was the same air of pulse-pounding tension and teamwork that Karl associated with the emergency room. Except in this case, if they didn't accomplish their goal, the patient would be dissolved.

Karl shifted position closer to the worm-thing, trying to cut the remaining sticky residue from the back of Lucy's leg. That hand-sized area finally seemed to be all that held her to the wall, and she flailed in a chaotic effort to get away from the wall and out of the path of the worm.

"Get me the hell out of here!" Lucy yelled.

"We're just about there," Karl said.

The worm moved closer, more green residue turning to mist in front of it. Closer.

"Pull!" said Karl. He hacked at the remaining bond between Lucy and the wall. He shifted position, closer to the worm, to get more leverage, and he pulled her leg away from the wall, applying greater and greater force. Robert and Alis both maintained a hold on the edge of a nearby hole and pulled on Lucy's outstretched hand.

The worm loomed larger, a steamroller just centimeters away. The patch holding Lucy's leg to the wall was smaller than the palm of a hand. Smaller. Almost gone.

But the worm was right there. No more time.

Karl planted his feet on the wall and pulled just as hard as he could.

Lucy stifled a cry of pain.

The worm was there. No time left.

Lucy's suit came unstuck. She and Karl popped loose from the wall and tumbled into the cramped area. Karl's foot grazed the worm as he spun to safety.

"Wow!" Lucy cried. "Am I leaking?"

By the time Karl stopped his tumbling and made it back to where Lucy and Alis and Robert were, Alis had already checked the back of Lucy's leg. "I think you're okay," Alis said. "But there's a small section that looks a little wrinkled. Let's play safe and put a patch on it anyway."

"Fine by me."

Karl watched the worm obliviously continue its sweep, already a quarter of the way through the outline of where Lucy had been stuck. At least it didn't seem to be a threat to anything that wasn't on the wall. Behind the worm, the wall was perfectly clear and dark.

Karl pulled himself upward through a hole in the ceiling and felt a little less claustrophobic in the taller level. Far away on the wall, he thought he could see a different worm making a cleaning run on this level. He moved to watch Alis complete the brief repair.

"Okay, I think that'll do it," Alis said seconds later. "Let's get out of here."

"Amen," Lucy said.

Karl led the way upward, moving through progressively bigger holes into taller and taller levels.

"Karl!" Alis said suddenly.

"What?"

"Just stop right there and hold still."

Karl's arms lay flat on the level above, his torso in midair. He felt Alis twist one of his boots.

"You'd better patch that boot, just in case," Alis said.

Karl pulled himself up to the next level. He bent one leg and pulled his boot into the pool of light shed by his helmet lamps. "Wow!" The side of the heel was gone, as if he'd held the boot against a grinding wheel for a minute or two.

"I bet that worm dissolved it."

"I bet you're right." Karl took two patches from a shoulder pouch and applied them both.

As he worked, Lucy approached. " 'Wow' is right. You three got me out just in time. Thanks."

"Hey, what are teammates for?" Karl decided he was glad he hadn't known for sure how dangerous the worm was to suit material until now. "You guys go on ahead, and I'll catch up. We still don't know how often this whole process repeats itself."

Robert was already on the level above. Alis and Lucy followed, and by the time they were on the next level up, Karl was following them. At least in the low gravity, Karl wouldn't be putting a lot of stress on the heel. As he moved to catch up, he tried not to think about what the consequences would have been had his foot moved a few centimeters closer to the worm. He could fix only so much damage with little pieces of fabric and adhesive.

They made good time getting back to the main level, despite Karl constantly imagining that he'd seen a flash of light from the central column or thinking he'd caught a glimpse of one of the worm-things approaching fast from the darkness.

"I see one of those air lock doors," Robert said seconds later. "I don't know if it's the one we came in, though."

"Let's go for it anyway," Alis said. "I want to get out of here ASAP."

"Sounds like a good plan to me." Robert's occasional bristling at taking orders from a woman seemed to have vanished.

Karl reached the main level in time to see the others still on their way to the exit, and he scrambled to catch up, careful to avoid the holes in the floor.

"Come on; come on," Robert said. "Open up!"

Just as Karl was starting to imagine them being locked inside this huge chamber forever, trying to avoid getting stuck to the wall and vaporized, Robert said, "All right!"

Robert and Alis were through the door before Karl was

even halfway to the door. Lucy followed. In the doorway, she turned and looked back. "Hurry, Karl!"

"I'm hurrying; believe me."

Karl moved closer to the door, his pulse accelerating. *Please don't shut the door,* he thought. *Please don't leave me here.*

Ten more meters. Five.

He reached the door and he was through it, moving so fast he ran into Robert.

"Hey!" Robert cried.

"Sorry about that." Karl didn't feel sorry at all. If he'd known he'd be able to soften his impact by running into Robert, he wouldn't have bothered to brake.

He turned to see the air lock door, and thankfully it had already closed.

Alis opened the far door. Beyond it was the familiar tunnel that circled the chamber. Karl had been irrationally worried that it would lead them someplace else in this crazy topsy-turvey place.

Alis and Robert exited, followed by Karl and Lucy. The air lock door irised closed behind them.

"I could use a nap," Lucy said.

"Me, too," Karl said.

Alis said, "The transport pod takes long enough to get from one place to another that we may as well take a break while we're riding."

No one objected as Alis started walking along the tunnel floor. Karl followed, feeling so turned around that he had no idea whether they were taking the shortest route. He was relieved enough to be out of the chamber that he didn't even care. He could have checked their coordinates and matched them to the map, but it felt good just to walk mindlessly for a few minutes.

The tunnel changed hardly at all as they walked. They passed another circular door to the chamber before they reached the circle on the outside wall. At that point Karl double-checked their current position against the spot where they had come out of the transport pod, and was happy to see a match.

Alis sat down. "Take a quick break if you like. I just want to take a look at the latest map the *Ranger* sent down."

Karl lay down as if in a large hammock, his back resting against the tunnel wall and his feet propped against the opposite wall. He flipped on the map display and took a look.

Details of Cantaloupe's interior were continuing to increase in resolution and contrast, though the overall result was still more like a fragmentary and ancient flat-Earth map than a modern collection of data measured in millimeters instead of leagues. Like a row of street lamps shining through the fog, though, the data made the unknown less intimidating.

Lucy said, "I can see more of the path the probe took. It's clearer, a little like a tiny scar."

Karl looked at the scar in his map display. The top end was more diffuse than it had been, as if it were being healed, but the bottom end met another blotchy volume deeper into Cantaloupe's body. "I wonder if the probe was directed to where the blotchy area is, or if the area's blotchy because the probe damaged it."

"No clue. But the transport pod can take us a lot closer. Maybe even close enough to find out."

"Sure, what the hell," Robert said. "We might as well get more screwed."

"You want to die sooner?" Lucy asked.

Robert didn't ask her to elaborate.

"Let's go," Alis said. "Maybe we can learn something new at the next stop."

Sure, Karl thought. *As if we learned a lot here.* Alis had enough trouble with Robert already, though, so he said nothing.

The door to the transport pod opened when Alis touched

it, and a half-minute later what was left of the team were sealed into the pod and on their way even deeper into the interior. The pod spun up to its normal rate, and Karl settled back.

"Is anyone else getting hot?" Lucy asked after several seconds. She sounded uncomfortable, almost sick.

Karl felt fine, and he checked his suit thermostat. Twenty-one degrees C. "I'm okay."

Alis and Robert were fine, too.

"Well, something's wrong then. I'm burning up. It's coming up on twenty-five degrees."

Robert said, "Maybe your suit was damaged when we cut you loose."

"Turn over," said Karl.

Lucy turned so the back of her suit faced the center of the pod.

"I think I know what the problem is," Karl said. He ran his glove over a mass of plastic-like remnants left from Lucy's encounter on the wall. "The goop that glued you to the wall is covering your heat exchanger. Your suit can't drain your excess body heat."

"This can't be happening!"

Karl dug out his knife and started hacking at the edges of the goop. Slivers fell away under the blade. "I think we can clean it off enough. For now, try to relax. Minimize your pulse rate. Meditate if you can. Just try to keep your metabolism rate as low as possible."

Robert and Alis dug out their knives and went to work on other sections of the dark black rippled rectangle that should be shedding Lucy's excess heat faster. The idea of someone overheating in this cold environment seemed to fit with the overall crazy experience.

Chipping away the goop was slow going, especially because all three of the workers were trying to make sure they didn't accidentally slip a blade through someone else's suit.

"I can't take much more of this," Lucy said after a time.

Karl had cleared an area no larger than the palm of his hand. He tried to cut even faster, first slicing goop away from the top of the ripples and then digging in the channels for the harder-to-remove stuff. He wished the heat-exchanger panel were flat, but it would have had to have been three times as large to dissipate as much heat as the rippled version with its extra area.

"Lucy," Karl said after a long silence.

No answer.

"Lucy, we need to know you're all right," Robert said. "Can you count slowly?"

Lucy finally started counting, but her voice made Karl nervous. She missed numbers and stuttered, sometimes pausing for ten seconds between numbers.

Their efforts had cleared a black grid showing through the green goop stuck to her back, but the bulk of the heat exchanger's area was in the channels.

Karl was suddenly aware that Lucy hadn't said anything for over a minute.

He shook her body. "Lucy, hang in there." He went back to cutting, but Lucy was still silent.

13 ▪ M A L I G N A N C Y

Alis kept chipping away the gunk stuck to the back of Lucy's suit, trying to go as fast as possible and still not risk cutting Karl's or Robert's hands as they worked on the same surface. Lucy had been silent for at least a couple of minutes, and Alis was all too aware of the possible meaning.

The transport pod continued its uniform spin, creating the trick with inertia that kept them drawn to the wall. They continued dropping deeper into Cantaloupe's interior.

"I'm getting hot, too," Robert said.

"Good," Karl said. "That means you're carrying your load." Karl's words were ragged, as if he were carrying a heavy log up a hill.

Alis kept cutting away material as fast as she could, the back of her brain now wondering if the tension so evident in

Karl's voice was the result not just of exertion, but of a hidden emotional attachment to Lucy. When it came right down to it, Karl and Lucy could be lovers for all Alis knew. As soon as that thought materialized, Alis was aware of something else even more amazing. Somewhere in a part of her brain she'd been fairly successful in ignoring came a twinge of pain, of—it took a moment to identify—jealousy.

She kept up her pace as if nothing had happened, but inside she was suddenly faltering. Jealousy made no sense. No sense at all. Karl had turned her life upside down. Anger was what she felt for him. But if he loved Lucy, then . . . *Stop it,* she told herself. *This is insane. Even if I were attracted to Karl, he's not attracted to me, and we're all going to be dead in a couple of days.*

More green chips fell away from the black heat exchanger at Lucy's back. *Please don't die, Lucy. Not after Belinda and Daren. That would be too much.* If they all died in a sudden burst at the end, at least she wouldn't have to face the aftermath. But too many people had died already.

"Did you say something?" Karl asked suddenly.

"Who are you talking to?" Robert asked.

"Shhhhh."

Alis could hear nothing but the sounds of forced breathing. Then a new sound. A soft moan. "Lucy!"

The three of them kept chipping away at the clogged heat exchanger with renewed vigor. With luck, they had cleared enough of the surface that it was able to lower the temperature inside the suit.

A minute later Lucy moaned more loudly.

"Hang in there," Karl said. "You're going to make it!"

Alis's hand was nearly going numb from the pressure she was applying to the knife. Now that Lucy seemed to be on the way to recovery, Alis slacked off just enough to let feeling start creeping back into her hand.

Her thoughts veered back to exactly the place she'd told

them not to go, and she wondered if she were so petty that she'd feel attracted to Karl just because he might be involved with someone else. Please don't let her be that kind of person. Were there things about Karl that drew her to him?

She tried to imagine how she'd feel about Karl if she knew he really was innocent of causing the Tokyan Station accident. To start with the most petty reasons, she actually did like the way he looked. He wasn't handsome in the video star mold, but she did like the boyish face that suggested he still knew how to play, even though she hadn't taken time to play for a long time. He prodded Robert a little too often, but Robert was the kind of guy who needed it. Karl could obviously step easily into a leadership breach, but he was supportive of her as the team leader, but without being sycophantic or patronizing. He was strong-willed, brave, and inventive. A team of people all like Karl would be a formidable force.

Lucy moaned again and said, "Is it hot in here or is it just me?" Her words were slightly slurred, but she had never sounded so good.

"You're going to be all right!" Alis said. "We've got most of the heat exchanger cleaned."

"Thanks, folks," Lucy said in a more serious tone. "I owe you a big one."

"What's your suit temperature?" Robert asked.

"Twenty-three. And dropping. Twenty-two point nine."

Karl said, "I think we should get the rest of this gunk off your heat exchanger just to play safe, but at least we can slow down now. What about if I take the first shift and we trade off every five minutes?"

"Good, Karl," Alis said. She leaned back, finally letting herself relax a bit, watching Karl continue working. After Lucy had recovered, he hadn't said anything that made it seem that he was any closer to Lucy than a teammate. *Get your thoughts off this,* she told herself. *Survival deserves total attention.*

She activated the display of Cantaloupe's interior and located the blinking indicator. Its color had changed from the normal yellow to a red that indicated it was her last known position rather than her current position. Until the transport pod stopped spinning, the navigation system wouldn't be able to keep up with the calculations. The system was supposedly able to handle a suited body spinning through space, so she supposed the wider excursions in position on the inside wall of the transport pod probably fell just outside of the design constraints. For a second she considered the idea that if the pod were falling at a rate determined by the pull of gravity, she could theoretically position herself in the center of the pod and hang there while the navigation system updated her position, but the situation didn't merit the effort of conducting the experiment. She'd find out all too soon how far below Cantaloupe's surface they were.

Robert took over from Karl and kept clearing the surface of Lucy's heat exchanger. Karl lay back with his helmet near Alis's.

Alis looked back at the display and the track the probe had left in its wake. "You know," she said, speaking mainly to Karl but aware that everyone could hear, "if we go with the evidence that Cantaloupe is in a sense a large living body, even if it's one designed to transport a large population, what the probe did was like a dissection of a living body. Operating on a live patient without consent."

Karl said, "I wonder if Cantaloupe feels pain. Obviously portions of the body react to the presence of damage or intrusion, but that's not necessarily the same thing."

"I hope it doesn't feel pain. The probe must have been inside for a long time, and some of the damage must be ancient. What puzzles me is the absence of people—alien beings. It makes sense that Cantaloupe would have self-repair mechanisms, but the presence of this transport pod and some of the tunnels definitely suggests the presence of beings not a lot larger than us. You'd think they'd get sent out to repair damage that can't be handled with the normal defense mechanisms."

"Could be they're all in suspended animation. At the speed Cantaloupe is moving, interstellar journeys are awfully long."

"Maybe. Or maybe they're all dead. I'm also curious about where the probe stopped, and if it's still active. It went a lot farther than any of the others. Maybe that means it had a different design. Maybe it penetrated far enough to damage the crew's quarters."

Robert moved away from Lucy. "You still going to take a turn?"

As Alis moved into position and started scraping more gunk off Lucy's heat-exchanger panel, Robert went on. "I'm more curious about when we hit the sun. Just call me selfish."

"You're selfish," Lucy said.

"Interesting way of showing gratitude," he said.

"Hey, I'm grateful. Believe me. But this isn't one of those things where I have to be your slave for life and grovel all the time now, is it?"

"Just a minute," Karl said. "We're thinking."

"Very funny, for a man."

Alis continued scraping gunk off the panel, thinking about how much easier this would have been with the aid of a sandblaster. At least the surface was finally looking pretty clean. "What's your temperature, Lucy?"

"Just about back to normal. I feel a little tired, but otherwise okay."

"I imagine we're all a little tired."

After a pause Karl said, "What if there is no crew?"

"You mean what if they're all dead or gone?" Alis asked.

"No. Maybe there never was a crew."

"Good going, Karl," Robert said. "No one's said anything really stupid for more than an hour. I'm glad you were willing to step in and level things out."

Lucy ignored Robert. "If there never was a crew, then Cantaloupe exists for its own sake? But it seems so *designed.*"

"It could still be the product of some design process. I'm not saying it's necessarily a natural life-form. Like you say, all these access tunnels and transport pods make it seem that whoever built it, or grew it, wanted access. Maybe they needed to be able to move around inside to make small tuning-level design changes or unanticipated repairs, or just to be able to see firsthand how the creation came out."

"What would be the purpose of designing something like this?"

"No idea at all."

Lucy said, "It could be a *Pioneer* plaque on a grand scale. Something just to tell other civilizations that there's someone else out there."

"But it's so huge," Robert said.

"Could be they built it for the long haul," Karl said. "The probe did a lot of damage despite how large Cantaloupe is. The smaller Cantaloupe is, the easier it is to be damaged by some civilization sending out probes."

"Well," Alis said. "Maybe we'll learn a lot more at the next stop. Whether there's a crew or not, we still have no idea how it gathers energy, or if it has its own supply. Does it ever change course, and how, or was it just essentially shot out of a cannon, like *Pioneer*?"

"There's an interesting thought," said Karl. "If we could find a control room, and somehow tell Cantaloupe to change course—"

"Good luck," Robert said. "That would be like an ant getting into a car and applying the brakes."

Alis didn't think the possibility was quite that remote, but finding the control room in time might be impossible, even if such a place existed. She applied a few more knife strokes to Lucy's heat-exchanger panel, then finally leaned back. "Lucy, I think you're back to normal."

"That's probably too much to hope for," Karl said good-naturedly, "but if her suit's back to normal, that's a good thing."

Lucy reacted to the light tone of voice. "So, Karl, you want me to take a knife to you now?"

"I'm fine, but Robert's got an ugly hangnail you might want to take a look at."

"I'm going to take a nap," Robert said. "Don't wake me until the next stop, all right?"

Another voice sounded. "This is the *Ranger,* calling the interior team," said Captain Fernandez. "I hope you're making your way back to the surface. The GSSC ships have arrived with their deflection explosives. This object is a lot larger than they've had to worry about before, but it's also much less dense. They're trying to figure out what approach to use— some way to deflect it without blowing it apart—and the result is going to be some confusion and false starts.

"We still have almost twenty-four hours before the last possible detonation time. I'm betting I can make them wait until nearly the last minute, but you need to get out. I'll update the map as soon as they pick potential detonation points.

"Another GSSC team has matched orbit with a large rock in the asteroid belt, and they're working on a backup plan to deflect the asteroid's orbit just enough to force a collision between it and Cantaloupe. I think it goes without saying that this new alternative has a lot more potential for damage. The rock they've picked has enough mass that the collision would be like a .45 slug hitting a grape.

"So get the heck out of there now. That's an order. *Ranger* out."

Alis let out a deep breath and said softly, "We'd love to follow your orders, sir."

"Is it depressed in here?" Lucy asked. "Or is it just me?"

"How does your suit feel now?"

"I think I'm okay. Since the suit was able to get me down

from overheating, I think it'll be able to handle any exertion level I care to try."

"Good." Having left the conversation on a more positive note, Alis let the silence lengthen. She closed her eyes. She still couldn't check her navigation display because of the transport pod's rotation, but she guessed they were two-thirds of the way to the next stop.

Despite the feeling of fatigue that permeated her body, she couldn't keep her eyes closed. She called up the latest map display and started reexamining it.

The transport pod route showed up better than it had before. So did other apparent routes. She traced backward from their present position to see if the transport route came close to the surface. It didn't. They had entered the path near its highest point. She turned the 3-D image, looking at other routes. She couldn't find one that got much closer to the surface than they had been when they found this route.

The network of transport pod routes, if that was what all the similar lines were, formed an image that could have been roughly approximated if someone had taken a dozen rubber bands and stretched them all into irregular orbits that came very close to the center of the volume. About ten of them seemed to pass through a small volume near the center of Cantaloupe, as if they were all subway routes connecting to the edges of a central terminal.

Between their current position and the "terminal" was the stop closest to the area at the bottom of the line indicating the probe's path, an area whose mottled texture made it seem more and more to be diseased or damaged in comparison. On the opposite side of Cantaloupe, the two large spheres were even better defined than last time, but their purpose was as foggy as ever. They were lined up so a path from the center of Cantaloupe passed through the centers of each small sphere in turn, but she could find no value to that information.

Very near the center of Cantaloupe was another area that

stood out from the featureless gray that constituted ninety percent of Cantaloupe's volume. That small volume, perhaps as big as the *Ranger,* was shaded with the reddish tint that said the density was significantly lower than average within Cantaloupe. That volume was located fairly near the "terminal," so she assumed there would be access to that area if they were still alive in a few more hours.

She closed her eyes again, waiting for this stretch of the trip to stop, thinking again of two dead companions. For a moment she looked for a word like "compatriot" that didn't imply as much friendship. *Now that's stupid,* she told herself suddenly. Why try to distance herself? Maybe she didn't know them all that well, but they were people she would have liked to have known a lot better. And they had been her responsibility.

Maybe that was why she looked for distance. So she wouldn't have to feel guilt and sadness at their death. Those two reactions were a marked change from the steady anger that had been seething in her for too long.

One of her teachers in high school had told her there were really only two emotions; either you felt good or you felt bad. For a time, she'd believed the teacher, but a month or two later the class bully had been hit by a car and died in the hospital. Alis had felt some guilty pleasure that she wouldn't have to deal with the kid anymore, then self-consciously analyzed her reaction. She came to the conclusion that if she felt the same emotion when a classmate died that she did when she received the top score on a test, she didn't like being the person who had those feelings. Differentiating between pride and relief, for instance, let her feel more comfortable with both reactions, and feel better about herself.

Alis shifted position. Once she'd started thinking about death, it was difficult to think of anything else. After her dad had died, she'd spent more and more time with her border collie. Puffer had eventually come down with a fatal liver condition when she'd been about fifteen and Puffer had been about eight. Puffer had been her best friend, able with just a snuggle or an excited bark to communicate his joy in being with her, displaying a friendship that was unconditional. Her human friends, on the other hand, always seemed to place conditions. She'd insisted on going with her mom to the vet the day they made their last trip there. She knew intellectually that stopping Puffer's pain was the kindest and most loving thing she could do for him, but looking into those trusting brown eyes just twisted her insides into coils of pain.

Belinda and Daren had trusted her, too, at least in the sense that they agreed without complaint to participate in the mission. At least she hadn't been compelled to watch their eyes as they spent their last moments accusing her of letting them down.

Alis suddenly pulled back. Her emotions were getting out of control. She was imagining feelings Belinda and Daren likely never had. She blinked furiously, thankful that her helmet concealed her face from the others. She took a few slow, deep breaths.

"Feel that?" Lucy said.

Alis was suddenly nervous that she'd done something to betray her emotional state, but then she felt the alternating push of gravity as she was first lighter, then heavier, then lighter. The pod must have been slowing down for the next stop.

"Damn," Robert said. "I wanted a longer nap."

Alis said, "Maybe it's time we all took a stimulant."

At first Alis thought Robert's medical background might push him to give a short speech about possible addictions, or damaging their bodies by running too long on imaginary energy.

"I suppose so. If we might all be dead in twenty-four hours, what's the harm?"

"Good point," Lucy said dryly.

Alis turned her head and found the water tube. With her eyes she activated the stimulant dispenser. Her next sip of water was slightly sweet, and seconds later she began to feel more rested, as if she had been treating her body well during the entire mission instead of adding high stress to long hours.

Karl was still silent. She'd expected that he'd join the conversation as the light-heavy cycles increased as they approached the new destination. "You all right, Karl?" she asked after a moment.

"Yeah." His voice was tired.

"You don't sound all right."

"I'm fine."

His voice was more convincing the second time, but something in his voice made her ask again. "You sure?"

He hesitated. "Maybe I'm a little depressed. The funny thing is, if you can call this funny, that what's bothering me isn't the idea that we might all be dead tomorrow. What's getting me is that I won't be able to tell anyone else what Daren said about the accident, so not only will I be dead, but everyone will go on thinking I'm an incompetent and careless jerk. Kind of silly, huh?"

"Not silly at all," Robert said. "You *are* an incompetent and careless jerk."

"Give it a rest, will you, Robert?" Alis said abruptly, surprised that she was defending Karl. "I don't think it's silly. We need to stay focused on finding a way out of here alive, but it'll be hard not to think about—well, dying, and how we're remembered. If we do die, I imagine we'll be remembered as explorers who gave it all we had."

"Except for me," Karl said. "I'll probably be remembered as the guy who screwed up at Tokyan Station and the jinx who probably made a fatal error that doomed the rest of the team."

"Probably true," Robert said. "You'll talk us to death."

Karl suddenly leaned forward and said very quietly and

menacingly, "Robert, I've taken a lot from you in the interest of maintaining the peace, but I'm just about at my limit. Don't make me do something that would feel real satisfying now but would probably seem like a poor idea in retrospect."

Robert was apparently learning when to say nothing.

Karl fell silent, too, as Alis realized that he wouldn't have been talking if she hadn't prodded him out of his silence.

The vibrations grew steadily stronger, to the point that in the light-gravity cycles, Alis felt as if her body might float away from the wall. The heavy-gravity side of the spin cycle felt like almost two gees.

At last the gravity ripples damped, and the pod slowed its spin rate to a halt. When the actual gravity was the only force on them, Alis knew they were much deeper than before. Here the gravity was even more diminished, enough to make sure that if you released a bag of marbles they'd all eventually wind up on the floor, but it could take quite a while.

Alis reached for the transport pod door and hesitated. "Everyone ready?"

No one objected.

Alis touched the door and it irised open. Beyond lay a flattened tunnel about a meter tall and three meters wide, as if someone had stepped on a gigantic hose. The tunnel walls were fairly smooth, and a uniform pink. She pushed herself into the tunnel.

In the microgravity, her perceptions played a few tricks with her head, and for an instant she felt she'd just arrived in the middle of a vertical tunnel and she was about to plunge headfirst into Cantaloupe's core. Then just as quickly, the illusion flip-flopped, and she felt the tunnel was horizontal.

Ultra-gently she drifted toward the floor of the tunnel. The gravity was so light that, in the absence of a roof, a light push-up motion would probably have resulted in at least a triple-gainer. Her helmet lamp illuminated a series of widely spaced grips running as far as she could see of the length of the tunnel. The grips would make it easy to make progress through the tunnel despite the ultra-low gravity.

One by one the others joined her in the tunnel. Karl said, "I sure hope this isn't a subway tunnel."

Alis's navigation unit was functioning again, and her current position was where she had expected it to be. She marked the location on the display. The area she had targeted as their destination, where the final probe might be, lay in front of them. She grabbed one of the rungs and easily pulled herself forward. "Let's go."

The others followed. The effort was easy, as just an occasional tug was needed, more to keep them off the tunnel floor than to pull them forward.

Ahead of them, beyond the reach of their helmet lamps, the tunnel was dark. Behind them the darkness was much closer. Alis blinked her eyes into telephoto mode and stepped up her light sensitivity. The fade between the tunnel surface brightly illuminated by helmet lamps and the darkness farther ahead became more gradual, and the view was more jittery, but aside from that, the view was basically the same.

A blowup of the 3-D map of Cantaloupe's interior, superimposed with a current-position dot, soon said they had traveled halfway from the transport pod to their goal. A shadowy trace indicating the tunnel they were in passed right by the mottled area of interest, then continued straight for such a long distance that gravity would not always be perpendicular to the floor.

By now the stimulant had kicked in at 100 percent. She felt vigorous, alert, ready for anything. She just hoped they didn't run into a situation that would require an energy reserve that she didn't really have. The stimulants served pretty much the same purpose as a fresh coat of paint on a rusted-out car. They'd help for the short term, but eventually they wouldn't be able to change reality.

Alis overshot an oval on the left wall. "Whoa! I think we're already there."

For a moment there was an orgy-like clump of bodies twisting against each other as they all tried to grab a rung and halt their forward motion. Lucy was rearmost, so when they were all stopped and reoriented, she was closest to what seemed to be another door.

A few seconds later, all four of them drifted sideways in the tunnel, facing the doorway as if they were four guppies all intent on a piece of food submerged in the water.

"Go ahead and open it," Alis said. From the corner of her eye she could see Karl grab the closest rung.

The oval door irised open more like a cat's eye than a human eye. On the other side was what seemed to be another air lock chamber. As Lucy floated inside, followed by Robert, Alis reflected on her luck that she lived in an era where most explorers went into new environments wearing pressure suits that took care of air, water, food, waste, and temperature. Some of the pyramid explorers and even more of the arctic explorers would have had significantly longer lives with the protection she sometimes took for granted.

When all four of them hovered in the small air lock, like guppies hiding in a fake cave, the door behind them irised closed.

"I feel like I'm in a torpedo tube," Karl said.

Alis reached forward and touched the oval in front of her. It irised open.

At least the view on the other side of the door looked nothing like the rotating disk area. Alis pushed herself gently forward, sure they should be careful, worried that this place was every bit as dangerous as the rotating disk area, but totally unsure where to expect the worst.

After she'd scanned horizontally, she looked above and below her. She could have been floating in something between an enormous beehive and a huge coral reef with endless pockets and passageways up, down, around, and through. Most of the passageways were large enough to comfortably admit a suited human. She peered through one passageway and concluded that at the other end of a passage a little longer than her height was another pocket perhaps three meters in diameter.

Karl pointed at a different passageway. "If I'm reading my display correctly, I think the probe is in roughly that direction. I'm assuming the brightest dot is the probe. It's pretty near the end of the line that looks like the path it cut along the way."

Alis started double-checking what Karl had said while Robert said, "This place could be hell to find our way out of. It's a giant three-dimensional maze."

Karl said, "To start out, I could tie one end of my rope here and—oh, I just had a better idea."

Alis finished studying her map, and came to the same conclusion Karl had about the direction they needed to go.

Karl went on, obviously excited about coming up with a solution to the problem of getting lost. "Here's all we have to do. Designate one of us to take up the rear. Take that person's video camera and a helmet lamp, and mount them on the person's foot so we have a clear view of what we're leaving behind. Then, when we're ready to go back, we play the recording in reverse and use it as a guide to get us back out."

"That's actually a pretty clever idea," Robert said.

Hearing Robert compliment Karl, even if obliquely, was almost as strange an experience as being in this place, Alis decided. And she agreed. Given that they probably didn't want to make cuts or marks on the scenery, in case that might summon some defense mechanism, the camera solution did make a lot of sense. "Good, Karl. You're the designated follower. Can you get the camera and lamp mounted by yourself?"

"It might be easier if I had help. Maybe someone can tie them to my boot."

Lucy and Robert ended up working together to accomplish the task. In the microgravity, it seemed easier for Lucy to hold the camera and lamp against opposite sides of the boot while Robert maneuvered the coil of rope. After a couple of minutes, Karl looked like he'd had a skiing accident and had one foot in a cast, but the camera and lamp were secure.

"All right," Alis said. "Let's move."

She kicked off toward an opening in roughly the direction they wanted to go. When she reached the passageway, she gripped both sides of the opening and aligned her body with the passage. The blue-green material gave a little, as if the structure were carved from an apple. She wondered if deeper into the surface it became harder, but she had no desire to attract defense mechanisms by cutting into it.

She tugged gently on both sides of the opening, and her body slid through the passageway, not even touching the sides. Fortunately, the chamber on the other side wasn't much larger than the first chamber. If she got stranded in gravity this low, it could take a while to get back to a surface she could kick off from.

From the new chamber, she had seven choices, and she pushed off toward the one closest to the direction she wanted to travel, which was about fifteen degrees up and twenty degrees to the right. She reached the irregular opening and pulled herself into the new passageway. The effortless motion made her feel she was scuba diving in still, totally clear water, but without the resistance.

The next chamber had only three other passageways, and the one beyond that one had nearly three-quarters of its area Swiss-cheesed by passageways. She kept constant watch on their position and the bright dot ahead. She hoped this area had nothing in common with scuba diving surprises like backing into a shark.

Gradually, as the foursome wound its way through grottos and crannies, the chambers grew larger and more distant from each other, as the passageways lengthened and became more twisted. Alis pulled herself through a passageway about five times longer than her height with two bends along the way. It occurred to her that if she had to get back to the door without the aid of Karl's video recording, she may as well give up right then. Other than a very weak sense of up versus down, she was completely disoriented. She switched her helmet viewer to see the view from Karl's camera and was comforted to see a view pulling back from an irregularly shaped passageway.

As she pulled herself through the next passageway, she put her hands against the walls and slowed to a stop. "Wait just a minute. I'm looking at the wall here. The texture is different from what we've seen." She angled her body to get a clearer view with her camera. From a recess where the wall of spongy blue-green material pulled into a pocket came the gleam of something shiny. The smooth exposed surface, no larger than the palm of her hand, was a coppery red.

She continued on her way. The bright dot was growing nearer.

The next passageway was twice as long as the last, with a narrow spot near a bend in the middle, and at first she thought she could manage to get through, but then she thought about the larger bodies behind her. "Sorry. Let's back up. I don't think we can all make it through this one."

Behind her, people slowly edged back out. She pushed herself gently backward through the passageway.

After they regrouped, Alis picked her second-choice passageway, which turned out to be even longer, but at least stayed wide enough to admit them all. She saw more frequent patches of the coppery material.

Alis stopped as her head emerged from the passageway. She looked around the new chamber, feeling like a grouper about to dart back into its cave. This chamber must have been twenty meters across. Getting to the mouth of the next passageway would involve either a fairly long jump or a rock-climbing–like jaunt.

She went for the jump. Poised at the mouth of the passageway, she planted her feet just below the lip and leaped. She actually overcompensated for gravity and hit the wall just a little higher than her destination. Fortunately, the material forming the walls was just spongy and irregular enough that she was able to get a grip and avoid bouncing off and falling slowly to the bottom of the chamber.

She pulled herself into the passageway and left her boots sticking out into the chamber. "Come on ahead," she said. "You can use my boots for a grip."

A few seconds later, Robert's hands fumbled at her boots and pulled. She kept her position by holding her outstretched hands against the tunnel walls.

"Okay," Robert said, "I'm stable."

Alis pulled deeper into the passageway and let Robert help Lucy next.

This passageway was so irregular that Alis thought it might wind up in a dead end, but after maybe thirty meters, she could see a darker open space ahead. Her map said they should be very close to what might be the probe.

Seconds later, she stopped at the mouth of the passageway and looked out at what reminded her of pictures of blight. The blue-green textured surfaces she'd grown accustomed to had turned a milky white in most places. The coppery red shiny surfaces she'd seen once in a while here occupied almost a quarter of the space, showing through the white surfaces like spots on a dog. But the coppery red surfaces were tinged with green, as if corroded.

Alis moved out of the tunnel and clung to the side of the textured surface so the others could see. On the far side of this chamber, the passageway level with her was much larger than normal. Through it she could see what looked to be occasional sparks lighting the darkness, as if a welder were at work.

"I hope they find our recordings," Robert said. "They'd never believe us if we just told them what we've seen in here."

Karl poked his helmet out of the passageway and looked around. Lucy perched nearby.

"Let's go see the fireworks," Karl said.

The fireworks came from the same direction in which the probe should be. Alis leaped across the large chamber, and she knew before she was halfway there that she hadn't kicked accurately enough. In slow motion, she hit the wall about a meter over the top of the passageway. She tried to grab hold so she could just work her way down, but the surface here was tougher, more like dried leather. She bounced off the wall and fell to the bottom of the chamber.

As she fell, Robert jumped for the passageway. He was luckier, perhaps gaining the benefit of watching Alis's trajectory. "Two points!" he said as his outstretched hands went into the passageway.

Men and sports, Alis thought, then erased the judgment as she realized the most competitive person she'd ever known was a female bounce-ball player on Tokyan Station. Marlee would probably have loved this environment, danger or not.

Robert moved farther into the passageway, and Lucy had made the leap, too, before Alis was able to regain control. She made a short series of jumps and entered the passageway behind Lucy. Behind her, Karl made the leap.

"Strange stuff over here," Robert said.

Just seconds later Alis was able to see past Robert and Lucy and find out what was making all the sparks. Robert was right.

The most normal-looking part of the scene was the missing probe. It still had its forward-facing equipment exposed, as if it had been busily cutting its way through Cantaloupe right up until the moment it died.

The rest of the scene was much less familiar. Alis moved out of the passageway so Karl could see, too.

The probe had apparently cut through what vaguely resembled a tree branch that joined the two sides of this chamber, lodging between the separated halves. Perhaps the reason it was still here was that, jammed in that position, with its cutting mechanism of no use to it, it had finally run out of energy.

As Alis watched, ooze formed on both halves of the severed branch, and both globs of ooze began moving closer together, starting to form a cover over the probe and a bridge between the two halves of the branch.

Motion to her left. A long coppery-red cable swung ever so slowly from a pivot point overhead. The free end came closer and closer to the probe. Several long seconds later, it hit. Sparks flew. The cable was flung backward in the same line it had approached.

When she could see the surface of the probe again, she could tell that the ooze that had been forming over the surface of the probe had been burned away.

The four of them continued watching in silence. The cable was slowly flung up to maybe a forty-five-degree angle, and it started down again. More ooze was forming on each side of the branch.

Karl said, "I see a déjà-vu coming."

So did Alis, and they were both right. Contact with the cable produced more sparks, and the newly formed ooze was again burned away.

They watched another two cycles before Lucy said, "Looks like a perpetual motion machine."

Robert said, "Maybe this is why the repair never was completed. Somehow the probe did some damage that Cantaloupe had never anticipated, and—it seems—the defense mechanisms have gotten locked in an endless cycle."

"If all that's true," Karl said, "maybe we could pull the

probe out of there, and Cantaloupe could finish the repairs it-self."

"Could be," Alis said. "Anyone see a downside to trying to help?"

"Only that it'll take some time," Lucy said. "But it's not like we've got a great chance of getting out of here anyway."

Alis assessed the rest of the chamber. This one was per-haps fifty percent bigger than the last, still small enough that one could easily jump from bottom to top in the tiny gravity, but large enough that jumping precisely wasn't easy. Almost all the wall surfaces were the brittle-looking white, or the tar-nished copper showing through in patches. Below the damaged branch running the width of the chamber was another hori-zontal branch, perhaps ten meters below, running at right an-gles to the one above it.

"You know," Karl said, "this situation is a good argument that there's no one alive inside here. You'd think that a situa-tion like this—damage that's not getting repaired by normal mechanisms—would call for manual intervention."

Lucy said, "Unless everyone's in suspended animation."

"Or there might never have been anyone in here."

"Let's get the damage fixed and worry about that later," Robert said.

The cable swung into the probe again and more sparks flew. Alis watched as small particles fell to the bottom surface of the chamber. That surface was slightly darkened, but there was no significant accumulation of debris, as if it were all being reabsorbed into the chamber walls.

Karl said, "Maybe we can use the rope to pull the probe loose."

"Sounds reasonable," Alis said. "I'm not crazy about the idea of getting too near it. Go ahead and unwind it from the camera."

Karl found another passageway, and he entered it halfway to allow Lucy and Robert access to his boot. Moments later

Lucy pulled loose the last loop. Karl remounted his camera and lamp while Alis made absolutely sure she could identify the passageway they'd come through.

When the others were ready, Alis made a careful leap to the edge of the lower branch. She gauged the jump just right, and moments later she straddled the branch. The others moved into position to join her.

14 · NUCLEUS

Karl felt more comfortable when his full helmet lighting was restored. He finished coiling the cord and fixed it to his belt. As soon as Lucy completed her jump to the lower branch spanning the chamber and moved out of the way, Karl followed.

His easy jump was slightly too low, but the gravity was so slight that he had an easy time of pulling himself on top of the branch. He straddled the branch, held his legs tight, and looked up.

He was just in time to see the reddish cable reconnect with the probe, producing another explosion of sparks reminiscent of fireworks. Some of the upward-shooting sparks helped illuminate the top of the chamber, and from his new vantage point he was able to get a better view.

The ceiling was much higher than he'd thought at first.

An irregular grid of reddish cables formed a Junglegym framework, and it was one of those reddish cables that had been severed. The other end was stubbier and motionless. Karl couldn't tell if the swinging end of the cable was long enough to reconnect with its counterpart. The uppermost point in the swing still left a couple of meters between the severed ends.

"It's amazing to think this cycle might have been going on for centuries," Robert said.

"Yeah," Lucy said. "You'd think some defense mechanism or healing function would have fixed the damage long ago."

Karl looked up at the slowly swinging cable. "I suppose the fact that the probe damaged two related areas is the key. Maybe Cantaloupe can repair virtually any one thing that goes wrong, but it can't necessarily handle any possible combination of multiple failures. What's even more surprising to me is that the cable has been able to flex that many times without breaking."

Alis said, "I suppose that implies the possibility that the cable is constantly being repaired. The repair mechanism hasn't been able to get the cable back into place so it can heal together, but apparently the individual sections are in good shape."

Robert said, "Well, I'm not sure whether we should try to fix the cable first or pull the probe out of there first."

"How about this," Karl said. "Try dislodging the probe first. If it's easy to do, then worry about the cable. If the probe doesn't come loose easily, then we try to do something about the cable. It could be that when we fix one of the problems, Cantaloupe will be able to fix the other."

"Makes sense," said Alis.

"Maybe we can loop the rope over the top of the probe," Robert said. "Then we can loop it under this branch and tighten it."

"Anyone with a better idea?" Alis asked.

"No," Karl said, "but it's not going to be easy in low gee to make the throw."

"Let me try." Robert held his hand out for the cord. Karl gave it to him.

Robert moved farther out on the branch, to get closer to the probe above. When he was in position, he made his first throw. The gravity was so weak that the rope pretty much just traveled in a straight line and bounced back in the same line as soon as it had fully extended. Robert tried again with the same result.

Robert tried a different way. He let a long length of rope dangle beneath him as he tried to get it moving in a pendulum motion that he could magnify. Again the low gravity made the job too difficult. The cord swung so slowly that Robert's efforts to generate a pendulum motion instead just served to make ripples in the cord.

Karl said, "How about if I jump up to the level the probe is stuck on? You can throw the cord at me, and I can drop the other end over the branch."

"I'm not crazy about anyone getting very close to the probe," Alis said.

"Me, neither, actually," Karl said. "You want to send Robert?"

Alis hesitated, watching Robert's attempts with the rope for another long moment, then said, "Go for it, Karl."

Karl moved to a point from which he could jump and safely avoid getting near the probe or the sparking cable. He carefully got to his feet, feeling as if he were balancing on a slick log. He jumped.

He must have been getting used to the small but non-zero gravity, because the jump was just right. He gripped the upper limb and pulled himself back into a straddling position. He was just in time to see the cable swing gently back onto the probe.

This time the sparks were less like a distant and pretty fireworks display and more like standing too close to a welder. Karl instinctively leaned back. A few of the sparks took trajectories directly toward his faceplate. Two of them made it all the way and bounced off the permalex. He looked closely but saw no sign of damage.

Karl tilted to one side of the branch until he could see Robert. "Okay, toss me the end."

Robert's first toss went under Karl. He tried to snag the line with his boot, but missed.

Robert tried again. This time the toss was perfect.

"Great." Karl took up the slack, then dropped the coil on the opposite side of the branch.

Robert couldn't quite reach the other end, but Lucy could. The rope was just about the perfect length for what they needed to do. If Lucy wrapped her end underneath their branch and they tied the two ends together, they'd be able to start twisting with a tool kit wrench, tightening the loop until a good amount of tension was built up. All they needed now was for the top of the loop to be positioned over the probe.

Karl gripped a length of the cord in front of him and tried to throw it toward the probe. He managed to get it only halfway.

The red cable arced into the probe again, spraying more sparks.

"No problem," Robert said. "We can get it the rest of the way." He and Lucy began to whip the rope back and forth so the ripples would push the cord where they needed it. The loop over the branch slithered toward the probe.

All looked promising until the rope snagged just a half-meter from the probe. Robert and Lucy both continued flipping the cord, but a short section of the cable seemed stuck on something.

"One of you try pulling," Karl said.

Lucy let Robert have the honor, but despite Robert's steady pressure and follow-up yanks, the cord didn't budge. Then Lucy tried, too, with the same lack of success.

"Looks like I'll need to free it," Karl said.

"Aren't there any other choices?" Alis asked. "I don't like

the idea of you being in range of that electrical discharge."

"I'm open to hearing other suggestions. While you're thinking, I'm going to time the cycle."

While Karl measured the cycle, no other suggestions were offered. "That cable sparks against the probe every forty seconds. I should have time to get close enough to free the rope and get back."

"I still don't like it," Alis said.

"I don't either, but I haven't heard any alternate suggestions. Does 'I don't like it' mean 'no'?"

"Just be careful."

"I will. But it's not like whatever we do here is going to make much difference in the long run."

"Don't say that."

"Whatever you say."

Karl got ready to move fast. In some situations, low gravity is advantageous to fast motion. Here it wasn't, not when he'd like to have more friction. In one gee, he could just run over to the rope, pull it free, and run back.

The next cycle was about to the start. The red cable was falling toward the probe.

Seconds before the cable hit, Karl was already moving forward, his legs still straddling the branch. Sparks filled his view, telling him he was much closer than he wanted to be. And then the red cable was arcing back up, giving him almost forty seconds to do something he hoped would take only ten.

At first, the rising cable seemed to move even more slowly than before as Karl edged closer to the cord.

He reached the cord. The rope seemed to have sunk slightly into the surface of the branch. Karl grabbed a section of the cord a quarter of the way down the side of the branch, and he pulled.

"The cord's stuck to the surface," Karl said.

He yanked upward on the end of the cord, and it slowly began to pull free. Along the top of the branch, under the rope, was a sap-like substance. Apparently the branch was secreting the material as a repair substance.

The cord was halfway loose, and the red cable was still in its upward swing, nearing the top.

Karl squeezed his legs tighter against the branch as he increased the tension on the rope. It was almost free. The red cable reached the top of its swing. He'd used up half his time already.

"Hurry, Karl!" Lucy said.

The rope came free. Karl pulled on both sides and tossed the loop forward. Slowly it settled over the top of the probe.

"Good going!" Robert said.

Even as the rope was settling onto the top surface of the probe, Karl was starting to move back to safety.

At least he tried to move back. But he was stuck. The inside of his left thigh was stuck to the side of the branch. "I'm stuck!" he yelled.

The tip of the red cable was falling again, extremely slowly at first.

"No!" Alis said.

If Karl could have reached the rope, he could have had them pull him free of the sap or whatever sticky substance he was in. But the rope was out of reach now, just close enough to be tantalizing. He pulled away from the branch, risking a fall, risking a tear in his suit, risking anything so he wouldn't be there when the red cable completed its swing.

No good. He lifted his right leg and planted his foot against the top of the branch. He pushed. He pushed harder. Suddenly he could feel something give. His thigh was pulling way from the branch.

Too slowly. He was pulling free, but the red cable was coming closer and closer.

"Hurry, Karl!" Lucy said.

Karl was pulling free too slowly. He suddenly knew he'd never make it in time.

He kept pushing, and in the last second or two before the red cable reached him, he wasted some energy saying, "I didn't cause that accident, damnit!"

The suit popped loose.

In higher gravity, he might have fallen away fast enough to avoid the red cable, but in higher gravity, the fall would have been fatal.

The cable hit. Sparks flew.

A searing pain jolted through Karl's thigh. He was falling.

Free fall made him think he was dying, and the pain was the only thing that said he wasn't, so for just a moment he welcomed the agony. A buzzing in his ears was something he recognized only in retrospect as the worried shouts from his companions.

He drifted in darkness, his eyes shut against the pain. Was his suit ripped? The pain made him think his leg had been severed and the suit was flooding his private atmosphere into the surrounding public vacuum.

Karl fell. Zero gravity intensified the feeling of detachment from the real world. Darkness beckoned.

Just enough of his rational mind kept functioning to remind him that even in the low gravity, a long fall could still generate enough inertia to—

He hit. He realized that he must have been breathing earlier because suddenly he couldn't breathe again. The wind was knocked out of him, and he was left in that strange state where the muscles responsible for filling the lungs with air somehow seem paralyzed right when they are needed the most. More faint buzzing noises sounded from far away. He was in zero gee again, having bounced off whatever he'd hit.

Just when he decided his inability to breathe came from the fact that his suit was open to vacuum, he finally managed a small gasp, then a larger one, sucking precious oxygen back inside. He hit again, but this time the blow was much softer.

Pain still boiled on the outside of his thigh, where the cable had hit, but for the first time he could make out voices.

"Get that patched!" said a voice that sounded like Alis's. She sounded so far away she could have been on Cantaloupe's surface.

Part of his brain registered another aftershock as he hit and bounced again. The aftershocks were more closely spaced now as his body finally crumpled against the ground. He should have been an accountant. This was just too much crap to take.

"I'm hurrying," said a voice rather like Robert's except for being even more remote then usual.

"Karl, can you hear us?" Lucy asked. She seemed closer than the others.

"I think so," Karl said. At least he thought he said it. No one responded in a way that made him think he'd been heard, so he didn't know if he'd imagined it or if his transmitter had died.

Some of the pain receptors in his leg must have gotten tired of screaming out their message. That could be good or bad, he decided. He couldn't tell if part of his leg had quit complaining of pain or it was simply numb.

"Can anyone hear me?" Karl said.

"What?"

"Can you hear me?"

"We can hear you, Karl!" Alis sounded so happy that he wondered if she'd just heard good news from the *Ranger.*

"Quit moving," Robert said. "I've got to patch your suit."

Karl hadn't been aware that he was moving, but once Robert mentioned the fact, he realized he was backpedaling his legs, as if tying to push himself away from danger. He willed himself to calm down and lie still. He decided most of his body had obeyed his commands, but his racing heart was obviously disobeying orders.

He could feel some pressure on his thigh. He clenched his teeth as the pressure changed to a new spike of pain. It happened again.

"All right," Robert said. "Your suit's holding now. You lost a little oxygen, but I don't think it was enough to make any difference. How do you feel?"

"My leg feels like someone shot me. Apart from that I really feel pretty crummy."

"You've never been actually shot, right?"

"Actually, I have. My dad owned a bunch of guns, and my little brother figured out how to pick the lock on the gun cabinet. Maybe he watched too many episodes of *Mangy Mike*. He thought he'd just found a neat toy. Fortunately, he didn't hit anything vital. I got even with him, though. Boy, did I cry."

"Er, well, can you be more specific about the pain?"

"Like on the Richter scale or something?"

"Where precisely does it hurt?"

Karl did his best to point. "From here to about here, I think."

"Does it feel hot or cold?" Robert asked.

"Hot, I guess."

"Is the pain stable. Pulsating? Is it going away?"

"Pulsating. Tell me the truth, Doc. Am I a hypochondriac?"

Robert ignored the comment. "Damn, I really can't do much in this environment."

"How are you with autopsies?" The pain intensified, and Karl's eyes watered. He sniffled, feeling like a sick kid.

"You're going to be fine, Karl," Alis said.

Karl's watering and blinking eyes made it difficult to deliberately control his helmet display, but seconds later he was able to call up the suit diagnostic display. Most lights were still green, but a couple of yellows were troubling. One yellow indicated the heat-distribution function was operating in a degraded condition. Marginal but temporarily acceptable. The other yellow said his left boot heater was marginal.

Robert said, "I'm going to transmit a prescription for your suit to dispense. The next time you take a drink of water, take a big gulp to dilute the taste. Keep drinking more frequently than normal."

"Got it. What's on the menu?"

"Painkiller, antibiotic, anti-inflammatory, with a couple of things on the side."

"Somehow it doesn't seem a good medical choice to label something with the word 'killer.' Shouldn't you people call it an 'anti-pain' or 'pain suppressant' or something?"

"I'll pass your comments along to the name designation council."

"There is such a thing?"

"Get serious."

"Is he going to be all right?" Alis said.

Karl quit babbling because he was interested in the answer, too. A medical status light flashed on his helmet screen, and he took a big gulp of water. The sweet-and-sour water taste made him take a second gulp, and that one was refreshingly neutral. Karl prayed that his suit diagnostic had evaluated correctly and that his suit's recycling and recovery system hadn't been damaged.

Robert hesitated. "I don't know. The suit's no longer leaking, but you can see the burn marks. Whether it will protect his leg adequately or not I don't know. And I can't really tell how much damage has been done to his leg."

Karl found himself wishing they had chosen a private communication that he couldn't overhear. He formed a mental image of burned skin plastered against melted pressure-suit material and thought about how painful it could be just to remove a large bandage tape. He could feel the soft touch of air moving against his right foot, but no matching sensation in his left.

"I'm sure you're going to be fine, Karl," Lucy said.

"I hope you're right." Karl arched his back and craned his neck to get a view of the probe.

When he first looked up, something seemed wrong with the picture. A large object moved slowly down from far above, as if an elevator in an invisible shaft were dropping toward them.

"Watch out!" Karl cried. "The probe is falling!"

Three sets of helmet lamps whipped upward. Karl tried to roll himself farther from the point of impact. His ears filled with the sounds of startled noises and swearing. Everyone tried to scramble out of the way, hustling and making very little progress in the low gravity, like pets on a slick floor.

Karl tried to ignore the pain throbbing through his leg as he completed two revolutions. He stopped and looked up again. The probe was still falling, moving faster, looking larger. Karl was safely out of its path, and Lucy was the last one out of the impact zone. He started to relax, then remembered that the probe could bounce. He rolled over again, two more times, his eyes watering with the pain.

He stopped again, just in time to see the probe hit the "ground" without landing on anyone. The probe was so massive, and the surface it landed on so inelastic, that it hardly bounced at all. In slow motion it rose to a height of less than a half-meter before it fell back in a leisurely motion that finally damped out after just one more impact.

"Everyone's all right?" Alis asked.

"Safe and sound," Lucy said.

"I'm okay," Robert said.

"I've had better days," Karl said. "Can we go home now?"

Alis cleared her throat. "Thanks, Karl. That could have done some serious damage."

"My pleasure."

"What's happening up there?" Lucy asked.

Karl rolled onto his back so he could look up toward the

top of the chamber. He squinted, trying to make out what had changed.

"Cantaloupe is repairing itself!" Alis said. No doubt she was looking at the top of the chamber with the benefit of telephoto eyes. "The branch the probe severed is growing back together. That reddish cable is slowly bending back into place. It looks like the two ends might meet in another minute."

"But we didn't do anything," Lucy said.

"Maybe Karl did. His body blocked the cable from hitting the damaged area around the probe directly. That must have been enough to break the cycle and let the branch heal itself to the point that it ejected the foreign matter—the probe."

"Makes sense," Robert said. "If the cable's constant flexing kept it from being repaired, breaking the cycle might have helped it start recovering, too. In the human body, if you're trying to cure two unrelated defects, you can wind up with problems like the drugs used for each problem interacting with each other. It could be that Cantaloupe's design allowed it to repair either problem but that the combination of the two was so unexpected that the cycle would have continued forever unless interrupted."

"Look," Lucy said. "The chamber walls up there. The texture or the color is changing."

"You're right," Alis said. "The pale white surfaces are gradually turning pinker. It could be that this damage was just the most visible portion."

Robert said, "Right. Stabilize a palpitating heart, and the prognosis for the entire body is greatly improved."

"Of course we don't know if we've just repaired the heart or just dealt with a blister," Lucy said.

"True," Alis said. "But I think we have done some good. Whether it's in time to make any difference, I don't know."

Robert said, "Whatever happened, the changes are happening rapidly. Look at the walls."

Karl did so, trying to ignore the constant pain. The walls

had almost completed a transformation from white to pink.

Lucy said, "Has anyone wondered whether these passages are normal or not? If they're only here because of the damage, or if they're enlarged because of the damage, we could be out the air lock without a thruster."

Alis responded instantly. "You're right. Let's get out of here."

"Yes, our work here is complete," Robert said. The levity in his voice was new to Karl's experience.

Alis said, "I've got Karl's recording queued up and ready to roll in reverse. I'll take the lead. Lucy, you next. Robert, you third so Karl can hang onto your ankles if he's too weak to keep up."

"Just a suggestion," Lucy said rapidly. "Let me jump up and cut loose as much cord as I can, in case we need it later."

"Good," Alis said. "Move it."

Karl thought he had the energy to keep up, but as he pushed himself upward, even the small expenditure of energy gave him a headache he hadn't noticed before.

Lucy was back shortly with two pieces of cord coiled on her belt. Everyone fell into place without argument. Alis had really turned out to be a good leader. Karl realized that some other mission, working under the virtually unavoidable threat of death, might well have fallen apart by this stage, dissolving in a quagmire of mutiny and just plain bickering and dissention. Maybe their success at functioning as a team was due to resignation and curiosity, but Karl thought there was more to it.

Pain surged through his leg again and somehow set up additional sympathetic pain in his head. Once he had a grip on Robert's ankles, Karl blindly held on.

After a series of long seconds, his head entered a passageway. He clung to Robert's ankles as he felt his body pulled through the passageway, bouncing back and forth off the walls. Somewhere in the foggy back part of his brain, he wondered if the passageway seemed tighter than it had on the way in. At one point pain turned his leg into a part of his body he wished he could just lop off.

In an atypical moment of clarity, he supposed the real measure of the pain was that his concern for having the pain end outweighed all other considerations, such as whether they reached the air lock alive or if they got out of Cantaloupe alive.

Another bump hit his leg. He screamed.

"Karl?" A tinny voice sounded like it was coming from Mars. "Karl? Can you hear me?"

After a time, Karl decided he was the Karl being talked to, and that Robert was the one talking to him. "I asked you never to call me here." Karl giggled.

"Karl, grab the rope. You let go of my ankles. I'm going to have to pull you out of there with the rope. Reach out. Feel the cord. Grab it." A pause. "Grab the rope, Karl!"

Karl supposed he must have followed directions, because moments later, Robert said, "Good show. Now hold tight."

Karl's body began moving through the narrow passage again, and the reflected light from the wall in front of his face was bright to the point of being painful.

He shot out of the tunnel like a torpedo exploding from a sub tube. For a time he fell, and for a time he hurt very badly.

Someone, Robert he assumed, tied his hands together and pulled them over his head. "Okay, I've got you now. We'll be out of here soon."

"That's nice. Where are we?"

"Just relax."

Karl felt his hands yanked over his head. Not very relaxing. He was in free fall for an unmeasured time, then drawn toward a dark hole and pulled inside, wondering if this was some memory regression to the birth canal.

His leg bumped against something again. Pain flared, this time mercifully letting the world recede to a small point of light and then disappear.

. . .

The world rumbled. Karl shut his eyes tighter. A flickering thought said maybe he was coming back from the verge of unconsciousness during a high-gee burn.

Fog dissipated a bit. Maybe he was just waking up after a bad dream.

No, this hadn't been a dream, he concluded. He didn't sleep in his pressure suit.

Part of a tunnel wall slid by his view, and in a rush everything came back to him. Trapped inside Cantaloupe. Injury. Threat of Cantaloupe being exploded by asteroid-deflection devices. Threat of burning up in the sun. He wished he could go back to sleep. What a crummy day.

Something yanked on his hands. He was still in diving posture, hands over head, still being pulled along, presumably by Robert.

"Are we there yet?" Karl asked.

"Thank God, Karl," Alis said. "We were afraid you were—" She stopped suddenly, probably realizing none of the choices were very good bedside chatter or confidence-inspiring. "I'm glad you're awake."

"How are you feeling?" Robert asked. For a moment Karl felt he was in an altered reality, because Robert had said something to him without using his normal disdainful tone, but then he remembered that Robert actually had started being civil to him a little while earlier.

"Better. Maybe the drugs are working finally."

Robert went on, still using a manner he might have used with someone he actually liked or respected. "I wish I'd been able to apply a topical medication, or give you some injections. The oral stuff takes too long, and it's tougher to target a specific area of the body."

"No problem. I hate needles."

"We're almost all the way out, Karl," Lucy said. "At least

we think so." Lucy sounded concerned, too. Lucy had always been less reserved than Robert, so this wasn't as much of a change for her, but the difference was still noteworthy.

"Only about a minute left on the recording," Alis said. "Brilliant idea, Karl." Alis's praise was the biggest surprise, as if he'd come out the other side of the rabbit hole and things were no longer what they seemed to be.

"That's me. Karl, the boy genius. Karl, the guy who stuck his leg in an electrical outlet." His head emerged from the passageway, and Robert gave him a yank toward a new destination. In a couple of seconds, Karl managed to catch up with recent events.

Alis actually gave a short laugh, and the sound of it was remarkably pleasing. Karl had been convinced that inside Cantaloupe he would encounter things never seen or heard before, and he'd been right. "You did great."

"Robert, I think I can manage on my own now. Want to cut me loose?"

"We're not far now, and I don't know that you won't have a relapse. Let's just finish up this way."

Karl would rather have been on his own, but at least Robert hadn't responded with a flat authoritarian "no" that would have increased Karl's determination.

The rise out of the fog seemed to have slowed. Karl felt much more alert and able than he had a few moments earlier, but he still didn't feel he could pass a written test at much past the third-grade level. There seemed to be an ultra-thin and clear membrane between him and the real world, a filter that allowed words to flow back and forth but still kept him slightly at bay, slightly off balance.

"I can see the air lock," Alis called.

Another yank on his arms carried Karl farther through the passageway. He felt like a fish on a hook.

Lucy said, "Is it just me, or do the surfaces seem a little pinker than before?"

"I think you're right," Alis said. "It's as if this entire area is getting healthier."

"I agree," Robert said, "but I'm still unsure why no one has come to fix the damage before us."

"Maybe we'll get a clue at the next stop. I would think there has to be a control room of sorts."

Lucy said, "If there is a control room, I'd be happy if we could get a clue about how to get out of here."

"Like an ejection seat?" Robert asked.

"Anything. Matter transmitter, escape pod. If nothing else, if there's a transmitter, we could maybe let the *Ranger* know where we are, and they could cut us out."

"Maybe things have improved on the outside," Karl said. "We haven't heard from them lately. Wouldn't the captain give us another warning or two before they blast?"

"Er, Karl," Alis said hesitantly, "he called again while you were out. We don't have a lot of time left."

"How much?"

"You don't really want to know."

Strangely enough, Karl found he agreed. Maybe it was the drugs. He'd been a pariah for so long, it just felt good to be accepted by three people.

His body exited another passageway, and he was pulled through a chamber and toward the mouth of another passageway. This chamber was much smaller than the ones near the epicenter of damage.

Karl bumped his leg on the way into the new passageway. There wasn't much pain, but the feeling was still troubling, more like hitting a numb spot than hitting healthy skin, and he couldn't just reach down and push and prod his leg to see how it actually felt. He tried to let his body relax and travel freely through the passage. The last pull on his arms brought him just to the opening to the next chamber, with his arms and upper chest sticking out into the opening. On the other side of the chamber, Alis had the air lock open already.

"Okay," Robert said. "Let's get rid of the rope." His gloves looked awkward for the task of untying the rope, but he just pulled on a loose end, and the slipknot came loose neatly.

Karl flexed his arms, working out the start of a cramp, and wondered if he'd been underestimating Robert just because of the man's anger. "Thanks for dragging me all this way, Robert."

"Thanks for sticking your leg in an electrical outlet so I didn't have to. How are you feeling?"

"Not a lot of pain actually. But a little woozy."

"You may stay a little woozy. I've programmed your medical dispenser to give you some antibiotics and painkillers at periodic times. If you get so drowsy you stop responding to us, I'll back off some. I've also set up a monitor program to warn me if your vital signs vary too much from normal. At the moment, your body temperature is up almost a degree."

"Well, I'm glad that's not my suit malfunctioning. Yet."

"You guys ready?" Alis asked. She and Lucy were already in the air lock.

"I think I'm ready," Karl said.

"Go ahead," Robert said. "I can help if you need it."

Karl pulled himself out of the passageway mouth, more grateful than ever for the ultra-low gravity. He started to pull his legs under him so he could make the jump, and felt a flare of the pain he'd hoped wouldn't bother him again.

"Are you all right?" Alis asked.

Karl hadn't thought he'd made any sound, but he guessed he must have. "I think I'm okay. Just a little twinge. Here goes."

Karl pushed off, thinking that the short span and the microgravity should combine for a trivial jump. He knew he'd missed even in the instant he jumped, the same way he knew when a basketball shot was just leaving his hands that he would miss. He hit the wall about a meter below the air lock.

After a short embarrassed silence, as Karl fell slowly toward the floor, he said, "Stupid game."

He recovered his balance on the floor and assured everyone he was fine for another try. This time he underestimated his kick and shot a little too high, but Alis was able to grab his belt as he fell past the opening. She dragged him inside.

"Thanks," he said. "I feel like I'm one of those newborn animals in the nature shows. You know, a tiny deer walking around on stick legs."

"I've had some experience with that myself," Alis said. "Join the club." In a transcript, the words might have sounded harsh, but there was a warmth to the words that Karl had never heard before, as if she really was commiserating without any bitterness showing through. She set him down gently on the air lock floor.

"Thanks," Karl said again. "Sometimes I feel nostalgic for things I've done in the past but haven't done recently. I don't think this place will ever make my list." *Unless,* he thought, *it would be for the time that Alis thawed out.* Then again, the possibility of growing enough older that he'd be capable of looking back at this time as a distant memory seemed pretty unlikely.

Robert's suited body appeared in the air lock door, and Karl pulled him inside. Alis let the door iris shut.

Karl let himself relax again, aware that he could fall asleep all too easily.

Lucy opened the far door, and moments later all four of them were in the tunnel beyond. The tunnel seemed to be just the way Karl remembered it, an infinitely long drainage pipe with pinkish sides, and rungs on the bottom. Alis made sure Robert followed Karl so someone would notice if Karl didn't keep up. Alis said, "Are you going to be okay getting back to the transport pod, Karl?"

"I think so. I pretty much only have to use my arms."

"Can I count on you to say something if you're having trouble?"

"Sure. I'll just let out a whine."

"Right." Alis's undercurrent of amusement left Karl feeling she didn't picture him as a whiner. He felt a bit better than he had a moment earlier.

Alis moved into the lead as they headed back toward the transport pod. Lucy followed her, and Karl followed Lucy. He gently tugged on one of the rungs in the floor, and pulled himself forward in a gentle arc. After a few imperfect jumps, he was able to twist his hands just a little when he pulled, and his feet stayed in the air, without thumping against the tunnel floor each time.

Karl settled into a comfortable pattern, keeping up with Alis and Lucy. After a while the monotony of the rhythm made him sleepy, but he fought to stay awake and keep from being any more of a burden.

"Are my eyes tired," Lucy said, "or are the walls changing color?"

Karl blinked and opened his eyes wider. Alis and Lucy skidded to a stop, and Karl braked his forward motion. When he was stopped, he flipped on his back and lay there looking at the ceiling illuminated by his helmet lamp. He tried to keep his eyes open.

Over the course of a half-dozen long and leisurely blinks, with his eyelids staying closed for several seconds each time, Karl saw what Lucy was talking about. The surface of the ceiling was making a very gradual transition from pink to purple.

"I see what you mean," Alis said.

"Me, too," Robert said.

"Karl, are you okay?" Alis asked.

"Fine. I thought I said I could see the change. I guess I didn't, huh?"

"Not that I heard."

Lucy said, "I wonder if Cantaloupe is dying. Maybe they've already set off the deflection explosives."

"I doubt it," Robert said. "My display says the most recent map update was sent down just a few minutes ago, so we're still in contact, and I can't imagine the captain forgetting to tell us."

"Me, either," Alis said. "I wonder if the damage we repaired—or Karl repaired—was in an area that affected much more than just the immediate surroundings."

"Certainly possible," Robert said. "With humans, the entire body can be almost paralyzed with pain by an ant's-head-sized calcified stone in a kidney. A small tumor in the wrong place, and you can't even speak coherently. The probe's damage could have kept a vital part of Cantaloupe from responding to other damage, or kept it from performing routine maintenance."

The color change continued as Robert spoke, the walls turning a deeper shade of purple.

"So we might have pulled a thorn from a lion's paw?" Karl asked.

"Maybe," Robert said. "But it could be the lion will never have any comprehension of that fact. And if it grows more fully conscious, it might even conclude that *we* are the source of the damage."

"What, and just destroy what helped it?"

"Human bodies have been known to reject organs they vitally need, let alone destroy foreign substances."

A few days ago, Karl might have taken Robert's assessment to be the negative expression of a pessimistic personality. Today the view just seemed prudent and reasonably cautious.

"Let's get moving," Alis said.

Karl really wanted a nap, but it felt good to be moving, if for no other reason than defense mechanisms might find them more easily if they stayed in one place. They resumed their journey, their motions vaguely like those of scuba divers swimming the length of a long drainage tube. Karl wondered how far they might be from sharks.

15 ▪ OBSTRUCTION

When the knock sounded on his cabin door, Captain Fernandez flipped instantly from standby catnap mode to operationally ready. "Come in."

The cabin door slid open. Martina Binotell set her large frame into the visitor's web and let the door close.

The captain stayed where he was, in his bed-web. The time was in the middle of his sleep shift, but that hardly mattered now.

"I hope you're happy with this one," Martina said. "I really think it's the best we can do."

Captain Fernandez gave her no encouragement, but if she really thought this was the best they could do on short notice, it probably was. She was the very bright leader of the asteroid-deflection team. Fernandez had run her in circles, partly in an effort to find the least-damaging alternative, and partly to delay the impact as long as possible. If he tried to delay much more, he knew he'd be talking to Martina's boss and her boss's boss with no delay beyond light speed. "Show me."

Martina unfolded a pocket screen and snapped it flat. On the screen came up an illustration sequence showing a large sphere labeled "Cantaloupe." Approaching it from a distance was a section of a sphere, about a thirty- or forty-degree arc, with the concave face heading toward Cantaloupe.

Martina said, "We detonate when we're about one radius out from the surface." On the screen an explosion sent a cloud of dark dust toward the surface of Cantaloupe, discoloring about a tenth of the area of the sphere.

She went on. "The device will be steadily accelerated for several hours before it reaches the impact point. That inertia will add to the inertia provided by the explosion. The back-thrust from the explosion should neutralize most of the container's forward motion, assuming it doesn't also blast it to bits. Bottom line: we pepper a huge area instead of creating a huge force in a tiny spot. Almost the same total push."

Good, Fernandez thought. A standard device placed against Cantaloupe's comparatively soft surface would be like shooting a watermelon. This way they had a chance of diverting Cantaloupe without fragmenting it, and that would reduce the risk of the crew being hurt. He watched the sequence replay as he considered whether he could ask for any more delays or fine-tuning, and concluded he'd probably pushed Martina all the way to her limits. "When could you deploy?"

"Impact will be no more than four hours after you say go."

"Go."

Martina lifted her wristcomp to her lips. "Go." As a male voice said, "Got it," she relaxed for the first time since the captain had known her. She pointed to the space on the far side of Cantaloupe from the planned explosion. "You'll probably want to be in this area with the rest of my ships. Anywhere else, and I wouldn't want to be your insurance company."

Alis checked the time again, impatient to get back to the transport pod. Ahead of her the dark tunnel filled with light at the speed she traveled. Behind her, Lucy, Karl, and Robert kept up their regular motions that kept their bodies traveling through shallow arcs from one rung to another.

As she kept watch for the transport pod door, she let herself slip into a moment of introspection. Why the impatience? Hours ago, maybe even days ago now, she'd felt resigned to being trapped inside Cantaloupe for the remainder of her expectedly short life. Now she felt the need to hurry, as if her actions of the moment really would matter.

The change puzzled her. She'd never put much stock in psychic abilities, so she doubted her new feelings were the result of some hidden message saying that if only they hurried they would get out of here alive after all. In fact, a true focus on saving life would probably leave her obsessed with whether Cantaloupe was still on a collision course with Hamilton Station. Four, or even six, lives wouldn't cause more than a possible rounding error on the number of lives that could be lost.

That thought helped her realize that she was, in fact, focused on her own life, and the lives of her remaining teammates. Now of all times she actually found herself wishing she could get to know Karl better. Maybe if she'd known him better before the accident, she would have had an easier time believing what he had to say.

Karl was driving her faster. Karl in pain. If a few days ago someone had told her she'd react this way to Karl, she would have had a hard time replying without expletives. She tried to further break down her reactions. Was this an injured teammate kind of thing, or was it Karl in particular?

She tried to imagine that Robert had been the one injured, and she reached her oddest conclusion yet. It was Karl. If Robert were injured, she guessed she'd be concerned and feeling guilty and all the other things she felt, but she really didn't think she'd feel the same hand-at-the-back-of-her-neck fear. She hadn't cried when Belinda died. She wasn't sure if she'd cry if Robert died. But somehow the idea of Karl dying now seemed beyond her limit.

"Hey, hey, hey!" Lucy said.

"What?" Alis blinked a couple of times.

"We're here. You overshot."

Alis suddenly registered the fact that the circular patch she'd just gone by was the transport pod door she'd been searching for so diligently. She sure was doing a great job. "Sorry. Distracted, I guess." She grabbed the next rung and this time, instead of giving it a light push to keep herself aloft, she grabbed it and hung on. She did a somersault ending with her heels bouncing on the tunnel floor.

By the time she pivoted and looked around, Lucy already had the transport pod door open and Robert was helping Karl get inside.

"Thanks for all the help," Karl said softly. "I feel really old or really rich."

Alis's original dislike of Karl would have been easier to maintain if his injury had turned him into a constant complainer, more like Robert seemed. Instead, his good humor gave her the impression that the real Karl wasn't much different than the public Karl—not that bad a guy.

Alis reached the pod door and followed the others inside. A few seconds later the pod started rotating again. Alis settled into a more comfortable position as the artificial gravity increased and the pod sides became a vaguely cylindrical floor.

A muffled groan sounded for just a second, barely long enough to identify, but the voice belonged to Karl.

"You okay in this gravity, Karl?" Alis asked.

"Now I am. For a moment there I thought I had glued all my leg hair to the inside of my suit."

"Let me take another look," Robert said.

Robert took Karl through a another detailed series of, "Does this hurt?" and, "How does this feel?" Karl's answers were mostly, "Okay," with an occasional, "That smarts," and a, "Don't touch me there."

Alis called up the latest 3-D interior map and tried to concentrate on it while Robert reassessed Karl's condition. The path ahead was even more well defined than before. They were headed right for the center of Cantaloupe.

If the collection of thin lines ahead were all transport routes, the paths of more than a dozen transport pods all passed through a sphere surrounding a seemingly open volume perhaps a few hundred meters across. It looked to Alis as if they could exit the transport pod they now rode and enter any other transport pod. Unfortunately, the map still showed no sign of any transport pod route reaching all the way to the surface.

She kept scanning the other areas of the interior. As with the rest of the features in the display, the two adjoining spheres on the far side of Cantaloupe showed up more clearly now. The enhanced view now available to her was showing shadowy features inside each sphere, but for some reason the level of detail was significantly inferior to that of regions elsewhere inside Cantaloupe. She wondered if the material on the surfaces of the two spheres was a better conductor than the rest of the insides of Cantaloupe, and hence a bigger barrier to the scanning transmissions.

The huge chasm they'd stopped at earlier and a symmetrical chasm on the other side of Cantaloupe showed up more clearly now, too. Other large features had come into view, giving Alis the strengthening feeling of looking at a scan of a body, not a scan of a ship.

What the scan still failed to reveal was any area Alis could convince herself was a living space. No apparent crew, and no apparent passengers. Just the huge bulk of Cantaloupe and its internal mechanisms.

"All right, Karl. You can relax again," Robert said. "I'm making some adjustments to your medication flow. You're doing as well as can be expected."

"Thanks, Doc." Karl sounded sleepy.

The "private message" chime sounded in Alis's helmet. Alis accepted the call, and Robert started talking only to her. "I'm afraid he doesn't look too good. I'll do the best I can, but—"

"But?"

"Well, at least I can keep him mostly free from pain. But it's all so hypothetical at this point. We could all be dead at any time, and my guess is that at the latest we'll all be dead in a couple of days when they hit us with an asteroid, or if we're lucky we'll die a couple of days later when we fry in the sun."

"As you say, all that's still hypothetical. What about Karl?"

"I can't really do anything for him, not without an operating room environment and getting him out of his suit. His leg is burned pretty badly, and toxins in his blood are increasing. Besides that, his suit leg isn't working reliably. I give him maybe twenty-four hours. Thirty-six if he's incredibly lucky."

"That long before he loses the leg, you mean?"

"That long before he's dead."

Alis was stunned. She had trouble finding the breath to say, "That can't be."

"I wish it weren't, but we're out of our environment here. When you put a human body in a life-suit, you can put the combination in a place where you can't normally breathe, where you can't light a match, where you'd freeze or boil in thirty seconds. But when something goes wrong, we're pretty fragile actually."

"This just can't be," Alis said softly.

"I'll keep monitoring him, and I'll let you know if my opinion changes."

"Please do."

The "private message terminated" chime rang, and Alis stared through the map display, seeing nothing but fuzzy overlapping lines.

She wondered how Karl would react to the truth. Maybe the medication would make him resigned, the way Robert sounded. Or maybe he'd be filled with anger and disbelief.

Karl groaned, then turned the groan into a painful laugh, the way people do when a sudden pain places them squarely between wanting to laugh and cry. The end-of-trip vibrations had started again, and Karl's leg was obviously an early warning indicator.

"You okay, Karl?" Alis asked when he fell quiet.

"Yeah. Just thought I'd have a longer nap before we got ready to disembark."

"We're coming up on what looks like a central terminal. We might be able to head any direction we want to, if we knew a way out."

"I'd settle for whatever has the longest non-stop flight. I'm still feeling a little tired."

"You hungry? Maybe a little nutrition would help."

"I might suck some pills later, but right at the moment I don't feel all that hungry. Maybe I'm just bored with the suit rations."

"I know what you mean. I could go for a real meal right about now."

"I wish we had time for a stop at Alfredo's on Tokyan. They make lasagna that you'd expect to have to trade precious metals for."

"I love their food, too," Alis said, surprised. She wondered if she and Karl had ever been in the restaurant at the same time.

"The last time I was there, I asked to go back and see the chef. He's a short guy, but when I told him how much I enjoyed the meal, he looked twice as tall."

Free fall caught Alis off guard. She realized the pod had stopped its rotation and they were evidently at their destination. At this point gravity was either zero or so small that Alis probably wouldn't have enough patience to conduct a test.

Beyond the pod door was a milky-white "floor" that gently rolled down and out of sight in every direction, as if they were floating on the surface of a small, round asteroid. The "ceiling" was about two meters over the floor and maintained a constant height. A grid of recessed handles on both surfaces, obviously designed to aid transport, was yet another detail that said Cantaloupe was designed.

Alis looked back at the transport pod. The circular door was off center on a thick column that joined floor to ceiling.

Karl surprised Alis again with the indication that he wasn't content to just be an injured hanger-on but instead was still thinking and observing. He said, "This could well be the starting and ending point for a round-trip transport pod. A few sections of the route still aren't filled in on my map, but it looks to me like all the transport routes are essentially big circles that hit here once. None of the circles seem to touch each other."

Alis took another look at her map. The transport routes weren't simple circles, and at many places different routes came close enough to one another that tracing a given route took some concentration, but after carefully following a couple of them she came to the same conclusion that Karl had. "So you're saying that if we got back in right here, we'd eventually retrace our route?"

"That's my guess."

"But that doesn't help us," Robert said. "The route never got close enough to the surface. None of them do."

"Didn't say we were saved," Karl said. "Just made an observation."

Alis said, "According to my map, the nearest other transport tube is that way." She pointed. "Let's just make sure."

Lucy in the lead, they moved off in the direction Alis had pointed, pulling themselves gently from handle to handle. In no more than a minute Alis could see another column joining floor to ceiling. The other column was indeed another transport pod housing.

Alis looked at their present location on the map and followed the route by eye. "This one doesn't even come as close to the surface as the one we were on."

Lucy said, "The one that seems to approach the surface most closely still only comes within maybe a kilometer. That looks like a small gap compared to the whole, but it's still a lot of digging."

"But if it were close enough that we could talk to the *Ranger* again," Robert said, "maybe they could dig us out."

Alis stared at the map for a long moment. So close.

Karl cleared his throat. "You know there's another way the captain might know where we are, even if we can't talk to the ship."

"And that is?" Alis was suddenly all attention. Such a statement coming from, say, Robert, she might have met with a more common "oh, prove it" attitude, but Karl didn't seem to spend as much time saying things merely for shock value.

"The map we've got is pretty detailed by now, given how long data's been collected. The changes from version to version are pretty subtle. I've just been flipping back and forth between the previous map and the current version. In fact, I've got the two set up to flip back and forth several times a second."

"And?" Robert said.

"And the two views are pretty much identical except for pieces of noise here and there. The difference between the two views is pretty much limited to noise in the system, and the actual differences. We've been moving. We're changing the map. Look at where we are right now."

It took Alis a few seconds to give the right commands to her suit computer, but soon she was looking at a flickering set of two maps, the current map and the newest version, flipping back and forth between the two views. The two large spheres off to one side of Cantaloupe showed substantial flickering, as if maybe the readings inside them were much noisier than the rest of Cantaloupe's interior. She homed in on the current location of the team, and suddenly she could see the flickering Karl had talked about.

"I see it," she said. "Our presence along that last section of transport pod route shows up as a barely noticeable change from the last map. If Captain Fernandez notices this, too, he might even be able to track our progress."

"Great," Robert said. "Now we can move around and spell out giant letters?"

Alis was about to say something cutting in response when Karl said calmly, "Good imagination. If we all keep thinking about possibilities, no matter how outrageous they seem at first, maybe we can find a way to turn this to our advantage."

"Hmm," Robert said, making a noise that Alis took to mean that Karl's suggestion had had a positive impact, defusing the condescending moment and deflecting Robert toward a more useful way of spending his energy. At the very least, Robert made no follow-up sarcastic remarks.

Lucy said, "So that means we should get as close to the surface as we can, and then keep moving around?"

Karl said, "That could be the best way. At the moment nothing better is occurring to me, but that's no guarantee we can't find anything better."

"So which of the transport pod routes do we want?"

"Not yet," Alis said. "I want to explore the inside of this sphere before we leave."

"Why delay?" Lucy asked.

"For one thing, ten or twenty minutes won't necessarily make much of a difference. For another, this thing is at the very center of Cantaloupe. Its physical location implies a degree of importance. You wouldn't want to be within five meters of an explanation for Cantaloupe's existence and never know it, would you?"

"If we die because we're trapped in here too long, and we can never tell anything that we found out, that makes the question one of those tree-falling-in-the-woods questions, right?"

"Well, I for one am curious," Karl said.

"Good," Alis said. "Come on, everyone. Follow me." Alis took off without waiting for any more dissention. A few seconds later she looked back and saw three followers. She turned her attention ahead, some of her confidence returning. She double-checked the map and corrected her course slightly to the right. The blip on her map was closer now. She passed another transport tube column from floor to ceiling and kept pulling herself along gently. When the light was right, and her eyes slightly off focus, the milky surface below her could have passed for clouds. She'd never had a flying dream this strange.

In hardly more than a minute, they had traversed almost a quarter of the perimeter of the central sphere. Ahead, Alis finally saw a disruption in the milky surface of the sphere. Seconds later the four of them pulled to a stop where they surrounded a dark, round spot on the floor, as if they were in some surreal campfire dream where all the light came not from the central fire, but from the heads of the campers. Alis decided she'd been awake too long.

"Another rabbit hole?" Robert said.

Alis moved her gloved hands over the surface.

"Well," Lucy said, "no go. I guess we'd better hit the road."

Alis was just about to reply when her hand touched a

slightly darker spot right at the center of the disk. Abruptly the disk divided into a couple dozen triangles all meeting in the center, and a slowly growing hole appeared in the center as the triangles all pivoted inward from hinges on the perimeter of the disk.

"Almost like a Venus's-flytrap in reverse," Karl said.

Alis aimed her helmet light into the gap. She could see nothing except a flat white surface about two meters inside. Openings on two sides led inward, but they cut off line-of-sight inspection, as if the foursome stood at the doors of a video theater.

"Maybe it is a trap," Lucy said.

Alis shook her head. "I can't accept that. I can't accept the idea that some life-form would design something this large for that simple purpose."

"I don't know," Lucy said. "The pyramids were pretty large and they contained traps."

"Okay," Alis said. "Anyone who wants to stay out here is welcome to do that. Don't leave any earlier than ten minutes from now."

Alis pulled her body past the rim of the disk and let the motion angle her downward through the hole. Another moving shadow on the wall ahead indicated that at least one person was following her.

The wall ahead of Alis curved, and she pushed her way deeper. Shadow fragments told her at least two people had followed her inside.

She made another turn. Her eyes widened and her breath came more quickly. Something ahead of her was emitting light.

Alis twisted through another couple of bends and reached the volume at the very center of Cantaloupe. Suspended before her lay an enormous spherical hologram. She'd been examining so many versions of computerized maps of Cantaloupe's interior, she knew instantly what this was—Cantaloupe's own view of itself.

"Wow," Karl said softly.

Alis flipped off her helmet lamps. One by one, three other pairs of lamps switched off, and the huge hologram took on even crisper definition. The outer shell was tinted lime green. The transport pod routes stood out sharply in bright yellow. Thousands of other details their scans hadn't identified made Cantaloupe's insides seem as crowded as a 3-D view of Tokyan Station.

The hologram filled virtually the entire volume of this central space. The dark walls were all heavily rippled, as if Alis were looking at a magnified view of acoustical tile.

Alis floated at the edge of the hologram, suddenly aware that during her intense inspection she had let go of the wall. Her body slowly floated toward the edge of the hologram, and as she came in contact with the green shell surrounding the spherical body, a large circular cutout in the shell formed and she could see more clearly into the interior.

She made sure her suit recorder was still functioning, and she placed a marker that would let her easily go back to this position in the recording.

Alis floated farther into the hologram.

A network of brown tendrils extended through almost the entire volume of Cantaloupe. As the tendrils neared two trunks on opposite sides of the center, they grew larger, with fewer tributaries, and the analogy of veins and arteries in the human body was impossible to ignore.

"It really does look like something alive, doesn't it?" Karl said.

No one disagreed.

The two symmetrical chasms, one of which they had visited, were both tinted a dark blue. They both came even closer to the surface than Alis had thought before inspecting Cantaloupe's own map. She triggered a brief puff from a suit jet and drifted closer to where one of the chasms came closest to the surface.

"Maybe we could get out that way," Lucy said. "That comes closer than any of the transport pods do."

"I don't understand," Robert said. "I admit this thing looks more like something alive than something designed to be, say, a generation ship, but a significant portion of it simply has to be designed, the result of deliberate creation. I can't imagine many natural life-forms have holograms at their center, rungs for visitors to climb on, and elevators."

"In a way," Karl said, "Cantaloupe is a bit like you, Alis."

"Really? How do you figure that?"

"Both of your bodies are mostly organic, but you both have manufactured elements. You have your new eyes, heart. Cantaloupe has elevators."

"Oh, that makes sense," Lucy said.

"I'm not expressing myself very well," Karl said. "I'm just trying to say that a mixture of natural design complemented by artificial implants isn't necessarily outside of our experience."

"True," Robert said. "Cantaloupe could be some natural life-form that some race has altered. Or it could be something they engineered from scratch. But assuming it's been engineered, it doesn't seem like the goal was a generation ship. Even on this display I don't see anything that looks like possible living quarters."

"Unless the residents are a lot different from us," Lucy said.

"Doesn't that almost go without saying? Still, you wouldn't think such a large structure would be needed if the goal was to transport microbe-sized life. The tunnels and rungs suggest a life-form that's at least on the same order of magnitude as our own bodies, and we've still seen no sign of life like that or living space for bodies that size."

Lucy said, "Bodies our size are still microbe-sized compared to Cantaloupe. If Cantaloupe is somehow a huge life-form, maybe even self-aware, trying to communicate with it is like a microbe trying to communicate with a human."

"Perhaps. But my vote is that Cantaloupe is an artificial creation, a living construct, a single enormous organism, not a vessel for some smaller creatures. Perhaps some of the tunnels are just access paths for the designers so they could inspect their handiwork directly."

As Alis drifted through the huge display, she discovered another feature of the hologram by accident. One of her gloved hands touched a section of yellow transport pod display. When she pulled her hand back, a translucent sphere formed around that point, and the edge of the sphere kept pace with her hand. The farther back she pulled her hand, the larger the sphere grew, and inside the sphere was a growing magnification of the volume that had been at the center. "Look at this."

Inside the magnification sphere, the yellow line grew faster and faster, as if the magnification control was logarithmic. A second later the yellow line had turned into a straw, and then a pipe almost one-tenth actual scale. As long as Alis moved her hand in and out on the same line, the sphere continued to shrink and grow so its surface was near her glove. When she moved her hand at a right angle, along the surface of the magnification sphere, the sphere disappeared and the display looked as it had before.

Karl called to the others. By moving his hand, he magnified a section of the display along their route. At first the insides of the magnification sphere gave the impression of clouds slowly re-forming. "This is where we repaired the damaged area. It seems to me this says two very interesting things."

"And they are?" Robert said quickly when Karl paused for some reason. Alis hoped the pause wasn't because the pain was intensifying.

Karl continued, his voice sounding more frail to Alis. "One, repair is proceeding at what seems to be a pretty fast pace. Two, this display is dynamic. It's showing us what's going on right now, not just some static display from centuries ago. It must be directly linked to sensors all through Cantaloupe's body."

Alis moved off toward the two spheres on the opposite side of the display, suddenly realizing that she might be able to confirm a hunch that had been at the back of her mind for some time.

On the bridge, Captain Fernandez pointed to the sparkles at the center of the flickering hologram. "See. Right there."

Martina Binotell squinted and stared for a long moment. "Well, if that really is them, why are they are the center instead of somewhere near the surface? They don't seem to be trying very hard to get out."

The captain shook his head. "I don't know. Nussem is a smart one, so there must be some reason. The only good thing is that they're pretty unlikely to be hurt by the deflection blast. I was worried they might find a way out right at the wrong time. I gave them a head's up, but there's no safer place for them right now."

The captain looked at the time-to-impact countdown. Four minutes and fifty-two seconds. Below the timer was a real-time view of Cantaloupe's surface. On the far side of Cantaloupe, the explosive probe was still accelerating toward Cantaloupe.

He was looking at a magnification of the hologram map when simultaneously he saw motion in his peripheral vision and Martina Binotell said, "What's going on here?"

On the screen showing Cantaloupe's surface, something extraordinary was happening. An enormous curved fissure had formed in just a few seconds. Captain Fernandez had to remind himself that he was looking at an image of something a hundred kilometers wide, because the image made it seem as if something as small as an orange was fissuring.

The fissure raced along the surface. When the crack

stopped lengthening, it must have been fifty kilometers long. The fissure was narrow, well under a kilometer wide, corresponding to one of the two chasms they'd seen in the scans. The fissure was about as curved as a weak smile, and the line was wavy, as if made up of a series of much smaller alternating curves.

Captain Fernandez enlarged a view from the explosive probe, showing the far side of Cantaloupe. A matching fissure had formed on that side, too. He and Martina Binotell watched in stunned silence. Seconds after the fissures stopped growing, the texture of the darkness along the length of both chasms changed. Something shiny was moving, coming out.

"Abort the explosive," Captain Fernandez said. "Deflect the probe!"

"I don't know if there's time," Martina said. Her statement was government-issue cover-your-ass rather than an argument, because she instantly gave the command.

The probe had been accelerating hard enough and long enough that it had reached almost ten percent of the speed of light. Watching the view from the probe's camera gave Captain Fernandez a rare feeling of helplessness. Cantaloupe grew larger and larger in the view, as the surface slipped ever so slowly sideways. The probe's camera had pivoted to keep facing the surface, while the body of the probe had turned ninety degrees so the thrust would curve the probe away from the collision point. If they had been in time.

"You disarmed the explosive?" the captain asked, his gaze riveted on the too slowly changing view.

"I sure did. But if the probe hits the surface, all bets are off."

The captain leaned forward. As motion continued along the length of the chasm, what first looked like a fence formed a low wall many kilometers long. The material forming the fence seemed shiny and gossamer thin, with dark struts every kilometer or so. One end of the fence grew taller and taller, and before long one end of the surface extended several kilometers up into space, and the taller end must have reached ten or twenty kilometers.

Captain Fernandez felt his face and neck tingle as the surface kept extending farther and farther into space.

Alis clung to the cavern wall, watching the display in amazement. As soon as the changes in the displays of the two chasms started, she and the others had backed off for a broader view of the display.

"You think we triggered this?" Lucy asked.

Alis didn't volunteer a guess, and neither did Karl nor Robert.

"I still don't understand what's happening," Robert said.

Neither did Alis. Cantaloupe was apparently ejecting material from the twin chasms into space. A very thin substance stretched between a leaf-like network of ribs was pushing farther and farther into space from both chasms. The material in space was shaded red, while the slowly moving subterranean material was shaded blue. As the material reached the surface, some accordion effect seems to be operating, because for every unit of motion in the blue material in the chasm, the red leaf seemed to extend five or ten units out from the surface. She thought of an Oriental fan slowly growing as it extended.

"Wings," Karl said softly. "No. Solar sails."

16 ▪ PREGNANCY

Feeling hazy partly because of the pain and medication and partly thanks to the amazing view before him, Karl watched the display. An enormous pair of what seemed to be solar sails kept growing from opposite sides of Cantaloupe, like a set of wings.

"I think you're right," Alis said softly. "They do seem to be solar sails."

Karl had to keep reminding himself that Cantaloupe was a hundred kilometers in diameter. It was too easy to imagine these wings were actual size. Even at actual size in the hologram, they were longer than any wings Karl had ever seen. At maybe a hundred kilometers each, from Cantaloupe's surface to the tip, these wings were of a size that took his breath away and made him question whether he was hallucinating. He decided he wasn't, but the decision was a close one.

Simply amazing. These wings would be large enough to eclipse entire countries if Cantaloupe flew between the Earth and the sun. They were big enough to completely wrap some moons, like a giant's game of rock, scissors, paper.

"Do you think this is what's really happening right now?" Lucy asked. "Or is it a recording or a demonstration?"

Alis said, "Indications are that everything else in the display is probably real-time, so my guess is this is really happening."

Robert laughed. "I bet Captain Fernandez is as close as he ever gets to excited."

"I don't know," Lucy said. "I wouldn't be surprised if he tells us he expected this all along."

Karl's leg hit the wall softly. Pain lanced through his leg, and kept moving all the way up through the top of his skull. He tried not to cry out. Seconds earlier he had jetted away from the center of the display so he could get a better view, and the growing sense of awe had let him forget about everything but the solar sails. The pain was his penalty for forgetfulness.

"Karl, are you all right?" Alis asked.

Apparently he hadn't been able to keep from crying out. "I'm fine. I just bumped into the wall." He had to pause as another wave of pain, like an aftershock of the first one, overtook him. "I didn't mean to be so careless." He fired a short blast from his chest jet and stabilized his position next to the wall.

Robert said, "You didn't seem to hit very hard. I think I'd better increase your medication."

"If you increase it much more, I won't be able to stay awake. I'll be more careful, okay?"

Robert hesitated. "Okay, but take it easy."

Karl would have pointed out how gentle his collision with the wall had been, but he didn't think that would help his case. "You got it."

Attention slowly moved from Karl back to the hologram display, and he felt more at ease.

By now the display of the wings had grown so far out from Cantaloupe's body, the images tricked Karl's eyes into thinking the display went well beyond to walls of the central cavern.

He caught himself just before hitting the wall again. It took him a moment to figure out what was happening. "We're decelerating. It's the solar sails. Cantaloupe must be starting to slow down."

Simply amazing," said Martina Binotell.

Captain Fernandez shook his head as what seemed to be wings kept extending farther and farther into space. He wasn't able to give the sight as much attention as it deserved, because his gaze was mostly fastened on the view screen showing the image from the explosive probe. He had so many recordings running, he was capturing several gigabytes of information every second.

The sunlit view had ramped back through five magnification stages in the last two minutes, and the image of Cantaloupe's surface still seemed just as large as before. The surface continued to slip sideways at an increasing pace, but there was a lot of surface to cover between the present view and the edge. The ship's computer gave an impact projection showing a yellow error band. Two-thirds of the band was on Cantaloupe's rim; the remaining one-third, which looked more like a tenth to the captain's nervous eye, was in space. The only reason the error band existed was that the *Ranger*'s computer didn't know precisely how much fuel was left on board, so its mass was slightly uncertain.

The probe was well outside the diameter of the wings when it had only a couple of seconds left to travel. Spotting it visually would have been about as easy as spotting a bullet, had they been on the other side of Cantaloupe.

During the last second of flight, a sliver of black space showed for the first time in the probe's display. The sliver widened. The screen went black.

"Oh, God," Martina said.

Captain Fernandez swallowed hard. He looked over at a display of Cantaloupe's far side, a view taken from an orbiting probe. Even as his eyes started glancing in that direction, perhaps to see a giant plume of ejected material exploding away from the surface, he realized his error.

The screen hadn't necessarily gone black because the probe was dead.

Sure enough. In the next second, the automatic gain control on the probe's camera did its work, and pinpoints of light flooded the screen. Stars. The probe was looking at the stars ahead.

"It made it!" Martina cried.

"Yes," said the captain. He was sure he looked calm to Martina, but his pulse was racing, and he felt way too warm.

The probe had actually missed.

The captain was totally uninterested in the probe now, but he knew he'd have to answer to the bureaucrats if it weren't accounted for. Instead of just letting it go and concentrating on the view unfolding before him, he took time to give the command for the probe to pivot an additional ninety degrees and start braking. It probably didn't have enough fuel left to entirely shed its velocity out of the system, but he would have done the best he could.

On the main screen, Cantaloupe's wings kept extending.

"We'd better give it a wider berth," Captain Fernandez said. He pulled slowly back until the *Ranger* was moving away at one gee. Automatic zoom in the primary screen kept Cantaloupe's body the same apparent size as they pulled back, so

as Cantaloupe's surface features flattened, the captain noticed
the familiar illusion of stars being ejected from the circular rim
of the horizon. He gave a single command that ordered all the
orbiting sensors to switch on their thrusters, changing their orbital velocity so they would pull away from Cantaloupe. Later
on he'd command them to reverse thrust to enter a new higher
and slower orbit.

Martina Binotell was slowly shaking her head in awe.
She must have become aware of her reaction when the captain
looked at her, because she stopped.

After several silent minutes, Cantaloupe's wings seemed
to reach their maximum breadth. Now fully extended, they
both slowly began to fan out into a configuration that gave
them even more surface area. When, after several more minutes, they reached their fullest area, both wings slowly pivoted
five or ten degrees, forming a configuration that should push
Cantaloupe off its present course. Both wings flexed gently
against the solar wind.

Captain Fernandez spent little of his life looking back, but
at that moment, he knew the recordings of this event were ones
he'd replay again and again.

With a *ping,* a new display popped onto an unused screen.
Cantaloupe had, in fact, changed course slightly. The ship's
computer-generated vectors showed its current path, as well
as change vectors. The wings shifted position again, and new
vectors came up on the screen.

Cantaloupe was altering its course to avoid the danger in
its old path. It would miss Hamilton Station, but now it was
heading directly for the sun.

Alis watched the hologram as the enormous wings shifted position ever so slightly. "You know what this means," she said.
"If Cantaloupe has the ability to make course corrections, it's
not going to hit a space station. Surely if it can maneuver, it

also has some mechanism for seeing where it's going." Her skin tingled. She was still struggling to accept all the new information and implications.

"Makes sense to me," Robert said. "But this is probably bad news for us personally. The wings, or solar sails or whatever you want to call them, are also a clearer indication to the people outside that at least to some interpretations Cantaloupe really is alive. They might have been willing to cut us out if we got close to the surface before, but now, four lives probably seem pretty small in comparison to cutting open the only alien visitor we've ever seen."

"He's right," Lucy said. "We've got to get out on our own. Somehow. Talk about your good news and bad news. This really is a first contact situation, and we're right in the middle of things, for God's sake. But our lives are worth next to nothing now, in comparison. There's probably no danger to any of the stations now, and no danger to Cantaloupe itself. There's no way anyone's going to damage Cantaloupe now to try to save us."

Karl cleared his throat. "Look, I know I'm going to be a burden. You three can move a lot faster if you just—"

"Shut up, Karl," Alis said, but the tone she used wasn't the same tone she would have used with the same words a week ago.

She hesitated, then decided she didn't care if she sounded stupid and brought up what had been on her mind. "There might be another way out."

Robert and Lucy both made prodding noises when Alis had second thoughts. She went ahead. "We need to look at part of the display. I'm moving to the space that contains the two spheres. Meet me there." Alis let her back jet give an ultrasmall blast. A few seconds and a few stabilizing blasts later, she floated next to one of the two spheres. Soon Lucy and Robert floated nearby. Robert floated sideways, but in this context up and down were pretty arbitrary, and he didn't bother to change his position. In the hologram, the spheres were both surrounded by green shells that made seeing into the interior difficult.

Alis said, "I think I know what these two spheres are. I want you to do what I've done already and tell me what you see. Retrieve the first interior map that shows these two features, and compare that map to the current map. Flip the display back and forth the way we did to see noise in the newest map."

She waited. A half-minute later Lucy and Robert both made sounds indicating they had made the comparison and perhaps found it interesting. "Okay, what do you see?"

Lucy said, "Both spheres seem a little bigger now than before."

Robert said, "Looks that way to me, too."

Alis said, "I noticed the same thing. And of all of the interior of Cantaloupe, the volume inside these two spheres is the murkiest on the current map. Any theories for why that should be?"

Lucy said, "Because the material surrounding them is more opaque to scanning."

"Or what's inside is pretty uniform," Robert said.

Karl said softly, "Change." He was on her wavelength.

"Change. I think Karl's right. What's inside those spheres could be changing over time. If that were true, a slowly accumulating scan of their interiors wouldn't find as much repeatable data from each scan, so the map would be indistinct, unreadable."

"And that means?" Lucy said.

Robert made a sudden "*mmm*" sound as if he'd made the connection. He was the medical doctor, so maybe that gave him an edge over Lucy.

"Think about it," Alis said. "We have a creature with a spherical body. Inside that body are two much smaller spheres that seem to be growing, changing."

"Twins," said Karl.

Lucy gasped. "Oh, my God. You're saying Cantaloupe is—pregnant?"

Alis caught sight of motion beside her. Karl had moved to join them. She looked back at the hologram of the nearest small sphere, and she reached into it. The surface disappeared, and the interior was revealed.

"You're right," Robert said in a hushed voice. "This is amazing."

Inside was what looked rather like a smaller version of Cantaloupe, complete with a smaller network of veins and arteries, or whatever they were, transport pods, the central core.

Karl started laughing until the pain apparently choked off the response. When he could talk again, he pointed. "Look. Look there."

Karl had to move until his glove penetrated the shell around one of the spheres. He moved slightly forward and pointed. "There. See those two tiny little round nodules? The babies must be born pregnant!"

Alis saw the pale green, almost invisible nodules just as Karl spoke. "Amazing."

Robert was closer to the other sphere. He reached through its shell to expose the interior, and it was, in fact, a replica of the first one. Twins indeed.

Lucy said, "I grant you this is fantastic stuff, but you said something about a way out."

Alis said, "Think about it. We're inside a pregnant creature. The babies have grown measurably in the last day or two, and they already constitute a significant portion of Cantaloupe's mass."

"You're saying Cantaloupe is close to giving birth?"

"Exactly. And if the twins are coming out soon, maybe we can go with them."

"You could be wrong about the timescale," Robert said.

"For all we know, the babies grow rapidly to their full size and then mature for centuries before being ejected."

"That's possible, but I think the twins are still our best bet. Maybe our only bet. None of the transport pods comes close enough to the surface for us to cut through fast enough, and the *Ranger* probably isn't going to be willing to cut now that they have an indication that Cantaloupe is alive. Do you see a better course?"

Robert's silence held his answer, and no one else volunteered any opposition.

"Robert's right about us not knowing the timescale," Karl said finally. "It's even possible that if we start moving right now we'll be too late because Cantaloupe's only minutes from giving birth. There's no way to tell. But there's also no other real hope for getting out."

Alis said, "I agree. We need to move fast, just in case."

"That's all the more reason to leave me—"

"Shut up, Karl," Alis said with a smile. "The first thing we need to do is get a good map of where we're going." She picked the transport pod that went closest to the smaller versions of Cantaloupe. Moving as quickly as she could in zero gravity, she traced the route, moving her hand toward the route and pulling it away far enough for the magnification bubble to give a reasonable level of detail. Once the information was recorded on video, they could always replay sections and blow the display up even more on their own.

She found the stop nearest the twins on the transport pod line, and blew up the display between there and the nearest twin. Running between the two areas of interest was a twisty, irregular tunnel that reminded her of a 3-D view of a stretch of intestines. She moved along that tunnel, getting a better view of each section.

"Okay, let's move," she said. "And, Karl, if you give me any more crap about leaving you behind, I'll shut off your comm channel. We're going to get out of here—all of us."

"Aye, aye, ma'am." Karl's voice carried a tone that Alis took to be relief—relief that he had made his offer and now he could feel less guilty.

Alis jetted back toward the place she thought they had entered the central chamber. "Robert, you've got the watch until we're on the transport pod. Make sure Karl's with us."

"My pleasure."

Alis switched her helmet lamps back on as she entered the path back out. She was grateful that this time her sometimes-reliable, sometimes-terrible sense of direction had cooperated with her. A minute or two later they were all back in the white layer surrounding the central chamber.

Alis consulted her map, re-oriented herself, and turned right to face the way she wanted to go. The others followed.

A couple of minutes later, she stopped before another transport pod stop. "Double-check me on this to make sure this is the pod that takes us toward the twins. We *really* don't need to be on the wrong route."

A few seconds later both Lucy and Robert confirmed the location. She pressed the center of the circular door, and it opened.

Only when all four of them were inside and the pod had started its familiar rotation did Alis allow herself the time for doubt.

17 ▪ QUIESCENCE

Alis shifted position in the pod. The rotation had reached normal speed several minutes earlier, but she was gradually feeling pushed to one side, something she hadn't experienced in the other trips.

Robert said, "It feels like we're accelerating, too, not just rotating."

"You got it," Lucy said. "On the way down, we mostly just fell. Probably the farther out we go, as the gravity increases, the pod will have to be lifting all the way. The pod must be rotating horizontally now."

Alis reached a slightly more comfortable position. She wondered how Karl was holding up, and suddenly realized she'd heard nothing from him after the point when they entered the pod. Not entirely sure why she didn't just start speaking, she blinked on a private channel and said into the silence, "Karl, are you all right?"

Nothing.

"Karl, how are you doing?"

Finally a soft chime indicated Karl had accepted the private call. A moment later he said, "Fine." The word sounded stressed.

"Are you sure? You don't sound fine."

"I'll be okay," he said. His body lay quietly across from Alis in the pod, but his voice sounded as if he were simultaneously lifting a few hundred kilos.

"Have you been talking to Robert about more medication? You really sound bad."

"If I'm unconscious, I'm no good to anyone."

"You can use a break. We'll carry you if we have to; it's not like the gravity's that high anyway."

Karl said nothing for a significant part of a minute. During that time, the AGC (Above Ground Crew) boosted the silence and the sound of his painfully labored breathing. Finally he said, "Will you make me a promise? I know you don't owe me anything."

"What's the promise?"

"If you have to—have to leave me behind—will you just tell me? Don't leave me sleeping without saying something."

"I promise."

The sound of Karl's breathing seemed to ease just a bit, but he said nothing more.

After a couple of minutes, Alis said, "What's behind that request? We wouldn't just leave you anyway."

"Nothing. I guess I just like closure." Karl tried to make a short laugh, and it turned into a painful series of noises that could have been laughter or crying.

"Tell me. Please. I won't tell anyone else."

She thought he wasn't going to answer, but the pain must

have worn down his defenses, because at last he said, "My dad left us when I was six. I found out the next morning when Mom told us. I haven't seen—him since. It just didn't seem like a very—fair—way to leave."

"God, Karl. I'm sorry."

"It was a long time ago."

Not long enough to stop hurting, she thought. "I promise you, we won't leave you."

"No. It's okay to leave me. You'll probably have to. Just don't go without saying—good-bye." Karl swallowed. "That won't slow you down too much."

"I promise you." Alis's hand moved, seemingly of its own volition. She became aware of the urge to touch Karl's hand, to put an arm around his shoulder, to make some actual contact. The moment seemed unreal, with her lying in her suit and Karl lying on the other side of the pod, not even his eyes visible at the moment. She realized he must have darkened his visor deliberately.

Not giving her action a conscious thought, she blinked her eyes into telephoto and heightened the contrast. She could see Karl's face hazily through the gray helmet face. His eyes were clenched closed, and a tear ran down from one eye. She couldn't tell whether the cause was the current pain, the past hurt, or both.

Something twisted in Alis's gut, and she seemed to share the same pain. Only an instant later she realized she was prying. Abruptly embarrassed, she blinked her eyes back to "normal" and could see no more of Karl than Robert or Lucy could see. She wondered if Karl had sensed the invasion.

A moment later, almost as if Karl had been aware of her observation, he said, "Thanks, Alis."

She suddenly felt even more guilty, wondering if he were somehow aware of her having first seen him and then ceasing to look. That was silly. Obviously he was just thanking her for the promise. She had to clear her throat. "It's no more than you'd do for me."

"I still wish I'd never been in that shuttle. It's been hard, obviously, that other people thought that was pilot error or whatever. That you thought it, too, was—" He coughed. "I didn't like that very much at all."

Somehow what Karl said summoned up images of deathbed statements, things said in the last few minutes of life, said when the burdens of pain and fear somehow bit into the ability to lie and tore it out of the body.

"I believe you, Karl. Call me gullible."

"I don't think that. You're a very smart lady, Alis. I really wish I could have met you under different circumstances."

So do I, Alis thought. "You're talking like you're going to die. I won't let that happen."

"We don't always do what we start out to do."

Alis reflected on the possibility that the twins wouldn't be leaving Cantaloupe soon enough to save them, and the odds that they might leave too soon, or that they might leave at the right time but crush the team on the way out. She was trying to force her thoughts away from the subject when she realized how strange it was that she and Karl could carry on a private conversation right in front of Robert and Lucy. For that matter, Robert and Lucy could be having their own conversation and she'd never know. "Try to get some rest, Karl. We may need our strength."

"Right." Karl started to laugh and cut it short. "I may be called upon to exercise my superpowers and punch a tunnel to the surface."

Alis said nothing, but she smiled.

A few moments later, Karl said, "Thanks, Alis. I feel better. Ordinarily I don't see myself as a whiner."

"You're not whining. You're just human."

As the pod continued upward, Alis asked herself if she'd

been the one whining, complaining about the surgery, the implants. Maybe she had overreacted. But the fact that she had those feelings, that reaction—in a twisted way that said she wasn't what she was afraid she was. A machine wouldn't have those concerns. Maybe the "only human" expression applied equally to her.

She still didn't know where being human ended and being a construct started. People had resorted to false teeth before genegrow made them obsolete. They'd worn hearing aids and eyeglasses before surgery and gene splicing had eliminated the need. Was an artificial heart any worse than a transplant? If she were now some artificial construct, she seriously doubted that she'd feel the anger, the curiosity, and—for the first time in far too long—hope.

Her new eyes never tired out, and that had formerly been the first way she knew she was fatigued. In the conversation lull she grew more aware of how sore her arms felt and how easy it was to let her eyelids slip closed. The idea of sleeping in the suit didn't even feel uncomfortable. She drifted.

Alis lurched awake as the pod slowed its rotation and came to another stop.

The gravity was still light enough to assist in another orgy-like jumble of bodies bouncing around the interior of the pod.

"We're not at the right stop yet," Robert said.

After waiting a couple of minutes, they came to the conclusion that the pod wouldn't resume its journey until the door had been opened and allowed to close. The theory proved true.

As the pod settled into its regular rotation again, Alis went back to sleep more quickly than she had as a child. She dreamed of amusement park rides, spinning space stations, and washing machines.

. . .

When they finally stopped at the right exit point, Alis still felt as tired as before, but now she also felt the sleep-deprivation annoyance of being roused from sleep far too soon.

The pod door led to a chamber that was a rough sphere twice as tall as Alis, its interior surface a smooth, turquoise-like textured blend of green and brown. On opposite sides of the sphere were circular openings to similar spheres, as if they had wound up in the middle of a string of hollow pearls all fused together and with the string missing.

Very few words were exchanged as the team exited the pod. People always seemed stiffer than normal while wearing pressure suits, but Alis felt Karl looked the worst. He pulled his body where he needed to go, and his legs just floated along with the rest of his body, with no apparent motion anywhere below his chest.

If Karl died, that would bring the losses to half of the original team. She supposed that if she and the others made it out without Karl, there would be some cruel jokes about Halfway Nussem, but she didn't care a bit about that possibility. Losing Karl would be a crisis all its own, and it would be the most painful thing she'd experienced since the accident. In fact, she suddenly realized, his loss would hurt worse than the accident. At least she was here and still alive, her brain and intellect intact.

Perhaps because she was tired, perhaps because of the introspection caused by her conversations with Karl, she experienced one of those perception flips similar to the sketch that shows either an old woman or a young woman, depending on perspective. She was suddenly unsure why she had reacted so strongly to having a few replacement parts. Especially while she was inside this suit, no one else would be able to tell whether she was "normal" or not.

"That way takes us toward the twins," Robert said.

He was pointing to the round exit on her left.

"Fine," Alis said. "Karl, are you ready for this?"

"You bet." His voice held a quality that suggested forced optimism had swamped out most doubts.

"All right then. Robert, you take the lead, then you, Lucy. You next, Karl, and I'll follow."

Robert pulled himself through the round opening in the side of the chamber. When it came Karl's turn, he made it through on his own, but he still moved stiffly, as if his knees were locked. Alis pulled herself through behind him. The opening was about a meter wide, so there was no risk of getting stuck. The next chamber lacked the transport pod door between the two exits, but was otherwise quite similar.

Alis was able to wait until Karl left the chamber and then leap the moderate gap, to land in the far exit. Karl was the slowest, because his condition required him to pull himself through the opening, maneuver across the curved floor, and pull himself up and through the next opening. Alis tried to think of a way to construct a litter or something else that would ease Karl's effort, but nothing seemed appropriate. The low gravity was just enough of a factor to prevent an easy time of it.

The repetitive nature of the trip was enough to make it boring despite the sense of urgency that kept them from lying down and sleeping for twelve hours. Alis had plenty of time to wonder why the pod didn't come closer to the area they were headed for, and to conclude that there would always be a million things they didn't understand about Cantaloupe. The idea that Cantaloupe was apparently about to be a mother of sorts still seemed as alien as everything else.

Alis took occasional glances at their current position in the map display, just to make sure they were still going in the right direction. The rate of progress looked encouraging only when the magnification level was set extremely high.

The gap did finally narrow, though. Without looking at

the time, Alis couldn't tell if the trip had taken them an hour or five hours. When Robert said, "It looks like we're here," she thought it was the most wonderful thing Robert had said to her. And it could have been.

A minute later the foursome hovered in another intersection. The tunnel they were in dead-ended at a large circular area that seemed to be a closed door. The door exhibited the same rippled edges around its circumference that the transport pod doors did. To the left and the right, a smaller corridor extended far enough in both directions that helmet lamps wouldn't penetrate all the way.

Karl carefully let his body settle to the floor while Lucy approached the door. She paused with her hand raised, as if ready to knock on the door.

"Any objections?" Lucy asked.

"Go for it," Alis said.

Lucy touched the center of the door. Alis had grown so accustomed to the transport pod doors opening to touch that she was surprised when this door, assuming that was what it was, stayed closed.

Lucy pressed harder. Robert moved forward and touched the door all over, like someone deliberately trying to leave fingerprints. The door remained closed.

"Maybe we need a coded knock," Karl said.

"Maybe it's not a door," Lucy said.

"Or maybe it's locked," Robert suggested. "That actually might be a good sign. If our assumptions are right, and if these two newborns are about to fly, it could be the area is off-limits for the time being."

Alis said, "It could be off-limits all the time. Maybe we are supposed to have a password or something." She looked down each of the side corridors. According to her recording they must run along the perimeter of the cavity. "Lucy, take a look down the corridor to the left. See if you see anything like another door. Robert, take the right side, will you?"

The two of them acknowledged her command and moved off in opposite directions. Alis stepped forward and pushed on the circular surface before her, then felt stupid. As if her touch was special, or Lucy and Robert hadn't done it "right." Sure enough, nothing happened.

"It was a good try," Karl said with a smile in his voice.

In the past, Alis might have felt laughed at. Now she felt laughed with. "You never know."

Karl said, "I've done the same thing too many times. A friend has a broken calculator or a phone that won't connect. I always want to hold it in my own hands and try to make it work before I believe someone totally trustworthy and accept the fact that it really is broken."

Alis let herself slide to the floor near Karl and simultaneously slipped into a somber mood. "My mom found my cat dead one morning. Pepper was almost sixteen and she'd been listless for a couple of months despite everything we did, but I still couldn't believe it until I'd seen her myself."

"Must be part of our skeptical nature. If we believed everything people told us, we'd be pretty easy to manipulate."

"Maybe," Alis said slowly, "sometimes we're too quick to disbelieve what we're told."

"I've been told that can happen." Again the smile in Karl's voice carried through clearly.

Alis let her thoughts drift a minute or two, then said, "Lucy, Robert. Give it five more minutes, then come back if you haven't found anything."

"Roger," said Robert.

"Wilco," said Lucy.

Alis got back up and pushed on the doorway again, still without results. It just didn't seem fair that she felt more full of life than she had in several years, and now death had chosen this moment to breathe down her neck. She kicked at the door, succeeding in doing nothing more than knocking herself off balance and stumbling backward.

"Kick it again for me, will you?" Karl said.

"I would if I thought it would do any good."

Lucy returned just before Robert did. "This must be the only nearby door," she said. "How do you want to cut through it?"

"I've been trying to think of another way," Alis said. "I suppose it'll grow back and repair itself, but I really don't like the idea of just hacking our way through with a knife."

"Wouldn't have to," Robert said. "We can slice through with a cutter. We'll probably need the extra power anyway, and it's not like it's worth saving for later."

Alis shook her head. "I'm not objecting to the particular instrument; I don't like damaging Cantaloupe."

"Like you said, it'll grow back."

"You have an opinion, Karl?" Alis felt silly for an instant, asking advice from someone under her command at the moment, especially Karl, but she realized his opinion was important to her.

"I think they're right. This is one of those times that delaying a painful decision isn't going to help. We might even be too late already."

Alis turned toward Robert, who had a hand cutter all ready to use. "Start cutting."

Robert flipped the switch, and a bright flare of blue light made Alis's faceplate darken and her pupils contract.

Alis said, "I want everyone ready to move through as soon as the opening is wide enough."

Alis slowly got to her feet as she watched Robert's cutter burn a slow line through the surface of the door, something like an old safecracker cutting through a vault door.

At first Alis thought Robert was cutting a big circle, but then she realized his medical training had helped him make a smarter decision. The curve was not coming full circle, but instead was going to wind up looking like a crescent moon. They would be able, she assumed, to bend the flap back, go through, and let it seal back into place so the healing process would be as simple as possible.

Alis guessed that Robert had cut about three-quarters of the intended cut when Lucy squawked.

"Something's moving!" Lucy cried. "What the—"

Alis turned her helmet lamp on Lucy, who was twisting back and forth. Lucy's boots were completely covered with a milky-white slime. In just the second or two Alis watched, the slime oozed higher.

"I don't like the looks of that," Karl said. He struggled to get upright.

Alis followed the direction of Karl's helmet lamp. The floor of the corridor behind Lucy looked lumpy, and alive. Milky-white fluid oozed from the walls onto the corridor floor. Its surface rose and fell, as if they were watching the surface of a boiling liquid, but each rise and fall carried more of the mass toward the team.

18 ▪ REPRODUCTION

Alis risked a quick glance away from the corridor floor and the oozing crud. What she saw raised her adrenaline level even higher. More milky-white ooze was rippling toward them from that direction, too. Only the large winding corridor they had taken here from the transport pod was still clean. They couldn't go back, though. If they did, they might never be able to get through in time.

"Keep cutting, Robert!" she said. "We'll deal with this."

"You're sure?" Lucy asked. She brought out her own cutter just before the ooze spread up her suit leg and reached her knee. The fingertips of her left hand glove had stuck to the ooze.

Alis grabbed her own cutter from her wrist, pulled the cable out several centimeters, and snapped the instrument into her palm. She switched it on. Her feet were already immobilized even though she'd been trying to keep her feet moving. The stuff made her feel like she was a fly caught in superglue as the stuff wicked up the surface of her suit. The level of the stuff on the ground was still below the top of her boot.

She drew the cutter's blue flame along the ooze, trying to cut through the trap without exposing her suit to the heat from the tip of the oxyacetylene flame. In a panicky instant, as if she'd felt a spider land on her in the dark, she almost lost control of the cutter and cut through her other glove.

From the corner of her eye, Alis saw that Robert had finished his cut. He held the flap open with one hand, and with the other he was helping cut away the ooze.

She looked back and realized that Karl was the worst off. He'd been sitting down when the ooze started flowing, and he was almost half-buried by it already.

She swung her cutter again and again, finding just the right speed—fast enough to make progress, and slow enough that the flame bit solidly into the ooze.

The ooze was plastic-like in some ways. The untouched ooze flowed like heated plastic, and after it had adhered to a surface long enough it became more like rigid plastic. When she sliced a barrier with her cutter, the barrier seemed to act like hard plastic and prevent further flow, at least temporarily.

Karl stopped moving. He'd never been able to get to his cutter since it was near the ground to begin with. His suit seemed to be almost growing into the surface of the tunnel floor.

"No, damnit!" Alis yelled. She finally cleared enough of the ooze that she could move again, stepping onto scorched areas of darkened ooze. She reached Karl's body.

"We've got to hurry," Robert said.

"We've got to get Karl," Alis said. It was an automatic statement, not really an argument, but more of an explanation of cosmic truth for the benefit of someone who wasn't thinking clearly. She sliced time after time around Karl's suit, coming so close that once she was afraid she'd cut through his sleeve. Maybe the ooze would serve as a patch if she had.

A quick glance told her Lucy was still cutting, using long strokes to form a barrier to the ooze coming from one of the tunnels.

After what could have been half her life or twenty seconds, Karl was moving again. She pulled his cutter loose from its holder and pressed it into his palm. Seconds later he was working away on the ooze on the far side of his body. Thankfully, she realized the ooze was viscous enough that not much had flowed under his suit.

"Come on!" Robert called. Alis glanced up again and almost panicked. Rolling toward them like a slow-motion wave in molasses was a miniature tidal wave of more ooze.

Karl was almost free. She couldn't leave him when they were this close.

Karl didn't agree. "Get out of here! There's no time!"

Alis had never found it easier to disagree. "Keep cutting. You're coming with us!" She released her grip on the cutter and it switched off.

Only Karl's foot was still trapped. She locked grip with Robert and pulled Karl toward her, hoping that his foot would come free without more cutting being required.

Only when Karl screamed did Alis realize she was bending his injured leg at a horrible angle. The new wave of ooze was almost on them. She reached forward with her cutter on again and made more quick cuts. Behind her, Lucy had already gone through the opening Robert had cut in the door. Robert was half in, half out, reaching toward her.

There was no more time. Alis turned off her cutter and gripped Robert's gloved hand. With her right hand, she grabbed Karl's hand and one last time she pulled as hard as she could.

Karl screamed again, but there was no help for it. She kept

pulling, praying it wasn't just her hopeful imagination that told her his body had shifted closer.

The ooze was right there, no more than a hand's width from engulfing Karl all over again. His scream cut short and he fell silent, probably having blacked out from the pain. Alis had tears in her eyes as she pulled again. Karl's cutter died as his grip loosened.

She reeled backward into Robert. Had she lost her grip? No, Karl was still with her! "Yes! Pull!"

Robert pulled her through the opening, and she pulled Karl through after her. She tumbled backward, suddenly afraid there was ooze on this side of the gap, too, but she felt no sticky resistance except from the remnants already on her suit.

Lucy was at the cut flap as soon as Alis was aware they had to deal with the opening. "Help me!" Lucy struggled to put pressure on the edge of the flap as it bulged toward them, as if the ooze was trying to get through. Seconds later, Alis and Robert joined her, all of them having trouble applying pressure because their feet skidded away in the light gravity.

Ooze started showing through the seam. Alis snapped her cutter into position and started forming a bead along the gap, almost like welding.

"Yes, that's got it!" Lucy yelled with relief.

Soon Alis was convinced Lucy was right. All along the cut seam, bits of ooze slowly seemed to melt into the wall itself, resealing the damage.

"Antibodies?" Alis asked.

"Good bet," Robert said, his voice still showing signs of stress. He talked louder than necessary, his speech ragged. "Apparently my cutting through the door wasn't on the approved list."

"Karl?" Alis said. "Karl, are you all right?"

No answer. All Alis could hear was the echo of his screams as she had twisted his bad leg and pulled as hard as she could.

"He's alive," Robert said. "His vitals are lousy, but he's not dead. I'm not sure how much longer he can hold on, though."

Slowly the surface they were pushing on began to flatten, as if they were pushing on the side of a large balloon that was losing air. Alis pulled one hand away from the closed tear in the wall, then pulled her other hand away. She stood back from the wall. Lucy and Robert backed up and stood on either side.

"Looks like it's going to hold," Alis said.

No one disagreed as she turned to find Karl. His body lay just a meter away, his legs all dirty with the dried slime.

Gently, she rolled him over on his back, hoping she wasn't aggravating his condition. She tilted her head to one side so she could get a better view inside his helmet. His lips were parted and his face had a blue tinge that looked decidedly unhealthy, but his chest slowly rose and fell, and he was apparently at least temporarily free of pain thanks to the oblivion of unconsciousness.

Robert knelt beside her and moved in for a closer look.

Alis rose and inspected their surroundings. The wall opposite the door was only a couple of meters away, about a meter on the other side of Karl's body. About five meters away to both the left and right, walls ran from the floor to the ceiling about ten meters overhead. They were trapped in the tall, thin rectangular space.

How would they get past this space, Alis wondered. As she looked blankly at the far wall, she recalled the hologram details and began to smile. The wall's color was familiar; it was roughly the same shade of beige as the outside of Cantaloupe. And this surface held the same dimpled pattern. "This is one of the twins," she said, moving toward the "wall." "We're here!"

Three steps took her next to the far surface. As she took the last step, the floor gave out from under her.

Alis cried out as she lost her balance. She fell forward against the surface of the twin and pushed herself backward as hard as she could.

Still off balance, she reeled all the way back until she hit the wall they had just sealed shut. She bounced forward and regained her balance. The lights from her helmet lamps joined the spots already formed by lights from Lucy and Robert, and she watched the floor slowly extend until it met the surface of the twin again.

Alis moved forward carefully. "Hold onto my arm, will you?"

Lucy took hold.

Alis took another step and reached forward with her other leg. She touched the tip of her toe against the floor right next to the twin's surface. The surface of the floor retracted, in a plant-like fashion. She touched the open edge of the floor, and it retracted farther until there was a gap almost a half-meter wide.

Alis angled her helmet lamp down into the dark. The space below looked like another rectangular volume just like the one they were in. She took her foot away, and after a couple of seconds the floor moved back into its fully extended position.

"Wow," Lucy said softly.

"Strange," Alis said.

Alis looked at the short walls extending from the wall they had come through over to the surface of the twin. The texture of that wall looked a lot like the mottled rubbery texture of the floor. She moved to the nearest short wall. Standing well back from the twin, and leaning on the side of the twin, she touched the wall right next to the twin's surface.

The short wall retracted just the way the floor had. Beyond the opening was another similarly sized cavity.

Alis looked up at the ceiling, and concluded that every surface would retract when called upon to do that.

Robert said, "So we're in a waffle-iron grid that's holding the twin in place."

"So it would seem," Alis said. "Maybe once the twin starts moving out, the friction keeps all these supports retracted."

"That could be bad news," Lucy said. "I hadn't thought very far ahead, and I just figured somehow we could maybe just get to the right part of one of the twins' surface and we'd be pushed out ahead of it. Right here, on the side, we'll just be brushed off by these baffles. We'll be stuck floating somewhere here inside with no guarantee that we can get out before the birth canal—or whatever it is—closes."

Robert said, "We can start moving from compartment to compartment, so we're at the point farthest out from the center of Cantaloupe."

"Might work in theory," Alis said. "But that's a long way to go, and we've got an injured man. Besides that, we don't actually know if this twin moves out of the birth canal like a ship moving out of dry dock, or if it somehow turns while it's moving."

The group was silent for a moment before Alis said, "There's got to be a way. We can't have come this far to fail."

Seconds after she finished speaking, the floor lurched.

"What was that?" Robert asked.

"I don't know," Lucy said, "but I don't like it. What if it means the twin is ready to start moving right now?"

"I think it does," Alis said. "Look."

She held her arm extended toward the twin's surface, her finger just a centimeter away from it. In the light next to her finger, she could clearly see the twin's surface was moving slowly upward.

Alis stood petrified for long seconds, watching the surface in front of her finger. The twin they stood next to really was moving upward, apparently ready to exit the womb. The section of the floor closest to the twin's surface slowly retracted as it sensed motion.

"You're right," Lucy said. "It must be leaving." She grabbed at the slowly sliding surface. "And we're going to be left here!"

Alis shook free of her surprise and touched the surface, hoping for a surprise. Maybe the newborn's skin would be soft enough that they could just grip a fold and hang on. No such luck. The surface was much like Cantaloupe's outer surface—the skin wasn't rock hard, but more like an orange peel made from something that felt indestructible.

Robert felt the surface, too. "We've still got our cutters. We could carve out a pocket and let it carry us out."

Alis glanced back at Karl's unmoving body, option after option racing through her brain. "I can't do that. It would feel like cutting up a baby."

"But that's not—"

"I know it's not reasonable. It's just the way I feel. You do it for yourself if we can't think of anything else."

"It's accelerating!" Lucy said. "We need to decide fast."

Alis stared at Karl's inert body. "Glue!" she said suddenly. "You saw how that slime acted when it came in contact with our suits. How it reacted to heat. We can reheat the slime that's still stuck to our suits and glue ourselves to the side."

"Whatever we do, it's got to be now," Robert said. "Give it a try."

The three of them simultaneously flipped on their cutters and spread apart.

"Robert, your suit has the least amount on it. You can get some from Karl's suit, I bet."

Alis and Robert moved to Karl's body as Lucy started carefully melting some of the slime still on the side of her boot.

Without damaging Karl's suit, Alis and Robert were able to quickly separate a large chunk of the sticky slime that had solidified, almost like what would come out of a hot glue gun.

"Wish me luck!" Lucy said.

Alis turned.

Lucy lay on her back at the edge of the floor nearest the rising surface of the twin. She had her cutter's flame playing over the solidified slime on the outside surface of the boot closest to the twin. In virtually a single motion, she snapped off the flame and crushed her boot against the twin's surface. It took only a second for the gooey ooze to solidify again, and Lucy was slowly dragged upward by her boot. "Ooohhh!"

"We have lift-off," Robert said in awe.

"I think it's going to hold," Lucy said. She kicked at the twin's surface with her other boot, and the glued boot held. She was halfway to the retracted ceiling already.

Alis and Robert watched her all the way to the ceiling. The lip of the ceiling retracted even farther when the obstruction of Lucy's boot hit it. Her body slid past the conforming section of the ceiling, as if her body were going through some alien car wash.

Seconds later she was out of sight. "I'm still all right! I think we're finally going home!"

For the first time, Alis genuinely let herself hope this would all work. "Give me health checks every minute until you're out."

"You got it. Here's another divider. And I'm going under it okay, too!"

Alis turned to Robert. "You ready?"

"Let's get Karl stuck first so you don't have to do that by yourself."

"Thanks. I just hope he can make it through all this without killing him."

"He's too near dead for me to predict it anyway. We just have to do the best we can."

Alis forced her thoughts onto the immediate problem. "Let's glue the backs of both heels so he doesn't have a dangling leg or all the pressure on one leg."

"Right."

They kept Karl on his back and bent his body at his hips, legs in the air, heels facing the rapidly rising surface. Simultaneously Alis and Robert played their cutters' flames near the solidified slime at the back of each of Karl's heels.

"You ready?" Alis said.

"Yes."

"On three. One—two—three." On "three" they slapped both of Karl's heels against the rising surface. Alis kept pressing Karl's boot against the surface until it rose too high.

She had a sudden image of his heels coming loose and seeing him fall, then fall through the gap at the floor, falling deeper and deeper into Cantaloupe. Miraculously the boots held.

"Hang on," Alis said to herself. "Hang on."

"Still healthy," Lucy called.

"Time to go," Robert said.

Alis waited until Karl's body had vanished above the ceiling gap. "Right."

She lay on her back and copied the action Lucy had taken. A couple of meters away, Robert did the same thing, heating up a glob of solidified slime next to his boot.

"Here goes nothing," Alis called. She pulled the cutter away and slammed her heel against the bottom of the upward-sliding surface. As she was yanked upward, she remembered to release her grip on the cutter and let the flame die.

Robert said, "I'm on the way, too!"

The surface continued to accelerate upward. Alis felt she hit the ceiling lip twice as fast as Lucy had earlier. She strained to keep her free leg against the surface. It wouldn't take much more speed to turn an awkward collision with a divider into a deadly problem.

"Still—urgh," Lucy yelled. Then silence.

"Lucy, are you all right?"

No answer.

Suddenly unsure she had made the right decision, but past the point of being able to change it, Alis hung on, her body rigid. The dividers came faster and rougher, and she felt like a cookie under a heavy rolling pin.

Within a minute the dividers were coming as quickly as picket-fence boards at 100 kph. Her head was repeatedly slammed forward and back until she felt she'd hooked her heel to a rocket rising through a tornado.

Her head slammed back against the supposedly cushioning surface of the helmet one more time, and she blacked out.

. . .

Captain Fernandez stared at the main view screen.

Next to him, Martina Binotell said for about the eighth time, "My God."

Without taking his gaze from the image, the captain reached over and toggled the ship-wide announcement channel.

He cleared his throat, still watching the screen, then said, "Those of you who don't happen to be watching right now might want to turn on your main viewers."

He supposed that, given the first contact situation and the recently extended solar-sail wings, hardly anyone aboard wasn't already at a view screen. He could imagine, though, that if a couple of the crew had collapsed with fatigue in their bunks, and given how little he engaged in hype, and how seldom anything would jog him out of his routine, anyone not already at a screen would rush to switch on the view, as if he'd said, "This is absolutely amazing. Turn those switches right now!" Despite being convinced that everyone was watching already, he couldn't help himself. He added, "I'm serious. This really is quite something."

The main view was currently driven by the transmission from a probe about ninety degrees away from the *Ranger*'s current position, because it had the best view. Cantaloupe's wings had shifted back from their fully extended positions, and an enormous section of Cantaloupe's surface seemed to have twisted sideways. A miniature version of Cantaloupe was emerging from the newly formed gap and was already almost halfway out. It moved faster and faster. From a different angle, the scene was reminiscent of a moon rising over the horizon, coming up faster than astronomical events were supposed to happen.

The event was being recorded by more than two dozen different instruments, in a half-dozen portions of the electromagnetic spectrum, and still Captain Fernandez felt compelled to look at the controls again to make sure the recorders were still on.

The captain said not one more word during the time it took for the small globe to move all the way out of the cavity within Cantaloupe. When the view from a probe to one side showed a band of black space between the two, the captain was aware of how stiff his neck was from staying in the same position the whole time.

"Still no word from the team?" he asked. It was a stupid question since any call would have drawn his attention immediately, but he'd been so absorbed in the view he thought he should double-check.

Martina shook her head, then said, "My God," again.

The small version of Cantaloupe had already started to extend its wings. The wings came out more slowly than Cantaloupe's wings had extended, and this small version was a bit jerkier.

The captain shook his head in wonder.

"My God," Martina said again.

A second globe was pushing up past Cantaloupe's surface.

Captain Fernandez had seen the scans, and knew there were two globes down there, but he was amazed all over again. Suspecting someone's pregnant is a lot different from being there in the delivery room.

Martina didn't say, "My God," again until the second youngster was already out and starting to spread its wings. By that time, the first youngster had its light-sail wings almost under control.

The circular opening in Cantaloupe's surface started sliding closed. It took almost twenty minutes before the surface looked exactly the way it had a couple of hours earlier.

Captain Fernandez looked pointedly at Martina.

"No, sir. Still nothing from the team."

. . .

Alis came to in free fall. She blinked several times, feeling grateful that the dream about falling from the moon to Earth had been just that: a dream.

Her head hurt.

To one side she could see Cantaloupe's surface. She was outside!

But no, that couldn't be entirely right, because she could see Cantaloupe above the horizon. Cantaloupe was there in space, and it had wings. What enormous, glorious wings.

The twins! That was it. She was stuck to one of the twins. And Karl was nearby. Or he should be nearby.

"Karl!" she shouted.

No reply. She bent at the hips so she could see past her feet.

There he was! Karl's heels were still stuck to the surface, his body floating, drifting, as if he'd been dropped into the ocean with cement shoes. Farther past Karl, much farther, was Lucy's body. And to Alis's right was Robert.

"Robert? Lucy? Karl? Are any of you awake?" The real question, the one she was afraid to ask, and that didn't make sense to ask, was, were they alive?

"This is Alis Nussem, calling the *Ranger*. Can anyone hear me?"

The near-silent electronic hiss was the most depressing sound she'd ever heard.

20 ▪ T W I N S

Alis's head cleared some during the next few minutes, so the primary remaining symptoms of the ordeal were the sensations of starvation, fatigue, sleep-deprivation, and pain in her head, neck, and shoulders.

She was feeling fairly well-adjusted to the idea of floating in space with one boot stuck to the side of an enormous baby Cantaloupe when her body was slowly pressed against the "ground." The twin she was on must have been positioning its solar-sail wings to deflect its path away from the sun.

She'd been considering trying to unstick herself from the surface and move to Karl or Robert, so she could at least convince herself they were alive but still unconscious. She could try that now without the earlier fear of floating loose from the surface and not being able to reach them, but she didn't know how long the twin's acceleration would maintain the sense of gravity.

She didn't have much to lose, she finally decided, so she sat up and got her cutter ready.

Her hand shook from the fatigue and the effort to hold still. She was trying to decide how much risk she was taking of ripping open her suit while trying to free herself when a pair of feet landed on the surface just in front of her. The feet were attached to a suited body.

Someone else was here. Someone from the *Ranger*!

Her brain must have been foggier than she'd thought, because it took so long for the fact that they were being rescued to register.

Someone else landed to her left. The first person leaned close to Alis and touched helmets.

"Your receiver must be down," a male voice said. "We've been trying to tell you we were on the way."

"Is Karl alive?"

"We'll check on the others. Just stay calm."

"We're stuck to the surface. We heated up some slime and used it like glue. A cutter will get it off, but be careful, okay?"

"You got it."

As if Alis's body decided on its own that now the team was in the hands of capable help she could go to sleep and coast, she lay back and remembered nothing more from that time.

When Karl woke, he couldn't tell whether he was aboard the *Ranger* or back in sick bay on one of the orbital stations. All he knew for sure was that the gravity wasn't close enough to one gee for him to have been on Earth.

The lack of pain worried him more than anything, because he took that to be a sure sign that he was under heavy medication.

His first visitor was a brusque doctor who told him he was aboard the Tokyan Station and that he had been out for more than a week but that he was going to be "just fine." The leg would heal eventually, but not as fast as it would have if he'd been a teenager.

His memory of events inside Cantaloupe was coming back steadily, but when the doctor left him with sped-up video of the twins leaping and soaring on their solar-sail wings, a feeling of amazement and disbelief was unavoidable. Cantaloupe and the two little ones had maneuvered into a couple of very tight planetary turns that had aimed them back toward the sun and given them more time to use their enormous solar-sail wings to slow down.

Later in what he thought was the same day, he had his first visitor, Robert.

"I'm told you're 'doing fine,' " Robert said.

"I heard that, too, so it must be true. I would have thought the doc would have given a compatriot a more complete diagnosis, though."

"He did. But it still boils down to 'doing fine.' "

"Thanks for getting me out."

"How do you know I helped? I might have voted against it."

"Just a hunch. I don't think you would have showed up here if you were still as angry as you had been aboard the *Ranger*."

"That's true. I don't really know what happened back here, but I do know what happened on Cantaloupe and I don't know that we'd be having this conversation if you had let us down in there."

"Thanks, Robert."

Robert handed him something. A card. "It's just a little get-well card."

Karl opened it and read the names and notes from people aboard the *Ranger*. He saw some friendly words from people who'd never been friendly to him. He looked up at Robert. "Did you have to forge some of these?"

Robert smiled. "No, but I did tell people what happened down there."

Karl swallowed. "This means a lot to me. Thanks."

Robert nodded.

Karl looked back at the card. Even Captain Fernandez had signed it with a curt, "Get well, Karl." And Alis had signed it, adding, "Thanks for what you did."

Karl closed the card and said, "So, what do the experts think about all this?"

"Lots of different theories. Naturally, people were pretty surprised to see the video we brought back. When I look at it, I have a hard time accepting any theory of Cantaloupe having occurred naturally, but there are people claiming that, too. To me it's pretty obviously an engineered life-form, but there may never be a consensus. The theory I like best is that Cantaloupe was designed to explore the galaxy by replicating itself at intervals and maybe reporting back. I'm betting that after a period of soaking up lots and lots of solar energy, Cantaloupe and the twins will leave here, and they might not all go the same direction."

"That sounds as good as any theory to me. I'd like to meet whoever was capable of designing it. For that matter, the probe that did all the damage implies the existence, or at least the past existence, of another race. And the larger probe, the one that soft-landed on the surface, probably came from yet another source. I guess we're not as alone as we thought we were."

Karl's doctor returned for some tests.

Robert put a hand on Karl's shoulder. "Look me up when you get out of this place. I'll buy you a drink."

"You got it."

A few more people from the *Ranger* and a couple of Karl's friends stopped by that day, but Karl gradually realized there was one person he most wanted to see. Unfortunately, it was the one person least likely to show up: Alis.

More doctors made more tests, periodically assuring Karl he would be, "just fine."

That night, what seemed to him like the middle of the night because his sleep schedule was so confused, he watched the recording showing the twins. He had a few new recordings by then, showing more of what looked like frolicking when sped up enough. Cantaloupe itself was more massive so it moved more slowly. The video gave Karl the impression of an old bald eagle with a couple of young sparrows that had somehow imprinted.

He was watching the recording loop for probably the fiftieth time when he became aware of someone else nearby. He turned his head. He smiled tentatively and his chest tightened. "I was hoping you'd stop by."

Alis moved from the doorway and stepped into the room. As if she didn't know quite what to say, she nodded at the video. "They make quite a sight, don't they?"

"They sure do. It feels good that we might have helped."

Alis nodded. She looked back at the video, still apparently uncomfortable and not knowing what to say.

Alis moved for the door. "Well, I'm glad you're feeling—"

"You really have to go?"

She hesitated at the door.

"If you're still angry with me—"

"No," she said quickly.

"I'm really glad to see you."

"You are? I was afraid that after all—"

"That's past. I can understand how you felt. I probably would have been the same way."

"I don't think so." She moved back into the room. "I saw you at what's probably your worst, and you did pretty well. I think I misjudged you, and I'm sorry—"

Karl was too embarrassed to let her continue. "Look, that's past, all right?"

"All right." Alis sat beside the bed and looked back at the screen.

Karl watched her for a moment. "You know, you have beautiful eyes?"

"Oh, please. I—"

"I know what you're going to say. Your eyes are cameras, they're artificial, that kind of stuff. That's not what I'm talking about. I'd say the same thing if you had your old eyes."

"How do you know? You never saw me then."

"Because I'm not talking about physical appearance. What I see in your eyes is how you act. Some people roll their eyes upward when someone says something dumb. You keep your eyes motionless so the faux pas seems to go unnoticed. Some people walk around with a vacant stare. You're constantly examining the world around you. Some people look around when they're in a conversation, distracted by everything. You watch the person you're talking to, so that person feels your attention is strong. If the eyes are the window to the soul, that's not because of how they look, but how they watch."

Alis looked directly at Karl and finally said, "That mission probably saved my life."

"Come again. I thought it almost cost you your life."

"Maybe 'salvaged my life' is a better choice of words. You know how sometimes you can pick at a scab so often that it never heals, but if you forget about it for a while, next thing you know, it's gone? Maybe I had to have something keep my attention diverted, to knock me out of the orbit I was in."

"And that orbit was?"

"I don't know. But I found out some things inside Cantaloupe. I found myself caring for someone again, really wanting things to work out for that person."

Karl looked at her open gaze and he didn't have to ask her who she was talking about. His cheeks felt warm, and he felt better than he had in a long while.

"And the idea of Cantaloupe having twins," Alis went on, embarrassed again. "The idea of us helping Cantaloupe recover so that could happen." She hesitated. "This is going to sound really, really stupid."

"I really, really doubt it."

She looked back at the screen. "Looking at the twins. They must mass more than some small moons, but they're children. You can just see how they're playing and experimenting with flight. It—this whole process has reminded me—that at some point—I might actually want children of my own."

"That doesn't sound stupid at all."

"But there's more. With all the surgery, the new eyes, the heart, the—well, you know the list. With all that, I've had days—a lot of them—where I felt more like a machine than a woman. But a machine wouldn't want to have children."

"I really doubt it."

Karl watched the small versions of Cantaloupe rise and fall toward the sun as their solar-sail wings curved to and fro. He looked at them, and he remembered the first time he'd ridden a bike. He turned back to Alis. "You know the great Italian place here on the station. I'd love to have dinner with you when they let me out of here, if—if you're interested in that."

"I'd love that, too." Alis took a quick involuntary breath, and she smiled.

On the screen, children played, even more gracefully than they had an hour ago.